PUFFIN CANADA

THE DROUGHTLANDERS

CARRIE MAC is an award-winning author who has moved too many times to count. For now, she lives in Pemberton, a very small town nestled in the mountains north of Vancouver. Her first novel, *The Beckoners*, won the Arthur Ellis YA Award, is a CLA Honour book, and is being adapted for film. *The Droughtlanders*, nominated as a Best Book for Young Adults by the ALA, is the first book in the Triskelia series.

ALSO BY CARRIE MAC

TRISKELIA

Retribution

The Beckoners

Charmed

Crush

Triskelia Book 1

THE DROUGHTLANDERS

CARRIE MAC

PUFFIN
CANADA

PUFFIN CANADA

Published by the Penguin Group

Penguin Group (Canada), 90 Eglinton Avenue East, Suite 700, Toronto, Ontario, Canada M4P 2Y3
(a division of Pearson Canada Inc.)

Penguin Group (USA) Inc., 375 Hudson Street, New York, New York 10014, U.S.A.
Penguin Books Ltd, 80 Strand, London WC2R 0RL, England
Penguin Ireland, 25 St Stephen's Green, Dublin 2, Ireland (a division of Penguin Books Ltd)
Penguin Group (Australia), 250 Camberwell Road, Camberwell, Victoria 3124, Australia
(a division of Pearson Australia Group Pty Ltd)
Penguin Books India Pvt Ltd, 11 Community Centre, Panchsheel Park, New Delhi – 110 017, India
Penguin Group (NZ), 67 Apollo Drive, Rosedale, North Shore 0745, Auckland, New Zealand
(a division of Pearson New Zealand Ltd)
Penguin Books (South Africa) (Pty) Ltd, 24 Sturdee Avenue, Rosebank, Johannesburg 2196, South Africa

Penguin Books Ltd, Registered Offices: 80 Strand, London WC2R 0RL, England

First published in a Puffin Canada hardcover by Penguin Group (Canada),
a division of Pearson Canada Inc., 2006
Published in this edition, 2007

1 2 3 4 5 6 7 8 9 10   (WEB)

 Canada Council   Conseil des Arts
for the Arts   du Canada

*We acknowledge the support of the Canada Council for the Arts which last
year invested $20.3 million in writing and publishing throughout Canada.*

*Nous remercions de son soutien le Conseil des Arts du Canada, qui a investi
20,3 millions de dollars l'an dernier dans les lettres et l'édition à travers le Canada.*

ISBN-13: 978-0-14-305666-9
ISBN-10: 0-14-305666-2

Library and Archives Canada Cataloguing in Publication data available upon request.

Visit the Penguin Group (Canada) website at **www.penguin.ca**

Special and corporate bulk purchase rates available; please see
www.penguin.ca/corporatesales or call 1-800-810-3104, ext. 477 or 474

for Justin Santry—a true quester

There are worlds within worlds
where both dreams and nightmares take form,
and within, your imagination comes to life.

GUY LALIBERTÉ, *CIRQUE DU SOLEIL*

[ONE]

KEYLAND

1

❦

E li leaned forward in his seat, his heart pounding as he watched the young acrobat near the halfway point along the highest tightrope. He heard the flap of wings first, and then he saw the bird. It was just a little pigeon but it was heading straight for the acrobat, who teetered forward, surprised, as the bird swooped. His balance faltered; he leaned back to correct it and nearly lost his footing again. Eli gasped, unaware until then that he'd been holding his breath. The pigeon disappeared up into the rafters, but just as the acrobat regained his balance another pigeon dive-bombed from above. The acrobat stumbled backward, and then, as the crowd's gasps lifted into cheers, he fell to the concrete floor far below and landed with a thundering crack.

Seth, Eli's twin, whistled to someone across the stadium and stuck a triumphant thumbs-up in the air. Eli bet it was Seth's friend Maury, who trained homing pigeons as a hobby.

Eli couldn't look away. He gripped the brass rail and stared at where the boy had landed, head first, just out of reach of the circus hands who would've caught him had they been allowed to use the safety net. Sometimes Chancellor East allowed the Night Circus several nets, or one big one, or just one small one, or sometimes none at all. He liked that the acrobats never knew just how much peril they'd face before each performance.

"That way, they're always off guard, and we're guaranteed a bit of blood sport every now and then." He'd explained this to Eli once while they watched a pair of circus hands drag another trapeze artist out of the ring after he'd fallen, landing on a crate and busting his leg in two places, the bone jutting out like an evil joke. The boy had screamed something awful as he was dragged out of the ring, and the crowd had stamped their feet with delight until finally he'd passed out. Eli remembered the way the boy's leg had flopped beneath him so strangely, as if it didn't belong any more.

"Look." Chancellor East swept his arm across the sea of Keylanders, whose eyes danced with the adrenalin that came with the excitement and the screams. "This is why I won't let them attend to the injury first. Other Chancellors might disagree, but I know what my people come to see. This, just as much as the choreography of it all."

Eli stared at the fallen acrobat as the other performers rushed to his side screaming. There were no nets tonight. Minutes before the show began Chancellor East had confiscated and destroyed them, forcing the Night Circus to perform without any safety measures at all.

"I'm in the mood for a little excitement," he'd said as the crowd settled in their seats.

And so he'd gotten his wish.

Now the other performers were weeping and moaning behind their masks, but still, not one of them bared their face, and why would they? Keyland Guards lined the perimeter, waiting for even the slightest infraction.

Chancellor East gnawed on his pipe. "You'd think they'd all died, the way they're carrying on." He nudged Eli's father. "That would be convenient, wouldn't it?"

"Quite, Chancellor," Edmund laughed. "But then there'd be the bodies to deal with."

"Well yes, there'd be that," Chancellor East said. "Always an issue, isn't it?"

Below, the Night Circus performers were on their knees, clutching each other and keening around the crushed body of the young acrobat.

Eli pulled his eyes off the grotesque scene to have a look at the stands full of Keylanders who'd all risen to their feet for a better look. There was something in their eyes—all of them, even the little children and the prim ladies in their fancy hats—a rapture of sorts. But not his mother. Eli looked behind him to where she sat with her gloved hands covering her mouth and her eyes turned downward, fixed on her lap.

The sound of marching drew Eli's attention back to the ring, where the Guards were closing in tighter, batons drawn. A girl, Eli could tell by the shape of her, rested her head on the boy's bloody chest for a moment before lifting his mangled head into her lap. She was wearing a costume matching the boy's, and had been standing at the base of the ladder, ready to go up just before he'd fallen. The girl pointed up at the Chancellor and screamed. "Why? Why do you—?"

A burly clown clamped a hand over the girl's mouth and pulled her away as the Guards uniformly squared their stance and raised their batons. The girl kept screaming behind the clown's firm hand, but she let herself be led away by him and several others wearing costumes like hers.

"They're such animals. Really, why all the fuss?" Chancellor East leaned his fat belly over the rail. "Get on with the show!"

Seth leaned farther over the rail. "I want a better look. Get out of the way!" he yelled down to the performers still keening around the body.

Chancellor East gestured at his sergeant below. The sergeant shouted, and the Guards steadied their shields. The performers rallied one another to stand and back away.

"Roll him over!" Seth hollered. No one moved.

"You heard him!" Chancellor East bellowed. "Turn him over!"

Eli's stomach rode a wave of pity that peaked with nausea as two circus hands reluctantly stepped forward and rolled the boy's body.

"Aw yeah, look at that!" Seth laughed as the stands tittered with excitement. There were more oohs and aahs over this than any of the gravity-defying acts of the evening. Eli didn't understand it. "The whole back of his head is caved in. Look at it, Father!"

Lisette, the twins' mother, finally stirred. She pulled Seth away from the rail.

"Seth, please." Her voice shook. "Show some decency. He may be a Droughtlander, but he was still a boy, like you."

"Yeah right, Maman." Seth shrugged her off.

Chancellor East frowned. "Lisette—"

Edmund glanced at the Chancellor and then squeezed Lisette's shoulder. "Now why would you say such a thing, my dear?" he said, cutting the Chancellor off. "What has gotten into you? It's just a Droughtlander, no better than a rat."

"*Oui. D'accord.*" Lisette worried the scarf at her throat as the boy was carried out of the ring, a wake of blood darkening the cement. Edmund raised a disapproving eyebrow.

"English, Lisette. How many times must I remind you?"

"Sorry," Lisette murmured. "Of course. I was just startled by the blood, that's all. It's made me a bit queasy."

Eli took his mother's hand. She was trembling, and would not look at him.

"And now, on with the show!" Chancellor East chomped on his pipe and gestured for the Guards to retreat. The performers bowed in his direction and then took their positions to finish the show. The Chancellor settled back in his throne. "Can't be wasting any more time. The rain is coming early tonight, is it not?"

Edmund looked at his watch. "Scheduled for ten, sir."

"Well, if I end up getting soaked, I'll blame you, my friend." The Chancellor let loose his tobacco-stink laugh as the stands of Keylanders took their seats and rustled impatiently. As engaging a distraction as the grisly death was, everyone was still mindful of the time. All of the Eastern Key was there, dressed in their finery. No one wanted to get caught in the rain, and because it was scheduled for ten, no one had brought an umbrella.

Lisette pulled her hand away from Eli's and excused herself as the lights dimmed. "I still feel a little queasy." She pecked Edmund on the cheek. "I'll walk through the gardens, get some air. I'll see you at home."

"Do you want me to come with you?" Eli asked, eager for a reason to leave that wouldn't set Seth off on a fit of bullying.

"No," Lisette said, and then again, more firmly. "No. Thank you, Eli, but no. You stay and enjoy the rest of the circus."

The spotlights swept back to the centre ring and the circus resumed, but Eli could not sit still, and nor could he watch. For him, the show had been ruined by the boy's fall. It seemed he was the only one, except for his mother, who could not sit back and enjoy the circus after such an event. Every other Keylander, the entire stadium full of them, was acting as if nothing had happened. Eli just couldn't do it. Not this time.

"I'm going to catch up to Mother," Eli said as he slipped past his father's seat.

How could anyone watch the rest of the circus? Before when there'd been a fall or some other spectacular circus accident, Eli had always been able to stay and enjoy the rest of the show, but something about this night was different. His heart was still pounding, there was a strange ringing in his ears, and he felt nauseous and hot as he stumbled into the corridor behind the Chancellor's balcony.

Eli hesitated there, turning back for one last glance at the ring. The performers were barely lurching through their routines now, their usual grace ripped away by fresh, raw grief. And the boy's blood centre stage, with bloody footprints coming and going from it as the performers were forced to pass through it. And Seth—Eli couldn't bear to even look at him. He'd been bored all evening but now practically hummed with anticipation, his knee bouncing as he waited for another disaster, the chances of which were good now that the performers were disabled by shock and sadness. He'd had something to do with it, Eli was sure. The thumbs-up, the whistle. Seth was always looking for trouble, and manufacturing it where there was none. Almost sixteen years of being Seth's twin, and Eli could not have felt any more disconnected to another human being. Eli turned and rushed down the stairs and out into the night, hungry for air that wasn't metallic with the aftertaste of tragedy.

LATER, HIS HEAD A LITTLE CLEARER, Eli decided not to try to catch up to his mother and instead headed home via the outer ring road so that he could sneak a peak at the Night Circus camp. It was set up just outside the Key walls, and Eli had always loved its brightly painted caravans and enormous Clydesdales with their sleek coats and manes braided with ribbons. Sometimes he'd watch the Droughtlanders practising, juggling flaming batons, balancing on each other's shoulders—the one on top, always the littlest, leaping from one human pyramid to another—or the tightrope walkers practically dancing on the taut line they'd set up between the two largest caravans. It was like watching a fairy tale come to life, seductive and buoyant. That was what he needed to get the haunting images of the boy's crushed skull and the bloody footprints out of his mind, a little colour and a lot of whimsy. Eli spied on the camp each time the Night Circus came to the Eastern Key. There was something about the bustling compound that thrilled him, and terrified him at the same time, mind you. He always kept a safe distance to avoid any sicks and he never let anyone see him, not from the circus or from the Key. How could he explain his interest to Edmund? And what would the performers think if they saw the Chief Regent's son gawking at them as if he cared?

Eli was still trying to shake the horrific images out of his head when he was surprised by the sight of his mother hurrying ahead of him, her long coat flapping, shoes clacking on the cobblestones. What was she doing on the outer ring road when she'd said she was going home through the gardens? Had she just changed her mind? Or had she lied? Either way, Eli was curious to know where she was headed with such purpose after having left the stadium such a shaky mess.

Eli slipped into the shadows and decided to follow her. He stayed about a block back and trailed her all the way to one of the barred slits in the wall used to monitor the Key's perimeter. This one was beside the service gate, the one the Night Circus had used to bring in their equipment earlier that day. The ground was still muddy from the foul antibacterial rinse each member of the circus and every animal and all items that entered into the Key were doused with before being allowed to come in. Eli's head hurt. It always did when he came anywhere near the rinse.

He squeezed his eyes shut, trying to ease the pain. There it was again—the fall, the bloody footprints, the girl screaming up at them. Eli opened his eyes. The pain had worsened but the horrors were gone for the moment, replaced by the shocking sight of his mother speaking to someone through the bars. What was going on? There was only filth and disease on the other side! Lisette was crying, more so than he'd ever seen her cry before. The old woman she was speaking to had her mask pulled down, revealing her sun-weathered face and dry, cracked lips. She was crying too. Eli watched, horrified, as his mother, the wife of the Chancellor's Chief Regent, embraced the filthy Droughtlander awkwardly through the bars.

"Maman!" Eli screamed. "Get away from her!"

Lisette spun on her heels, surprised. She gulped back a sob and waved him away. "Stay back, Eli!"

Eli stopped in his tracks, not sure what to do. Pull her away? Call for help? Run? Lisette said a few more words to the old woman, and then kissed her on both cheeks before retreating. Kissed her! As she walked slowly toward him, Eli glanced at the alarm on the wall by the gate. Should he pull it? If he did, the Keyland Guard would come and deal with his mother's severe and confusing violation. Perhaps it would be best left to them, considering Eli had no idea what to do.

Lisette wiped her eyes. "Are you spying on me?"

Had she gone mad? Eli reached for the alarm. He should pull it, right now, without another thought. It was law, after all. But there came the other thought. This was his *mother*.

"Eli?" Her eyes were locked on his hand, hovering at the alarm pull.

"And so what if I am? What are *you* doing with a filthy old Droughtland cow?"

"Don't be rude, Eli."

Rude? She's talking about his manners when she's violating *law*?

"If I pull this, you go in front of the Star Chamber."

"True."

"Why shouldn't I pull it?" Eli's stomach knotted. His mother's fate, her life even, rested with his decision. Eli had never wielded so much power in all his life. It was overwhelming, and foreign; he didn't have a clue what to do with it. Except give it back somehow, give it away, so it wasn't his problem.

Lisette broke her stare. "Come, *mon fils*. Let's go home." She rearranged her cloak and started walking. Eli stared at her, stunned, and then ran to catch up with her at the corner.

"Aren't you going to explain? Aren't you going to report that you touched a Droughtlander? I saw you, Maman! You *kissed* her!"

"You don't know what you saw. Not really." Lisette stopped. "I came to tell her of the boy. She was close to him."

"What? What are you talking about?"

"Eli, would you really report me? Do you think you have it in you to put your mother in front of the Star Chamber?"

Eli hesitated. This sounded like a trick question, like when his father posed such challenges with only one answer in mind he was willing to hear.

"I . . . I don't know."

Lisette touched his arm. "I don't think you are that kind of person," she whispered.

Her hand. The hand that had touched a Droughtlander was now touching him! He yanked his arm away and scrubbed at it furiously with his shirt.

"Maybe you're wrong! Maybe I am!"

Lisette started walking again. Eli followed her, still astonished at what had just happened. They passed another alarm, and Eli paused before it to see if his mother would notice. She didn't even look back. He felt the cool pull beneath his fingers and tested the give, tugging just enough to feel it catch. Any more and the alarm would sound, setting off an unknown chain reaction that would catapult his life, and his family, into an unforeseen darkness. That's not what he wanted. He loved his mother, as strange as she was acting; he loved her, and furthermore, he trusted her. He hoped. Eli carefully released the pull, dropped his hand, and backed away. He might love her, but he was angry with her, too. Very angry.

Eli followed her all the way home, his rage and confusion growing with each step. She ignored him, walking with her chin up, her arms swinging casually. They passed three more alarms, and at each one Eli slowed, baiting her, waiting for her to beg him not to pull it. There was no reason why he shouldn't summon the Guard. She could be bringing Droughtland sick right into their home. They could all die!

By the time they reached their gate, Eli could only hope she knew what she was doing. His mother was right. He wasn't the kind of person to turn her in, and at that moment, he hated himself for it.

"I won't report you. Not right now anyway," he announced as he held the gate open for her. He tried to muster a stern tone. "But I insist that you be doused before I will allow you inside the house."

Lisette reached to touch him again.

"Don't you touch me! I mean it!" He scooted out of the way. "I won't let you inside until you're doused!"

"The need for such measures is greatly exaggerated, *mon fils*." Lisette climbed the front steps. Eli wrenched a lantern stand out of the ground and blocked her way.

"I can't let you inside, Maman! You might be infected. That woman was *outside* the walls, she wouldn't have been doused!"

"Eli, stop." Lisette grabbed the end of the lantern stand and moved it effortlessly out of her way. Eli could not believe his lack of will. He really, truly was the mama's boy Seth loved to claim he was. Seth would impale their mother before letting her in, but not Eli. Once a coward, always a coward.

"I know more about these matters than you, Eli."

"How? What do you know about it?"

"That woman was a cook in my house when I was a child. We have stayed in touch."

"That doesn't mean she's safe! That doesn't mean anything at all!"

Inside, the hall light went on. The new maid opened the front door. Eli locked eyes on his mother and shook his head, silently imploring her not to go inside. Lisette winked. She pulled off her cloak, handed it to the maid, and stepped inside.

"Are you coming in, Master Eli?" the young maid inquired after waiting an awkwardly long time at the open door, the cool air raising goosebumps on her slender arms. Eli wanted to say no. He wanted to tell the girl, a new and timid addition to the house staff, to evacuate the rest of the servants and run for her life. Instead, he stabbed the lantern stand back in the ground and went inside, praying that his mother knew what she was doing.

2

Eli watched anxiously those first few hours for any sign that his mother was falling ill. She didn't mention anything about her detour when Edmund and Seth came home. Instead, she sat in the parlour with them, quietly sipping her tea and working on her needlepoint while Seth recounted the grisly event for the tenth time, Edmund went on about some new complicated property tax Eli didn't understand, and Eli sat in stunned silence, his tea cold, his cookies untouched. Lisette seemed fine. But how could that be? Luck? Providence? Or had she contracted a sick that took longer to present?

For the next several days Eli monitored her and the rest of the household for any symptoms, anything unusual. Maybe his mother wouldn't get sick because she was so healthy. Maybe it would be one of the staff, or someone with a weaker immune system, like the twins' tutor who always seemed to have a snivelly nose or Cook's husband who could barely take care of the coaches any more for his arthritis. When the new maid didn't appear behind his father's chair at breakfast one day he dreaded that she was lying dead in her bed in the cellar, but she'd only fallen back to sleep after being awakened by the staffminder on her rounds. The worry was driving Eli mad.

What Eli knew of Droughtlander sicks came from the stories he heard, mostly from the house staff—stories shared between them as they prepared meals or worked the grounds, stories that were hundreds of people old, shifting shape with each telling so that by the time they reached the tightly protected world of the Keyland elite they were the weight and breadth of myth and Eli didn't know how much of it to believe.

There was a sick that made you spout curses and a sick that made your arms and legs rot off, sicks that stole only babies, sicks that stole only women, sicks that couldn't care less whom they took in the dead of the night, stealing breath or mind or blood or limb. There were tales of sicks that passed through water, sicks that passed by meat, and stealthy, wicked sicks borne by air. The last Eli was afraid of most. The Key walls were high, but not high enough to stop the wind carrying filthy Droughtland air over top and with it untold pathogens. Eli knew his worry was unfounded. It was rare, very rare, that a sick happened this way, and when it did, or was thought to have, it could never be proven that it came over the walls. Usually there was a trail of contact established that verified someone's laziness with washing or dousing or their violation of proximity laws. The proximity laws were supposed to take care of the airborne sicks. Those ills needed closeness, the intimacy of a hug or someone coughing nearby, but still, Eli worried. Before every rainfall the Key was coated in a fine layer of Droughtland dust that Eli was sure was infested with sick, although the Chancellor had regular tests done that supposedly proved the dust itself was harmless. Still, after the rain was summoned and cleansed the Key, Eli felt safer being outside.

Eli's absolute favourite time to be outside was actually during the rains. No one else went out in them; they didn't have to, and sometimes the cloudseeding results were unpredictable—and on rare occasions dangerous, like when a newly hired cloudminder attempted to erupt a hailstorm before it reached the Key. The outcome had been thunder and lightning and hailstones the size of bricks, unprecedented damage to Keylander property, and one fatality—the labourer who'd been sent out after the Chancellor's granddaughter's puppy, which had taken off at the first crack of thunder. Hailed to death.

That cloudminder, an unfortunate, harmless geek with a bad sense of cloud navigation, ended up in front of the Star Chamber and was imprisoned indefinitely, which everyone knew meant he'd been executed somewhere and his body disposed of discreetly.

The current cloudminder was very good. Accurate and dedicated. He made sure everyone had a weather schedule so that daily life could be planned accordingly. The rains were usually scheduled for the middle of the night, but sometimes a rogue storm heading their way required diversion, or a particularly bad dust storm had covered the Key with Droughtland filth and the Chancellor decreed a daytime action. The silver iodide pellets would be shot up into the clouds and shortly afterward the rain would begin, or the storm would be diverted, or the clouds would part, depending on the recipe, timing, and velocity applied by the cloudminder.

THE RAINFALL CAME ON TIME, right at ten, while the maid was pouring the second round of tea. She removed Eli's untouched cup without comment and backed out of the room with an unnoticed curtsey as the rain streaked the tall windows. It rained until dawn, as scheduled. Eli hadn't slept at all. He'd stayed awake all night listening to the rain, worrying about his mother, about everything, the image of the boy falling to his death replaying over and over, heightening his worries into an unnerving panic.

At dawn he pulled on his housecoat and boots and crept up to the rooftop garden with his spyglass to watch the Night Circus leave. They collapsed the tents, packed up their gear, and bustled around in near silence as the sun rose over the hills. They wouldn't get far before the heat made it too hot to travel, but then, Eli didn't know where they were going.

The cart with the boy's body was parked in the middle of the ring of wagons, his corpse cinched in a bag painted turquoise with orange and purple swirls on it, as if he were his very own sunrise, or sunset, perhaps. All packed, the caravans pulled out, the wheels creaking, the horses shuffling, the walkers with their shoulders slumped, all of them glancing back at the Key. They were too far away for Eli to see their expressions, but he could imagine the grief, the anger. Two held back, holding hands, staring at the gates of the Key. Eli adjusted the spyglass, but he couldn't really see any better, and they were wearing their masks. He thought it was the old woman, though, and a girl, their skirts rustling in the wind. When the caravans were far enough away that the dust had settled a bit, they turned and walked off into the Droughtland, still holding hands.

ELI DIDN'T SLEEP that night either. In fact, he didn't sleep for nearly a week after the circus left. He felt ill with exhaustion. His vision was watery, his skin prickled with fatigue, and he couldn't concentrate on his lessons, but he did have to admit that it seemed, thankfully, as if no sick had invaded his home from his mother's blatant disregard for Keyland law. Lisette seemed fine, if that was the word for it. But she wasn't fine, really. She was different, but not enough for Eli to think it was a sick of any kind. She was changed, somehow. Depressed, maybe? Or tired? He wasn't sure, and he didn't want to ask. There was something about her, and the way she looked at him, that made him nervous and want to keep his distance. It was as if she was about to ask him to do something huge, and he wanted nothing to do with it. It was bad enough that he'd done nothing about seeing her with the Droughtlander that night. That was huge enough.

The night Eli was finally able to sleep he slept a thankful, dreamless, solid sleep and woke with the achy unease of not having slept enough. He felt as though he could sleep away the rest of the year, but instead he forced himself to get up and pad his way across to the window, where he saw the ominous black clouds of an unscheduled storm hovering low over the horizon. Eli quickly got dressed and hurried downstairs.

It was before breakfast, but already the cloudminder was in a closed-door meeting with Edmund and Chancellor East in Edmund's office. Eli put his ear to the door and discovered that the cloudminder believed some unknown force was trying to move the storm west, when in fact it was one of theirs, according to international sanctions, even though it was unscheduled and rather alarming in scale.

Eli backed away from the door as his mother descended the stairs.

"Has spying become your new hobby, Eli?"

Eli leaned against the wall, arms folded. "Fraternizing with Droughtlanders yours?"

"You're not going for your run this morning?"

Eli shrugged. "I slept in."

"You've missed your morning run for almost a week, Eli. Are you not feeling well?"

"I've been a little preoccupied with someone else's health, actually. How are you feeling, Maman?"

"I'm absolutely fine. Now, I'm off to work." She smiled; it was cheeky, dismissive, and made Eli want to scream. "Tell your father I won't be home for supper. I've already informed the kitchen."

Lisette was a botanist, a valuable Keyland occupation given that reviving and evolving unique agriculture from the abandoned rainless regions was considered a lofty, important task. Without the botanists, such delicacies as cocoa beans, mangos, bananas, and oranges would be an extinct echo of the past rather than the rarest of rare delights they were now.

"Is that all you want me to tell Father?"

Lisette smiled again, crooking her finger at him. He leaned in. She kissed his cheek. "Yes, that's all."

Eli wiped his cheek. "Don't touch me!"

Lisette's calm shifted. She beckoned Eli to follow her outside. On the front steps, she gripped his shoulders.

"When are you going to stop?"

"Stop what?" Eli twisted out of her grasp.

"Acting like some lowly Guard pawn, which you are not and never will be!" She glanced up at Seth's window. "That's your brother's job in this family."

It was strange to hear her talk like this. For a moment, Eli wondered if there was a sick he hadn't heard of, one that subtly bent the mind in odd directions.

"I expect more from you, Eli."

Eli scowled. "I don't know what to expect from you any more."

"Nonsense."

"Nonsense? After what I saw? You must be really dumb, Maman, because I am fully aware of the laws and the consequences of breaking them and I'm just a kid."

"You are not just a kid. You are my son." Lisette pinned her hat in place. "And I won't stand here and have you talk to me like this." Her words were firm, but her assured exterior was cracking. Eli could tell because her accent was getting thicker. "I am your mother. *Et tu me respecteras en tant que tel.*"

"Chancellor East's nephew turned his mother in."

Lisette's cheeks reddened. She'd been close to the Chancellor's sister. She'd worked at the gardens too, in floral heritage. She'd left the Key one night to meet a Droughtlander. Her son had followed her and seen it all, and had reported her. The Chancellor himself was waiting for her upon her return. He didn't bother with the Star Chamber. He simply sent her back to the man she'd been with and forbade her ever to return again. The stories of her starvation and subsequent death were many and varied.

"What do you want from me, *mon fils?*"

"The truth! Why were you talking to that old woman? Who is she?"

"I told you. She was our cook."

Eli shook his head. "I don't believe you."

Lisette shrugged. "*C'est la vie.*" She hurried down the walk and hesitated at the gate. "You will go for your run daily, Eli. And you will train with Gulzar daily as well. He tells me you have not been to the gym or the stables for almost a week."

"Like I said, I've been a little—"

"Enough." Lisette lifted a gloved hand and shook her head. "No excuses. As I said before, I expect more from you, Eli. This petulant nonsense is getting tiring."

Eli bristled, but said nothing as Lisette pushed through the gate, shut it with a gentleness that implied fury, and strode down the street without looking back. Eli watched her until she was out of sight. Why did it seem that truth had taken a very real shape and was hidden in her cloak pocket? He wanted it. He wanted the truth, and wished it were as simple as stealing it.

FOR HOURS THE STORM STRETCHED in a tug-of-war between west and east, gaining ground and then rolling back into its own darkness. Eli watched out an attic window. Who was trying to harness the storm, and without permission? If it was one of the Western Keys, there would be fierce debates when the legislature soon met. It was the Eastern Key's turn to host the annual session, and Eli had to wonder if the battle over the storm had something to do with that, some kind of political statement or terrorist activity. He knew that Edmund had hoped Eli would show a passion for politics, and sometimes Eli could feign interest, but mostly the legislature seemed like a bunch of brats pounding on the tables and talking over each other, and Edmund's job seemed a series of tedious meetings and public appearances. Let Seth be the political poster boy . . . he was headed that way anyway, what with his obsession with the militia. Times like this, though, Eli did wish he had a better idea of what was going on. Usually he didn't care, but when it came to renegade storm fronts, it started to get interesting.

Seth would say it was the Triskelians. He believed, as did all the Guard initiates, that Triskelians were the most dangerous of all rebel factions. To hear Seth tell it, the Triskelians were responsible for every evil deed and all seemingly natural disasters. Seth often came home from initiate rallies talking about Triskelia, the supposed rebel front, but Eli couldn't really believe that any Droughtlander would have the skill or health or wealth to do much of anything other than wait for death and pray that it came quick and in the least painful incarnation as possible. It's not that he thought Droughtlanders, or Triskelians in particular, were no better than rats, that wasn't it. It was just that he couldn't imagine such an exhausted, sickly people organizing anything that would actually pan out. To hear the kitchen staff talk, which Eli did whenever he could as they had the tallest, bawdiest tales of all the house staff, Triskelia was either a religious cult for the feeble-minded or a myth born of drug-induced visions and the misplaced idealism of Droughtlanders with potent imaginations.

"And just as well," Cook had once said, gently directing her staff back to their tasks. "I wouldn't want some Droughtland filth thinking they have any right to what we got here in the Keys. Them's that are born into it, or them's that are lucky to get culled to work before getting a sick, it's hard enough making the food go round as it is."

Recalling what Cook had said reminded Eli of something else, a realization that made his blood quicken. His mother's family never had a cook. They'd run a bookshop in the Northwestern Key and had lived above it in a tiny apartment with a kitchen—according to Lisette's stories of her childhood—no bigger than a sailboat's galley, and while Eli had never been on a sailboat, he'd seen pictures. The kitchen had been tiny, and their income had been modest. Two facts that did not add up to a cook of any kind.

Eli bounded down the stairs and out the front door, followed closely by Bullet, the dog Seth got as a puppy and had trained to be a guard dog, a project he'd long since lost interest in. Bullet, on the other hand, had long since decided that Eli was the kinder master of the two. He followed him everywhere, unless he was fenced inside the kennel behind the stables. Gulzar rushed out of the stables as Eli and Bullet ran past.

"Whoa, whoa. What's the hurry, Master Eli?"

"I have to talk to my mother."

"She'll be home later! Join me on a ride before that storm arrives? And what about your training?"

"Later, Gulzar. I have to ask her something." Eli took off out the gate.

"Master Eli! Come back! Please!"

Eli shook his head and ran faster, his breath settling into a familiar pace, his muscles loosening. He'd missed running. It felt good, as if his worries were slipping away with each step.

ELI STOPPED ACROSS THE STREET from the gardens. His sweat cooling, his breath evening out, he watched the gates from the teashop across the street. There were two gates. One opened into the Key's gardens, enjoyed and accessed by all, especially young children brought there by their tutors and nannies. Eli and Seth had spent many afternoons there, first with their nannies, and then with their tutors. They'd had a few women tutors over the years, but they'd had an especially hard time keeping Seth in line. Because of this, Edmund had long insisted on male tutors, and so Eli had spent hours and hours of sunshine and blue sky watching them flirt with the young nannies of the Key while Seth dominated the children's games Eli was never included in. That was not the part of the garden Eli was interested in today. He wanted to get into the botanical garden where his mother worked.

The environment inside the long glass greenhouses was carefully monitored, with traffic kept to a minimum to avoid introducing foreign bacteria to the fragile ecosystem. Eli had never been in the greenhouse where his mother worked long hours each day. His parents had been talking about him studying botany lately, this after Eli had failed the accounting exam that would've set him on the path to become a financial advisor with Keyland Finances. Accounting was Edmund's second choice for Eli after Eli had failed to demonstrate the leadership qualities required to follow Edmund into politics. Eli hadn't exactly leapt at the idea of being a botanist either. Sometimes he wished he had the sense of purpose Seth had. Maybe he *would* go into botany. It could be interesting. And it was important work, befitting the son of the Chief Regent. Eli laughed at himself. He'd likely fail at botany too. It was Seth's job to excel. It seemed he was always ahead of Eli, and if Eli ever did manage to do something better than Seth, Seth hounded him so hard that Eli never bothered to try to outdo his twin any more. Let Seth shine. Eli couldn't care less. What he wanted right now was to get into the gardens. Eli laughed at himself again. If he had shown a little more interest in taking up botany when Lisette had suggested it, he wouldn't be stuck for a way into the gardens right now. That's the way life seemed for Eli though; always behind by a few steps. Never on top.

Mustering what little courage he could, he crossed the road and approached the gateminder.

"I need to see my mother, Lisette Maddox."

"I know who your mother is." The gateminder passed him a slip of paper and a pencil. "Leave a message."

"I'd like to see her in person."

"Would you now, Master Eli?" The gateminder fixed his eyes on him. "It is Master Eli, isn't it? You're not the other one?"

"Seth has blond hair. Now, I would like to see my mother. Please let me in!"

The gateminder slowly rose from his post. He stretched his arms above his head and yawned before stepping outside. He was putting on a show, and it was not lost on Eli.

"Just let me in."

"Quite the storm brewing over there. Not on the schedule. Bit of a rogue, I guess."

"Let me in, please."

"Well, I'll go let her know that you're here." The gateminder checked that the gate was locked before starting down the path to the greenhouse. He meandered slowly, stopping here and there to smell the flowers, tie his shoelace, and have another stretch. Eli wanted to throttle the man, or at least holler after him to hurry the hell up, but he resisted. He sat on a bench to wait, with Bullet lying at his feet, asleep.

IT WAS OVER AN HOUR before the gateminder reappeared with Lisette and let him in. Without a word she turned on her heel and headed back down the path to the greenhouse. Eli smirked at the gateminder and followed her. Bullet bounded ahead of them, disappearing into the lush bush surrounding the long greenhouse. Lisette kept a couple of paces ahead of him. If he sped up, so did she. She kept her chin high, and did not say a word until they reached the door.

"Bullet stays outside." She gazed at Eli, a strange and tender look on her face. "I don't know what to do with you, Elijah. What am I supposed to do with you?"

Eli balked at the sound of his full name, but then he reminded himself that he'd come here to ask *her* questions, not the other way around.

"You didn't have a cook when you were a child, did you?"

"*Quoi?*"

"That woman at the window can't have been your cook. You never had one!"

Lisette unlocked the door and led him into an anteroom.

"Take your shoes off and put these on." She handed him a pair of boots. "Does your brother know you're here?"

Eli shook his head.

"Your father?"

Eli shook his head again as an uneasy feeling crept up his spine. Once more it was as if she, and she alone, was keeping the truth from him.

"And this." She handed him a long smock similar to hers. "Over your clothes."

She led him into the greenhouse where the air was hot and moist, so cloying it was almost difficult to breathe. The massive glass building was full of brilliant greens, and the pungent aromas of tree and vine fruit were so strong that Eli thought if he stuck his tongue out the air would taste sweet.

"This is all too soon," Lisette said as she led him down the length of the greenhouse. "The others say that the time has come, but I think it is too soon."

"Too soon for what?"

Lisette shook her head, as if in conversation with herself, oblivious to Eli. "It's all gone so wrong. It wasn't supposed to be like this. Not at all. If only . . . "

"If only what?"

Again Lisette shook her head. "I must trust. I will trust." She stopped and took Eli's hand in hers. "*Mon fils.* I do trust you. I always have."

"What is this about?"

Lisette held his gaze for a long moment. "Do you trust me?"

"Of course, Maman."

"But you haven't, lately."

"Because you—"

Lisette gripped his hand tight. "You and your brother are so different. When you were little I treated you the same, teaching you compassion and empathy without your father knowing. I watched him make you hunt, and deny your friendships with the staff's children, and teach you to be so cruel to the labour, and I hoped my teaching would at least end up in a balance of sorts. That my attention to the soul and the heart and the body would result in compassion and critical thinking and understanding and strength."

"But I *don't* understand, Maman." There was a crashing sound in Eli's ears, a panic pounding against his skull. This was not right. This was the way things went in stories just before it was all about to collapse.

"Just trust. Right now I just need you to trust." Lisette took his other hand too, her eyes wide. "This is all how it was always meant to go, only it is happening sooner than I'd hoped, and without your brother. Despite my influence, he is too much like your father. I don't know what will come of all of this, but I can only pray that you will come to understand, and will not make hasty decisions."

"You're scaring me, Maman."

"Good." She let go of his hands. "Then you will not take any of this lightly. I don't believe you are ready, but at this point, there is no choice."

"Ready for what?"

"You will see." Lisette pulled a thin lever that looked like part of the irrigation system. A section of the back wall slid back, revealing a narrow, dimly lit hall. "Follow me."

She didn't have to say it; there was no way Eli wasn't going to follow her into the mysterious corridor. Heart pounding, mind spinning, he followed her down two flights of stairs and another even narrower hall that eventually opened into a large room, lit only with lanterns and candles. As Eli's eyes adjusted to the dimness, he made out rows of tables strewn with books and maps and what looked like equipment of various kinds being repaired or taken apart. And people—there must have been a hundred of them at least, all of them quiet, looking up at him and Lisette standing on the landing. No one was dressed in the smartly cut clothes of the Keys; they wore the tired tunics and threadbare pants of the Droughtland instead, a look Eli associated with sicks and filth. One by one, they stood.

"Who are they?"

Lisette ignored him, and instead addressed the crowd. "This is my son. This is Eli."

"Where's the other one?" someone called from the darkness.

"He is not ready."

"He might not ever be!" someone else called. Eli squinted into the darkness, but could not place the voice. "How long will we wait?"

"I don't have all the answers." Lisette waved. "Please, go back to work. Time will take care of the rest." No one moved. All eyes were on Eli, who felt the shudder of collective wariness.

"Time?" Another voice from the dark. "We don't have much more, Lisette."

"Silence, please."

"Who are these people?"

"Rebels." Lisette sighed. "They live here. There are bunks along the wall."

"*Rebels?*" What did this mean? What was going on? Eli's mind raced with questions doused in fear, but he wanted to appear calm, he knew somehow that he *needed* to be calm, so he held back. "H-how d-do they get in?"

"There are a few ways." Lisette led him to a chair. He glanced behind him. Slowly the people sat down again, their murmurs and grumbling an unnerving undercurrent to the quiet. Finally Eli sat. "You don't need to know what you don't need to know. Yet. So? What do you think?"

Fear? Shock? Surprise? Eli wasn't sure. Something about all this was not surprising in the least. He wasn't so much unnerved as tremendously curious. And he felt privileged that his mother was showing him this—whatever it was—when it was clear that neither Edmund nor Seth knew about it.

"What do you think, Eli?"

"About what? I don't know what all this is, I don't know who those people are, I don't understand what you're doing down here. I have no idea what to think!" Eli dropped his head into his hands as a man approached out of the shadows. Eli glanced up at him. He glared at Eli. Several large men, all with formidable scowls, flanked the man.

"Why today, Lisette?"

"Gregor, this is my son. Eli."

"I *know* who he is, but why is he here, now of all times?"

"After what has happened, can you know when the time would be right?" Lisette shrugged. "Everything has changed now. His curiosity was becoming dangerous. He knew there was something to be discovered. Didn't you, Eli?"

Eli nodded, although he didn't know what he was discovering, even now. All he'd known before was that Lisette was keeping something from him, but he'd had no idea that it was something so clandestine as this. This, this was huge, and Eli didn't know what to do with it. Gregor motioned for the other men to leave them. When they'd retreated into the shadows, Gregor leaned in close, his breath oniony.

"We have waited a long time for you, but it was never to happen like this. By being here you are swearing yourself to silence. If you don't keep the silence, we will keep it for you, understand?"

Eli nodded, wanting to pull away from Gregor's smell but afraid to insult him.

Lisette put a hand on Gregor's shoulder. "My son is not one who can be bullied."

Oh, but he certainly was one to be bullied, by Seth, their father, other Keylander children, tutors and nannies and maids, even the children of tutors and nannies and maids. Eli silently thanked his mother. She was creating a space for him to become someone new down here in this strange, dim world.

No one knew him here. No one knew how he'd spent days at a time in a darkened room as a child, crippled by migraines, how he'd wet the bed until he was twelve, how he'd clung to Lisette's side whenever meeting someone new, even children younger than him.

He'd spent fifteen years as the weak one, the coward, the crybaby, the sissy, the mama's boy. He was going to turn sixteen soon, so why not be someone new? This was his chance. Eli did his best to ignore the urge to vomit.

He rose, squared his shoulders like Edmund always did, and extended his hand.

"Pleased to meet you, Gregor."

Gregor sneered. "We don't shake hands here." He stepped back. "Lisette, I hope you know what you're doing. Are we to expect a surprise visit from the other one too?"

"No. Not yet. Master Seth is far too content with his war games. He wouldn't think twice about telling his father." Lisette touched Eli's shoulder. "I don't know what to do about Seth, but we've always known Eli would join us at some point, did we not?"

"But not this soon! And not at a time like this. Just keep him quiet." Gregor backed into the shadows, leaving a wake of disapproval behind him.

"Waiting for me? You knew that I would join what?" Eli sat back down. "What is all this?"

"This is a rebel cell." Lisette poured two mugs of tea. "More specifically, this is the rebel headquarters for the Eastern region. I am the leader of this cell."

Eli wanted to clamp his hand over his mother's mouth and make her shut up. The things she was saying! If Edmund or anyone found out what was going on down here, they'd all be executed—Gregor, his mother, everyone! And what about Eli? He knew now. He would be executed too. But if he were to tell, could he have his mother spared? What would happen to her if this secret room was discovered?

Lisette watched him. "You're excited?"

Eli nodded.

"And afraid?"

"I don't know what to think."

"But how you *feel*, you're afraid?"

"Yes."

"And?"

"Conflicted, confused." Eli dropped his head into his hands. "Father says there are no real rebels, but then Seth is always going on about that cult Triskelia. Although Cook says it's all just a myth."

"It is no myth." Lisette lifted down a stack of books from a shelf. "And Triskelia is not a cult."

She opened a thick book and pointed to an illustration of a hollow triangle with an S-curve radiating from each corner. "This is the symbol of Triskelia. The symbol of the rebels. The symbol of our people, Eli."

Our people? As far as Eli had ever known, the Keyland elite were his people. This secret room, the people in it, everything his mother was saying, seemed so unlikely, yet all of it—even the unknown—was so alluring that he could almost imagine letting go of what he thought he knew to be truth in exchange for the truth his mother held. It all resonated within him somewhere, like an echo of his own voice. He traced the triangle with a finger. If this was the symbol of his people, then who was his mother? Who was his father, really? And who was he?

3

~~❧~~

Lisette wouldn't answer any more questions until after Eli had read the massive book she placed before him: *The True History*. It was like the dry tomes the tutors fed him, going back to the livestock diseases and avian influenzas, global warming, water commodification, corporate war, overpopulation, all the factors that Eli already knew contributed to the need for forming the Group of Keys.

"But I know all this!" The last thing Eli wanted to do was read when this underground labyrinth begged to be explored. "I want to know what's happening now!"

"You don't know all of it." Lisette patted his head. "Keep reading."

"What about time? They said they didn't know how much more time there was, and you want me to take precious time and read this?"

"Time is always precious, and yes, we don't know how much time we have, but it could be lots. And it might be none. Read."

And so Eli read, distracted by the quiet bustling of the underground population and the creaking of the building that seemed to practically breathe with the secrets it kept in its bowels. He wanted to run up and down the lengths of tables and workbenches, drinking in the sights, meeting the people, gleaning what he could. Lisette sat with him, though, working on something, keeping an eye on him. And so he read. Chapter after chapter of what he already knew.

And then suddenly she was right. The very next chapter accused the founders of the Group of Keys of annihilating eighty-two percent of the world's poorest populations by biological and environmental warfare. Eli had never heard of that. Nor had anyone mentioned that cloudseeding had been used as an intervention in civil wars happening in lands where the Keys had investments or large interests in their natural resources such as oil or water. Furthermore, the Keys had severely modified the weather, totally unbeknownst to the battling regimes or their insurgents who were variously assaulted by monsoons, blizzards, or heat waves—all deadly and environmentally debilitating.

The technique had also been used to induce drought in already struggling countries so that the floundering governments were forced to sell their water rights to the Group of Keys in the hope that they'd provide water for their people at a reasonable cost. It was reasonable to begin with, but as the prices were jacked up based on the supposed rising costs of shipping the water in the "unfortunate ongoing drought," clean water became unaffordable and the Group of Keys managed to extinguish another ten percent of the world's population.

The chapter after that talked about how little infrastructure survived with only eight percent of the world's population left to manage it. The Group of Keys had been prepared for the loss of labour in their third world sweatshops, but not for the long-term impact. Slowly the world's material goods degraded, and there were no replacements since there was no labour to produce them. The Group of Keys adjusted though, forming the enclaves and moving their families and staff into them, erecting walls to keep out everyone else. Eli was back on familiar ground now, although shaken at the thought that the Group of Keys was responsible for the death of ninety-two percent of the world's population. If all this was really true, giving up the Keylanders as *his people* just got easier.

Eli kept reading. The Keylanders' goal was to resurrect the leisure class. As long as they had good food and water, beautiful estates and civilized society with loyal staff, why bother pursuing the plastic nuisances of the past? Had such rampant consumerism been all that ideal? Radiating computers and car exhaust, slavery to email and phones? The Keylanders were reviving the easy times enjoyed by the ruling class centuries before: tea parties on perfectly manicured lawns, stormy nights spent playing cards in cozy parlours, afternoons at the piano or with friends, a pantomime at Christmas. The Group of Keys had only to ensure one thing. Rain. And they did that by perfecting the art and science of cloudseeding, redirecting the weather patterns so that what precipitation there was would fall on the Keys, leaving the land between the Keys parched.

The land between became known as the Droughtland, and the people struggling to survive in it, the Droughtlanders.

ELI GOT THAT FAR THE FIRST DAY. When it was time to go home he hadn't found out any more about Triskelia or what exactly his mother and the others did under the greenhouse, but he did leave armed with knowledge that shook the very definition of the society he lived in and who he believed himself to be. The strangers working below the gardens all silently watched him as he left, and as their gazes bore into his back he felt both small and limitless.

On the walk home he and Lisette barely spoke. Eli's mind was booming with all he'd learned and seen that day, and Lisette had made it very clear as they'd headed back up into daylight that she would not tolerate any reference to the rebels outside the secret room. As they turned the last corner before their estate, she stopped.

"What will you tell Seth?" she whispered. "About where you've been all day."

"He never asks."

"Good. I don't have to tell you again that he is not to ever know about any of this, do I? Or your father?"

Once again, Eli wanted to ask. Ask everything. Ask about her and his father, ask how she got involved, what they were planning, was she even a botanist at all? Lisette saw his curiosity building like a belch.

"Shh. Not here," she said as a crack of thunder resounded and the first fat drops of the storm fell. She looked up at the sky. "Another one lost." She ushered Eli into the doorway of a closed shop. "These are dangerous times, Eli. If anything should happen to me, I want you to promise that you won't try to go to the greenhouse alone. It's not safe. If for any reason you need anything, I want you to know you can talk to Gulzar."

"Gulzar is a—?"

"Shh." She nodded. "No more talk. Not at all. I will let you know when it is safe for you to come again."

"How?"

"We'll say you've decided on botany after all." Lisette looked pleased with herself. "That you want to follow in your maman's footsteps. A bright beginning to a promising career. Your father will be so pleased that you've finally settled on a direction. He's been so worried about your aimlessness."

"Aimlessness." Eli's stomach flipped. He'd been made aware of many things that day, but he wasn't sure what he truly believed, or wanted to believe. He doubted he had any more direction than he'd had that morning. In fact, he felt about as lost as he thought was possible. "I have no idea what is real any more, Maman. Do you realize that? Do you understand what you're asking of me? Do you understand what it's like to have what you thought of as your life be turned upside down and replaced with the strangest things?"

"I know this is all overwhelming." Lisette patted his cheek. "Of course it is. But I trust you. And you must trust me. There is no going back to ignorance, *tu comprends*? I promise that it will all make sense with time."

"I need it to make sense now!"

"In time, Eli." She stepped back into the street, the heavy rain quickly darkening her cloak. "Now come, let's go home."

Home. What was that, if not another lie? Where did the deceit end and his life begin? What did this mean for his family? His father? Seth? How could he keep all of this to himself?

BUT ELI SOON DISCOVERED that he was surprisingly good at keeping secrets, or rather, the secrets keeping him. The weight and breadth of what he'd seen was a colossal beast he was afraid of releasing. Whenever possible he answered his father in one- or two-word sentences, spoke as little as he could get away with to the house staff and his tutor, and didn't speak to Seth at all, unless it could not be avoided. But Seth rarely had anything to say to him, so keeping something from Seth was actually very easy. But to Gulzar, whom he spoke to the most of all, more than his mother or tutor or anyone, he didn't know what to say.

At his mother's orders, he met Gulzar for a training session the morning after he'd been below the gardens. The early morning mist was thick and the grass slick with dew as they set off for a run across the rolling hills that stretched out behind the main house. Usually they chatted easily as they ran, partly as a way of making sure they were pacing themselves. But today, with each question from Gulzar, Eli quickened his stride.

"You came back late yesterday," Gulzar said as they descended into the orchard. "Where were you all day?"

"Nowhere." Eli took a sharp turn back up the hill.

"Where are you going?" Gulzar stopped. "We're not even halfway!"

Eli kept running. He couldn't lie to Gulzar, not knowing that he was a part of it somehow. If only he knew how much Gulzar knew, and if it was safe to ask him. Back at the gym above the stables, Eli quickly jumped into the shower before Gulzar returned. Gulzar was waiting for him at the wall of free weights.

"Why did you change out of your gym clothes, Master Eli?"

Eli shrugged. "I don't feel very good. I'm going to skip the rest of the workout."

Gulzar let a long moment stretch before answering. "As you wish." He opened the door for Eli. "Perhaps you'll feel better tomorrow."

"I hope so." Eli clutched his gym bag to his chest and rushed out into the fresh morning air.

IF HE COULD HARDLY HOLD BACK with Gulzar, it was the opposite at the house. In his father's company, or Seth's, he might as well have had his lips sewn together, he was so reluctant to talk. Or maybe it was the lack of opportunity. Seth rarely spoke to him at all, and Edmund even less. Seth was wrapped up in his Guard initiate ceremonies and rallies, counting down the days to their sixteenth birthday, the day he'd be able to move to the Keyland Guard base and begin his training to become a full-fledged member of the Guard.

As for Edmund, his time was filled with whatever Chancellor East filled it with. Lately, it was the upcoming legislative session that would see the Chancellors and their Regents and staff from all eight North American Keys descend on the Eastern Key for a month of political debates and lavish celebrations. It was a busy time.

And what of time? If it was so much the essence, why wasn't Lisette summoning him to the gardens again? When would she? When could he ask her more about the people working there? Who were they? Where did they come from?

Days went by, and Lisette behaved as if nothing had ever happened. Her act was so seamless that Eli wondered more than once if he was crazy and had imagined it all. But it had happened. As little as he'd been introduced to, he knew it was all real. Fleeting and compelling and very real. He wanted more. And he could not wait. Every morning he asked if he could go to the gardens with her and every morning she said no.

"Not yet, love."

"But when?"

"I will tell you when." And off she'd go, leaving Eli with his curiosity like a gut ache.

She gave him nothing. No signal, no hints, no nothing. Finally, when he could stand it no longer, he cornered her. She was playing the piano in the drawing room, fumbling over a difficult piece of music.

"When can I go with you?" he asked as the music crescendoed louder. "I have to know."

"You're not to bring it up." Lisette waited for another loud section before continuing in a whisper. "Too dangerous. Might arouse suspicion. Be patient."

Forced patience was twisting him into knots. Eli's stomach could not deal with the stress of uncertainty and anticipation—those were foreign things to him. Everything in the Key was predictable, planned. He'd only ever anticipated Christmas and birthdays. Nothing like this.

THEN, AT SUPPER ONE NIGHT, just after the power plant had been mysteriously tampered with, Edmund set down his fork.

"Darling, now don't be alarmed, but I need to ask you something of great importance." They were dining by candlelight, which was usually a pleasant change, but now Eli could hardly swallow. He forced himself not to look at Lisette.

"Yes, Edmund?"

"Do you know anything—anything at all—about what happened at the power plant?"

"Why would I?"

"Well, I'm not generally at liberty to discuss such matters, but you should know that the Guard is investigating the gardens for a possible link to the attack."

"Attack? Is that what we're calling it?" She took a sip of water. "Oh dear, should we be alarmed?"

Eli was impressed by his mother's calm command of herself. Inside, he was reeling with fear for her, for the people living below the greenhouse, and for himself. He felt as if he were wearing his new knowledge like a dishonouring badge. As if all Edmund had to do was glance at him to know exactly what was going on.

"It's the Triskelians!" Seth blurted.

"There is no such thing," Edmund growled. "Don't talk nonsense."

"Come on, Father, if the Guard believes it, why don't you?"

"These *rebels*," Edmund shook his head, "aren't intelligent enough to organize anything of any significance or power. I'm inclined, as is the

Chancellor, to believe it is the work of one or two deviants, who will be caught and dealt with in short order."

"Well, then." Lisette helped herself to more meat. "It doesn't sound like it has anything to do with the gardens at all, does it?"

"The Guard seems to think so." Edmund straightened in his chair. "Colonel Grey has asked me personally to mention it to you, and to ask you to keep your eyes and ears open while you're at work. You might see or hear something that you wouldn't normally think unusual, but in these times, it would be helpful if you reported to me each night anything you think might be relevant."

"I will."

"You'll keep your eyes open? Take notice?"

Lisette folded her napkin and smiled. "I've just said I will, haven't I?"

ELI KNEW BETTER than to ask again about when he'd be allowed back below the gardens. It wasn't likely to happen any time soon, he presumed, not since the power plant incident, and probably not until well after the legislative session came and went and the Guard relaxed a little. To distract himself, and to hopefully learn more, maybe something that would be helpful to Lisette and the others, Eli made it his business to eavesdrop on his father and the Chancellor when they met in Edmund's study.

To do this he had to excuse himself from lessons, so just as Professor Wood was about to begin a history lesson, he'd ask. The twins' latest tutor—they never lasted long—was a pale stick of a man who assumed that Eli had a bladder infection, and so didn't say anything about Eli's frequent requests to use the bathroom.

"Professor Wood?" Eli said one day as the young man pulled out the history texts Eli had taken as truth until so recently. "May I please be excused, sir?"

"Of course, Master Eli." Professor Wood blushed. "I've told you before, there's no need to ask."

"Does it hurt when you piss, *Eliza*?" Seth smirked. "Do you have to sit down like a girl?"

"You mean like you do every time?" Eli immediately wished he hadn't said it.

Seth stood and wiggled his fingers as a come-on to fight. "Come right up to me and say that again, Eliza. I'll make it so it hurts just to blink, never mind piss."

"That's quite enough, Master Seth." Professor Wood stepped between them. "Please take your seat."

Seth glared at Professor Wood as though he'd changed his mind and would far rather pop him now instead of Eli, but Seth had been warned by Edmund that if he drove off yet another tutor he'd be kept back from the Guard until he could "manage himself more appropriately."

Seth tried to let it go, and he almost succeeded, but he couldn't quite resist. "Shut up, Woody," he muttered as he sat.

Now anger coloured the tutor's cheeks. "I'm afraid I'll have to speak to your father if you insist on harassing either myself or Master Eli about his unfortunate condition."

"You mean you got a pissing problem too?" Seth asked.

"You know very well what I mean." Professor Wood nodded at Eli. "You're excused, Master Eli."

"Thank you, sir." Eli doubled over a little and winced. "I'll be sure to tell my mother about your kindness and consideration."

"Suck up!" Seth called after him as he left the room. "Be sure to wipe the brown stuff off your nose before you come back or you'll stink up the whole room with it!"

ELI RACED DOWN THE STAIRS to Edmund's study, where his father and the Chancellor had been camped out all day for the second day in a row. Each time Eli put his ear to the door he'd heard nothing of interest, mostly dull planning about the upcoming legislative session. This time, however, was different.

"No, Edmund"—the Chancellor's tone was furious—"*below* one of the greenhouses, not actually *in* it."

"But there is no 'below' any of the greenhouses," Edmund said. "I should know; I cut the ribbon on opening day. I've had several tours. There's not even a crawl space, let alone some far-fetched secret chamber. Are you sure this isn't just some rumour out of the Guard? You know how they can be."

Eli held his breath, not sure if he should run to the gardens and warn his mother immediately or stay put and hear more.

"My sources are not wrong about this," Chancellor East said. "The gateminder has proven his loyalty before."

That weasel! Eli put a hand to his mouth. His mother! Gregor! The others! How much time was there? He had to *do* something!

"Well then, what is to be done about it, sir?" Edmund must've been pacing the floor; some of what he said was clear, but then other bits were barely audible. Eli mashed his ear against the door.

"You have several options," his father was saying. "You could call in the Guard and have them raid the greenhouses in their rather clumsy, blundering manner, or you could leave it for a while, perhaps send an eye or two in to learn the inner workings, and then raid it."

"We could ask Lisette to be an eye," Chancellor East said.

"We could."

Eli sighed with relief. That meant his father didn't suspect her, didn't it?

"But there are other options, Edmund." The Chancellor said this with a glee that was clearly detectable, even through the door.

There was a pause, and then Edmund spoke. "What do you have in mind, sir?"

"Blow the whole thing up. Make it look like the *rebels* did it! Isn't it brilliant?"

There was another pause, this one much longer. "Brilliant, sir."

"It is, if I might say so myself."

"However, it would be problematic, Chancellor."

"What?" Chancellor East growled. "Why?"

"The botanical garden would be destroyed, and with it all the years of work. You are aware that our exotic fruits bring in a full ten percent of our trade from other Keys? And that's not including tobacco or coffee beans."

"I know that. What do you take me for?" There was the familiar chomping gnaw as the Chancellor chewed on his pipe. "That is the beauty of it. No one would ever suspect the Group of Keys to be responsible for such a heinous act of terrorism. And wouldn't the people of the Eastern Key, of *all* the Keys, despise the rebels for ruining decades of vital agricultural gains? All of a sudden we'd have the strongest Anti-terrorist Keyland Organization of all the Keys on this continent! Wouldn't that be grand?"

"Yes, sir." Edmund's response was not enthusiastic in the least. "Grand."

"Of course, you'll make the arrangements, Edmund. I don't want to know all the details. Plausible denial, you understand. I leave it up to you. I want it done before the legislature convenes, of course. I don't want the Chancellors here when it happens, but I would appreciate their sympathies and generous donations toward rebuilding afterward, when they're here to behold the shocking ruins of what had once been the most glorious gardens in all of Keyland."

"Yes, sir. Of course." Eli heard his father ease into the old leather chair behind the desk, and then the familiar creaking as he spun his cherished glass globe on its axis. The plan had to be stopped. Eli closed his eyes and imagined the globe moving under his father's fingers, spinning so fast that the etched landmasses blurred into each other like clouds. That's what this felt like. Out of control, stormy, and going too fast. It had to be stopped, but how?

ELI FOUGHT THE URGE to run straight to the gardens, beat up the gateminder, and warn everyone. But he had never beaten anyone up, and he didn't know how to open the back wall to the hidden stairs. There was no way he could do anything without sparking a suspicion that would no doubt spiral into severe, unspeakable punishment for everyone involved, including himself. And so he fretted all afternoon, roiling with worry and helplessness. When it was time for Lisette to come home he waited outside for her, his heart pounding like heavy footsteps on stone. When he saw her turn the corner he ran to her, and in a flustered, hushed spill of words reported the conversation he'd overheard.

"We knew it was only a matter of time." She sounded calm, but she'd pulled off her gloves and was twisting them anxiously in her hands. "That's why we rotate locations. It will only take a week or so to prepare the next cell."

"We may not have a week, Maman! It could happen any day before the legislature and that's only two weeks away!"

"We can't talk like this." Lisette glanced down the street behind her. The sidewalks were scattered with shoppers and others heading home, and still others simply out enjoying the sunshine. "Not here." And with that she headed up the walk to the open front door where the new maid was waiting to take her cloak. Eli followed slowly, not sure if he could trust himself to keep silent. He slumped against the door while his mother handed the girl her hat and gloves with a smile. When the girl slipped off toward the kitchen, Eli took one more chance.

"You can't go back, Maman!" he whispered. "Not ever. It's not safe!"

Lisette replied in an even quieter whisper. "I must, Eli. To get everyone organized, and to keep your father from suspecting anything. How would it look? I've gone to the greenhouse every workday for the last seventeen years and then all of a sudden I don't?"

"You could pretend to be ill."

"They need me, Eli."

"But what about the bomb?"

"I'm not the only person to consider in this matter." Lisette smiled as the maid returned with a tray of tea and biscuits.

"Thank you, dear. We'll take it in the parlour."

The maid curtsied before retreating again. When she was well out of earshot, Lisette cupped her hand to Eli's ear and whispered again. "There is a whole network of rebels to keep safe. I will not be there when it happens, if it happens at all. There are secret ways to leave. No one will be there."

"Do you promise?"

She nodded, and then winked at him as Seth bounded down the stairs, dressed in a crisply pressed Guard uniform. "Mother!" Seth cried, having abandoned what he now called the babyish Maman just days before. "My uniform came! Look!"

"I see that." Lisette nodded. "And you look positively dashing, Seth."

Seth turned in front of the mirror at the bottom of the stairs. "I do, don't I?"

As Seth ran down the hall to present himself to Edmund, Eli grabbed his mother's hands in his. They were cold, and felt frail, not like the hands of someone who could handle all of this. "Maman, you can't go back! Please!"

"I won't be there. Everyone will be safe." Lisette winked at Eli again as Seth paraded back down the hall toward them. "I promise."

4

The next morning Eli was waiting for his mother by the door when she left for the gardens.

"Don't go, Maman," he pleaded as she pulled on her cloak. He followed her outside.

"Don't worry, Eli." She went on tiptoes to kiss his forehead. "How tall you are."

"Don't." He pulled away. "Don't treat me like a baby."

Lisette sighed. "We have at least a few days. Your father isn't one to make hasty decisions, especially not of this magnitude. I will urge everyone to work quickly."

"I will worry, Maman."

"Of course you will." She patted his cheek with her gloved hand and then fastened her cloak. "I'll see you at dinner, *mon fils. Je t'aime.*"

Eli watched his mother until she turned the corner, and then he plodded along to the dining room for breakfast, feeling as helpless as an infant. Seth was already there, sitting at their father's place. He tilted the chair back and rested his feet on the edge of the long polished table.

"What's with the face?"

Eli took the chair farthest from Seth and poured himself a cup of tea. He added a heap of honey and stirred.

"Aw, is widdle Ewiza sad? Poor baby." Seth lifted his feet and let the chair crash down. The young maid standing ready by the kitchen door jumped, startled. Eli stirred his tea slowly, clanging the spoon against the cup, willing himself to ignore his brother.

"Stop it, Eli."

"Stop what?"

"Stirring your tea like that."

"Is that another one of your rules?" Eli clanged the spoon with zeal. "Now I can't even stir my tea without your permission?"

"Stop it!" Seth yanked the spoon out of Eli's hand and threw it at the wall. Again the maid flinched. She looked over her shoulder, unsure if she should summon help or not.

Eli saluted his brother. "Sir! Yes, sir!"

Seth leapt out of Edmund's chair and lifted his hand as if to salute, but instead he whacked the back of Eli's head so hard his head jerked forward and his teeth rang. The spot where Seth's Guard initiate ring hit stung viciously.

In just over three weeks he and Seth would turn sixteen, and Seth would move out of the house to the Guard base. Eli resisted the urge to rub his head. Three more weeks. Eli couldn't wait until he could count the days on his fingers.

Edmund came in then, a folder of papers in hand. He claimed his seat where Seth had been sitting just seconds before. Eli wished he'd held his tongue so that their father could've caught Seth usurping his place. Both boys bowed their heads slightly and murmured in unison, "Good morning, Father."

"Boys." Edmund kept his eyes on his paper and extended his hand out, palm up. The maid took a step forward but stopped when Edmund shook his head. "You can fetch my eggs and bacon from the kitchen. One of my sons will fetch my tea and toast."

Eli stared at his father. What had he done about the gardens? Anything yet? Surely not, judging by his calm. But then their father was always hard to read. Sometimes impossible.

Seth shoved Eli. Eli shoved back, so Seth shoved Eli right out of his chair. Edmund glanced up coolly. "Sooner than later."

"Yes, Father." Eli glared at Seth as he gathered himself off the floor and went to fetch Edmund's tea.

"Marmalade, this morning, I think," Edmund said as he accepted his cup.

"Yes, Father." Eli buttered two pieces of toast. Seth passed him on his way out and grabbed one of the pieces.

"Yes, *Father*," Seth whispered. "Yes, Father, anything you say, Father, but please don't make me join the Guard, I might chip a nail."

"Like Maman says," Eli whispered, "smart ones don't join the Guard."

"Mother never said that."

"Oh yes, she did. Ask her yourself. She says anyone who joins the Guard might as well be a sheep. She says the Guard is just one big baby game of follow the leader. No original thought required. No thought required period, just blind, boring obedience. Her words exactly."

"If Father wasn't in the room I'd kick your face in."

"You're all just sheep. You know nothing." Eli barely whispered it. "Baaa."

"Later, Eliza." Seth snatched the other piece of toast just as Eli finished spreading the marmalade all the way to the edges, the only way Edmund would accept it. Seth waved it in Eli's face before taking a bite. "You just wait."

THE EXPLOSION HAPPENED two hours later, as Professor Wood was just about to begin another history lesson and Eli was just about to excuse himself. At first Eli thought it was thunder, but no rain had been scheduled and there hadn't been any rogue storms on the horizon earlier. As the blasts continued, Eli knew. He also knew at once that his mother was dead. Seth and Eli ran to the tall bay window and stared in awe at the flames and smoke rising up from where the elegant gleaming greenhouses had stood just moments before. Shattered glass rained down on the Key.

It seemed like ages before the smoke and dust even began to clear. There was nothing left, just a great crater of rubble in the middle of the now devastated gardens.

"Maman," whispered Eli.

"Oh, she's fine," the professor said too quickly. "She got out, surely. I'm sure she's fine."

"The rebels did this!" Seth balled his hands into fists. "There were rumours at the rally last night. Rumours that rebels were inside the Key."

"Maman." Eli slumped against the window. "She was in there, Seth."

"I'm going down." Seth pulled on his uniform jacket. "Have you seen my cap?"

"Don't you care that she was in there?" Eli looked up at his brother. "Don't you care that she's dead?"

"Of course. Don't be stupid." Seth rooted in his jacket pockets for his regulation blue cap that identified him as an initiate. "That's why I'm going. To see what I can do. To help, rather than sit here crying like a baby. Maybe she's still alive, maybe she needs help. But you're just going to stay there, bawling your eyes out, aren't you? Not me." Seth saluted the portrait of the Chancellor above the door. "I'm going to do something about it."

Eli stayed at the bay window watching the gardens the entire day, until it grew dark and all he could see was the glow of the labourers' lanterns and the deeper orange glow of the fires that still burned. At some point Cook sent up a tray of food, but Eli left it untouched except to give Bullet the slice of roast. Eventually he fell asleep, his head leaning against the cold window, his knees pulled up, Bullet lying across his feet. He dreamt of Gregor and the damp shadowy room below the greenhouse. Eli was looking for his mother in a maze of dim corridors. Gregor was helping him, but they couldn't find her anywhere.

A low growl from Bullet woke Eli in the middle of the night. Edmund stood in the doorway, his face shadowed by the hall light behind him.

"Your mother is missing."

"She's dead!" Eli's dream only confirmed it as far as he was concerned.

"We don't know that for sure." Edmund stepped into the room. "There's no body."

"How can there be? There's nothing left!" Eli glared at his father, wishing he had the courage and strength to throttle the man with his own bare hands. This man, whose hand was on Eli's shoulder in a misplaced gesture of condolence, was responsible for Lisette's death. "How can you—?"

Eli choked back his words of blame, taking note of the glimmer of anger in his father's eye, illuminated by the light of the moon. His instincts screamed, Don't say anything more! But Eli couldn't resist.

"How can you actually believe she's still alive?"

"I can hope, Eli. I expect you to do the same. As the Chief Regent's son, it's your duty."

Eli covered his face with his hands, desperate not to let loose the furious, insane bark of a laugh threatening to escape.

"Hope," Eli spat instead. "Look at it, Father. Hope?"

The two of them gazed at the smouldering remains of the once beautiful gardens. It was Edmund who finally broke the taut silence.

"Go to bed, Eli. It's very late."

"I'm staying here."

"Then I'll leave you. I'll speak with you when you're less upset."

"When will that be?" Eli looked up. "Can you tell me that? Can you?"

"It's time for bed, Eli."

"No, Father, I really want to know. When will I be less upset?"

Edmund retreated to the door.

"Oh, you can't tell me? That's something you don't know?" Eli watched his father's eyes narrow in an acute anger he'd never seen before, not even in Seth's often blazing eyes. "Fine," Eli whispered, chastened somewhat, afraid but still fuming. "Just go away."

Edmund disappeared without another word. It was the first time in Eli's life that he'd ever had the last word with him. As far as Eli knew, no one besides the Chancellor himself had ever had the last word with Edmund. This anger, this grief—the two of them together wiped out any fear or respect Eli had ever held for his father.

WHEN SETH CAME BACK the next morning, his Guard jacket covered in mud and ash, his cap caked in chalky fire retardant, Eli had not budged. He'd stayed awake since his father left, and was now watching the smouldering wreckage in the cool grey light of dawn.

"We didn't find her."

"Did you find any bodies?" Eli thought of Gregor, his strongmen, the multitude of quiet curious eyes on him that day.

"Forty-three labourers." Seth's voice lacked his usual arrogant inflection. For some reason, this made Eli nervous. "And the three other botanists."

"Did you see the bodies yourself?"

"Not all of them. The sergeant told us in the debrief this morning. He said Mother probably wasn't there, judging by the debris."

"The body parts, you mean."

Seth looked away and shrugged. Eli immediately felt sorry; Seth would've seen gruesome horrors in the night, sights far worse than Eli could imagine. However, Eli didn't feel quite sorry enough to apologize.

"She *was* there. I saw her leave, same as every day."

"Maybe she *said* she was going to the gardens, but went somewhere else instead."

"Is that what Father says?" Eli had been struggling to place his father in this mess. During the long hours before dawn his mind had soared through the possibilities. Edmund as innocent. Edmund as ignorant. Edmund as hapless accomplice. Edmund as murderer.

Seth shrugged again. "People are talking."

"About what?"

"I'm not at liberty to say."

"Tell me, Seth."

"Let me put it this way." Seth leaned forward as though he was going to whisper, but he didn't. "It's about Mother and *Gulzar*."

"What about Gulzar?"

"Well, apparently, Father ordered one of his men to keep an eye on him for the past eight months. They were lovers."

Lovers? They were not lovers. Eli had to stifle a laugh. His mother? Gulzar? Not likely.

"That's ridiculous." Eli shook off any doubt. "Gulzar helps us in the gym. And he minds the horses, that's all."

"I've seen the two of them behind the stables. Close, like they'd just been kissing."

"Never." *If anything happens* . . . through the murky waters of confusion and grief, Eli recalled what Lisette had said after she'd showed Eli the room below the greenhouse. *You can talk to Gulzar.* Eli thought fast, but not smoothly. He needed to clear Gulzar of any suspicion.

"They were probably just talking about the horses. She was probably explaining something to him. He's going deaf, you know. Something congenital. Runs in his family. Sometimes I have to shout so he'll hear me. I mean, you wouldn't know that, because you never ride any more, and you work out with the Guard, but he's gone really very deaf." Eli's skin prickled with fear. If Gulzar was found out and punished, Eli would have no one to turn to. No one at all.

"You know what I think?" Seth stood at the window, staring at the rubble. "I think Mother was just waiting for the perfect chance to leave us. The explosion was her opportunity. We'd all think she was dead, and she and Gulzar could live happily ever after."

"But where?"

"Well, it would have to be in the Droughtland, wouldn't it? She couldn't hide in any of the Keys. Everyone knows who she is."

"Has anyone asked Gulzar about all this? Have you even talked to him?"

"How could I?" Seth folded his arms and levelled a chilly smirk at Eli. "He conveniently left to console his mother somewhere in the Droughtland before the Guard could bring him in. Apparently, his father was a labourer in the gardens and died in the explosion." Seth laughed. "A likely story, don't you think?"

Eli's heart sank. No Gulzar, no information. No idea of what to do next.

"Poor Eli," Seth crooned. "Mommy's favourite wasn't even worth staying for."

A MEMORIAL WAS HELD two days later for the three other botanists, pointedly excluding Lisette. There would be no service or recognition of any kind for all the labourers who perished. What was left of them was incinerated, the ashes dumped outside the Key walls for anyone who wanted to claim a bucketful.

At the memorial Eli was positioned beside Seth, who stood beside Edmund, who was carefully poised at Chancellor East's right as he droned on about the evils of Droughtland rebels and the increasing threat of the Triskelian cult and the heinous act of terrorism they'd committed against the good and noble and peaceful Keylanders and their precious Agricultural Regeneration Program.

" . . . and now, in our time of challenge and grief, we must work together to ration what food we do have. We must be grateful for the generous outpouring from our neighbouring Keys. We must rally together in the face of terror and maintain our civility, our calm, and our dignity. Rest assured that the fanatics responsible for this act will be sought out and punished. They will be brought before the Star Chamber and duly tried and sentenced. As your trusted leader, I assure you, we *will* see them hang for the deaths of these three fine men."

Edmund had been ordered by the Chancellor to keep a low profile until Lisette's remains were found or her whereabouts could be determined, so he didn't speak at the memorial. He stood tall, shoulders squared, his jaw clenched the entire time, and did not say a word. Eli, listening at Edmund's study door, had overheard the Chancellor lecturing him the night before.

"Why didn't you keep her home when you gave the order for the bomb?"

"I have reason to believe she'd been lying to me about going to the gardens every day. I don't believe she was even there."

"Then where did she go that morning?"

"I have reason to believe she's been meeting the stableminder." Edmund said each word slowly, in such a manner that there could be no doubt as to what he was implying.

"Oh dear. Hmm. Yes. You'll want to keep quiet about that, old boy. Rumours like that would certainly not help the Chancellor-in-waiting. What would the people think? A next-in-line who can't maintain order or loyalty in his own home?"

Edmund was silent then too. The Chancellor continued. "Let's keep this under our hats, shall we? We'll say she's disappeared and presumed dead in the explosion. Such a loss to two fine boys and to you, too, our beloved Chief Regent. A terrible tragedy."

"Yes, sir. A terrible tragedy."

Eli felt a swell of rage so vast he had to brace himself from collapsing. Did his father really believe that? After the hand he'd had in it all?

"We'll give it another day or so until we announce it. If she shows her face in the meantime, see to it that she is immediately and discreetly dealt with, however you see fit."

"Yes, sir."

There was a long pause. Eli heard the Chancellor's silver tobacco tin open, and then the strike of a match.

"Tell me, Edmund, do you really think she's gone off with him?"

"Yes. I do."

How badly Eli wished that to be the truth, however sordid.

"It's an embarrassment, isn't it, old boy?" The Chancellor thumped Edmund's back. "Best kept between you and me. You're a grief-stricken widower, now. Act the part."

"Grief stricken, sir."

The thing was, Edmund did sound genuinely grief stricken. Furthermore, he began to weep. The Chancellor cleared his throat and made ready to leave in a sudden embarrassed hurry.

"Have we dealt with all the rebel bodies?"

Edmund must've nodded.

"Good, good. I'll, uh, leave you to it then."

Eli slipped into the darkness of the dining room as the Chancellor opened the door.

"I'll see you at the memorial. Best you say nothing, keep your head down, riddled with grief, all that. Try to get some sleep, Edmund. You look terrible." The Chancellor took a puff of his pipe. "Then again, looking terrible will work in your favour. Keep it up."

In Eli's opinion, his father didn't look as terrible as he should, considering. He'd given the order for the bomb that no doubt killed his wife and the mother of his children. Eli sank to the floor and closed his eyes. His father couldn't really believe that Lisette had run off with Gulzar, could he? Surely he must be saying that because he's ashamed of what he'd done? Eli's tears started again. He would have to leave this place. He could not bear it in his father's house any longer. If his mother was still alive, he would find her, even if it meant leaving the Key.

5

A week later, Chancellor East officially announced in front of a packed coliseum that Lisette was missing and presumed dead, another victim of the tragic bombing. Edmund stood at his side, eyes at his feet, bracketed by his sons, while the Keylanders, delighted at any excuse for a dress-up outing, listened with rapt attention, offering appropriate sympathetic murmurs as the Chancellor spoke.

Afterward, Edmund stood by the main exit, shaking hands and receiving consoling hugs. Eli had tried to get out of this wretched length of make-believe, but Edmund had clapped a firm hand on his shoulder and wordlessly guided him to where he was to stand and do the same. Seth, dressed in his uniform, was loving the attention, especially from the girls of the Key, who each pecked him solemnly on the cheek.

Allegra, the Chancellor's granddaughter, had been appointed to support Edmund and the boys through their "difficult time." She was an elegantly tall young woman, only five years older than the boys. She stood beside Edmund, receiving the cards and offerings of food. Seth kept glancing at her, Eli noticed. He probably wished she was in the lineup to give him a kiss too. Eli was disgusted by the whole process and ached to get out of there.

It was time—Eli decided in the carriage when they finally left the coliseum—that he at least try to talk to Seth. He needed to know if Seth knew anything from the Guard's rumour mill, if he knew for certain that

Lisette had left with Gulzar, or if she was dead, or truly missing. As well, he'd made the very hard decision to tell Seth what he knew in the hope that Seth might find it in himself to join him in his search for their mother and seek justice for her death. It wasn't that he wanted Seth to come along, but he had to admit it would be safer not to go alone. He hoped the idea of justice would appeal to Seth, but the hope was faint. Although the Guard advertised justice they were in fact about strong-arming to get their way, regardless of right and wrong.

Eli was filled with dread at the idea of approaching Seth, but with Gulzar still gone there was no one else and Eli very simply had to start somewhere. He found Seth in his quarters that evening, where he was once again sorting through the trunk of supplies he would take with him to the Guard base on their birthday. He'd taken out the dress uniforms, the navy blue towels, and the pyjamas and was carefully repacking them for what must've been the tenth time.

"One more week and I'm out of here." Seth set a stack of towels back into the trunk. "I'll be able to hunt down the Triskelians myself and bring them to justice. Each and every one of them. Too bad you're such a wimp, Eliza, or you could come with me."

"Yeah, too bad." Eli stood in the doorway and watched his twin, physically identical in every way except that Seth's hair was blond like Edmund's whereas Eli's was chestnut brown like Lisette's. "I know something, Seth." Those first words were promptly followed by the metallic taste of regret. This was not going to work. What had he been thinking?

"Congratulations! I knew you had to know *something*. What do you know? How to finally count to five?"

Eli ignored the comment and took a moment to collect his thoughts. What he'd been thinking was that if there was anyone else, any other person Eli thought he could confide in, trust, he would. He had no close friends, not like Seth who couldn't walk a block without running into one of his adoring fans. He was the one who had friends enough for a full game of baseball, and girls lined up waiting to dance with him at the socials. Eli had no one. He'd had a best friend for a short while when he was eight, a boy named Justin who was tall and quiet and wore glasses. But Justin's family had relocated to the Northeastern Key and that was the end of that.

As for the other Keylander children, Eli had never been interested in their sporting games, or Guard make-believe, and the few times Edmund had forced him to join in, Seth had turned the group against him and Eli had ended up in his mother's lap in tears. Would Gulzar ever come back? Could Eli wait and see? It was a gamble. What if Seth was right and he was out there with Lisette? Right here, right now, with nowhere else to turn, there was no one but Seth. What a sad, scary reality.

Eli tried the words out in his head once more, and then repeated them out loud, exactly the way he'd rehearsed them in front of the mirror.

"What I know is that the rebels did not bomb the gardens."

Seth laid the last towel back into the trunk and then unwrapped his rifle from its oilcloth.

"Sorry to be the one to tell you this . . . no wait, I'm not sorry to be the one to tell you, in fact, it gives me great pleasure to be the one to tell you that you are categorically insane." He took apart the gun and began cleaning it.

Eli had to persist. It would be worse if he stopped now and was forever wondering if he could've convinced his brother of the truth. He owed it to Maman to at least try.

"Chancellor East ordered the bombing because there was a rebel cell below the greenhouse. He wanted it to look like an act of rebel terrorism in order to boost Keylander patriotism, get aid from the other Keys, and get rid of the rebels, all at once. Maman was a rebel organizer. She was killed in the bombing, Seth. The bombing *our father* ordered. He *killed* her."

Seth wordlessly put the rifle back together. Then he walked over and shut the door, locking the two of them inside the room. He poked Eli in the chest with the tip of the gun and backed him up against the wall with it. He moved the gun up to just under Eli's chin and whispered, "Say that one more time, or to anyone else, ever, and I will kill you."

"But it's the truth!"

"You don't know what you're talking about!" Seth jabbed the gun at Eli's throat. Eli gagged. "If I killed you right now and told Father what you said, I would be seen as a hero and you would be seen as some crazy traitor. You talk shit, Eli. Dangerous shit."

"Fine. Then shoot me." Eli couldn't see any other way out. If he really was alone in this, he was already as good as dead. Stay and live a lie. Go and likely die. His eyes widened as Seth's finger slowly tensed against the trigger. Eli squeezed his eyes shut.

Click.

Seth laughed.

Eli blinked.

"It's not loaded, you pathetic loser." Seth pulled the trigger again. "We don't get bullets until after basic training. Any idiot knows that." He lowered the gun and took a step back. "Conversation over. Say any more about your retarded theory and I'll report you. The Star Chamber's executioners' guns are loaded, in case you didn't know that, which you might not, considering how blindingly stupid you are."

Eli felt his bladder betray him.

"Unreal." Seth shook his head. "You really are a baby. Get a diaper, Eliza."

Eli slid to the floor. Fear and rage and humiliation and a confusing relief all fought to dominate his emotions. When he spoke, his voice quavered.

"You'll make a really good—" Even after everything, Eli was just about to say *sheep.* He stopped himself. *Just leave,* he instructed himself. *Leave now while he thinks you're retarded. Leave!* He could almost hear the word in Lisette's voice. *Leave, mon fils! Tout de suite!*

"You'll make a really good Guardy, Seth." Eli stood, horrified about his smelly, wet crotch. He slowly unlocked the door, praying that he had the willpower to say nothing more.

"I will." Seth grinned. "I know that."

"Goodbye, Seth."

"Before you leave to get changed into clean panties, Eli, and I'm doing this just as much for you as for Father, you have to promise not to tell anyone the shit you told me. You've got to realize what lies like that would do to Father. It would destroy him and his future as Chancellor, and mine too, because I can guarantee you that you will never, ever, be Chancellor."

"If Maman isn't dead, where is she?"

"With Gulzar, you idiot."

"How can you believe that so easily?"

"Because of all the times I've seen the two of them together when they had no reason to be."

"You can't believe Maman was a rebel? There's not even a tiny part of you that can believe that?"

"That is the stupidest thing I have ever heard you say." Seth placed his gun back into the trunk. "And that's pretty remarkable, isn't it?"

Go. Eli stepped into the hall. *Go! Go without saying another word!* But he just couldn't. He turned back.

"I'm leaving, Seth. I'll look for Maman, and if I don't find her, I'll find the rebels and join them."

"You do that . . . " In one unsurprising move, Seth pinned Eli to the wall by his neck. "And I will kill you. You can't screw it up for Father and me like this. People are already beginning to believe that Mother ran off and left us. That's bad enough, isn't it? If you go, I will make sure you never come back. You will die in the Droughtland."

Eli could barely breathe, but so what? He'd die here by Seth's hand, or in front of the Star Chamber, or he'd die in the Droughtland. What difference did it really make? It would come soon enough, no matter. And perhaps his death would be for the best.

"Promise you'll keep quiet!"

Seth leaned his forearm harder against Eli's neck, lifting him off the floor and onto his toes. As his vision blurred and his blood slowed, Eli realized that death might come for him soon, but that he very much would rather die at least trying to find Lisette than like this, at the hands of his brother, with his pants soaked with piss.

"I promise," he croaked as his vision blackened.

Seth dropped his arm. Eli collapsed to the floor.

"Never forget." He jabbed a finger at him. "You promised. If you break that promise, I will personally make you pay."

Eli lay curled on the floor, heaving, starving for breath.

"I swear, I will hunt you down myself and make you pay. Beside, you wouldn't leave." Seth kicked him in the side. "You wouldn't last one hour out there. But you just might get the chance if I decide to tell Father what you told me. And if you dare mess up the legislature, if you say anything to any of the delegates, I'll kick you out of the Key myself."

WHEN GULZAR suddenly reappeared at the Key gate at dawn three days later, the Guard descended on him as if he had an army behind him and was not, in fact, alone and unarmed and, with a legion of guns pointed at him from the top of the wall, standing very still with his arms up. They doused him from afar and then a squadron of Guardies rushed him, restrained him, and delivered him directly to the Justice Hall.

The first Eli heard of it was at breakfast. News had travelled from the milkminder to the maid that fed the chickens to the kitchen help to the new young maid, who told Eli with such urgency that he half-wondered if she knew something significant. Eli dismissed the idea. She probably had a crush on Gulzar, that was all. It was that thought that gave him the idea.

"Do something, Master Eli! They might not let him get to trial!" She pulled on his sleeve with a familiarity that would have her severely punished if Edmund walked in. But his father wasn't there, she told him; he was already down at the Justice Hall. Eli didn't know what to do, only that he had to do something. He had to talk to Gulzar, and he couldn't do that if the man was going to be executed.

Eli left his breakfast and ran to the compound of buildings that housed not only the penitentiary but also the Star Chamber and Government House. At first he wasn't even let past the first desk, but when he raised his voice and hollered for his father he was ushered out of the austere lobby and into the corrections office. He was told to wait, and not to move.

Edmund eventually emerged from a small room at the end of the hall, his shirtsleeves rolled up, sweat on his brow. Was Gulzar in there? Were they trying to beat information out of him?

"What are you doing here, Eli?"

"Gulzar's innocent!" Eli grabbed his father's arm.

"Nonsense!" Edmund pried Eli off. "What makes you say that?"

"I've met his father!" Eli prayed that Edmund wouldn't ask for a name. "His father *did* work at the gardens."

"When? When would you have met him?"

"Maman brought me to the gardens just a few weeks ago. She introduced me to him. He was a weeder, and had black hair and a lot of missing teeth." Eli hoped he sounded more convincing than he felt.

"That may be," Edmund said. "But I have other reasons to believe he was involved in your mother's disappearance, not just the question of whether this father of his was ever employed at the gardens. Go home."

"Father," Eli continued, "I know what you're talking about, but let me assure you. I was with them often, and I can tell you that Gulzar is in love with one of the maids. Maman told me he was just about to ask this girl to marry him."

Edmund rolled down his sleeves. "Tell me more."

"You can ask her yourself."

"Who is she?"

"The new maid. She's about my age, with red hair. I don't know her name." In fact, she'd just told him her name was Francie, but it would be unusual for Eli to know a servant's given name, so he left that part out. "You can ask her. She's back at the house, distraught at the idea that you might have it wrong. She can't be consoled, sir. The staff doesn't know what to do to get her to stop crying. She's hysterical. I'm afraid she might hurt herself!"

Edmund jammed his hands into his pockets and stared at the wall for a moment before sighing. "I'll look into it," he said as he disappeared back into the room.

Eli sat, then stood, then paced, then sat, and so on until his father emerged from the room with a very gaunt Gulzar behind him, escorted roughly by two towering Guards.

ELI AND EDMUND took the Chief Regent's carriage back to the house while Gulzar and the Guardies rode behind them in an open cart. Edmund didn't speak during the short trip. Eli was thankful for that, because the charade was shaky no matter how he looked at it.

When they got to the house Edmund ordered the Guards to keep Gulzar outside until Edmund was ready for him. Eli followed his father into the kitchen, where the maids were consoling Francie with strong tea and fresh hankies and tender pats on the back.

"Clean her up, then I want the lot of you, and every single female house staff, lined up in the dining room." He approached Francie and lifted her chin with a finger in a gesture that was both threatening and tender. "You are to look like you haven't shed a tear. Not a single tear. Understand?"

Eli's heart pounded. He'd figured his father would bring Gulzar in and ask him to pick out his girl. Eli had guessed this back at the Justice Hall, but he hadn't had even a discreet second to give Gulzar any kind of signal as to whom he should choose.

The girls and women lined up in the dining room, each carefully maintaining a neutral expression, as ordered. Seth, who'd been sleeping until just moments before, raced down the stairs as Gulzar was escorted in, hands bound behind his back. Seth roared, rushed forward, and punched him in the face. Gulzar reeled back, his lip split and bloody.

"How dare you even set foot in here?" Seth was about to slap him, but Edmund hauled him off.

"Control yourself!"

"But Father, how can you—"

"There may have been a misunderstanding, Seth. We are about to find out. Now, if you want to stay, you will have to behave like someone befitting your position, or you will remove yourself to your room."

"I'm sorry, sir."

Eli wished Seth had stormed off in a huff so that he wouldn't have the opportunity to remember that Eli had told him Gulzar was going deaf.

Edmund and more Guards kept a sharp eye on the women, ensuring that none of them gave any kind of signal. They'd been threatened with expulsion if they so much as moved an inch or raised an eyebrow, so, not surprisingly, they were all statue-still, eyes closed, as ordered.

"Which one is it?" Edmund demanded as the Guards shoved Gulzar into the room.

"My love!" he cried and threw himself at Francie's feet. "My one! My heart!"

Francie opened her eyes and looked beseechingly at Edmund, tears back in full force. He reluctantly nodded his permission and she hugged Gulzar and covered his face with kisses. The other women tittered, but were immediately shut up by one bark from Edmund.

"I thought you were dead!" Francie wailed. "I thought I'd never see you again!"

Eli cringed. She was overacting, but Edmund didn't seem to notice. He dismissed everyone until just Seth and Eli remained in the room with Gulzar. How had Gulzar known who to choose? No matter, he'd done it. How, who knew? Edmund clasped his hands behind his back and addressed the man in a voice crisp with fury.

"There is only one reason why I am letting you come back to work for me as usual. The reason is that I do not want to confirm the rumours that you had anything to do with my wife's disappearance. With you back at work for all the Key to see, they will finally let go of the ridiculous rumour. And since I know the rumour has travelled to the other Keys, you will be sure to be front and centre during the legislative assembly so that the Chancellors and their Chief Regents and their staff can carry back to their Keys that it is business as usual at the Maddox estate. Understood?"

Gulzar nodded.

"Then go."

Gulzar left through the kitchen. The brothers and their father listened to Francie carry on her renewed hysterics upon seeing Gulzar again, until Edmund leaned in and ordered Gulzar to make his way to the stables immediately and to stay there, and for Francie to retreat to her bed until she could handle herself in a more appropriate manner.

Back in the living room, Edmund now addressed the boys.

"Your mother is dead."

Eli's muscles shuddered with the resistance it took not to lunge at his father and rip him apart with his bare hands. "How can you stand there and tell us that as if—"

"Enough!" Edmund cut him off. "Your mother is dead and there is nothing more to be said about the matter. Is that clear?"

The boys nodded. Edmund left the room. Seth followed him, leaving Eli alone. Francie popped her head out from the kitchen and gave him a big grin and two thumbs up before disappearing again. Eli glanced around the dining room where he and his family had shared so many meals. He ran his fingers over the worn, carved wood of Lisette's chair. He didn't know if she was alive or dead. He was confused and angry and scared, but he was sure of one thing. He would leave this place at the first opportunity, and if he never came back it would be fine by him.

With that determination in the forefront of his mind, Eli went up to the attic, dug out his father's old hunting pack, and began to prepare in earnest for his leaving. For the moment, Gulzar would have to wait. There'd be eyes on him right now, too many for Eli to slip past. At least he was back. There was a profound comfort in knowing he had an ally. Or he hoped he had an ally. Still, he must be cautious. Lisette hadn't explained how much Gulzar knew, or what exactly Eli could go to him for. But it was something. It was somewhere to start.

Eli slept better that night than all the wretched nights since he'd first set foot in the secret room below the gardens. He would speak to Gulzar. When the time was right.

6

༺❀༻

Eli yanked on his runners and headed to the stables the next morning. It wasn't unusual for him to go for a morning run with Gulzar, and it would be the perfect opportunity to talk to him. Eli was just about out the back door when he was cut off by Seth, coming out of the kitchen with a loaf of bread and a jar of honey.

"Where are you going?"

"Where does it look like?"

"You're not going to go meet that traitor?"

"He's been cleared, Seth. News flash."

"News flash, Eli." Seth dunked a finger into the honey and wiped it on Eli's cheek. Eli jerked back. "Gulzar's not allowed to train you any more. He's back to being just the lowly stableminder. And there's a Guard out there. If you're interested."

Eli felt the colour drain from his face, but he managed a nonchalant shrug. "I can just as easily go for a run by myself. I don't care. It's just that Mother liked him to coach us."

"That's right." Seth streaked his other cheek with honey too. "My. One might think that's a bit strange, having the stableminder act as personal trainer to the master's children. But seeing as she isn't here any more, things have changed."

"You have no idea, Seth." Eli yanked open the door and set out across the field before Seth could take it any further. Wiping at his sticky cheeks, he ran past the stables, slowing to catch Gulzar's eye. He was currying the horses, and looked up, but only briefly. There was a Guard leaning at the gate smoking a cigarette, his rifle slung across his chest. This would be harder than he thought, but it could be done. He would speak to Gulzar. He had to.

For the next several days Eli started each morning with a run, cutting across the field and heading out past the stables, and every day Gulzar was magically outside, if only to nod at him as he passed. Amazing that just a simple, understated nod could feel like sustenance. Eli wanted more, but every day the same Guard was there, looking bored and put out but still keeping an eye trained on Eli as he jogged past.

Meanwhile, the Key was a bustle of activity as preparations for the legislative assembly got well underway. Centre Street was swept and ordered off-limits so that it would be in pristine condition for the Grand Entry, the buildings were draped in the Keyland colours of blue and yellow, and each storefront was decorated with competing patriotic displays. The mess of the bombsite was not only left in shambles but covertly enhanced to make it appear even more devastated than it was.

Greenminders perfected lawns and trimmed hedges. Seamsters worked long days fitting gowns and suits for the Keylanders, and servants in every household, including the Maddox estate, raced around dusting and cooking and washing drapes that hadn't been cleaned since the last time the legislature was held in the Eastern Key seven years earlier. Two dignitaries were going to be guests for the month: the ancient Chancellor of the Southeast Key and her dour Chief Regent, who'd no doubt been waiting for the old woman to die for a very long time. Amidst all the activity, Eli gathered supplies quite unnoticed and made his own preparations. To leave. Security around Gulzar might never let up. He'd have to leave sooner or later.

He'd stowed the pack beneath his bed, filling it with candles and matches, a canteen, spare clothes. He snuck dried fruit and beef jerky from the cellar, a bag of oats, a sack of flour, and of course water-purification drops from the emergency supplies below the stairs. One evening when his father was dining at the Chancellor's, Eli slipped into his parents' chambers and helped himself to Lisette's silver ring with the opal stone, the one he used to rub against his cheek when he was small, and the double-strand pearl choker Lisette treasured. The pearls had been in for restringing the day his grandparents' shop and apartment had burnt down just before his parents met. Lisette's parents had perished in the fire, along with all their possessions. She often said that the pearls were all she had from before she was orphaned. Now Eli was as good as orphaned himself. These treasures he would keep forever. He would never part with them, no matter how poor or desperate he might become in the Droughtland.

ELI WAS AS READY to leave as he'd ever be the day the dignitaries began to arrive with their excessively decorated horses and carriages, parading down Centre Street led by the marching band. He'd kept his eye on the stables all day, and as he'd thought, the Guard was finally summoned to join the troops protecting the dignitaries and the various sites considered "high risk" for a terrorist attack. No Guard could be spared to babysit a stableminder. At last, Eli would have his chance.

While his father and Seth welcomed Chancellor Southeast with a high tea and a string quartet on the front lawn, Eli snuck out the back, taking his pack and two saddlebags to the stable. Bullet trotted behind him, clutching Eli's bedroll in his teeth.

Gulzar was brushing Chay, Eli's blind old horse. He stopped when Eli came in. The two of them grinned at each other. "Master Eli."

"Gulzar."

Gulzar pointed at the pack and saddlebags.

"What's all that?"

"I meant to come earlier, but that Guard just wouldn't leave."

"And he'll be back, once everyone is in and the Key is locked up. We don't have long."

"Long for what?"

"Whatever it is that you came for. Whatever these bags are for. My guess is that you're leaving."

"I am." Eli held his breath. He was counting on Gulzar's help to get him out of the Key. He could pack and prepare all he wanted, but he still had no way out without being noticed, and no idea where to go. He wanted to leave that night, with the festivities as a distraction, and he would need help. But had Lisette had a chance to tell Gulzar about Eli at all? That she'd mentioned Gulzar to him? That Eli had visited the gardens? Did Gulzar even know about the gardens? Or had Lisette suggested he could talk to Gulzar only because he was just a sympathizer and nothing more? Or maybe he knew nothing at all. Maybe she suggested Gulzar because she really was having an affair with him, and thought that he, out of anyone, might at least understand, might help the son of his lover. Eli squeezed his eyes shut and shook his head.

"Where to, Master Eli?" Gulzar looked him squarely in the eye. There was something to the look. A weariness Eli did not recognize. A sadness.

Eli held his gaze. "I don't know."

"Well, that won't do, will it? You must have some kind of destination in mind."

"Sort of, but I thought maybe you could help me with that?"

Gulzar's sadness darkened. "I'm afraid you're not going to find who you're looking for, Master Eli. I buried your mother."

"I knew she was dead." But he hadn't, or he hadn't wanted to admit it. Not until now. Eli's breath was tight and thin, as if he'd been socked in the gut or was being suffocated by a pillow.

"I wanted to tell you," Gulzar continued. "But it was too dangerous. The Guard believes it was my dad I took home. It wasn't, although, had they investigated, they couldn't have identified her. But I know it was your mother, Master Eli, there is no doubt."

"Don't call me *master*!" Eli blurted. In that moment he wished he could trade places with Gulzar. He wished he was just a stableminder, and that he'd never had anything to do with the Keylander elite. He wished his mother had never met his father. He wished he'd never been born at all. He wished he knew something for certain rather than nothing for sure, which was driving him mad.

Eli closed his eyes and leaned against the stable wall. "She really is dead?"

Gulzar nodded. "My mom saw to it that she had a decent burial, even though the headstone has a stranger's name. Her funeral was attended by many—hundreds."

"But not me," Eli said. "I wasn't there! She's my mother and I wasn't there! All this time, I've been stuck here. A coward, not doing anything, not knowing."

"Well, now you know for sure." Gulzar took Eli's pack and set it on the floor. "What's your plan?"

"I don't have one!" Eli kicked the pack. "I just know that I can't stay here any more. Not even one more night!"

"Do you have any idea what it's like out there? What it will take for you to stay alive? I can't go with you. They'd come for us if it looked like I had anything to do with your disappearance."

"Then just tell me what you know." He stared at Gulzar. "Please, will you help me that much?"

"I'll help." Gulzar led Chay back to his stall. "With what little time there is. But I can't tell you much. There are good reasons why we all know just a slice, so that if any one of us is caught, they can only glean so much under torture. I'm sorry I don't have that much to share with you. That was what your mother was going to do for you. Teach you. Show you. Bring you boys in as she'd always planned."

"Seth too?"

Gulzar nodded. "She was waiting for him to change his ways."

"That won't happen. Seth will never change. He's always been the warmonger of the family, so why would she think he might change?"

"She didn't want it to begin without the both of you."

"She didn't want what to begin?"

"The revolution. She wanted her children with her."

"Revolution?" The word was a mountain range, huge and rocky, reaching up into the sky, endless in all directions. It was impossible to think about. Not right then, when what mattered was getting out while he could. Time was thinning. He needed to get back to the house for the formal dinner before anyone noticed he was missing.

"My mother said there were secret ways in and out."

"That, I can help with." Gulzar nodded. "I can get you out."

"And then where should I go? Where are the rebels?"

"They're everywhere, Eli."

"Yes, but where are they based? Do they have headquarters? Where is it? Where should I go once I leave?"

"I don't know." Gulzar shrugged. "I would tell you if I could, but I'm told only what I need to know, and I've never needed to know that. All I can say is that it's west from here."

"Pretty much everything is west from here! How *far* west?"

"I'm sorry, Eli." Gulzar shrugged again. "I honestly don't know. But however far it is, you can't take old Chay. He wouldn't last a day."

"I know." Eli looked sadly at the droopy old horse he'd had his whole life. "I'd already decided to take Seth's horse."

"Saber?" Gulzar glanced at the sleek black horse, his muzzle hidden in a bucket of oats. "Well, Seth certainly won't miss him. I can't remember the last time I've seen him out here."

"He rides the Guard horses now."

Eli took a moment to say goodbye to old Chay. He scratched the horse's ears and gave him a pat on his bony flank, and then went to help Gulzar fasten the saddlebags onto Saber's saddle. Saber was a strong young Arabian, a fine specimen of a horse that Seth never deserved in the first place. Once Saber was ready to go, Eli told Gulzar he'd return as soon as he could. Then he reluctantly trudged back to the house to endure the dinner that was being put on in honour of the visitors.

He changed into his dress clothes and dragged himself down to the dining hall, where the string quartet had moved in from the lawn and was now set up in the corner by the fireplace.

Eli took his seat at the table while the others still mingled, holding onto tall flutes of champagne and picking at the hors d'oeuvres. Chancellor Southeast noticed him sitting all alone and approached him, leaning a little more on her cane than she had the last time Eli had seen her.

"Haven't you grown!" The pale old woman bent to kiss his cheek. Eli grimaced, and then tried to smile. He really had nothing against the old woman. She was a warm summer rain to Chancellor East's cold arctic storm.

"Hello, Madam Chancellor."

"Where were you earlier? I do believe you missed the Grand Entry, didn't you? I must say, I have the most gloriously decorated carriage of them all this year. It's in your carriage house, if you'd like to have a look."

"Maybe later, Chancellor. Thank you."

"Of course. Now, how about some dinner?" She banged her cane on the floor, gracelessly summoning the rest of the guests. "Come along now, let's eat!" She swept her gowns to the side and took the seat beside Eli. "I'm absolutely famished after all that travel in the Droughtland. It is stressful, sick people and highway robbers and filthy beggars and wretched wastes of life everywhere you look. Stress makes me terribly hungry, and besides," she whispered as the others came to the table, "the sooner all this festive claptrap is over with, the sooner I get to sleep."

Eli tried not to think about robbers and beggars and sicks. He let Chancellor Southeast's chatter drift over him, a cloud of blessedly distracting feistiness. She was the oldest person Eli knew. Everyone, except for the Chancellors, was relocated to elderminders on the eve of their sixty-fifth birthday so as not to be a burden to their families and so that they could enjoy peace and quiet in a community of their peers. Eli received letters and gifts from Edmund's parents, but he'd never met his grandparents. For them to leave the elderminders, or for anyone to visit them, would be to put the frail elderly at risk for sicks. It made the company of someone like Chancellor Southeast a novelty.

Eli was happier to sit beside her instead of any of the other stuffy guests, although Chancellor Southeast wasn't supposed to sit there. Her Chief Regent came up behind her, all in a fluster, wringing her hands like wet cloths.

"Chancellor Southeast, you must sit at the head. It's simply expected."

"I will sit where I like, thank you, Nuala. That will be all." She winked at Eli and waved off the skinny woman with the pinched mouth. Nuala pulled Allegra aside and babbled at her, but Allegra, in her role as impromptu stand-in hostess, didn't seem concerned about the new seating arrangements, or not enough to do anything about it anyway. As much as Allegra pretended to be the very definition of carefully controlled grace, Eli could practically see the nervousness dancing around her like a ring of imps. He hated her, if only because she was sitting in Lisette's chair. If his mother were sitting there, if none of this had happened, tonight would've been a delight. Fine company, a feast, and fireworks afterward. Lisette had been planning the meal for weeks, and now the food that was heaped on Eli's plate might as well have been so much horse dung.

As the others chatted and joked, Eli pushed the food around on the plate. He wished he could eat. He wanted to, and he should, considering that this may be the last real meal he'd have for a long time. This could be his last meal, period. He might be short hours away from death, given that he didn't have the medicines and armoured carriages and flanks of the Keyland Guard that the dignitaries used to travel the Droughtland. He was thankful for Chancellor Southeast and her distracting, ceaseless commentary on the meal and the other guests. She had sharp words for Allegra's choice of soup, but praise for her gown and the table decor. After dessert and tea was served, Eli helped her on with her cloak as everyone prepared to leave to watch the fireworks. Normally the fireworks were held in Chancellor East's garden at the other end of the Key, but tonight's display would be above the ruins of the gardens, a tribute to the tragedy. An opportunity to flaunt the debris, more like.

"Your poor mother," Chancellor Southeast said as Eli helped her to the door. The others had gone ahead and were waiting impatiently in the carriages on the street. "It's a terrible tragedy. She must've been so proud of you. You must be so sad for her death."

Eli fought back the tears he knew could come from just the mention of his mother. Before speaking to Gulzar, whenever Eli had thought of his mother, he remembered her as he'd last seen her, turning the corner to the gardens that day, smart and beautiful, the sun reflecting on her face, but now he imagined a corpse burned beyond recognition, buried in some Droughtland stranger's grave in the middle of nowhere.

"Yes," Eli murmured. "I miss her terribly."

Eli helped Chancellor Southeast into the carriage beside Nuala, who tucked a blanket roughly over the Chancellor's lap. The old woman swatted away her hands and patted the seat beside her.

"Sit beside me, young Eli. It's been so lovely to talk to you."

"No, but thank you." Eli shook his head. "I'm going to walk. I'll see you there."

BUT HE DIDN'T, of course. As he watched the carriages turn the corner, he thought very briefly about the possibility of travelling back to the Southeastern Key with the old Chancellor, perhaps offering himself as an apprentice to the botanists at her gardens. It would be a way to leave this place and still be a Keylander, but the idea faded as quickly as it had come, overshadowed by the sharp, clear memory of when he'd first laid eyes on that secret room below the gardens. There was another world out there. His mother's world. The rebel world. Triskelia. If it truly existed as a place, or thing, or movement, he would find it. He would find his mother's people, or die trying.

ELI TUCKED A NOTE for Seth under his brother's desk blotter and then made one last stop, entering the forbidden realm of his father's study. He headed straight for Edmund's treasured glass globe. He examined the etched lines that separated water and land, the small ridges that marked mountains, the raised stars that marked the Keys. He placed his finger on the Eastern Key and traced a route across the Droughtland to the waters off the west coast. It seemed an impossible distance. Vast, incomprehensible even, but somewhere between here and there, Eli would find the rebels.

Eli set the globe spinning with his finger and then got it going faster and faster, the iron axis squeaking as it picked up speed. Eli grew angrier as the globe spun faster. It was his father's most prized possession, handed down through six generations. It was one of the first representations of the world after the Group of Keys was formed and new borders were muscled into being. Edmund was not a typically sentimental man, nor did he typically get emotionally attached to objects, but to Edmund, the globe was priceless and irreplaceable.

Eli set both his hands on it to stop it spinning and then swept it off the desk. It smashed into tiny shards on the slate floor. Eli stared at it, his heart pounding, until a man's voice broke the silence.

"Eli."

Eli's heart lurched to a sudden, painful stop. He didn't dare turn around. Edmund? He couldn't even begin to conceive how his father would punish him for breaking the globe.

"There is no more time, Eli." It was Gulzar. Eli's heart started again in earnest, pounding and clattering in his chest.

"You shouldn't be in here."

"I had to make sure you were coming. Francie let me in." Francie peeked around the corner.

"What's she doing here?"

"It's okay, Eli. She's one of us."

"I packed you a meal." Francie offered him a package, still warm. "You didn't eat much at supper."

How many people knew? Who else was a rebel in his house? If he wasn't alone, perhaps he could stay. There was Gulzar, and Francie, and who knows who else?

"Maybe I should stay, and carry on from the inside." The smell of the food in his hands stood only to remind him of what he'd be going without if he left.

"Carry on with what?" There was an edge to Gulzar's voice that Eli had never heard before. "You don't know what you're talking about. You don't know anything!"

Eli couldn't argue. How could he carry on with an enigma? Nothing more than nuance? There was no fortitude in that, only a cowardly facade.

"It's time, Eli." Gulzar pushed him toward the door. "Saber's ready to go and the fireworks are about to begin."

Eli picked up the family portrait Edmund kept on his desk, although since Lisette's disappearance Edmund had turned it so that it faced his visitors and not him. In it, Lisette and Eli smiled casually at the photographer while Edmund and Seth stood at attention, their small smiles cancelled by their furrowed brows.

"Eli!" Gulzar whispered harshly. "We must go before anyone sees you!"

None of the servants had been given leave to see the fireworks, although they'd be gathering on the roof when they began, and hurrying back into position while the last sparks were still falling. "We must move quickly!"

"I'm ready." Eli slipped the photograph out of the frame and tucked it into his pocket.

AS SOON AS THE FIRST BURST of fireworks sounded, Gulzar, riding Lisette's horse, led Eli through little-used gates in private fields.

"I can't go this way!" Eli shook his head when he realized they were on a circuitous route heading for the service gate. "Even if you have a key, they'll hear the alarm when the gate rises."

"You're not going through the gate." Gulzar led them past the gate to the carriageminder's service house on the other side. He pulled open the wide doors and led the way into the darkness. "You'll have to dismount." Gulzar lit a lantern and then led Saber ahead of Eli toward the back wall. Eli looked down at Bullet, who looked back at him with a shared skepticism before reluctantly following Gulzar into the dark.

"Here's where we part ways."

"What are we doing here?"

"Getting you out." Gulzar grabbed hold of a tool hook in the wall and started cranking it. "Crank that hook there." He pointed to a larger one on the opposite wall. "Clockwise."

Eli turned the hook, expecting the wall to perhaps pull back like the false wall in the greenhouse. The wall stayed put, but in the silence between the fireworks he could hear what sounded like chain moving on metal cogs far below them. "Step to your left, Eli. Keep cranking." Eli did as he was told. "Watch the floor."

How could he not? It was collapsing, or more to the point, one end of a large square of the floor was tipping into the earth, becoming a ramp down to a tunnel below.

"Does this mean the carriageminder is a rebel too?"

"No, he doesn't know anything. This was put in when his grandfather was the carriageminder. He was a rebel, as was his son, but not the present one, as he's got a mouth on him as big as this hole."

"Will Saber really follow me into that?"

"He'll go if you go; he's a bit like Bullet that way."

"What if he balks?"

"Then your mother's horse will be happy to oblige. She's been this way a few times, but Saber's her colt, so I suspect he'll have no trouble in the tunnel. You see now that Chay wouldn't have gotten very far at all." Gulzar handed him the lantern. "Have a look."

Eli slid down into the tunnel. The walls were braced by wide planks, as was the ceiling, for as far as Eli could see in the small pool of light from the lantern. The floor was damp dirt. It smelled of mould and rot.

"Where does it come out?"

"You have three choices. Take the first right and then left and you'll come out near my village. Take the first left and then right and you'll find yourself at the nearest Droughtland market. Keep going and the tunnel ends just south of a major trading route."

"Which way should I go?"

"That's up to you. The less I know, the better, just in case."

"How far is it to your village?"

"You'll be in the tunnel for two days, any which way you go."

"Two days!"

"My advice is to sleep when you're tired and eat when you're hungry, because the darkness has a way of playing with your mind if you try to make hours out of it."

There was a gap in the fireworks just then. The two of them fell silent, waiting for the explosions and cheers to resume, but there was just daunting quiet on top of quiet.

"There's no more time!" Gulzar led Saber down the ramp and into the tunnel. The horse's breathing quickened and he tried to rear back, hitting his head on the ceiling. Gulzar grabbed a firm hold on his reins and spoke softly into his ear.

"We'll just have to hope he'll be okay in here. If he gets nervous, whisper into his ear, anything at all, doesn't matter what you say, just how you say it. Call Bullet in after you, if he's going with you." Eli took a couple of tentative steps into the tunnel and took Saber's reins from Gulzar. "Hold him tight until you know he's okay. If you let him go, you'll never find him. The three ways I told you of are just three of hundreds. He'll die in here if he bolts."

Eli wondered if that explained the smell of decay creeping from the tunnel. Bullet stood above them and whined as Eli disappeared from view, but before he could call for him or tell him to go home, the dog jumped down into the tunnel. Gulzar patted the dog, whispered a little something in Saber's ear, and then climbed out.

"If you go to the village, my mother's name is Falma. She'll know who you are. Travel carefully, Eli. It's dangerous out there. May luck and health be on your side."

"The same to you, Gulzar." Eli held the lantern up. "Thank you. For everything." Gulzar's face was a dim shadow, but his encouraging smile was as clear as anything, and was the last thing Eli saw as the floor settled back into place. Then Eli was alone in the stale black tunnel, alone except for Saber, who whinnied loudly, stamping his hooves in the dirt, and Bullet, who had already gained his night vision and taken off ahead of them into the pitch black.

[TWO]

DROUGHTLAND

7

❧

Eli had no way of marking time in the tunnel, but it felt as though whole days had been swallowed up in the stuffy dark before he stopped for the first time, just after the first junction, where he turned right, toward Gulzar's village and his mother's unjust grave.

He didn't know if going to the village was what he should do, but it felt like what he needed to do. He needed to see his mother's grave. He needed to make her death real, because it still felt as if he might wake from the nightmare of it all at any moment. Maybe by seeing his mother's grave, feeling the rough stone with the stranger's name on it with his own hands, knowing his mother's body was at some kind of uneasy rest, maybe then his mind would clear enough to make a plan. Right now he only wanted his mother, and if her grave was the closest thing, it would have to do.

An alcove, carved out of the narrow tunnel just past the junction, beckoned Eli to rest. He tied Saber to a long pole that ran from floor to ceiling and looked to be there for that purpose. There were crude bunks carved into the walls, and a table scattered with broken crockery and crumbling bones. Eli followed a wicked stench down a narrower tunnel that led off the alcove and found a toilet of sorts, or at least a deep pit with a seat built up around it and a nearly empty pail of lime dust beside it. Eli coughed back a gag, plugged his nose, and used the pit, tossing a scant handful of lime on top when he finished.

He unwrapped Francie's food package back at the little table. He was very hungry now and wanted to eat every last morsel, but he forced himself to divide the food into three portions. He ate the first, and then couldn't help but eat the second. He savoured each mouthful with his eyes closed. He could hear the dinner guests laughing, and the string quartet, so loud that he wondered if he opened his eyes he'd find himself right back at the feast, the rightful one, with Lisette in her place, smiling across the table at him.

Eli opened his eyes. He was still in the tunnel, and a rat was picking at his third portion. Eli sucked in his breath and slowly reached down for a rock as he kept an eye on it. He lifted the rock and smashed it down on the rat. It screeched. Eli lifted the rock again and brought it down on the writhing creature's head. Another pathetic squeal and it was dead. Eli used the rock to push the rat and the rest of the food off the table and onto the ground. Bullet sniffed at the rat and then gobbled up the rest of the food.

Eli's hands shook as he unrolled his sleeping bag onto one of the bunks. He'd never killed anything before. Whenever Edmund took the boys hunting, Eli was always sure to miss. This tunnel was making him crazy. Or was it?

After a restless night dreaming of explosions and fireworks, Eli woke to darkness, of course. The dead rat had collected a legion of flies and had started to stink. Eli couldn't wait to get far, far away from it. He rolled up his sleeping bag and set off right away, this time tackling the void ahead of him at a canter, his lantern offering him just a sliver of sight before he raced on. Saber was happier at this pace, as was Bullet, but Eli was happiest of them all at the thought that they were pounding nearer to Gulzar's village with every step.

At long last, just when he was thinking he'd go mad if he didn't get out soon, Eli noticed a change in the smell of the tunnel. There seemed to be more air, fresher air. He must be near the village. He slowed down, taking deeper breaths as the air became clearer and more abundant and the ghostly stench of the dead rat finally left him, just when he was beginning to think he'd have to live with it forever.

He rounded one more long curve and then the tunnel came to an abrupt end in front of him, a flight of stone steps leading up to a wooden door. Eli grabbed the handle and pushed the door. A shock of light assaulted his eyes. He let the door slam shut and groaned in pain, unable to open his eyes again, even in the dark. It was a good thing he didn't, because someone opened the door all the way then, letting in the violent light.

"Keep 'em closed!" It was a boy's voice.

Bullet started barking. Eli desperately wanted to open his eyes, but he resisted. "When can I open them?"

"I'll tell you when. No sooner, or you'll need looking at by the eyeminder. And call your dog off."

"Bullet, enough." Bullet stopped with a whine. "How about now?" Eli turned in the direction of the voice. "Can I open them now?"

"Not yet! Is that horse your beast?" The boy had come into the tunnel. "You want to sell him? I can find you a buyer, if you give me half an hour and a finder's fee."

"He's not for sale." Eli tightened his grip on Saber's reins. Bullet growled at the boy, and Eli let him.

"How about the dog? You selling him?"

"I'm not selling anything. Can I open my eyes now?"

"Oh no, if you do, they'll be shocked so bad you won't see for weeks. Maybe never."

"I want to get out of this tunnel."

"It'll cost you some coin if you want my help until you can open your eyes."

"Fine." Eli turned, hopefully out of sight of the pestering boy, and discreetly fished out a handful of coins from the pouch tied under his shirt. The pouch bulged with the weight of wealth, all taken from the copper box tucked in the back of his father's dresser under a pile of underlinens. "Here. Now take me out of the tunnel."

The boy took the money. "All right!" Eli could tell by his tone that he'd seriously overpaid him. "Anything you need. Let's go!"

"Take the reins."

"You have to get off the horse. Want a hand?"

"No!" Eli slid out of the saddle. "I'm fine."

"Sure. Right." The boy grabbed Eli's wrist anyway.

"Don't touch me!" Eli wrenched away.

"What, you think you'll catch a sick?" The boy waited for Eli to answer, but Eli couldn't think of what to say. "You either stay in here or take your chances out there." The boy sniffed loudly. "Pray to your highers if you think that'll help." The boy took Eli's wrist again, and this time, after taking a deep, steadying breath, Eli let him lead him up the stairs into the brightness.

"Keep 'em closed!"

Eli could hear people, lots of people, shouting and talking. And music coming from not far away. "Well?" The boy sniffed again. "What are you waiting for? Put on your mask."

"I don't have one." Eli's heart sank. How could he have overlooked such an obvious detail, especially after taking care to bleach the colour out of his rattiest clothes in order to fit in? "I . . . uh, I lost it in the tunnel."

"You can borrow one of mine." The boy slipped one over Eli's mouth and nose and tied it at the back. "For a price."

Eli held his breath for a moment, horrified that he was actually wearing a filthy Droughtlander's mask. But what choice did he have? He reminded himself that he was supposed to be reconciled to the idea of death. His death. But he wasn't, not at all, and that was very clear now that death was nipping at his heels. Eli paid the boy and then stumbled along blindly as he was dragged toward a noisy chaos of people shouting prices, hawking wares, bartering belligerently, with chickens squawking and the sound of children. Lots of children. There weren't supposed to be many children in the Droughtland. The few that made it to birth were supposed to die from all the infant sicks. Mind you, that was the Keyland spin on things. In that moment, Eli gave up what little he thought he knew of the Droughtland and decided he would find out for himself, for better or worse.

"Which way is Gulzar's mother's house? Do you know where she lives? Can you take me there?"

"Aw, what's he doing out already?" The boy squeezed Eli's wrist hard. "Shut up a minute. Don't say nothing."

A man's voice bellowed across the din. "Nappo!" The voice came nearer until it was as close as the boy's. "What're you doing away from the tunnel?"

"Helping this blind boy find his mother." Nappo sniffed again.

"*Gulzar's* mother," Eli said. "And I'm not blind, I'm just waiting for my eyes to adjust to the light. I've been in the tunnel two days."

"Is that what you told him, you lying little cheat?" The man put a hand on Eli's shoulder. "Open your eyes, son. Your eyeballs won't dry up and fall out, if that's what he told you."

Eli opened his eyes a crack. A burly man towered over him, greasy stains on his vest, bits of food stuck in his beard.

"Thank you." Eli's eyes watered a little, but they were okay otherwise. He held his hand out to shake hands with the man.

"That's funny," the man laughed, pointing at Eli's outstretched hand. "Good joke, that."

Eli let his hand drop. *We don't shake hands here.* That's what Gregor had said in the underground room. "Yeah, well, thanks."

"I apologize for Nappo there; he's a swindling little flea, so he is." The man grabbed hold of Nappo's collar and searched his pockets, pulling out Eli's coins and giving them back. "Tunnel-leaving is free, boy." He wiped at his beard. "Now, I'll be getting back to my meal. Nappo, you get back to the tunnel. All I ask is that you mind it for me while I have my lunch, understand?"

"But he was the first one in all the times I've minded for you, Pike!"

"I don't care," Pike hollered over his shoulder as he set off. "You stay at the tunnel until I finish my lunch, you hear? You got all the rest of the day to terrorize the market, boy. You owe me one hour a day."

"Thanks." Nappo glared at Eli. "Thanks a lot!"

The way they talked was different from Eli's. Their accent was looser, less refined, sloppier even than Keyland labourers. Eli put his mind to adjusting the way he spoke.

"Sorry." Eli covered the mask with his hand, afraid he might vomit now that he'd had a good look at the Droughtland filth that had touched him. Skinny bare brown arms and chest, riddled with long red scars and streaked with dirt, his nose red raw and dripping snot. He wasn't wearing a mask, and his eyes were rimmed in red wetness. Eli longed for soap and water, and fast. He spat on a corner of a handkerchief and scrubbed his wrist where Nappo had touched him.

"A lot good *sorry* does." Nappo made some gesture that Eli quickly caught the drift of, and then stalked off. "Piss off, you stupid wanker."

From that view, Eli got a look at the boy's equally scarred back and limp black hair, pulled into a ponytail that ended halfway to his bum. Eli had never seen a boy with long hair before. He was barefoot, his feet and legs also covered in the same scars, his heels dry and cracked, his only clothes a ratty pair of shorts patched with rags.

Then Eli was suddenly struck by what Pike had said. The market? But he wasn't headed for the market!

"Wait!" Eli turned, loosening his words as he ran through the crowd after Pike. "Is this really the market?"

"Another good joke, boy," Pike bellowed before disappearing into a large tent with the words *ale* and *meat* painted on either side of the canvas flap.

ELI LED SABER AND BULLET down the middle of a dirt lane lined with stalls and makeshift shops. The market went on for as far as Eli could see, all of it safely shaded from the brutal sun by a patchwork roof of tattered blankets and bits of scrap material. As he walked along he tried to make sense of the mask situation. Some Droughtlanders wore masks, but only a few, and they were more like the Night Circus performers' masks than the dull everyday ones he'd seen on occasion. The masks Eli saw in the market were decorated in bright colours, or in fanciful shapes, or were stitched with shiny beads or colourful feathers. Eli eventually gathered that the ones who weren't wearing masks all had the same long, ragged scars on them somewhere. Nappo had those scars, and he had touched him.

Eli dug in his pack for a bar of soap and then led Saber to a trough of water and let the horse drink while he wet his arms and soaped them up. He caught a look at his reflection in the water. His mask was just a patch of leather, the kind of mask Gulzar wore when he swept up mouse dung in the stables. The only difference was that Eli's had a pocket of lavender under the nose.

"Pay first, boy, and it ain't a bathhouse," said a man perched on a stool beside the trough. He was wearing a mask, and did not, as far as Eli could tell, have the scars.

"Can I get a pail to rinse with at least?" Eli said as he paid him.

"If you got the money for it."

"I'm good for it." Eli tried out the phrase he'd overheard down the lane. The man said nothing, so Eli scooped a pail of water and rinsed his arms.

"I'll charge double if your beasts keep at it."

Eli pulled Saber and Bullet away from the trough.

"Can I ask you a question?" Eli dropped three more coins into a jar above the trough. It was awkward speaking behind the mask; it felt almost rude, but Eli wouldn't dare lift it.

"No one's stopping you."

"Do you know of a village?" Eli struggled to think what direction Gulzar's village would be from the market. "North of here, I think."

"There are lots of villages north of here."

"I was in the tunnel, the one that leads to the Eastern Key, and I took the wrong turn. I meant to turn right, but I turned left instead." Eli thought back to the first junction. "No, wait. I did turn right."

"You saw the rest nook?"

"Yes! I slept there, and then when I woke . . . " Eli closed his eyes and tried to remember. " . . . That's when I must've got turned around." Eli was so angry with himself his knees went weak. He eyed an empty stool beside the waterminder. "Does it cost to sit?"

The man laughed. "It's free to sit, boy."

Eli sat, blanching again at being called *boy*. This was the second Droughtlander to call him that in less than five minutes. In the Key he was only ever addressed as Master Eli by anyone other than his parents or Seth. *Boy* was a term reserved for servants and labourers, no matter their age.

"I need to find a woman—"

"That does cost."

"Not a *woman*." Eli blushed behind his mask. "Well, she is a woman, I guess. She's my stable—" Eli cut himself off. "She's the mother of a friend of mine, and she lives in a village north of here. From the tunnel out of the Eastern Key, I was supposed to take the first right and then the first left after that. Do you know which one I mean by those directions?"

"Never been in the tunnel. Been here my whole life."

"But then how did you know about the rest nook?"

"Stories travel." The man took a coin from another customer and then tended the fire in two pits behind him, topping up the boiling vats of water hanging above the flames. Eli had read about such labour-intensive practices in Professor Wood's history books and was thankful for his water-purifying drops securely hidden in a saddlebag.

"This village you're looking for, what's it known for?"

"What do you mean?"

"Milling, weaving, poultry?" The man sighed. "The village trade, don't you know it?"

"I don't know anything about the village. I'm looking for a woman who lives there. Her name is Falma."

"Well, that's all you had to say, boy." The man laughed. "That's Talderton. Brickmakers."

"You know Falma?"

"I know *of* her, like everyone else."

"I know her son, Gulzar."

"Never heard of a son." The man helped another customer. "But Falma is the most skilled herbminder in the East, better than some life-minders even. People travel as long as it takes to be treated by her. She sells remedies here, but people travel to her if they can. Go talk to her niece. She minds the stall." The man gestured down the lane. "Fourteen down that way, on your left."

FALMA'S STALL WAS CURTAINED in fine purple linen, its counter a smooth blood-coloured wood. The line was so long that it trailed out of the market behind the stall and into the dangerous sunlight. Eli joined the tail end of it and dug in his pack for the hat he'd brought, one he'd stolen from Cook's husband, as all his own were too fine. He kept Saber on the side that would make some shade. Many ahead of him, and behind him soon enough, looked gravely ill, some of them with the long bloody wounds of the sick dripping down their legs and arms, others with sores they'd reach under their clothing to scratch, which made Eli want to scratch beneath his shirt too, although he had no cause to. Not yet, anyway. But then, he had no idea how long a sick took to do its nasty deed. But surely if he'd caught anything from Nappo he wouldn't be feeling it this soon, would he?

He began to think of all the diseases in the Droughtland and wondered how many could be passed on just by being in the presence of it. He kept his hands in his pockets, his face turned away from the ones who coughed a lot, and was thankful for Nappo's mask, especially the pocket of lavender under the nose. That eased some of the stench from so many unwashed bodies, seeping wounds, and the pungent ointments that some were dabbing on their sores. By the time Eli was next to be served he was sure he was already ill—probably dying. All that effort to get here and he was going to die on his first day out of the tunnels. He told himself it was inevitable. That he knew it was inevitable. At this point, death was the only sure thing. Not the how or when of it, but the certainty of it, indeed.

"Ailment?" Falma's niece was about five years older than Eli, slender, but not starved skinny. Healthy looking, with the same cinnamon skin as Gulzar's.

"I don't know. I just—"

"Ailment?"

"But, I—"

"Look, we don't diagnose here, we only treat. If you want a diagnosis, there's a lifeminder at the next market." She gave him a dismissive smile. "Next?"

"But wait, I just stood in line for hours to talk to you. Give me a minute, will you?"

"You see the line behind you? Does it look like I got a minute?" She folded her arms and looked Eli up and down. "You want my advice? Now, I'm no lifeminder, but I'd say you're too pale. Your skin is the colour of a Keylander. You look terrible." She turned to the two women preparing poultices behind her. "Doesn't he look awful? Like Keyland death warmed over?"

"Just listen to me for one minute." All this Keyland talk was making him nervous. He'd heard horrible stories in the kitchen, about Keylanders strung up and quartered by night bandits, getting their noses sliced open just because they were Keylanders, money or not. "I've been in the tunnels, that's all. I'm not sick. I'm looking for Falma."

Falma's niece stared, arms still crossed, the smallest of smiles on her lips. "Isn't everyone?"

Eli leaned across the counter and whispered. "If I could just have a word with you in private?" Eli could tell by her expression that her interest was sufficiently piqued.

"Well, girls, he wants a word without the two of you listening." Falma's niece winked at her helpers. "Maybe it's a condition he's too embarrassed to let you in on, eh? Something oozing in his pants?"

"It's nothing like that!" Behind him, the ones well enough and within earshot tittered, amused.

"Well then, what is it?"

Eli leaned closer, and beckoned for her to do the same. She rolled her eyes at the crowd, winning a laugh or two.

"I was sent by Gulzar," Eli whispered.

She lowered her voice. "How do you know Gulzar?" But Falma's niece didn't wait for an answer; she sucked in her breath and lowered her voice even more, to barely a whisper. "You *are* a Keylander, aren't you? I could tell by the look of you. I knew it!"

"I don't know what you're talking about." Eli felt the sharp announcement of panic rushing to his heart. "I just need you to tell me how to get to Talderton. I have to see Falma."

"You'll come with me." She hung her apron on a hook behind her. "I'm leaving for Talderton tonight." She held out her hand, fingers together and down, the way Keyland women did upon introduction. Her helpers noticed immediately.

"Getting fancy on us, Gidah?"

She winked at Eli and waited until he reluctantly took her hand in the formal manner. "Just having fun with the ghost boy, that's all." To Eli, she said, "I am Gidah."

"I am Eli."

"Well, girls, it turns out that Eli is a friend of Falma's after all." Gidah winked again. "He's taking me to dinner." Eli sure hoped no one took note of all her exaggerated winking. She was about as subtle as a signpost announcing just how very much he did not belong. But her helpers didn't seemed concerned, and the people lined up definitely hadn't taken notice; they were too outraged that she was closing early to care that she was playing Keylander as if it were a child's game. Maybe it was a child's game out here, like playing war was in the Keys. Eli had never much been into that, but he'd often watched the other children wield toy guns at the poor saps who had to be the Droughtlanders. But then, that wasn't war so much as extermination, popping them off as if they were vermin.

They're no better than rats. Who had said that the night of the circus? It was Edmund. Eli gritted his teeth, a sudden, fierce rage washing over him, strengthening his resilience. Death or not, life or not, Eli would go forward until it was no longer possible, and it wouldn't be for lack of will.

OVER DINNER, in the tent that Pike had disappeared into earlier and under the cover of noisy drinkers and a drum-heavy band with more enthusiasm than talent, Gidah made Eli tell her everything about life in the Key. She stared at him with rapt attention, drinking in every detail, right down to the place settings at the dinner the night Eli left and the gowns the ladies were wearing. Eli left out everything about his mother and father and the bombing. She'd asked about it, but he feigned ignorance, and she was obviously more interested in Keyland society than politics, so she hadn't pestered, thankfully. So long as it would get him to Talderton, Eli droned on about Keyland life until at long last Gidah stood and stretched her arms above her head.

"Someday I will marry a Keylander and get away from all this."

Eli resisted the urge to laugh. A Droughtlander had about as much chance of marrying a Keylander as Eli had of finding Talderton on his own. As they left the pub he tried to come up with a diplomatic way of setting her straight, but her dreamy grin stopped him. Why ruin a harmless dream when she obviously had so little else?

It was dark out, and much cooler, so safer to travel now. Eli turned to untie Saber from the hitch, but Saber, his pack, and the saddlebags were gone. Bullet lay fast asleep in a little bowl he'd dug into the dirt.

"My horse is gone!" Bullet bolted awake. He leapt up and growled at Gidah, baring his teeth.

Gidah backed away with a shriek. "Call him off!"

"Sit, Bullet." Bullet sat. "Why didn't you go after whoever stole Saber?" His tone was so fierce the dog cowered for the first time in Eli's presence.

"Was your horse locked?"

"Locked?" Eli ran in and out between tents, whistling for Saber. "How could I lock a horse?"

"To the hitch, with a lock, like everyone else."

"Saber? Come on, boy!"

"Look, I can't wait for you, Eli. Besides, your horse is probably long gone and sold ten times by now. It's not like this doesn't happen all the time."

"But my packs! My things!" Eli kicked the dirt. "I can't leave without them!"

"I'm really sorry, Eli. But I just can't wait for you. And honestly, I don't think there's anything to wait for."

"But my things . . . "

"I'm sorry, Eli."

"This place is just a cesspool of ignorance and lawlessness!"

"Wow." Gidah snorted, hands on her hips. "And all it took was a few hours for you to figure us out. How astute."

Eli stared at her.

"Yes, I know fancy words like *astute*."

"It's not that."

"Then what?"

"I just . . . " Eli shook his head. "All my things. My money. My gear! How am I supposed to survive out here?"

"I'm sure you'll figure something out." Gidah started walking toward the end of the market, where the Droughtlanders' carts were watched by cartminders. "Maybe you should just go home to Mommy and get more *things*. Get another horse while you're at it. I hear they're plentiful where you come from. Maybe next time you won't be so stupid and leave your horse unlocked outside a pub."

"I didn't know!" Eli screamed at her, raising the attention of several stallminders nearby.

"Well, now you do!" Gidah hollered in reply.

Eli had no choice but to follow her, of course. He might have money, but he had no horse, no clothes, no food, no supplies, and no clue; he couldn't let the one person he barely knew slip away, leaving him totally alone in the Droughtland. He trailed behind Gidah as she, ignoring him completely, made her way through the mess of ramshackle carts parked in no decent order.

"This git has had his horse stolen," she said to the cartminder on their way out. "And all his possessions. All he has left is this vicious dog. If you hear anything about this horse—it is very handsome, all black with a white diamond on its chest and fancy shoes—tell one of my girls and you'll be generously rewarded." Then she turned to Eli. "Well, pay the man, already. He's watched my cart for the whole week."

Eli scowled at Gidah while he counted the coins into the cartminder's gloved hand. Gloved or not, Eli wiped his hands on his pants as Gidah steered her horse and cart through the maze.

"Why don't you people park in *lines*?" Eli asked as they came to another dead end, blocked on three sides by carriages. "And why are the carts so wide? If no one can park properly it would at least help if the carts were narrower. Doesn't take a genius to figure that out, speaking of gits."

"Why don't you shut up about the way we dirty Droughtlanders do things and be thankful that I'm letting you come along at all?"

"You're only *letting* me come along because I'm paying you."

"That's exactly right, so shut up." Gidah finally navigated her way onto a wide dirt road, stretched out for miles in the moonlight.

"Fine, I will," Eli said. "And I won't answer any more of your stupid questions either."

"You think I care?"

Eli didn't reply. He stewed in self-loathing instead. How could he have *lost* Saber and all his gear? Gidah was right, he was stupid. Stupid beyond belief. He thought about the water drops and nearly wept. He would probably run out of money in a matter of days if he had to pay for clean water rather than use the drops.

Somewhere out there in the dusty night a wicked thief was dancing with joy at Eli's stupidity. Somewhere out there a filthy Droughtlander was touching the picture of his family—never mind *family*, Eli hadn't taken the picture for any other reason than it included his mother. As far as he was concerned he didn't have a *family* any more. Come to think of it, had he ever had a real family? Or had it always been a hollow statue of one?

Eli pushed the heart-crushing idea out of his mind and instead leapt on the image of a faceless, diseased thief slipping Lisette's ring onto his woman's finger and pocketing the pearl necklace to trade in the morning. Eli was going to cry. He simply couldn't help it. He turned away from Gidah and wept until he fell asleep, thankful that the clatter of the wagon masked his miserable sniffles.

Seth had not cried once since Lisette's disappearance. He lay awake most nights, hands behind his head, eyes wide open, searching the darkness for some explanation for what had happened. He would not name this search grief, though. He named it fury. He named it confusion. But he would not name it grief. He refused to grieve the loss of a mother who had betrayed his family and threatened Edmund's future, and his own. He refused to grieve for a woman dead or missing due to her own failures. Since Gulzar's return he didn't know what he truly believed, but he chose to believe that she deserved whatever she got, be it exile or death. How could she jeopardize Edmund's rise to Chancellor? How could things have gone from so perfect to so foul in such a short period of time?

Eli. That's how. He was responsible for all of it, Seth was sure. His toxic words had started the doubt. The drivel Eli had spouted that day about their mother haunted Seth, no matter how often he reminded himself it was all crazy talk from a brat who was too stupid to understand anything of consequence. He could not even know the meaning of consequence, that much was clear, not after what he'd done.

When Edmund and Seth had come home after the fireworks, Seth had found Eli's note on his desk and Edmund had found the smashed globe and the empty picture frame.

"Not a word," Edmund growled when Seth had come running with the note. "Not a word of this to anyone. Eli is joining the Guard with you, understand?"

"Yes sir." Seth nodded, doubtful anyone would believe that wimpy little tosser would join the Guard. He wasn't about to argue though, not judging by the expression on Edmund's face. "You watch, Father. I'll make him pay for this. I'll hunt him down and bring him—"

"Silence." Edmund snatched Eli's note from him and read it aloud. "*Someday you will value truth and justice, and then you will understand. Until then you will always be a disappointment to the cause.*" Edmund ripped the paper into tiny bits. "What does he mean by this? What *cause*?"

"I have no idea, Father. Maybe he's gone crazy. He must've, to break the globe. He knows what it's worth. Maybe Mother's death has affected him more than we thought?"

"Your mother," Edmund seethed. "My dearest *Lisette*. She is responsible for how that boy has turned out."

"What do you mean, Father?"

"Get out." Edmund quaked with rage.

"I'll do whatever you say, Father. I can find him. I can make him pay for this."

"Leave me," Edmund growled. "And not a word. Your brother has joined the Guard. He will die in a training accident, and we will bury him."

"But I can find him, Father! I can bring him back so he can be punished. We can make him an example."

"Don't flatter yourself. You could never find him." Edmund shoved Seth out into the hall. "Don't be a fool. Eli is dead to us. Do not mention him again. Ever." Edmund slammed the door.

"I will find him," Seth whispered to the door. "You'll see, Father. I'll bring him to you."

THE NEXT MORNING Allegra was at the breakfast table, pen and paper in hand, making a list for the First Ladies tea being held the next day.

"Good morning, Seth."

Seth frowned at her. They'd left her at her house the night before, so when had she come back? Early this morning? Or had she spent the night?

"Where's my father?"

"At the legislature, of course." She set her pen down and folded her slender hands in her lap.

"What are you doing here?"

She pushed the list at him and offered him the same smile that used to make him blush with desire. "Would you like to check my spelling?"

He had spent countless hours with other boys, spying on her at dances and feasts and game days and formal functions, one-upping each other about what they would do to her if they had her to themselves in a dark room. And now what? She'd become his father's whore?

"I don't care what you're doing." Seth backed away.

"Suit yourself." She shrugged and went back to her list.

Just as Seth left the room, she called after him. "I gather your brother has gone ahead of you to the base? Your father said he needs some extra training before the rest of you begin?"

"If that's what he said."

"Yes." Allegra paused. "That's what he said."

"What are you getting at?"

"Nothing. Nothing at all." She offered him that smile again. "Just trying to make conversation, that's all."

"Whatever." Seth rolled his eyes.

"Careful, Seth." Again, she folded her hands in her lap. "Your father told me to let him know if you disrespected me in any way."

"And have I?" Seth grinned. He had. He definitely had. He and half the boys in the Eastern Key had, in their dreams and in their empty bragging.

"Not exactly."

"Then we're fine." Seth gave her a casual salute. "Have a great day, Allegra."

HE MET PROFESSOR WOOD for lessons that morning, but before they could begin, Seth laid it on the line.

"No more lessons, Woody." Seth grabbed the lesson book and chucked it into the garbage. "We're finished."

"You don't have any say in the matter." Professor Wood retrieved his book.

"Go tell my father that I'm having a little holiday from studying before I join my brother at the Guard."

"Master Eli has not joined the Guard!"

"Talk to my father. No more lessons, Woody." Seth stormed out of the room and hollered over his shoulder. "You're fired!"

"Master Seth! Come back at once!" Woody chased after him. "I will talk to your father the instant he's home from the legislature!"

AND SO PROFESSOR WOOD was fired. Seth didn't know what had transpired between him and Edmund, but at dinner that night, while

Chancellor Southeast was being helped to her seat by Allegra and Nuala, Edmund yanked Seth out of earshot and whispered harshly, "If you think you can use your brother's disappearance to manipulate me, you are wrong. Is that clear?"

"But I didn't tell Professor Wood anything that he wasn't going to find out soon enough."

"No, you didn't. But you sent him to me thinking you have some kind of power. And you don't. I didn't let him go because I was afraid of you revealing the truth. Don't get me wrong. I let him go because he's a waste of money at this point. You won't be able to concentrate on anything other than the militia, I imagine. So make no mistake. You had nothing to do with this. Understood?"

"Yes, sir."

"I will not be blackmailed by my own son."

"Sorry, sir."

"If you ever try anything like that again, you will not be going to the Guard. Not now. Not ever. Understood?"

"Yes, sir." Seth took his seat, trembling with excitement. He suddenly felt taller than his father, taller than anyone else in the room. It was as if he'd shot up with the power of exerting his will, of defeating his father in this small way.

8

Eli and Gidah spent the brutal daylight hours nursing their grudges for each other in whatever shade they could find, whether in a coulee with a tarp strung up between long dead trees, or at the base of a rocky outcrop, or for money in the root cellars of strangers. On the second night they entered a stretch of tunnel that allowed them to travel through the day as well. The tunnel ended abruptly, and they were in the cooler dark of the Droughtland night again. Along the way Gidah provided a reluctant commentary of what Eli wasn't seeing—tunnel entrances, caves, huts built into the cool clay hills. Eli figured she was talking just to hear the sound of her own voice, but he didn't complain or tell her to stop. In truth, he was glad for her chatter; it made the time pass more quickly, and he was genuinely interested in what she was saying. He knew so little about the Droughtland that he was eager to glean as much knowledge as he could, although he was too proud to expose his ignorance by asking what she would no doubt consider to be stupid questions.

They reached Talderton at dawn three days later and found Falma at the receiving end of a very long line of sick people. Falma knew who he was immediately. She swept him into a hug as he stepped down from the cart.

"Gulzar sent word that you might come. Come in, come in!" She ushered him into a clay hut, which he was surprised to find quite cool despite the growing heat outside.

"Now, Master Eli, what can I do for you?"

"Just call me Eli, please."

"I see you've already learned a thing or two about being a Keylander in the Droughtland," Falma said. Eli wished that really was the case.

"No one calls anyone Master out here." Across the room, Gidah washed the road dust off her face and arms with dirty water from a small basin. "Out here, everybody is *equal*."

"Out here, everybody is *desperate*," Eli countered. "At least in the Keys no one has to lock their doors, or their horses for that matter."

Gidah joined them at the table, where Falma had laid out the wine and cheese and apples they'd brought from the market. "That's because if anyone was caught breaking one of your rules they'd go in front of the Star Chamber, right? They're all too scared to do anything for themselves. That's not freedom either."

"That's enough, Gidah." Falma patted her arm. "Why don't you get your horse settled and unpack the cart?"

"You're going to let him talk about us like that?"

"I'm going to let him get comfortable after such a long journey. Now go on."

"Sure, get rid of me. Who am I? Just your niece, that's all. Just family. Just blood." Gidah pushed her chair back with a loud scrape. "But let me tell you one thing, *Keylander*, I've changed my mind about marrying your kind. All it took was meeting one."

"Not like you would've even had the remotest chance anyway. No Keylander man would want you."

"Oh!" Gidah smacked his cheek. "You piece of Keyland trash!"

"I thought *trash* was a word exclusively applied to Droughtlanders," Eli said, and then wished he hadn't, as he hadn't meant to hurt Falma's feelings. He was about to apologize, but Falma stepped between them. Eli brought his hand to his stinging cheek.

"Go deal with your horse, Gidah." Falma hustled her toward the door.

"Fine, I will, but seeing as I'm not talking to that swine any more, would you mind asking him why is it," Gidah glared at Eli, who could hear her just fine, "if the Keylanders are such great and noble people, that his dead mother is buried here?"

Before Falma could chastise her, Gidah flounced out of the house, the sting from her parting words far more painful than the slap in the face. She'd known all along who he was, and hadn't said anything, which was merciful. That just made him feel worse.

"I WANT TO SEE her grave," Eli said after they'd eaten.

"It's too hot," Falma said. "Later, when the sun goes down."

"No." Eli shook his head. "I want to see it now."

"Eli, the sun is high. It's too hot."

"I need to see her now," Eli murmured.

"So be it." Falma sighed. "But you mustn't stay long. You can go back after sunset."

She gave him a wide-brimmed hat, donned one herself, and led him to his mother's grave. It was hot. So hot that the short walk was a cruel marathon. Eli glanced up at the sky. Not a single cloud. And no rain to look forward to. No cleansing storm to refresh the world.

A short fence skirted the plot, which was covered in the same red-brick dust as all the graves in the odd cemetery that wound like a boulevard between the huts of the tiny village. The headstone read *Nashua Opal*. Opal, like her precious ring. The ring he'd lost. Eli shook his head and said nothing. Falma left him there with a jar of boiled water and a brick of honey and oats, and told him she'd come for him in an hour.

All Eli wanted was to be still and sit quietly with what was left of his mother, a charred body and memories. Thank the highers for the memories, because imagining her corpse was almost unbearable. No, it was unbearable. All of this was unbearable, even the memories, if only because that's all he had left. He tried to clear his thoughts, the way she'd taught him. He steadied his breathing and pictured a blankness of warm light. He concentrated on it, gritting his teeth and frowning, but still, clarity wouldn't come. Flies buzzed at his head and cicadas squabbled in all directions like an insult. There was no quiet. No peace. No nothing, just shimmering heat and the wicked truth that everything that ever was was ruined.

There was no solitude either, just the facade of it. No villagers walked by; they would never leave their houses during the heat of the day, not even to catch a glimpse of the Keylander boy. But Eli could feel their heavy gazes, their curiosity poking at him like a stone in his boot. Falma had told him that they knew who he was, and had promised him that no one would even think to tell the Keyland Guard when they came through the village on their regular inspections. Eli wished he could trust her. He wished he could trust the villagers. But there was no such thing as trust any more. How could there be? He couldn't even trust in who he was, or where he'd come from, so how could he trust strangers to keep his secret? He squinted at the dark windows of the huts lining the street. He couldn't see anyone, but he knew they were watching, seeing how long he could stand the heat, or the grief. He couldn't stand any of it. He couldn't stand his life. Maybe he should just lay himself down across his mother's grave, if it even was his mother's grave, and let the heat take him.

Or maybe he should go back. Not home, there was no such thing any more, but to the familiarity, the safety of the Key. He could go to the Southeast Key, implore the Chancellor to take him in, claim that the tragedy of his mother's death had compelled him to leave but that he was ready to return. Eli sat with the thought crushing him like a boulder. He could not go back. He had to go forward, no matter if it killed him.

An hour hadn't passed, but Eli was done. He stared at the headstone, the stranger's name carved into the clay face.

"Nashua." Eli ran his fingers along the indentations of the crudely carved letters. "I wish it could say Lisette, Maman."

And then his grief fell away as if it were a cloak slipping off his shoulders, leaving him with an armour of rage. He wanted to scream at the dark windows with their critical eyes, at the cloudless sky, at Seth for his stubborn ignorance, at his mother for her lies and her leaving it all until too late. He wanted to scream at her for dying even, but most of all he wanted to scream at his father.

Eli balled his fists and wondered again, for the millionth time, if Edmund had truly known Lisette would be at the gardens that morning. Had he known about her involvement? Had he known that Triskelia was interwoven in his household like an invisible ivy?

Eli looked down the boulevard of headstones and graves with their garish mementoes and rickety fences. Somewhere beyond, across the dry death of the Droughtland, lay the lush green of the Eastern Key. It did beckon him, the sanctuary, the wealth, he wouldn't deny that. But he could not go back and would not go back. Seth wouldn't let him, and besides, Eli wanted to find his mother's people. He needed to know where she'd come from, what she believed, who she really was in the world. He'd failed to keep her alive. He could've stopped the bombing. But he hadn't. He'd do right by her memory now. Failing wasn't an option. He'd rather die.

Eli laid the bouquet of dried flowers Falma had arranged for him on his mother's headstone and then walked back to Falma's house, the heat a vicious gauntlet.

THAT NIGHT, Falma packed Eli a bag full of everything she and the other villagers could spare while Gidah fumed in the herb garden out back, watering the skinny plants with the villagers' meagre supply of grey water. The village had a pump, connected to a rickety series of pipes that hooked up to an overused underground spring far, far away, but there'd been nothing from the pump for days.

"It happens sometimes," Falma said when he'd asked about it. "It's never lasted longer than a week." She arranged the last of the food packages. "Now, I've packed you food enough for several days, if you ration carefully." She walked him to the edge of the village after supper so that he could flag down the transport carriage going west. "I also put in a satchel of medicinal herbs and tinctures. There are instructions for each, but I will pray to my highers that you won't need them. I'm sorry we couldn't spare more water."

"That's okay." Eli adjusted the heavy load on his shoulders. "Thanks for everything."

"I put in a special sweetcake for you. Gulzar told me about your birthday."

"It was yesterday!" Eli stopped. "How could I have not remembered my own birthday?"

"It's understandable, considering."

"That means Seth has joined the Guard." Eli could just imagine it, his brother all puffed up in his uniform, marching along like a good little sheep while Edmund grinned proudly in the stands. Did Seth ever think about their mother? Didn't he wonder about any of it? "He doesn't believe any of this," Eli said. "He doesn't believe Maman was a rebel."

Falma put a hand on his arm. "Eli, she was much more than a rebel."

"A rebel leader, I know."

"That too, but she was your mother. That always came first for her. Her children. That's why she waited so long, so that she could have her children with her. You must know that."

"We could've left sooner." Eli looked down the dark road toward the pounding of an approaching carriage. "If it weren't for Seth." A cloud of dust rolled out of the night until the long carriage, which was really just three carts precariously hitched together, pulled to a stop in front of them.

"Look forward, Eli. Be strong."

"I'll try, Falma," Eli whispered as the driver threw his pack gracelessly onto the floor of the cart. "Do you know *where* in the west?"

"If I did, I would've told you before now. Take care, Eli."

"You too." Eli climbed into the last cart. "And tell Gidah I'm sorry."

"I will. Be safe." Falma waved, holding the thin cloth of her cloak over her mouth as the dust swirled up again and the cart rolled away. Eli got as comfortable as he could, arranging his new pack as a pillow. He tied Bullet to it with a length of rope as an extra precaution. He should've tied Bullet to Saber in the market, but he hadn't thought of it. Let someone try to steal from him again. This time he was close enough to sic Bullet on them. Eli hadn't taught him to attack on command, that'd been Seth's doing, but now Eli was glad for it. It would no doubt come in handy.

Eli closed his eyes and slept, memories from past birthdays slipping into his dreams, happy snippets of singing around towering cakes and ripping through mountains of presents.

According to Keyland records, Eli had been dead and buried for two days already and had not lived to celebrate his sixteenth year.

Everyone was amazed that Edmund could sustain such stoicism, what with all the tragedy that had befallen his family in recent weeks. He was even able to deliver a eulogy, albeit a short one. Seth didn't bother to listen. It was all lies, cooked up and churned out. *Brave boy . . . died serving his fellow Keylanders.* It was enough to make him puke. The story was that he'd fallen off the climbing wall and broken his neck, so how, even in fiction, could that be construed as serving his fellow Keylanders? Seth had a hard time not laughing at the pageantry of it all. Especially the burial. That was particularly funny. Seth was a pallbearer, and as he strode past the crowds with the weight on his shoulders, he wondered if there were just rocks in the coffin or if it was actually a body. Seth didn't want to know. Or he did, actually, but he didn't want to admit it.

SETH SPENT THE NIGHT of their sixteenth birthday in the barracks at the Guard training compound between the Northeastern and Eastern Keys. It was the first night he'd ever slept away from home. He tossed and turned on the narrow bunk, listening to the sleeping noises of the other two dozen new recruits. The building next to his was also full of new recruits, but girls. He'd never seen so many people his age before that morning. He'd never seen so many girls before, ever. Seth had a difficult time keeping his eyes off them during the long registration process. He tried to remember that he was supposed to be in mourning, for his mother and Eli, but it was hard. He wasn't sure that Lisette was dead, and if Eli was, by chance or stupidity, he didn't care, so it was hard to maintain the solemnity Edmund expected.

"I'll leave you then," Edmund said after they'd completed all the paperwork and had carried the heavy trunk to his bed. "It's a long way back."

"Father." Seth pulled his shoulders back and saluted the man, who looked as though he'd lost an inch to his height in the days since Eli's disappearance. Maybe that's why Seth felt taller, because his father was actually shrinking under the mess of it all.

"No need for that." Edmund frowned at his son, and at the other boys who stared at Seth, wondering what he was doing. "Stand down. You look like a fool."

Seth's shoulders drooped. "Goodbye, Father," he said to Edmund's back as his father left the barracks.

Edmund had barely spoken to him since Eli had gone. The only reason he'd escorted him to the training camp was that it was expected. Seth doubted that his father's melancholy was the result of sadness. Humiliation, more like. Seth knew this because that's what he felt himself. Never mind sadness about Lisette and Eli, it was the deep horrifying humiliation that was hard to manage. If only Edmund would confide in him. They were alone in these lies. Just the two of them. And if Edmund would let him, Seth could be an ally of such value that his father would grow to depend on him. That was how it should be between a Chief Regent and his son. Not fractured like it was now.

Seth would make it up to him. He'd bring Eli back for Edmund to punish. They could lay it all on him, the bombing, Lisette's "death," and his own fake death. Seth would be the one to expose such deep-seated betrayal within the Key. And it wouldn't weaken Edmund's rise to power. On the contrary, it would strengthen it when the Keylanders could see that he'd turn in his own traitorous son to preserve the integrity and security of the Key. If only Edmund would let him prove his worth.

Seth turned again in his bunk, screwing his eyes shut to rid the image of Edmund gripping the iron axis of the smashed globe as if he'd like to beat his remaining son to death with it. It wasn't his fault Eli ran away, or Mother either, for that matter, if in fact she'd actually run away. The boy beside him, a great hulk of a Northern Keylander simply called Nord, whispered harshly in the dark.

"If you don't stop moving, Maddox, I'll make it so you can't move at all."

Seth fought the urge to leap out of bed and throttle him. Nord was much bigger than he was, and besides, Seth didn't know the rules here yet. He'd wait and get his bearings before he started to edge himself into place. There was always a hierarchy, and it was always an art to place yourself in it. It was all part of the dance of power, and it required patience. Seth understood such things, and so he should, considering his future.

Nord rolled over and glared at him. "Did you hear me?"

"I heard you." Seth thrashed under the covers once more, and with deliberate vigour.

"I mean it, Maddox."

"Sorry," Seth said, but he wasn't at all. Not about that, anyway.

9

A team of six horses sped the transport carriage through the night, finally coming to a stop in a long rickety shed at the side of the road. Eli and the other passengers each claimed a bunk along the wall and tried to get some sleep. Eli couldn't sleep, though. He sat outside in the shade of the building and watched a storm developing on the horizon, likely destined to release over the North Central Key. How cruel to watch the weather form and then never have it manifest.

The clouds hovered on the horizon for about an hour and then rolled back over themselves, surging northward. Eli wanted to run after them, if only to feel just a few drops of cool rain on his hot, dusty skin. It looked as though this stretch of Droughtland hadn't seen rain in decades. The only sign of life were the vultures tearing at the carcass of a horse at the edge of the road. Poor Saber. What had become of him?

DURING THE LONG HOURS on the carriage Eli paid close attention to the way Droughtlanders spoke. He tried to mimic their cadence and accent, but he still thought he sounded like a Keylander. It took so much effort to erase his pompous lilt when he talked, as he had in the market, that he was sure he sounded a little handicapped, so he just didn't speak at all. He didn't say a word to the other travellers who got on and off at the carriage stops, not even if they asked him a question. He just played dumb, and so people left him alone.

The first words he spoke were at dusk on the third day, about an hour out of the carriage rest. Even in the dusky light there was no mistaking what Eli was looking at in the distance.

"Saber!" Eli couldn't believe his eyes. "Stop the carriage! That's my horse!" It *was* Saber, in all his glory, albeit rather filthy, tied up behind an abandoned trader shop. Sitting astride him, or more accurately, slumped and apparently asleep on top of him, was a very small boy. Eli's packs and saddlebags were still cinched in place.

"Driver, stop!" Eli watched frantically as Saber grew smaller in the distance. "That's my horse! Someone stole him! And there he is! Stop!"

The driver slowed the horses. Eli grabbed his pack and climbed down, all the while keeping an eye on Saber, who was now just a dark speck behind them. When his feet hit dirt, Eli started running. Bullet loped ahead of him, barking.

As he neared, another boy emerged from the crumbling shack and headed for Saber. Eli ran faster, his muscles screaming from so many days of sitting on his butt, his lungs resisting the hot, dusty air. Bullet was well ahead of him, head lowered, ears back.

"Sic, Bullet!" Eli wheezed. "Get him!"

Bullet plowed across the remaining distance. The boy noticed him then, and threw himself onto Saber. He grabbed hold of the child and kicked Saber into a gallop. Bullet closed the gap and launched himself into the air, but he missed the boy and locked his teeth onto the leather stirrup. He let go and fell to the dirt as Saber cantered off.

Eli stopped running. There was no way he could catch up. He whistled the three notes Gulzar used to cue all the Maddox horses. Saber reared up, sending the two boys crashing over his backside and onto the dirt. He swung his head, searching for Eli.

"Saber!" Eli waved his arms and whistled again as Saber trotted back to him. "Here, boy!" Saber nuzzled his pockets and snuffled. "No apples. Sorry." Eli walked the length of him, checking him out. "Where've you been?" The horse was filthy, no surprise, but other than that he was in pretty good shape. Eli climbed into the saddle. From that height he could see the smaller boy lying still in the dirt while the older boy knelt at his side.

Was the little boy hurt? Eli went to investigate. As he neared he realized that he recognized the older one. It was Nappo, the boy from the market.

"You stole my horse!"

Nappo didn't look up.

"You rotten thief!" Eli jumped down to check the saddlebags. "And what about my things? Have you traded them all? Sold them?" Still Nappo didn't look up from the small boy. "Look at me!" Eli smacked Nappo's head. "Did you sell everything?"

"Just a couple things, to get us this far. I can explain. That day in the market—"

"Just shut up!" Eli rooted through the bags. So far, so good. "Shut up, okay? I don't want to hear it."

"But let me tell you first—"

"I said shut up!" Eli slid his hand down the inside of the saddlebag until he felt the satisfying nubs of his mother's pearl choker where he'd sewed it and her ring into the lining of the bag. Eli calmed a little and turned his attention to the younger boy, who was lying on his back, eyes closed, motionless. "Who's he?"

"My brother."

"What's wrong with him?"

"He just got thrown off a horse!" Nappo wiped his nose and glared miserably at Eli. "What do you expect?"

"But he wasn't moving before, either." Eli crouched beside the little boy. "What's wrong with him?"

"I don't know!" Nappo started crying, the tears cleaning two thin lines down his filthy cheeks. "He's been sleeping for five days. That's why I stole your horse. I was going to sell your things to pay for a herbminder, or a lifeminder if there was enough. Now he'll just die, like the rest of them!"

"The rest of who?"

"Mom. Dad. The villagers. Talia was the last one."

Eli navigated carefully between scars and found a pulse at the little boy's wrist, weak, but steady. He was maybe three years old, his nose caked shut with snot and dirt, his eyelids glued together with gritty, dried puss, the rest of him covered in the same scars as Nappo's. His little fist was closed tight around a strip of bluish rag that might've been a blanket once.

"Is it the scars?"

"No, those are from the skineater, from before. This is the sleeping sick. The rest of them died like this, sleeping for days and then their breath just leaves them. Talia told me not to let Teal get sick, but I couldn't help it. He must've caught it from her before she died."

"Who's Talia?"

"Our cousin. She took us to her village after our parents died and we lived there until they started dying and then she took us to live at the market, but then she got sick and died. I didn't know Teal was sick until I went back to him the day you came out of the tunnel. He was asleep and wouldn't wake up and that's why I stole your beast. To get help."

Eli took Falma's pack off his shoulders and rummaged through it until he found the linen with all the herbs rolled up in it. He opened it onto his lap and began sorting through the pouches of herbs and little jars of tincture. The instructions were hard to decipher, as Falma's writing skills weren't as honed as her healing skills.

"I said I was sorry," Nappo said.

"No, you didn't. You just told me why you stole him." Eli found instructions for a waking tincture and was trying to understand them. "Open his mouth."

"What are you going to do to him? What is that? Are you a herbminder?"

"No. Falma gave it to me."

"Gidah's aunt?"

"Yes, Gidah's aunt."

"Well, I am sorry about the horse. I guess."

"No, you're not. You're just saying that so I'll help you." Eli pried the cork off what he hoped was the right vial. "But I'm not helping you. I'm helping him. Open his mouth."

Nappo hesitated.

"Do you have a better idea?"

Nappo shook his head.

"Then open his mouth!"

"You better know what you're doing." Nappo pried open the little boy's chapped lips and held them apart while Eli let twenty drops of the foul-smelling tincture fall onto his tongue.

Finished, they both sat back and watched in silence, waiting for the boy to open his eyes.

"Nothing's happening." Nappo crouched over his brother. "Glad I didn't make the trek to see Falma in person if this is the best she has to offer. Glad we're halfway to the lifeminder instead. Glad I didn't—"

"He can't open his eyes if they're caked in muck." Eli tipped Nappo's water bladder over the boy's face.

"That's all the water we got!"

Eli smiled. So, Nappo either hadn't found the water drops or he didn't know what they were for. He trickled the last of the water over Teal's eyes.

"Aw, no! Don't do that. I don't got the money for any more!"

Eli wiped the gunk away from Teal's eyes and nose, and then cleaned the rest of the boy's face while he was at it. "This is your brother's life. Isn't that more important?"

Nappo threw his hands up. "Not if he's just going to die from thirst or water sicks!"

Just then, the little boy opened his eyes a crack. Nappo grabbed his brother's face in his hands.

"Teal? Tealy? You awake?"

"Thirsty," the boy croaked.

"See? He needs water!" Nappo kicked the dirt. "You think some magic spring might spout up or something? 'Cause all's I got now is the dirty stuff I been giving the horse."

"You've been giving Saber dirty water?" Eli walked over to the horse and stroked his neck. "We'll fix that, boy." He pulled off the saddlebag with the false bottom, where he'd stashed the drops and more cash.

He took the bladder of dirty water and a tin cup and went back to the boys. He filled the cup and added the drops. He waited a full minute, and then held the cup to Teal's mouth.

"You can't give him dirty water!"

"It's not dirty any more."

Nappo's eyes went wide. "You got those magic drops? Can I see?" He grabbed the cup. "Looks the same."

"That's because it's not magic, it's science." Eli took the cup back and let Teal take another sip. "Don't you know anything?"

Nappo stared at Eli for a long moment before wagging a finger at him. "You're a Keylander, aren't you? A Keylander! I don't believe it!" He looked around frantically, as if he expected an audience to appear and applaud his discovery. "What are you doing out *here*?"

Eli considered lying, but he badly wanted not to. He wanted to be able to ask stupid, dangerous questions of someone, he wanted to be honest, he wanted someone to tell his story to, what he'd been through, what he was searching for. He wanted a friend, and the only candidate for a thousand miles around was doing a strange little victory dance in the dirt. And besides, Nappo owed Eli, after stealing from him.

"A Keylander! A real, live Keylander!"

"I'm looking for the rebels. I'm going to join them."

"*You*? Join the rebels? The rebels will flatten the Keys, you know. There won't be any more Keylanders after the revolution. You'll all be Droughtlanders, like the rest of us, only we won't even be Droughtlanders, not after the revolution, we'll be Westlanders or Northlanders or Eastlanders or—"

"Or Southlanders, I know. That's fine by me." Eli tried to sound like he meant it, but he wasn't sure if he did. Who would look after the water? Who would monitor the gardens? And the weather? Would they all have to live like this? Covered in filth and disease, never more than a moment from death in any direction? And what about death? Whoever said any Keylanders would be permitted to live? Truthfully, Eli knew nothing of what the Triskelians had planned. Perhaps every Keylander would be killed. Eli wouldn't be surprised, and nor could he even blame them, not after generations of oppression at the hands of the Keylanders.

"The rebels won't kill *all* the Keylanders," Eli said. "Not the ones that comply. They won't, will they?"

"Nah, they're not murderers." Nappo wiped his nose and took a tentative sip from the tin cup. "Not like you Keylanders, who'd have us all killed if you weren't so afraid of the sicks and didn't need the clean ones for labour." Nappo lifted Teal's head so that he could get another drink. The boy started gulping, until Eli pulled the cup away.

"He shouldn't drink that fast, he might—"

But Teal threw up before Eli could finish explaining that he might do just that.

AS THE MOON ROSE HIGHER and Teal rested, Eli told Nappo the story of how he'd come to be in the Droughtland. Nappo listened as if it were a tale of mythic proportions, even though to Eli the whole thing just sounded desperate and lame. He didn't know how to survive out here. He didn't even know where he was going.

The night stretched on, until the first colour of morning snaked a line along the eastern horizon.

"We have to find somewhere to stay for the day." Eli stood and stretched his aching legs. "It will start to get hot soon."

"But where am I supposed to take Teal? I got no money. And now you're taking the beast." Nappo unstopped a little clay jar that hung from a piece of leather around his neck. He tipped a bit of grey powder onto his pinky and snorted it up his nose.

"The horse was mine to begin with," Eli said. "And what is that?"

"You don't know?" Nappo rubbed his nose and squinted at him. "You're all fancy fancy and you don't know?"

"Look, never mind, all right? I don't care what it is. We need to get going. I can take you with me," he said as he draped Teal over Saber's back, "but we should cover some ground before the sun gets any higher."

"I can ride," Teal mumbled, grabbing hold of the saddle horn.

"You can't ride," Nappo chided him, and then explained to Eli. "He's never been on a horse before this one."

"You'll ride." Eli patted Teal's back, feeling the heat of his fever through his thin shirt. "When you're well enough, you can ride him as fast as he can go."

"Promise?" Teal's eyes were still pussy and red.

"Promise, kid."

And it was a promise Eli intended to keep, if Teal ever did get well, that is.

WHEN THE SUN WAS HIGH enough to harm, Eli bought the three of them and the animals shelter in an underground bunker. The bunker was much cooler than outside, but it was still too hot for Eli to sleep, which is what he wanted all three of them to do, or at least the brothers, so that Eli could have a few moments of blessed quiet to think of what to do next. Then a thought occurred to him.

"Nappo? Are you awake?"

There was rustling from across the room. "Yeah, too hot to sleep."

"You don't know where the rebels are based, do you?"

"Right. Sure." Nappo laughed in the dark. "I know exactly where. I'll take you right to their door. I know the password too. It's 'Are you mad?' You say that right after you do the secret knock, which I can teach you too."

"I was just asking." Eli bristled. "You don't have to be such an ass."

"Nah, I know." Nappo yawned. "It's just that it was a pretty stupid question. And speaking of stupid questions, it's poppy dust."

"What?"

"Up the nose. Sniff. Snort. Dust. Powder. It's poppy dust. You should try some."

"No thanks." Eli didn't need to be high. With his luck, it'd probably make everything seem even worse than it was. And if it didn't make it worse, and it made everything seem better, that would be disastrous too, because then he'd get lazy and complacent. He wouldn't care, and if that ever happened, he'd rather be dead.

What a mess he was in. Maybe he should've stayed in the Key. But no, it would've been impossible to stay. His life was an impossibility. Nothing felt right. Nothing felt safe. Nothing felt smart.

He turned onto his side in the pitch black and nearly airless room, his sleeping roll under him barely softening the hard wooden bunk. His bed in the Key was vast and soft, with a wall of windows to look out of as he fell asleep, the stars like a bedtime story.

It wasn't entirely true that nothing felt right. It was that "right" now felt more like a question than a certainty. He had to keep going. He had to find his mother's people. As scary and overwhelming and daunting a task as it was, it was his, and the only thing he knew these days.

10

࿔

After moonrise, the boys woke and Eli made Teal a foul-smelling fortifying tea from Falma's herbs. As soon as Teal got a whiff of it he pursed his lips shut. It took Nappo holding him down and Eli prying his mouth open to get the tea down his gullet. The little boy was definitely improving, whether it was because of the herbs, or the water, or simply time, Eli wasn't sure, but he was glad.

They set off, Eli and Nappo taking turns riding Saber and holding Teal while he slept for hours at a stretch. They travelled slowly, what with only one horse and the three of them. Even Saber, as big and strong as he was, couldn't carry the three of them and all their gear and make good time, and so either Eli or Nappo had to walk.

Bullet was happiest when it was Eli's turn to walk. When it was, he trotted at his side, glancing up at him every few steps to make sure he was where he was supposed to be. When it was Nappo's turn to walk, Bullet ran ahead, or dawdled behind, nosing some interesting hole in the ground. The dog was never that far away though, and always had Eli in sight, as if he'd learned a lesson from Saber's disappearance.

THE TRIO TRAVELLED three nights like this. In the middle of the third night, when it was Eli's turn to walk and he'd trudged along in silence for hours while the brothers slumped forward on the horse, asleep, Eli suddenly stopped. Saber stopped too, waking Nappo, but not Teal, who snored steadily.

"I've had enough of this, haven't you?"

"Enough of what?" Nappo said.

"Walking!" Eli flung his arms out at the barren landscape, well lit by the nearly full moon, its yellow orb resting plump on the horizon. "We're hardly moving at all! And on top of it, we don't have the slightest clue where we're going!"

"We're going west, aren't we?"

"But *where* in the west?"

"What does it matter?" Nappo shrugged. "We'll find out sooner or later."

"Will we? How? When?"

"How would I know?"

"Well, we better find out soon, because I am not going to wander around out here forever and I am not going to die out here, either. I'm going to find the rebels and I'm going to join them, no matter what it takes!"

"Yeah, right." Nappo uncorked the little bottle around his neck. "As if."

"What's that supposed to mean?"

"You're crazy, you know that?" Nappo snorted a snatch of powder up one nostril, then the other. "Why don't you give up about the rebels? You're never going to find Triskelia. The reason the Triskelians have lasted so long is that nobody *can* find them, especially not a Keylander. They're everywhere and they're nowhere. The rest of us are happy enough with that. We know that when the time is right the revolution will begin and everything will be better."

"When will that be?" Eli laughed. "How many more people have to die? And what exactly are they waiting for? And why don't they show themselves?"

"They can't."

"Why?"

"Does everything have to have an answer?"

"Of course," Eli snorted. "How else do you make sense of the world?"

Nappo stared at him. "You expect the world to make sense?"

"Of course."

"This world?"

"Nappo—"

"Give it up, Eli."

"I won't."

"Then at least give up about Triskelia. The truth is that you could spend the rest of your life out here and never find them."

Eli didn't want to think about that. "They're cowards, aren't they? Too chicken to show their faces."

Nappo wiped his nose with the back of his hand. "You don't know what you're talking about."

"I know enough."

"You might think you do."

"When I find them, I'll kick things into action. I'll start the revolution myself." Eli's tone was solemn. "I will find them. I will, Nappo. I will not die out here first."

Nappo waited a respectful moment, and then broke out with laughter so loud that it woke Teal. "Yeah, right! And if you think they'll have you just because you say your mother was a rebel, you're in for a surprise. That is, *if* you ever find Triskelia."

"What's Triskelia?" Teal rubbed his eyes and sat up with a great big yawn.

"It's a myth," Nappo told him. "It doesn't exist."

"It's not a myth!" Eli nearly hollered. "Teal, it's not a myth. It's the city of rebels, and it does exist. We're going to find it, and they will take us in. It's out here somewhere."

Teal rested his head against his brother's chest and closed his eyes again.

"Me and Teal have to live out here," Nappo said. "You can always go back. You shouldn't tell him lies."

"And neither should you." Eli started walking again. As Nappo caught up, Eli said, "Why are you travelling with me, if you don't even believe in Triskelia?"

"Because you're feeding us."

"So you're just using me?"

"We're not as stupid as you think. We go where the food is."

"Well, if you're stupid enough to admit that, then you're not that bright either. Get off my horse." How could Eli have thought Nappo could be his friend? They might as well be from different solar systems they were so different. He might as well have a couple more dogs instead. They'd probably eat less at least. And they'd be quiet. "I said get off my horse! Both of you!"

"But Teal's asleep."

"I don't care." Eli pulled Teal down and set him unsteadily on his feet. Teal rubbed his eyes again. "Don't rub them, that only makes the infection worse." Eli waved a piece of clean linen in the boy's face. "I told you to wipe them with the cloth, you stupid pussy Droughtland brat." Had he thought it through, Eli wouldn't have said such mean things to a child, but he was tired and scared and frustrated, and so there it was, hanging in the moonlight between them.

"An' you're just a Keyland pig!" Teal launched a feeble kick at Eli's shin.

"Back off, Teal!" Eli gave him just a little push, but Teal fell right over.

"So, you're the big guy!" Nappo shoved Eli hard. "You Keylanders like picking on little kids? Huh? That's why you cower behind walls, because you know us Droughtlanders would beat your brains out if you set foot out here alone and without all your Guardies!" As Eli stood, Nappo shoved him again. This time Eli stumbled, but didn't fall. "You might have guns, but you don't got guts!"

"How about you? Using me for my money?" Eli yanked the brothers' meagre belongings out of the saddlebags and threw them onto the dirt. "This is the end of your free ride. I can make much better time without dragging filthy Droughtland trash along."

"Yeah, you could!" Nappo bundled their things into a dirty shirt and tied it in a knot while Eli climbed onto Saber. Then he squatted so that Teal could ride piggyback. He picked up their bundle and started walking west. "Let's go, Teal. We don't need him."

"Bye, dummy Keylander stupid head!" Teal stuck his tongue out at him. "We're going to tell on you!"

"You better not, or you'll be sorry!"

"Oh!" Nappo laughed. "We're trembling with fear!"

"You're not even going to say thank you? For anything I did for you?" Eli rode up to them. "Not even for saving Teal's life?"

"We would've managed."

"Teal was dying!"

"Look, don't you got someplace to be?" Nappo stopped walking. "All of Triskelia is waiting for you, isn't it? Better hurry up, or you'll be late for the revolution."

Revolution. He remembered when that word was a mountain range, impossible to comprehend. Now it was like a beast, slowly waking in his thoughts. Eli didn't say another word. He and Saber and Bullet took off at a canter, going as fast as the transport cart had at full speed with six horses. Eli never looked back, only ahead, hopefully toward Triskelia, sorry that he'd ever met the brothers in the first place.

Seth was currently sorry about a lot of things too. He was especially sorry that he wasn't bigger, as in big enough to take on the second-tier recruits, the ones chosen for their strength rather than intellect or Keyland status. Seth wished he was a second tier, along with Nord and his boys, who practically ruled the place. The second-tier recruits were supposed to have less status than the first, but Seth was fast finding out that while it may be stated in the Keyland Guard Handbook, page six, first paragraph, underlined twice by Seth's own hand, it did not play out in real life.

In real life, first tiers were considered too precious for combat. The most they could look forward to was a fancy uniform and a big desk and the privilege of one day being a higher rank than any second tier. But in training that didn't matter. Strength, stamina, and ferocity were key.

NORD MADE THIS VERY CLEAR, again, the day both first and second tiers were performing yet another obstacle course, this one three times as hard as the one before.

"Hey, Maddox!" he'd called from the top of the scaling platform, where he was balanced on the thin edge, a twenty-foot drop on either side, as confident as if he were standing on the front stoop of the mess hall. "You make it up in the time it takes me to recite the bit about Droughtland women in the Blue Book and I will personally see to it that you become an honorary second tier."

"No way, Nord." Seth gripped the rough rope, his hands still raw from the last time.

"You only get a chance like this once, Maddox."

"Give it a go, Maddox," Dakin whispered behind him. He was first tier too, and for good reason—his daddy was a Chief Regent, able to get him into the Guard despite his thick glasses and slight tremor in his left hand. "I'd kill for the chance."

"What do you say, Maddox?" Nord called from on high.

Seth glanced again at the palms of his hands, swollen and chafed. Now or never, do or die. "You're on!" He looked up at Nord, silhouetted by the sun. "Whenever you're ready."

Nord bowed. "I will now recite page thirty-six, paragraphs five through ten of the almighty Blue Book. You ready?"

Seth checked that the two corporals overseeing the course were still at the beginning drilling poor Lytton and his boyfriend—some little guy with no other name that Seth knew of other than "Lytton's boyfriend"— through the first leg of the course. Lytton's boyfriend was in tears. Served the little bender right. Seth looked up at Nord and gripped the rope. "Ready."

"Right, then. And I quote . . . " Nord laid on a Southern accent, mocking Sergeant Hatfield, their Droughtland Interface instructor. "Guard members are not to fornicate with any Droughtlander, either casually or for any sum. Droughtland women are especially to be avoided, as they carry the fatal skineater disease in their genital region. Droughtland women believe it is their duty to infect as many Guard members as possible by means of fornication. . . . "

Seth was halfway up the rope and his hands were on fire. He left streaks of blood on the rope as he climbed. He could see Nord's boots clearly, though. He was getting closer. He kept climbing, pushing himself up by his legs as much as he could manage. The first tiers below him cheered wildly, bringing the attention of the two corporals, who were now making their way to the scene at a flat-out run.

"Stop! You there, get down!" Seth kept hauling himself up.

Nord continued, "Droughtland females are renowned for their sexually provocative manner of dress." Nord swept his hands in front of him, gesturing as if he were reciting a famous poem. "From a very early age, Droughtland females are taught various skills used exclusively to lure Guard members into sexual acts which will prove fatal. This includes fellatio." The spectators roared with laughter at the way Nord pronounced it, exaggerating each syllable.

Seth's arms screamed. He just couldn't do it. He glanced over his shoulder at the corporals, hoping they'd get to him before it became obvious that he'd failed. He slowed a bit, sighing with relief when the corporals arrived, screaming for both him and Nord to come down immediately. Seth slid down the rope without using his hands, hugging the rope and letting himself down with his legs instead. Nord came down twice as fast and landed with a grin, bowing for the cheering lineup of recruits.

"That's a fail, Maddox!" he called as he was led away by one of the corporals and Seth was led away by the other. "There's no way you would've made it! You're just a pathetic weakling like the rest of the faggoty first tiers."

SETH COULD NOT LIFT his fork at dinner that night, which was only slightly more embarrassing than failing Nord's little challenge. Equally embarrassing was his punishment for the escapade: two weeks of singing the morning reveille, which was normally performed on a bugle. He had to *sing* it. Seth was sorry, also, for the fact that he could not sing. He was also sorry to see that second tiers were also favoured unofficially among the Guard higher-ups; for all of Nord's part in it, he only got a talking to.

The unfairness was excruciating. The only thought that kept him from erupting was that he would soon be able to hunt down Eli and mete out the punishment he deserved for the mess he'd left behind. Each night Seth dreamt that he found Eli in the Droughtland. Sometimes it took years, and they were both old men. Sometimes it was as if it had happened years ago. But he always found him in the dreams, and he never got away.

He dreamt that he captured him at gunpoint and took him captive, in a bizarre steel cage, to the Eastern Key where he was put on display at the Justice Hall for everyone to ridicule before his gruesome public execution. In the dreams, Eli was beheaded by Seth himself, even though beheading had long since fallen out of fashion and it would never be Seth who would gas him or hang him. In the dream, Seth held the machete poised above Eli for a long, delicious moment while Eli stared beseechingly up at him, tears streaming down his face as he writhed against the restraints. And then Seth chopped his brother's head off with the same ease as slicing an apple in half.

Seth sometimes smiled in his sleep, especially when his father, beaming with pride, cheered the crowd on as he stepped over Eli's severed head and came forward to praise Seth as he never had before. That was the single best part of the dream, the swell and warmth of knowing Edmund was proud of him. Dreaming of his father's pride and approval was enough to make Seth look forward to the escape of sleep each night.

11

⚜

As the sun rose, Eli settled in to spend the day out of the cruel light in a dirt bunker below a trader's shop. He couldn't sleep though; he was kept awake thinking about Nappo and Teal out there on foot in the steadily climbing heat. After an hour of tossing and turning, he decided to go back for them and at least bring them to the trader's so that he wouldn't spend the rest of his life wondering if they'd died because he'd left them behind in a huff.

Eli went upstairs to speak with the trader, an old man whose right leg was gone below the knee. Given that Eli was the first person who'd come by in four days, the old man wanted to chat.

"Can't sleep? Cellar too hot? You want to buy some more water?"

"I need a horse," Eli said in a way that made it clear he wasn't interested in chatting. "Do you have any for sale?"

The man shook his head. "No, but I could maybe get you one in a few days. There's some folks I know coming through in a week and they—"

"I need one now," Eli said. "What about the chestnut mare in the paddock? The thoroughbred?"

"I'm watching her for her mister. He's coming back for her."

"I'll buy her."

"She's not mine to sell." The man shrugged. "Sorry."

"How much *would* you sell her for?"

"You mean if she was mine?"

"No, I mean now. How much would it take to get you to sell her to me, keeping in mind that her mister will be back, and no doubt angry that she broke out of the paddock and ran away?"

The man smirked. "Well, that would be a terrible loss to the mister, wouldn't it?" He glanced slyly at Eli. "He'd want some compensation, wouldn't he?"

"He would."

"And there'd have to be something in it for someone like me, wouldn't there?"

"That's right."

"I guess that would make up a pretty sum, don't you think?"

"Name a price, man." Eli was getting tired of this dance. "I need the horse now."

"Come with me. I was just getting ready to move them into the stables." The old man grabbed his crutch and led Eli to the paddock. The mare was well groomed, her coat shiny, her muscles well defined. She was a fast one, no doubt. "Her name's Dawntreader, on account she does fine in the heat, or that's what her mister claims."

"Perfect. How much?" Eli opened his purse; not his main one with all his money in it, but the smaller leather one attached to his belt.

"Forty bills?"

"Agreed." Eli started counting.

"Wait, no!" The old man waved his crutch and hobbled forward a couple of steps. "I meant to say sixty. Yes, sixty, of course I meant sixty, slip of the tongue, my fault. Sixty."

"I'll take two sacks of feed as well then." Eli counted out six tenners. "And she better come with a saddle and bags at that price."

"Sure! Sure! I'll fetch them for you." The old man scurried off. "Made of handsome leather! I'll tell the mister they was stolen by night bandits. I'll tell him it was bandits that stole his beast too, why not?"

SHE WAS A MUCH TOO ELEGANT horse for a cumbersome name like Dawntreader, so right away Eli shortened it to Dawn. He rode her east, with Saber following. He could only hope to find Nappo and Teal before the sun grew too hot and he was too far out to get back to the trader's before succumbing to the heat himself. He'd had to tie up Bullet back at the trader's so he wouldn't follow. It wasn't too hot for him yet, but it would be soon. The dog had been distraught at being left behind. He pulled and strained against the tether, whining and barking. Eli hoped he wouldn't chew right through it and set off looking for him.

Thankfully, it didn't take very long to find them. They'd stayed with the road and had walked all night and made much better time than Eli expected. Nappo was trudging along, piggybacking Teal. He stopped when he realized it was Eli coming toward them, with not one horse but two.

"What do you want?" Nappo said as Teal slid off his back and ran up to Dawn.

"Whose horse?" Teal asked, happily accepting a nuzzle from her.

Eli climbed down and handed the reins to Teal.

"She's yours."

With that, Eli mounted Saber and started back the way he'd come. "There's a trader with a bunker about an hour west from here," he called over his shoulder.

"I got a horse!" Teal squealed. "I got a horse!"

"Wait!" Nappo helped Teal onto Dawn and then climbed up himself and caught up with Eli. "You can't do this!"

The word *savages* came to mind. "I believe the words you're searching for are *thank you*."

"You don't understand," Nappo said. "We can't accept the horse."

"Yes, we can!" Teal clutched the reins to his chest. "*You* can't say no. He gave her to *me!* She's my horse!"

"Tealy, we can't feed her, or water her."

"I gave you two bags of oats, if you'd bothered to look," Eli said.

"That won't last." Nappo shook his head. "We can't look after her. She'll die with us. You have to take her back."

"But she's *my* horse!" Teal slapped at his brother. Nappo pinned his arms down.

"I'm sorry, Tealy, but we can't keep her. She'd die because of us."

"No, she wouldn't!" Teal wriggled free and hit him even harder. "I hate you! I hate you!"

Eli had to smile. "Looks like he's feeling a lot better today," he said over Teal's screams.

"I hate you!" Teal pummelled his brother with his fists. "She's my horse. Eli gave her to *me!*"

"We can't take the horse, Eli." Nappo tried again to restrain Teal. "It's really nice of you and everything, but we just can't afford to keep her."

"Yes, you can," Eli said.

"You don't get it, do you?"

Savages or not, during the last couple of hours Eli had realized that the guilt he was feeling wasn't just because he'd left the brothers behind in the middle of nowhere with no means of getting out of the deadly sun. He wanted to make up for his behaviour the night before too. And now, thinking about it, he had to admit that it was shortsighted of him to give them a horse. Cruel even. And as for friends and allies, as much of a burden as these two were, he had no other prospects.

"Come with me. I'll feed her. I'll buy the water," Eli said. "I'm sorry for what I said last night."

"S'pose I'm sorry too," Nappo said.

"Truce?" Eli held out a hand.

"Never offer to shake hands, Eli. That's a dead giveaway." Nappo rolled his eyes. "Man, have you got a lot to learn."

Teal relaxed. "You mean I can keep her?"

"I guess," Nappo said. "For now."

"Yes!" Teal punched the air, lost his balance, and fell off the horse, landing with a thud in the hot dirt. Just as Nappo and Eli were about to help him, he jumped up and hopped around on his scrawny scarred legs, yelling, "I got me a horse! I got me a horse!"

"He seems okay, doesn't he?" Nappo said.

"Still scrawny for five, though," Eli said. Teal was so much smaller than any Keylander at that age. When he'd asked how old the brothers were, Eli could hardly believe the answers. He and Nappo were both sixteen, yet Nappo was nearly a foot shorter than Eli, and he was actually three months older.

"Are you sure you've got the years right?" Eli said. "I mean, isn't it possible that you might lose a year or two out here?"

"Your people are such hulking wastes of space because of the rain you steal, the good food and water you get growing up, and the fact that you never have to lift a finger. If you're born out here, it's best of luck to you if you live just one whole day. Your people have no idea what it takes to survive out here."

Eli wanted to tell Nappo never to refer to the Keylanders as *his people* again. He wanted to remind Nappo that he was learning what it took to survive out here so that he could find *his people*. His people were in Triskelia—his mother's people. He resisted saying any of it though. Their truce seemed tenuous enough as it was without launching into another debate.

"Point taken," Eli muttered, leaving it at that.

"Good. Come on, Teal! We got to get moving." Teal ran back to the horse, took Nappo's hand, and clambered up. They started west once more.

"And another thing," Nappo added after a few minutes of hot, muggy silence. "It helps to grow up healthy and strong if you get a good night's sleep. I bet you got a good night's sleep every night of your life, not worrying about sicks and water, never mind even getting to sleep in the first place, jammed in a tiny hut filled with stinking, snoring relations, someone grunting over somebody else in the corner. I bet you got your own room, huh?"

"I did."

"Yeah?" Nappo grinned slyly. "So who's telling who to shut up now, huh?"

"Shutting up, sir!" Eli saluted him, hoping it was received with the good nature he was trying for.

"At ease," Nappo said, which sent him and Teal into a fit of giggles.

Eli did not actually feel good-natured, not beyond the easing of his guilt about having abandoned Nappo and Teal to the elements. What he felt, for the most part, was rage, although who or what it was directed at he wasn't sure. At the Droughtlanders for accepting the worst life had to offer as normal? The Triskelians for letting millions die when they could start the revolution any time? Keylanders, for stealing the weather and hoarding the wealth? His mother, for not telling him the truth sooner and then dying before she could tell him more?

He knew he was mad at Edmund and Seth. That much hadn't changed. But his anger was bigger now, and seemed to be growing with every moonrise. He wondered if he'd be this angry forever, or if someday it would fade into a livable peace.

Or was this the manhood that would be his? This constant rage. This constant seeking. Unsatisfied. Confused. Alone.

12

❦

One comforting thought was that the farther west Eli and the brothers travelled, the more unlikely it was that Seth would track him down. Eli knew that Seth would love the opportunity to punish him for being a traitor, but he took comfort in Seth's stupidity, whether or not it was justified, and believed that after nearly a month in the Droughtland he fit right in. He listened intently to everything Nappo taught him, copying him carefully, asking lots of questions. Nappo admitted that Eli had perfected the accent and gestures. As far as looks went, his skin was tanned despite his efforts to stay out of the sun, his hair was sun-kissed a lighter brown, and he'd mostly surrendered to the filth that went along with daily life in the Droughtland. His hair was still shorter than most Droughtlanders, but he planned to tell a story involving a disgusting amount of lice, should anyone ask.

He never stopped washing his hands though. There may not be ways of avoiding all sicks, but he could do this one thing, and so he did, every chance he got. He hoped and prayed that by washing his hands he could avoid the skineater sick at least, and that's the one he was most afraid of now. He often stared at the brothers' skineater scars, imagining what it would be like to live through such a horrible, disfiguring sick. But he wasn't as afraid of sicks as when he first came out of the tunnel. He'd learned, or surmised, a thing or two about them, the most important being that they took the weakest: the elderly, babies, people already sick.

And that they weren't nearly so easy to catch as everyone in the Keys so staunchly believed. But even if he was among the least likely to get ill, Eli still harboured a healthy terror of all sicks in general, and the skineater sick most of all.

THE BROTHERS' SCARS weren't the worst he'd seen. He saw much worse, especially on the fringes of markets, where the terminally ill often lay dying, having dragged themselves away so as not to spread the sicks any farther. Riding into any market, Eli could gauge the level of sick in the area by the number of bodies rotting and the human bones scattered in the red dirt. At first he was repulsed, but then he began to be fascinated by the human decay, until one day he came upon a clean, sun-bleached human skull and gave in to the urge to collect it. The nightmares started that night and only got worse until he announced to Nappo that he was going to retrace their path to return the skull to the rest of its bones. Nappo managed to talk him out of doing that, and arranged instead for a traveller heading the opposite direction to replace it. After that Eli's urge to collect bones evaporated and his macabre fascination began to diminish—as did the number of corpses and makeshift graves as they travelled farther west, where there was much less sick.

AS ELI AND THE BROTHERS neared the looming mountain range of the west the days became thankfully cooler and the nights longer, until at long last they had to stop for only one more day before they could begin to travel in the daytime without the danger of the sun. It was almost daybreak as they neared a small market with its long billowing roof of patched cloth covering the neat rows of stalls. In the dawn light it looked like a giant colourful caterpillar in the distance.

"Let's stop!" Teal cried, spotting it first. "Can we? That's the first market in *so* long. Please?"

"You don't have to beg, Teal." Eli's mouth was already watering at the thought of fresh teacakes. "No one's arguing with you."

Droughtland markets never closed. Most Droughtlanders travelled in the night hours, so they were open all night, but some travellers needed a place to spend the long daylight hours, so they were open all day too. The first thing Eli noticed was that there were no corpses as they approached, not even one, or the remnants of one. The atmosphere of this market was friendly and relaxed, so much so that none of the resting horses were locked up. Nonetheless, Eli still locked up Saber and Dawn, as they were the finest horses of all and he had long since learned his lesson.

Once they were under the shade of the market they let their sunhats rest on their backs and pushed their masks into place. Eli put another drop of lavender oil onto his nose filter, preparing for the usual market stench of rotting produce, trash heaps, and sick, unwashed Droughtlanders. In Eli's opinion, Droughtland markets were the epicentre of all sicks, even though they tried to keep out the obviously contagious. That didn't account for the breathsick at all. Stealthy in its transmission, days passed before symptoms developed, and by then everyone in the vicinity was infected too. For all his hand washing and general good health, Eli would nonetheless be amazed if he found the rebels before he fell ill from something.

This market was different, though, and it wasn't just the horses; there was no stench, and no one was wearing a mask.

"Why isn't anyone wearing a mask?"

"They say it's all worse in the east." Nappo pulled down his mask. "It could be that there's no sick here."

"Is that possible?" Eli didn't want to take off his mask, although people were beginning to stare.

"You better take yours off too," Nappo said as he untied Teal's.

"What if I don't want to?"

"Well, they might think you're bringing a sick in. I seen a guy get stoned to death for that once."

"I seen it too!" Teal grabbed Eli's hand. "There was lots of blood. It was gross."

Eli often wondered about the tales the brothers told about the things they'd seen and lived through. How much of the gory details were true?

And how much was born of a couple of rampant imaginations eager to shock him? Yet the Droughtland was a brutal place, and he was new to it, so he pocketed his mask, hoping Nappo knew what he was getting them into.

ELI AND NAPPO BROWSED the stalls while Teal ran higgledy-piggledy, bumping into shoppers and traders and nearly toppling the breadminder's pyramid of freshly baked loaves. Eli bought two loaves just to keep the burly man from going after Teal with the stick he brandished at him.

"But I want more than this," Teal said, stuffing the bread into his mouth. "An' I'm thirsty, too."

They were all excited about a cup of cold tea, so they went on a search for the teaminder and found the stall in the middle of the market, surrounded by neatly laid out tables and chairs.

"Can I get an applecake too?" Teal reached up and helped himself before Eli could answer either way. "And one for Bullet," he said as he helped himself to another with his dirty hands.

"Just hold on!" Eli grabbed the second cake before Teal could feed it to Bullet, who'd decided weeks ago that Teal was the best thing to happen to him in a long time and was already salivating with anticipation. "Not for dogs."

Eli paid for the drinks and cakes. They claimed a table out front and watched the shoppers and stallminders go about their business in a peaceful manner that reminded Eli of Market Street back in the Key. Now full, Teal climbed into his brother's lap and closed his eyes.

"Can we sleep now?"

"We'll sleep tonight." Nappo shook him awake. "We need to stay up today, so we'll sleep when it gets dark. Remember how we used to sleep when it was dark? In the village? When Talia was alive?"

"Too sleepy," Teal muttered. "I want a Talia story."

"She's dead, Tealy." Nappo shook him again. "You have to stay awake now, or you won't be sleepy later."

"Come on." Eli pulled the boy to his feet. "Let's go buy the horses some oats, and some food for Bullet, and water, and whatever else you can think of."

"Another horse!" Teal was wide awake at the thought of it. "One for Nappo so I don't have to share."

"I don't think so." Eli handed Nappo two sacks of oats at the grain-minders. "We need to save our money. It has to last until we find Triskelia."

All the shoppers within earshot suddenly stopped and stared at him in horror. Then they started whispering to each other, pointing and frowning at Eli. Nappo pulled Eli around the side of one of the stalls as their voices grew into a loud angry tangle.

"What did you say that for?"

"What, Triskelia?"

Nappo clamped a hand over Eli's mouth. "Yes, that!"

"Why can't I mention it?"

"This is a *clean* market, Eli." Nappo took his hand away. "The Keyland Guard only ever spies in clean markets, so they won't get any of the sicks, get it?"

"You never told me about any clean markets!"

"Well, I'm telling you now!"

"So they might be here?" What if someone discovered him? Or worse, recognized him as Seth's twin? "In disguise?"

"Of course." Nappo lowered his voice. "They come to the markets to get information. They think they'll find out where Triskelia is if they hang around the markets long enough. But they're fools if they think anyone at a clean market would even utter the word, except for a bloody idiot like you." Nappo pushed him. "If you're lucky, they'll let you get away with it, but it'll take explaining. Stay here. Don't move."

"But it was a mistake! I didn't know. I'll tell them." Eli tried to push past Nappo, but Nappo was firm.

"I'll do the talking. You have no idea what trouble you're in." Nappo turned to the amassing mob that now blocked their path. "Brothers, sisters, I am sorry. This brain-blighted boy doesn't know what he's saying."

"But—" Eli tried once again to speak for himself, but Nappo held him back.

"His brain was sunstroked two days ago, when his horse died and he was stranded in the sun. He's spoken only gibberish since I rescued him."

"Seemed okay to me when he was throwing his money around," the breadminder shouted from the back of the crowd.

"That's right," the teaminder added. "And what's a Droughtlander kid doing with all that money?"

"His parents died, may they rest in peace with their highers, from the skineater sick. Those few coins is all that's left." Nappo glanced over his shoulder at Eli, the look in his eye far from confident. "He has moments when he's fine, but then his brain goes soft again. It must be healing from the stroke, right? It takes time—" Nappo's story was fraying at the edges "—for the soft bits to heal, like a burn." Nappo gulped as he registered the overwhelming skepticism. "Like a bruise, right?"

"We'll give him something to heal from!" The breadminder pushed through the crowd and grabbed Eli by the ear. "You a Guardy?"

Bullet lowered his head, growling, ready to lunge at the man. "Call off the dog, boy!"

"Bullet, down." Bullet crouched, still growling.

"I said call him off!"

"Bullet, no." Eli tried to steady his voice. "Teal, take him away." Wide-eyed and silent, Teal scooted forward and tugged Bullet away.

"Answer me, boy! You a Guardy spy?"

"No, sir, I—" The crowd roared with the force of a clap of thunder.

"And if you ain't a Guardy spy, why does that filthy word roll off your tongue so easy, huh?" Bullet bared his teeth and strained to pull free as the breadminder twisted Eli's arms behind his back. "No one calls nobody *sir* out here, boy."

"You dare use that word?" The breadminder's wife came forward. She was nearly as big as the breadminder. Eli wished that if trouble was going to find him that it had found him back east, where the Droughtlanders weren't so healthy and well fed. "Never in my life have I heard a Droughtlander use that word."

As the woman crowded Eli, Bullet started barking.

"I can't hold him!" Teal yelped.

Nappo grabbed Bullet's collar as he tried to explain.

"He knew a Keylander!" Nappo tried to get between the man and Eli, but Bullet was snapping and lunging for the breadminder. "Yeah, he worked for one and had to call him that." Nappo couldn't remember the word to repeat it. "That's how come he knows it."

"An' he's got so much money 'cause he's really, really rich!" Teal hollered, which brought a hush upon the mob while Bullet barked and growled.

"Tie that dog up before I slice its throat open," the breadminder ordered Nappo while he glared at Eli.

As Nappo tied Bullet to a post the breadminder's wife got right up into Eli's face, her cheeks red, her lips chapped, her breath yeasty.

"A rich Droughtlander kid?" She squinted at Eli. Eli felt as if he were literally shrinking inch by inch under her glare. "A rich Droughtland kid who talks fancy?" She grabbed his hand and spat on his palm, wiping it clean with her apron. "Look at this!" She yanked it up for all to see. A collective gasp rose from the crowd.

"Oh no." Nappo shook his head. "You're doomed, friend."

"What?" Eli asked, as the crowd took turns examining his hand. Already there were suggestions for punishment. "What is it?"

"Look at mine." Nappo held his hands out. "And Teal's." Teal did the same. Their hands were covered in scars and calluses, their deep grooves so filthy no amount of spit or cleaning would make them look any less dirty. Eli looked up at his pale, clean, perfect hands being yanked at and tugged by the strangers. His looked like a sculpture of a hand, even after these few endless weeks. His was not the work-worn hand of a Droughtlander.

The woman was lifting his shirt over his head now; someone else was rolling up his pant legs.

"There's not a scar on him!"

"Not anywhere!"

"Please, no!" Eli tried to stop the breadminder's wife from pulling down his pants, but she won, yanking them down to his ankles and then reaching to strip him of his underlinen too. "Please, stop!" She paid him no mind, and in an instant, Eli was stark naked in front of the crowd, hands pinned behind his back by the breadminder. The crowd fell silent.

"He's been cut!" The woman reached out as though she was going to touch him, but Eli twisted away.

"Get away from me!" He looked at Nappo. "What's happening?"

"No Droughtlander is cut, friend." Nappo tried to shield Eli, but the crowd pushed around him, snatching looks. "Your foreskin. You don't got it any more."

"I don't know what you're talking about!" He'd never heard of being "cut." He'd never seen another penis, not even Seth's, but surely they were all alike?

"I'm not so cruel as to have us all to stare at your poor butchered willy." The breadminder's wife yanked up Eli's underlinen. "We got our proof," she said to the crowd. "Now what'll we do with this Keylander spy?"

"Stone him!"

"Nappo!" Eli pleaded. "Do something!"

"Let him hang!"

"I'm sorry, Eli." Nappo hugged Teal to him as the crowd surged forward, imprisoning Eli in the middle while Bullet twisted and barked, straining against the rope, nearly choking himself with the effort to pull free.

"Don't worry, Eli!" Teal yelled, trying to calm the dog. "I'll look after Bullet for you! And Saber!"

"Leave him to the sun!"

"Gut him and leave him to the birds!"

"I'll see what I can do, Eli!" Nappo's voice rose above the rest. "I got your purse!"

"Don't leave me here!" Eli screamed as he was dragged out of the market and locked into a suffocatingly small clay box. The days here were cooler, but not so much that being trapped in the clutches of a full midday sun couldn't be fatal, if one was unfortunate enough to spend it as a prisoner in a tiny, windowless jail.

"Enjoy your accommodation." Eli recognized the voice of the bread-minder. "It'll likely be your last!"

"Please, sir—" Eli hit his head against the clay wall at his repeated stupidity. "I didn't mean to say that! I meant, please mister, please hear me. I'm just a—"

"Just a Guardy plant thinkin' you'll get information out of us." That was the breadminder's wife. "You Guardy slaves think you'll ever get information outta the clean markets? You'd do better to take your chances at the ones riddled with sicks. That would teach you to go snooping around. We'd all like to see your skin rot off, or maybe you'd just get the sleeping sick and die nice and quiet, no fuss, no muss." The woman came right up to the tiny hole in the door, the only hole in fact. It was smaller than Eli's pinky, but Eli could see her clear brown eye examining him from the outside. "Oh, I could see to it that you got the skineater sick. All I'd have to do is get me a bit of live sick flesh and drop it in here and the skin would be dropping off you like fleas off a Keyland dog so fast." Then she spat in the hole as best she could and left to catch up to the other stallminders who were convening to decide his fate.

After a few minutes, which seemed like forever in the hot box with increasingly little air, Nappo's dark eye appeared at the hole.

"What do I do?"

"Get me out of here!"

"I can't. They're convinced you're a spy! I had to tell them I didn't know you were a Guardy—"

"But I'm not!"

"That doesn't matter." Nappo's voice quaked. "I think they believe me, but maybe only because of Teal. If they think I'm with you, they'll kill us both and there'll be no one for Teal. They wouldn't send him away on his own, would they? He's just a little kid."

"I don't know." Eli didn't care if he sounded sympathetic or not. He cared about Teal's fate, sure, but it just wasn't his main priority at the moment. He was far more concerned about his own fate. "What are they going to do to me?"

"The breadminder's daughter said the last time they caught a spy they let him starve to death in there and then let beasts eat him clean and then they carved his bones into forks and knives and had a feast."

"But I'm not a spy!"

"I know that," Nappo said.

"I know it too!" Teal's voice popped up from out of sight.

"But it doesn't matter what we think," Nappo said. "You're the closest they've come in the eight years since the Market Council Committee for Keyland Spy—" Nappo disappeared for a second as he said to Teal, "You take off. Go give the horses some oats. I'll meet you there in a minute."

"But I want to stay with you!"

"I said go, Teal! Give us a minute."

"But—

"Scram, now!"

"Fine. But what if Eli's dead when I come back?"

"I won't be dead!" Eli yelled, his throat so dry the words came out cracked and dusty.

Nappo's face appeared again. "The breadminder's daughter says you're the first spy they've caught since the Council for Keyland Spy Torture and Execution started. They're pretty excited."

"You have to do something! I'm not a spy!"

"Maybe not, but—"

"*Maybe*?" Eli rested his sweaty head in his equally sweaty hands. "Don't you believe me?"

There was a pause, during which Eli truly believed all was lost, until Nappo spoke again.

"I believe you, Eli. But this is serious stuff. Imagine if the Group of Keys found out where Triskelia is. What if they thought it was more than a Droughtland myth? More than an imaginary land that we're wasting our time trying to find? They think it's just a made-up place, just some stupid Droughtland fairy tale."

"So you don't really believe it's a myth. Then it *does* exist."

Nappo lowered his voice even though they were alone in the blazing sun. "Of course it does."

"Then you believe in it? In Triskelia?"

"Of course I do."

"Why didn't you say so?"

"You're a Keylander, Eli."

"But I thought I was your friend!"

"Even still, you're a Keylander."

"This whole time, did you know where it is?" Eli thought he'd cry if Nappo said yes.

"No."

"Are you lying to me now?"

"I'm not lying." Nappo snorted a pinky of poppy dust. "I bet you want some of this right about now, don't you?"

"No. I do not."

"I could roll some into a leaf and slip it through."

"I don't want any of your dust."

"It'd calm you down."

"I don't want to calm down! I want to get out of here!"

"If I hear they're going to kill you, I'll slip you all the poppy dust I can find and you can beat them to it if you swallow it all at once."

"Nappo, they *can't* kill me." Eli dropped his head into his hands again, the sweat running into his eyes. He was too scared to cry, and too hot and thirsty to scream for mercy. "I'm not a spy. I'm on their side!"

"How're they going believe that?" The council debated loudly in the distance. "Look at them."

Eli squinted through the tiny hole. Beyond the watery heat waves the crowd was jittery with excitement, just as the Keylanders were when the Night Circus was about to begin. When the acrobat fell to his death, seemingly so long ago, none of the Keylanders had cared, except for him and his mother. This was no different. He could hardly blame them, if he was being brutally honest with himself.

"Tell them the truth."

"*Tell* them you're a Keylander?" Nappo's eyes widened. "Are you going crazy in there? They'd definitely kill you."

"Maybe." Eli was having a hard time breathing; what little air there was in the box was growing thin and stale as the sun climbed up the sky. "Maybe not," he wheezed. "It's the only chance. Tell them the truth, all of it. Tell them about my mother and father. Tell them about the bomb and the rebels. Tell them everything."

The jeering caws of corpse-hungry birds circling above and the excited sounds of the mob arguing Eli's punishment coloured Nappo's silence until he finally spoke.

"I'll try." Nappo's voice was very small. "But I can't promise it'll work. If it doesn't, I'll try to get you the dust before they come for you. Trust me, Eli, if it comes to that, use it."

If Seth and Eli were the kind of twins who could psychically intuit each other's experience, Seth would have delighted in Eli's predicament and then promptly arranged to go home. He would've liked nothing better than to go home and have it all be over with. Instead, he was learning how to keep secrets. He'd recently violated rule seven, section four of the handbook: *Exchanging monetary gifts or offering bribes for the purpose of status gain is strictly prohibited.*

Before now Seth had never broken a rule in his life, but then again, he'd never wanted for anything before. He'd always gotten everything he could ever possibly want. When it occurred to him that he could use his wealth to his social advantage, he didn't struggle very long with the fact that it was strictly against the rules. Instead, he paid Nord a full hundred to become an unofficial second tier. It was either that or suffer being Nord's favourite target for the rest of basic training.

Seth could have and would have paid him twice that much, but that was a secret he wasn't going to let Nord in on. Seth kept most of his money in his trunk, which was the first thing he'd ever locked in his life. Everyone was expected to keep their trunk locked, even though theft supposedly did not exist in the Keys. But this wasn't the Key, and so he kept only a little money tucked into the document pouch on the inside of his fatigues. If he ever actually made it into the field, he'd use that hidden pouch for top-secret maps, decoding chits, and bribes in case a Droughtlander caught him. By paying Nord, hopefully he'd avoid ending up at a tedious desk job beside the likes of Dakin, Lytton, and Lytton's boyfriend, never to see action up close.

Seth had found a way to get as much money out of his father as he could ever possibly need. The supply was endless and endlessly useful. All it took was some tiny mention of the disappearance of Eli in his weekly letter home. Every letter sent was answered by the arrival of a package within the week. They were put together by Cook, filled with her sweet biscuits and boiled candy, but there was always an envelope of money too, from Edmund, along with a brief note filled with words like *propriety* and *consequence* and always ending with *your discretion is appreciated.* The notes were always signed *Master Edmund R. J. Maddox, Chief Regent, Eastern Key.* Never *Father*, and absolutely never ever *With love.*

Edmund's gifts were definitely coming in handy. They bought him a larger serving at mealtime and they assured him top marks in all his classes, but best of all, and what he was saving for, was that he'd been told he could *buy* his way into the regiment of his choice after basic training. Seth knew exactly which one he wanted, so when it was time he approached Nord, who was supposedly the one who could make it happen.

"What?" Nord had a way of making everything, even questions, sound like an irrefutable statement. "You're in my light."

"Sorry." Seth stepped to the side so that Nord could check the shine as he polished his boots. The rest of the recruits were doing the same, polishing their boots. It was the last thing they did every night before lights out.

"Why don't you get someone to do that for you?" Seth glanced back at Lytton, who was doing Seth's boots along with his, for a price. "I could probably arrange something, if you want."

"Self-respect, man." Nord looked up with a reproachful scowl. "Some things a man's got to do for hisself."

"Right." Seth nodded like he got it, but he didn't. He hated polishing his boots. He'd maybe done it once since he got there. "Yeah. It's funny you say that, Nord, because that's kind of why I want to talk to you. The whole 'some things a man's got to do for . . . hisself' thing."

"Speed up or shut up."

"Right. Okay, well, remember a while back you told me you knew who I could pay to get into the regiment I wanted? Well, I guess I'm asking who that is, seeing as I should hook up with them before we're assigned. I hear the assignments are coming any time."

Nord put down his boots. "You owe me, Maddox."

Seth was prepared. He made sure no one was watching before he handed Nord his payoff.

Nord slipped the money into his pocket without counting it. "Follow me."

Seth followed two steps behind, which was the only way Nord would tolerate his company. He led Seth across the compound, through the gymnasium and down a hall that ended at the rear of the administration offices. Nord rapped on the door. A spindly man opened it and peered out, his eyes small and darty.

"Who's he?"

Nord and the man shook hands. "He's with me."

"Is that right?" The man opened the door wide, revealing the back room of the records office. "Well, come on in then and have a drink."

"Jakko is the janitor," Nord said.

Seth shook the man's hand.

"No, Jakko is the maintenance man." Jakko offered each of the boys a shot of strong-smelling liquor. "You pay me, I maintain."

"*He's* paying you this time." Nord downed his drink and shoved Seth forward.

Seth downed his own drink, grimacing at the bitter heat. He pulled out a handful of bills and offered them wordlessly to Jakko. The man laughed. "You want to maintain the general location of your face with this?"

"Sorry, Jakko." Nord glared at Seth. "Don't insult the gentleman, Maddox. Triple that at least, huh, Jakko?"

"And add another ten on top of that for sheer stupidity."

"I . . . uh . . ." Seth wondered what to say. It wasn't that he couldn't or didn't want to pay the man. He'd had no idea how much it would be, so he hadn't any left in his pocket. "Sure, hang on," he finally said, turning to leave the room so that he could fish the cash out of his document pouch in private. Nord clamped a hand on his shoulder.

"I know where you keep it, Maddox. You think you got any secrets with me?"

"No, Nord, it's just that I have to take my pants down to get at it."

"You can do that here." Jakko grinned. "We're all men."

Seth faced the wall and retrieved the cash as best he could without dropping his trousers all the way. After nearly falling over in the process, he handed Jakko the rest of the fee.

Jakko counted it twice before tucking it into the pocket of his overalls. "Now, down to business." He crossed the room and trailed his fingers along the wall of file cabinets until he came to the M's. He started flipping through the files. "What regiment do you want?"

"West Droughtland."

"What the hell for? The west is for real soldiers. Not the likes of you." Nord's question sounded like a real one that time. "Did the liquor land in the wrong spot?" He rapped his knuckles on Seth's skull. "Or is it really hollow in there?"

"Personal reasons."

"Personal death wish?" Jakko stared at him, having momentarily abandoned his search for Seth's file.

"Just do it, okay?" Seth folded his arms across his chest. He was not going to give Nord any more information. "That's what I paid you for, right?"

Jakko found his file and pulled it out. He ripped a slip of paper off a notepad on the desk and wrote something on it. "Another two tenners goes in with this."

"Who for? This has already cost me nearly a hundred."

"You don't think I can make the actual change, do you? I'm just the janitor." Jakko held out his hand. "This is for the administrator who can make your little death wish come true. You'll just have to fish in your pants again."

Seth turned his back to him and made quick business of getting the money. "If I don't get this posting, I'll have you severely punished."

"Oh. Please, sir." Jakko pouted. "No. Not that."

"I mean it!" Seth wanted to lunge at the man, drive his fist into his thin lips, and annihilate his condescending pout. "Screw me over and I'll make you pay! I can, you know, my father is Chief Regent—"

"Easy, Maddox." Nord pulled him back. "He's holding your destiny, man."

Jakko waved the little paper with the tenners folded up in it. "I could just keep this myself and let you land where you land, couldn't I?"

"Yes, you could, Jakko." Nord pulled Seth toward the door. "But you won't, because I bring you lots of business, right?"

Jakko dropped the note into the file and put it back into its correct spot in the drawer. "Your wish is my command, young Master Nord."

13

꧁

With the heat shuddering his eardrums, Eli strained to listen as best as he could to nothing really at all. The council had gathered too far away, and the drone of heat-drunk insects was a constant rave of sound. Every once in a while he thought he heard a proposed punishment rippling across the plain.

Hang him!

Sell him to the night bandits!

Send his head to the Guard!

Eli hoped it was all a kind of hallucination that the heat and lack of air was conjuring out of nothing.

Sometimes, and he knew he wasn't making this part up, the council's anger swelled well above the insect din and across the distance to lap at the clay walls. He couldn't make out words, just the dangerous grumblings of an angry mob.

Eli thought it would never end. But then it did.

The sun had finally set, and along with it the criminal heat. Eli lay slumped against the wall, dripping in sweat, delirious with hunger and exhaustion and desperate for something to drink. There was some kind of celebration going on, or maybe the drumming and music was just another hallucination. The drumming was hypnotic, tribal, and made Eli want to sleep and dance at the same time. Just as he slipped into a dream of Lisette beckoning him to follow her in the moonlight across the plain to where a throng of people danced in a sweaty frenzy around a fire, there was the clunk of the lock landing in the dirt, and the door opened. Eli forced himself to focus on the stranger's face.

A girl, with a kind smile and a plump, pockmarked face.

"What's happening?" Eli's voice was hoarse.

The girl smiled. Beatific. So kind. Pity at his imminent death? Or was it genuine? Or was all of this a mirage of an angel who wasn't really there?

"Just tell me." Eli crawled out into the night and collapsed on his back, gulping in the cooler night air.

"What?"

"Tell me how I'm going to die." Above him the sky was vast, the stars glimmering in the night like jewels. "Just tell me."

"You don't remember me, do you?" The girl was on her knees, bending over him, her hair falling forward.

There was something familiar about her, but Eli was too delirious to put a puzzle together.

"I'm supposed to know you?"

"My name is Lovely." She sat back on her haunches. "We didn't meet officially, but I was there in the market, at Gidah's stall. I was making poultices. When she came back, she told us all about you."

"So much for secrets."

Lovely brushed her hair over her shoulders. "You should be thankful for her big mouth."

"How so?"

"Come with me." She stood and offered him her hand.

Eli teetered a bit, and then found his footing. "Where are we going?"

"To the party."

Eli wrenched free. "Is this some kind of trap?"

"No." Lovely folded her arms and gave him a cool look. "I saved your life. They're not going to hurt you."

"Like I'm supposed to believe you." Eli started backing away. He could gain a bit of time if he just ran now, even as weak as he was, and even if he had to leave everything. "Where's Nappo? And Teal?"

"You don't have to run," Lovely said. "When I came, Nappo was telling them your story, and they didn't believe it, so I piped up and told them it was true. They believed me. Eventually, after interrogating me forever. It's a good thing Gidah had a crush on you or otherwise she might not have remembered so many details to pass on."

"Gidah had a crush on me?" Eli stopped. "I don't think so."

"Whatever." Lovely shrugged. "I'm getting back to the party."

"Party? For me?"

"Gidah did say you were an arrogant prick." Lovely laughed. "Thomas's eldest is getting married tomorrow. That's what the party is for. Come on."

"Why did you come get me? Where is Nappo?"

"Your buddy, once he was sure you weren't going to be skewered on a pole and roasted over a spit, got plowed. He's already had enough dust to keep him powdered for a week. He doesn't waste time, that kid."

"He's stoned?" Eli had been fighting for his life, and Nappo was getting high?

"Come see for yourself." Lovely started toward the fire, turning to beckon him, like Lisette had in his dream. He followed, trying his best to stay alert and aware of his surroundings, should he have to bolt. All this was a little too pat.

As they got closer to the bonfire and Eli could start seeing faces instead of shadowy threats, the band stopped playing, the revelry faded into silence, and once again all eyes were on Eli.

The breadminder stepped out of the crowd, his good clothes stained with sweat, his cheeks red with drink. He glared at Lovely.

"I told you I didn't want him here."

"Now, Thomas, don't be a bear," Lovely said.

Thomas turned his glare on Eli. "You hear what I said, boy?"

"Happy to oblige. I'm out of here." Eli started backing away, but Nappo stumbled out of the dark and grabbed his arm.

"Waita, wait a . . . wait. Minute. Hold a sec." He used Eli to steady himself. "Yeah, Eli, I was jus' gonna come getcha."

Eli peeled Nappo's hand off his arm. "Thanks for your help, Nappo."

"No, I was. Honesty. I mean, honest . . . ly." Nappo teetered. He flung his arms out. "Isn't it great? They're not gonna kill you . . . and it's all 'cause of me!"

Lovely put her hands on her hips.

"S'okay, so maybe she helped," Nappo slurred.

"Nappo can stay." Thomas budged between the boys. "But you are not welcome at my family's celebration. No Keylanders welcome here, no matter who they think they are, or where they think they're going. Consider yourself blessed by your highers, boy. We would've sliced you up for the dogs' supper if Lovely hadn't spoke when she did. You can stay in the market until your friend sobers up, but you are not coming to my baby's wedding party. And stay out of my way. Or else."

Eli wished he could ask why exactly they had changed their minds. Did they know Lisette? Did they know Triskelia? Or did they just feel sorry for him, about his family crumbling to pieces?

He backed into the darkness beyond the candle lanterns. The music started up again, and a young couple, dressed in shimmering silks and with smiles that shone like stars, held hands and began to dance while everyone cheered. They must be the ones getting married. Eli watched them dance. They gazed adoringly into each other's eyes and moved together with a fluidity and grace that ached with innocence. Would anyone get married if they knew the deceit? The betrayal? The tragedy? The loss? Eli would never marry.

Eli wandered along the nearly deserted market. The few night shoppers and stallkeepers were ignoring him now, so he didn't bother to lie too low. He found the horses, and Bullet, tied to a post, whining and wagging his tail meekly as if admitting he'd failed to keep Eli safe.

"It's not your fault, bud." Eli untied Bullet. Instead of his usual frolicking, the dog put one paw on Eli's knee and just sat, staring up at him.

"Yeah, it was a close call." Eli scratched Bullet's tummy. "And now I'm talking out loud to my dog." Eli glanced around. No one was watching. He sat in the dirt. Bullet climbed onto his lap.

"I'm not dead," Eli said, more to himself than to Bullet. "I'm still here." He thought he might cry from the relief, and from the catharsis of fear that had gripped him all day in that wretched box. And he may have, had Teal not run up to him just then with a gaggle of filthy, bright-eyed waifs, all clamouring for scary stories of the bloody Keyland Guard.

NAPPO DIDN'T SOBER UP until after the wedding festivities ended, which wasn't until two nights later. He'd mooched his way right into the thick of it, playing sweet with Thomas's youngest daughter, a lithe beauty called Tasha, and was enjoying the endless supply of free booze and poppy dust because of it. The only reason Thomas didn't have anything to say about it was that he was well hammered the whole time too, and was so hell-bent on not laying eyes on Eli that he didn't give a toss what Nappo got up to, Tasha or not.

While Nappo spent his waking hours tanked beyond comprehension and Teal romped around the market with his unruly gang of children, Eli stayed out of Thomas's way, hanging out along the edges of the market, drawing pictures in the dirt with a stick and gazing at the mountains to pass the time.

Somewhere on the other side was Triskelia. Unless he was wrong. Maybe they'd passed it already, or maybe it was within spitting distance—Eli had no way of knowing. But he had to keep going, and he only knew to go west. And he was still alive to try to find it, and so he would. Ever since his experience that first day in the market, when life became as fleeting as a shooting star, Eli had known he would try to find Triskelia at any cost. Or he would die trying. Which was certainly a possibility, if not inevitable.

Tasha kitted the boys out with food and goods and saw them off at dawn when Nappo was finally straight enough to travel.

"Please stay, Nappo! My father's not that bad." She wept as Nappo packed the goods into their bags. "He'd have you as a son-in-law, Nappo. He likes you well enough."

Nappo caught Eli's glance, and the two of them rolled their eyes.

"Maybe I'll be back."

"Please, don't go!" Tasha flung her arms around Nappo. "Stay with me, please!"

Again, Eli rolled his eyes as Nappo held her to him, and stroked her hair and kissed her long and plentiful, and then bid her farewell. Eli soon got sick of the production and rode ahead with Teal. Nappo caught up to them with Dawn, and winked at Eli.

"She's pretty hot, eh?"

"Her father wants me dead. Therefore the whole family is ugly."

"Thomas isn't that bad. He was really warming up to me by the end. At least I think he was." Nappo punched him. "You're just jealous because you didn't get any."

"Whatever, Nappo. I couldn't care less." Eli clicked and pulled on the reins, coaxing Saber into a trot. When Nappo kept up, Eli gave up on the snubbing. "Did you at least find out anything useful? Like where Triskelia is, or at least a general idea of where we should be going?"

"Nope."

"Great." Eli plucked Teal off of Saber and plopped him on the back of Dawn with Nappo. "That's just great." He worked Saber into a canter, and then hollered over his shoulder. "If you're looking for me, I'll be heading generically and indeterminately west. Still."

ELI HAD THOUGHT IT MIGHT take a few days to cross the mountains, but after two days of travel they were still nowhere near the peak of the first pass. It would take many days, maybe weeks, and even then, once they'd crossed the mountains, they wouldn't know where Triskelia actually was. Eli couldn't help but think that someone at the clean market must've known. Had it not gone so pear-shaped so quickly, had Eli managed to make allies instead of enemies, would they have left with information as precious as water? Would they be travelling toward the true Triskelia instead of aiming for the vaguest idea of it instead?

What would he do if they travelled as far as the ocean and *still* had no idea where Triskelia was? Eli could spend his entire life, however much more of it there was, searching for Triskelia and maybe never finding it, or . . . or what? Compete for food and water and work out here along with millions of others just as desperate? As they trudged up and up and up into the mountains, both the air and hope grew thin.

IT WAS COOL ENOUGH in the mountains that they were never without sweaters. They replaced their sunhats with toques, and were thankful for the mitts that Tasha had given them. After a week they reached the snowy summit of the main pass where a makeshift camp of travellers was set up.

It was a clean group, for the most part, although there was a family with the skineater sick that stayed far away from the main camp, up a hill in a little cave. They were waiting for the father and one of the sons to die before they'd move on. They weren't allowed to use the main fire, or trade with any of the other travellers. Eli felt sorry for the little girl who ran back and forth between the cave and the camp, fetching kindling and bread for her family. She was the youngest daughter, and wasn't sick at all. She'd be an orphan before long, and while Eli wished he could do something for her, he had to realize that he already had too many responsibilities for his steadily dwindling resources.

He'd passed countless orphans begging at the side of the road and had forced himself to harden against the urge to give them each a little something. If he had, he and the brothers would've been destitute in a matter of days. But this little girl—there was something special about her. She didn't have the dark, vacant eyes of orphans who spent their hours kited on dust. She was strong and eager. Each time she passed their tents she slowed, eyeing Nappo bashfully.

"She likes you," Eli said, grinning.

"She's just a little brat," Nappo said. "Maybe eight years old, that's all."

"She's stupid." Teal glowered at her as she meandered past again, a pail of snow in each hand. "She's dumb."

"She's dead, if she's orphaned before they get to Foothills Market." Eli watched her scamper up the slippery hillside to the cave.

"We're not taking her with us." Nappo punched Eli's shoulder lightly to get him to look away from the cave and the little girl. "If that's what you're thinking." It *was* what he'd been thinking. But it was a ridiculous idea, and besides, they were going in the opposite direction.

CARD GAMES WERE POPULAR at the mountain camp. In fact, betting at cards seemed to be the main purpose of the makeshift settlement. Nappo was delighted to have a chance to make back some of the hundreds Eli had spent on him and Teal so far. Of course, that meant borrowing from Eli to begin with.

"Twenty?" Eli had offered him five. "Isn't that a bit steep to be throwing away on cards?"

"I'm really good, Eli."

"He is!" Teal said. "I seen him win lots at cards before, at the market, when Talia was alive."

"Then why are you broke?"

"I'm really good at playing, but not so hot at stopping when I'm ahead."

"That's what he was mindin' the tunnel for," Teal said. "He owed Pike."

"I still owe Pike," Nappo muttered.

"Then no way, I'm not throwing away twenty just like that. We don't have an endless supply, in case you care to know."

"Ten, then. C'mon." Nappo looked nervously over at the main fire, where groups of four were forming for another round of Seduce. "I got to get in now, or I'm shut out till tomorrow. Come on, Eli, I'm good for it. Let me do this. I can pay you back, brother."

"A tenner. That's it." Eli handed him the money. "And I will personally stop you while you're ahead. Teal, you go with him, and when he's ahead, you run back here and get me, understand?"

"Okay."

"And don't get drunk!" Eli called after Nappo as he raced over and made the fourth in the last group. "Or stoned, for that matter!"

The game of Seduce was beyond Eli. He had no idea how to play it and even less interest in it. It had something to do with the Queen of

Hearts, like you weren't supposed to end up with her, or you were supposed to end up with her, something like that. There was something special about the ace of spades, too, but all Eli really knew was that the game was ruthless. Most of the fistfights he'd seen in the markets had been over the Queen of Hearts.

The game would go on for hours, so Eli built up the fire outside their tents and settled down to wait. He didn't want to go watch the game, because if you didn't know what was going on, it was dead boring to watch.

Eli took out the knife he'd bought at Foothills Market. Most Droughtlanders had one similar to it, even Teal did, although his was the blunt kind the children had until they turned thirteen and were given a proper one. Eli pulled out the first blade, the one used for cutting, or, as Thomas had suggested, slashing Keyland spies across the throat. He sharpened it with the flat stone he'd bought for that purpose. There was another piece to the knife too, a long narrow blade. Thomas had lots of ideas about how it could be used on spies too. As much as Eli didn't like Thomas, he did half wish the market would catch themselves a real Guardy spy, although he wouldn't wish the little clay box on anyone. Except maybe Seth, or Edmund. And Chancellor East. Or any number of Guardies, come to think of it, especially considering the stories of torture and cruelty he'd heard about the regiments that travelled the Droughtland. That little box would be a terrible way to die—slowly, the air vanishing as your blood thickened in your veins until you perished from the elements.

Eli was so engrossed in sharpening his knife and being mad at the Guard that he didn't notice the little girl slide down the hill from the cave. When Eli next looked up she was standing right beside him, shivering and silent.

"You shouldn't sneak up on someone when they're sharpening a knife, kid."

She stared at him, her earlier brightness entirely gone.

"Are you okay?"

She shook her head.

"Did your father die?"

She nodded.

"Do you need someone to dig the grave?"

She nodded again, and held up four fingers.

"*Four* graves?"

This time her nod was barely perceptible. She started back up the hill, and then stopped, not moving again until Eli reluctantly followed her.

"I can't go in," he said as they reached the mouth of the cave. "I'll get sick."

"Not if you don't touch their bodies."

"They're *all* dead?"

"My mom made a tea." Now she started to cry. "They all drank it, but she didn't give me any."

"What kind of tea?"

"This." She picked up a handful of dried leaves.

"Put it down! It might be poisonous to touch too."

The girl scattered the leaves and scrubbed her hands with snow while Eli glanced at the slumped bodies, all ravaged by the wide oozing wounds of the skineater sick. They had all been much closer to death than anyone at the camp knew.

"You can't stay here by yourself."

The little girl cried and cried, scurrying around the cave, tidying.

"We have to go tell the others."

She ignored him, so Eli left her there and ran down the hill. The Seducers didn't even stop playing when Eli reported the news.

"People die every day." A large man with a thick black beard looked up at him. "At least the mother was merciful."

"But what about the girl?" Eli said. "She needs someone to take care of her."

"We'll deal with it after the game, Eli." Nappo glared at him over his cards. "We're right in the middle of it."

"He's way ahead!" Teal piped from Nappo's side, where he was watching the game with rapt attention.

"Not ahead enough to quit," Nappo muttered.

"Tell your friend to piss off." The big man frowned at Nappo. "He's spying at people's cards."

"I am not! I'm trying to figure out what to do with the girl!"

"You're going to get me kicked out of the game, Eli." Nappo waved him away. "They're dead, right? So they can wait till the game is over."

THE GIRL'S NAME was Althea and she was ten years old. Eli dragged her away from her manic tidying and brought her down the hill. He sat her by the fire and gave her a mug of strong, sweet tea and covered her thin shoulders with a blanket. After reciting her name and age, all she did was stare silently up at the cave. Eli tried to get her to eat something, but the plate of bread and cheese just sat in her lap until Bullet helped himself to it.

That night's game of Seduce seemed to go on much longer than any other game Eli had seen. Finally, when the moon was at its highest, the man with the black beard cried out, "The Queen is dead!" and the game was over. Eli had forgotten all about his tenner, and at this point he didn't care about it either.

Nappo slunk back, hands shoved in his pockets, eyes downcast. "Sorry."

"He spent some on dust and lost the rest and he owes Trace forty more," Teal reported as the two of them helped themselves to the tea, kept hot over the fire.

"So?" Eli shrugged. "That's not my problem."

"Come on, Eli." Nappo looked like he was going to be sick. "Where am I going to get that kind of money?"

"Not from me."

"But Trace'll kill me!"

"So what?" Eli shrugged again. "I can't say that I care too much about someone who can shrug off a little girl and her dead family over a stupid card game."

"Stupid card game?" The man with the black beard came into the light of the fire. "You got my forty, Nappo?"

"No, he doesn't," Eli said.

"Eli, meet Trace," Nappo said miserably. "Trace, Eli."

"I'll wait." Trace took off his cape and settled himself near the fire. His arms were like sculpted wood, and under his leather vest was a muscular chest unlike any Eli had ever seen, except on some of the Night Circus performers.

"What are you lookin' at?"

"Nothing."

"You were lookin' at my muscles, yeah?"

"I guess."

"Yeah." Trace flexed his arms like a Night Circus strongman. "These are the same muscles that are going to break your face if I have to leave this fire without my money."

"Take it easy, Trace." Nappo handed him a mug of tea. "I'm working on it."

"You're not getting it from me," Eli said.

"Okay! Okay!" Nappo yelled. "So then shut up at least and let me think."

The three of them sat around the fire in an awkward silence while Teal ran between them, recounting the game hand by hand. "An 'en Trace had the bitch, but no one knowed it! An 'en she went around again and again, an 'en Nappo had her and he was all mad but didn't show it."

"Go to bed." Nappo grabbed Teal as he flew past again. "Now!"

"But you're stayin' up!"

"Now, Teal."

"But I got to finish telling about when you—"

"No one wants to hear it," Eli snapped. "Go to bed."

"You better go to bed, because if you keep talkin'," Trace said, "I'll sew your lips up with a piece of thread, right?"

Eli and Nappo glanced at each other and then glared at Trace, and Nappo said it for the both of them.

"You talk to my little brother like that again and I will—"

"You will, will you?" Trace stood, his fire-cast shadow plunging Nappo into darkness.

"Just don't talk to him like that." Nappo turned to tell Teal to get off to bed again, but he'd taken the hint and already made himself scarce.

"Down to business then." Trace took his seat. "My forty, or the boy."

"Teal?" Nappo paled. "You're joking, right?"

"I have a cotton farm. I need labour. I was going to buy more labour with the forty. You're getting a deal."

"No way!" Nappo looked frantically at Eli. "Come on, Eli. I learned my lesson, okay? I'll pay you back. I will!"

"You'll never pay me back."

"I will!" Nappo crossed his heart. "I swear! What more can I say? I promise I'll pay you back! Come on, just pay him. Please? I'll do anything!"

Eli sighed. He got up, went to the tent, and returned with the money.

"Now will you leave us alone?"

"So." Trace pocketed the forty. "How do you come by your money?"

Before Eli could come up with a story that would satisfy Trace, Nappo answered for him.

"He wins it at Seduce."

"Really?"

If there was one time he'd wanted to punch Nappo in the face, this was it.

"Yeah. I did." He tried again, with conviction. "I mean, I do."

"Then how come you didn't play tonight?"

"I was—"

"He only plays in the markets," Nappo blurted.

"A highroller? I wouldn't have guessed." Trace stood and fastened his cape. "If I see you in the markets, we'll play, right?"

"Of course." Eli nodded. "Absolutely." Eli hoped never to set foot in the same market as the Droughtland strongman standing before him. His muscles were so big he could barely cross his arms. "I look forward to it." Thank the highers that Trace was heading southeast to the land of cotton farms.

"Right. See you again," Trace said, and then he lumbered off into the darkness.

"Not if I have anything to do with it," Eli mumbled when he was well out of earshot.

Eli didn't say a word to Nappo as they set up Althea's tent by theirs. Nappo kept apologizing, but Eli wasn't having any of it. He got the stunned little girl to bed, and then went to bed himself, with Nappo carrying on with his apologies across the darkness from his own tent.

THE NEXT MORNING Eli woke to shrill screams. He stuck his head out his tent and saw Trace wrestling Althea onto his horse. Eli scrambled into his boots, raced over, and pulled her down. She clung to Eli and wept.

"Where are you taking her?"

"I bought her."

"From who? Her family is dead!"

"I paid for a proper burial, didn't I?"

Two men in the gathering crowd nodded. The taller of the two spoke.

"That's right. He bought her from us. We're burying the others, and for a good price."

The shorter one pulled Althea away from Eli and handed her roughly back up to Trace.

"You got a problem with that?"

"I was going to take her."

The crowd laughed.

"Just like that?" Trace snapped his fingers. "She's clean. She's worth something. There's many years' labour in her and you thought you'd just steal her like a horse?"

"I didn't know—"

"Never mind him." Nappo appeared and pulled Eli away. "He had a little too much to drink last night. Ride safe, Trace. Take care. See ya. Bye."

"I'll be seeing you in the market games." Trace winked at Eli. "Been a while since I played a highroller."

Eli forced a nod. "Right." He waved at Althea. "Bye, kid. Sorry."

Althea waved miserably, and then had to hold on with both hands as Trace took off west at a gallop, nearly sending her bouncing off the horse.

"I thought he said he had a cotton farm," Eli said, dismayed. "Those are southeast from here, right?"

"At the game he said it was blueberries," Nappo said. "That could be anywhere."

"I heard he had a poppy farm," Teal said.

"And that would be north," Nappo said. "That's the most likely. No wonder he's all secretive. He doesn't want anyone to know where it is, or it'd get raided."

AS ELI AND NAPPO AND TEAL packed up to leave, Eli kept his eye on the murky duo who'd agreed to bury Althea's family. They had a long breakfast, including plenty of booze in their coffee, and then they climbed up the hill and dug a sloppy, shallow ditch in the snow beside the cave. The whole chore took them a fraction of the time it took them to eat breakfast. Then they donned worn-looking arms-length leather gloves and dragged out the bodies and rolled them into the crude grave. The taller one stood up a bit straighter and looked as though he was saying something prayerful, but for all Eli knew he could've been reciting the names of horses he'd had or girls he'd loved. Then they slipped and tripped down the snowy hill and started in on lunch without so much as washing their hands.

"That didn't look like a proper burial to me."

"Would you quit looking for trouble?" Nappo whispered. "Just leave it."

"Me? What about you? We could've bought the girl if you'd told me that's how it works! And you cost me four tenners last night, five counting the one I loaned you!"

The two of them bickered and raged at each other all afternoon as they began their seemingly endless descent down the other side of the mountains.

14

~❧~

As creepy as he might be, Jakko was at least true to his word. Seth did get assigned to the West Droughtland Regiment, and so did Nord, much to Seth's surprise and sincere dismay. Seth asked him why the hell he wanted that posting.

"Target practice." Nord made a gun with his fingers. "Pow, pow! Where else am I going to get the chance to kill Droughtlanders on a regular basis? You think I want to stand around protecting the Group of Keys against nothing?"

"You'd be protecting them from the rebels."

"There are no rebels."

"There are so! They bombed my Key."

"A couple of flakes, that's all. There's no rebel Shangri-La, or whatever they call it."

"Triskelia."

"Yeah, that. No way. It's just a myth Droughtland dusters cling to, like some kind of religion. If it really existed, we'd be taught about it, right?"

"Yeah, I guess." But Seth did believe in Triskelia. *A couple of flakes* could not have organized the bombing of the gardens. He didn't know what Triskelia was, or who it was, or how many there were, or if it *was* just a bunch of flakes, but it was something to be reckoned with, he was sure.

SETH DIDN'T EXACTLY LIKE the commander of the West Droughtland Regiment, but he did have a healthy amount of fear and respect for the man. Commander Regis treated Droughtlanders like they were rats and his soldiers like they were prized terriers. Keep your rat catchers happy and you've got it made, that was his philosophy. At the first village they stopped at, after travelling three nights, Commander Regis rounded up all the young Droughtland women and had the medic examine them to find out if they were diseased.

The sick ones were sent away. The others were instructed to wash thoroughly with harsh soap provided by the medic, and then were ordered to dress in the best clothes they had and wait to be paired off with the men of the West Droughtland Regiment—and they were all men. Regis would not have any females in his regiment, and now Seth was gathering why.

The typically starving women were then ordered to sit and watch while the Guardies feasted on their usual rations as well as the last of the village's stores.

After dessert, Commander Regis lined up the girls, prettiest to ugliest.

"Yeah!" Nord rubbed his hands together. "Don't give me a dog, Commander. I'm your bitch forever if you give me one of the first, sir!" The regiment hooted and cheered as the Commander walked the line, inspecting the women.

"What about the whole Blue Book thing?" Seth whispered. The farthest he'd ever gone with a girl was some tongue and a grope under her shirt, so he was more than a little terrified at being paired off with one for the entire day. But he couldn't back out; Regis wouldn't let him live it down. He'd probably accuse Seth of being bent, and as terrified as he was, Seth wouldn't deny that he was intrigued and excited. He'd had his eye on several girls at basic training, but nothing had ever come of that except a few wet dreams, as much as Seth had tried. He'd begun to think he might be less good-looking than he'd always thought. The nice thing about Droughtland women was that it didn't matter what they thought of his looks. They had just one easy decision—be with him or be punished, simple as that.

"Ah, that's what the tests are for, Maddox." Nord wolf-whistled. "Guaranteed clean."

"But they're still Droughtlanders!"

"Just close your eyes and pretend they're not. Think of a Keyland girl you've had." Nord turned on him. "You a virgin, Maddox?" He said it loud enough for the Droughtlanders and the other Guardies to hear. What was worse? The hoots and jeers? Or hours upon hours alone with a Droughtland girl?

"I am not!"

Seth didn't have time to argue further; Regis was assigning the women in order of his favourite men, and Seth was right up there, but only because Regis was acknowledging the wealth attached to the son of a Chief Regent. Seth was given the fourth woman, after Nord was given the third.

Seth took her hand for a brief moment before realizing none of the others were holding their Droughtlander's hand. So he dropped it and followed her away from the feast, just as the others were following theirs. He stared at her from behind, planning how he would touch her when they got to wherever they were going. Were there rules? Was there a particular way he was expected to do this?

He watched her long, dusty black hair swish with each barefooted step. She was wearing a very short dress, just a tunic really. Her butt was round and bouncing and showing. Seth had to cover his crotch with his hands as he followed her through the village. Apparently, his body couldn't care less about the differences between Droughtland and Keyland girls.

She led him into a small dark hut, its only light coming in from one narrow window high on the wall. She crawled onto the bed and waited for him to join her. Seth stood by the door, his hands still covering his crotch.

"Aren't you going to say anything?" he asked.

"I can't talk unless you ask me a question." Her voice was scratchy, like someone who smoked a lot of poppy dust, or maybe she was sick after all and the test hadn't caught it.

"Are you sick? Your voice sounds weird."

"You took all our water."

Seth tossed her his flask and she took a drink. He waited for her to speak again, to see if her voice had improved or if she'd been lying about its being scratchy from thirst. She stared at him, eyebrows raised, until Seth remembered about asking a question.

"Is that better?"

"A lot. Thanks." Her voice did sound much better. "You going to stand there all day?"

All day. It seemed like such a long time. Seth shook his head.

"You seem—" She stopped herself.

"I seem what?"

"Nothing." She shook her head again and patted the bed beside her. "Can I have another drink of your water first?"

Seth sat on the edge of the fusty straw mattress and offered her the flask. She finished the water, and then looked questioningly at him.

"What?" Seth asked. "You can talk whenever you want. I don't care about this stupid question-first rule."

"That's not all the water you brought, is it? We'll need more than that, even if we don't—"

"We will!" Seth pushed himself off the bed, red in the face. "I'll go get more."

"I do that." She took Seth's flask and a jug from the table and went out into the brutally hot day, leaving Seth behind and befuddled.

By the time she came back from the regiment's water cart, Seth was determined not to mess up his first time. She brought him a mug of water. He put it on the little table beside the bed and they stared at each other for an awkward moment, and then Seth pushed her back onto the thin mattress.

He kneeled over her, absolutely petrified, closing his eyes and trying to recall the images from the book Nord kept under his bed at basic training. She waited, arms behind her head, clearly bored, watching Seth's eyebrow furrow in frustration. In the end, it was she who choreographed the occasion, which lasted all of a rather unbearable thirty seconds.

Seth rolled onto his back and stared at a fat spider crossing the ceiling. He thought he could sense the girl stifling a laugh beside him, but he couldn't be sure. The whole experience, as short as it was, left him furious and embarrassed. He got off the bed, fighting the urge to slap the puzzling expression off her face, and went to the window and yanked the curtain shut. The hut was now completely dark.

"Shut up and go to sleep," he ordered, even though she hadn't said anything.

After an hour of wrestling with regret and humiliation, Seth finally fell asleep. He tossed and turned beside her until the sun set and he slammed out of the hut to join the others at the horses.

It wasn't until they reached the next village several days later, and he'd been paired up with another Droughtland girl who told him her name without his asking, that he realized he never learned the name of the first dark-haired girl. She would always be his awkward, nameless, shameful first.

So much for avoiding Trace. Even though they travelled slowly, he was one of the first people Eli laid eyes on at the market in the valley at the bottom of the mountains, two weeks after they'd left the mountain camp.

"Don't let him see me!" Eli ducked between the horses when he spotted him walking by.

Eli managed to avoid Trace for over an hour, until they headed into the pub for lunch and there he was, set up at a table just inside the door.

"Hey there, highroller. Have a seat." He patted the chair beside him. "Wondered when you'd show up."

"Where's the girl?"

"Sold her. She cried too much."

"But you said you were going to use her on your farm!" Eli reluctantly sat down. "Do you even have a farm?"

Trace ignored the question. He summoned the tableminder and told her to bring drinks for the boys and to find one more man to join them. "Let's play."

"I don't feel like it." Eli folded his arms. "Who'd you sell the girl to?"

"What do you care?"

"You lied." A fourth player was approaching the table. Eli leaned close. "You don't have a farm, do you? Who are you, really? What do you traffic children for, huh?"

"Mind your own business." Trace winked. "And I'll mind mine. Now *play.*"

"I won't play with a childtrader. You're sick." Eli pushed his chair away from the table and stalked off, willing Trace not to follow him. He hoped he'd at least evaded playing by pulling that little stunt. Nappo followed Eli out of the pub, complaining all the while that he could've made them some money if Eli would just spot him a fiver.

"I'll triple it and then I'll quit the game, I swear," Nappo said as they hurriedly shopped the stalls for supplies. The sooner they got out of there, the better.

"Like at the camp?" Eli loaded another sack of oats onto Nappo's outstretched arms.

"I told you, I learned my lesson." Nappo hurried after Eli. "I swear I'll stop while I'm ahead. I won't drink or dust, either."

"You always say that, but then you still stick that junk up your nose."

"So?" Nappo shrugged. "Everybody does."

"Not me." Eli shook his head and lowered his voice. "That stuff makes your people lazy. That's why the revolution hasn't happened yet. You're too stoned to lift a finger. The poppy dust makes you not care."

"Hey, I care."

"Sure, you all care enough to talk about revolution. But that's it. Talk, talk, talk. And you can hardly do that for fear the Guard is spying on you. You know, the Keylanders have you all duped. You outnumber them by millions. There's just not that many Keylanders." Eli sighed. Nappo was craning his neck, looking off into the crowd. "Are you even listening?"

"Where's Teal?"

"Around here somewhere."

"Did he come out of the pub with us?"

Eli thought back. No. He hadn't. "Trace!"

Eli and Nappo ran back to the pub, where Trace tut-tutted the two of them and grinned.

"Left your beloved Teal with a rotten childtrader, didn't you? People like you make my job so easy."

"Where is he?" Nappo leapt at him, executing a fairly useless headlock. "What have you done with him?"

"He's at the bar, fool." Trace plucked Nappo off him with one hand. "Ordering food. He said he's had nothing to eat except pan bread for a week."

"He's lying! We feed him well."

"Nappo! You came back!" Teal ran through the crowd as best he could without tipping his enormous bowl of stew. "He said you forgot me. But you didn't, did you? Look what he bought me! You can have some."

Nappo shook the boy. "Don't you *ever* do that again, you understand?"

"My supper!" Teal cried as it sloshed onto the floor. "Do what? I never did nothing!"

"The boy's right." Trace grinned. "You two left him behind. That's not very nice. After all, he's only five. And quite the talker."

Eli grasped the boy's wrists. "What did you tell him?"

"I don't know." Teal stared at what was left of the stew.

"Excuse us for a minute." Eli carried Teal, squirming under his arm, outside and around the back where nobody would overhear. "Did you say *anything* about Triskelia?"

"I don't know. Maybe?"

Eli shut his eyes and sighed. "You knew that was a secret."

"But he said if he knew where we were going he could take me to you."

"He was lying, Teal." Eli slumped to the ground. It made so much sense. Trace was a Keyland spy. No Droughtlander was that healthy and strong! And he didn't have any scars either. He was no trader. He was a spy.

But why trade in children? That seemed a risky business to pick as a cover. Poor little Althea, just ten years old. What had Trace really done with her? Where was she now? Sold to a Key as labour? He tried to calm himself. That wouldn't be so bad, sending Droughtland children to the Keys. They'd be fed well, and kept safe. Worked hard, yes, but safe. The Maddox household had seen many labourers grow up in their service, and none of them had suffered for it. But then Lisette wasn't your average Keylander running an estate, either. Eli shook his head. Focus on the now.

"We're in big trouble, Teal." Eli sunk his head into his hands and took a minute to think. "Okay, listen carefully. I need you to go back in and try to get Nappo to come out *without* Trace. We have to make a run for it without Trace knowing. I'll meet you at the horses. Bullet will go with you. If Trace follows you, point at him and yell 'Bullet, attack!' Got it?"

"Bullet, attack!" Teal nodded sombrely. "Bullet, attack. Got it."

It took more than a little coaxing for Bullet to go with Teal. Eli could only hope that if it came to it, Bullet would obey the five-year-old's command.

MINUTES LATER the boys were on the run, horses galloping, with Bullet left behind keeping Trace at bay. It was almost an hour before the dog caught up with them on the road. Eli had worried that he'd seen the last of Bullet, that Trace would've wrung his neck, but there he was, running so fast it looked as if none of his paws were touching the ground. His muzzle and chest were bloody, but he wasn't hurt. It must be Trace's blood.

Eli praised the dog and lifted him onto the horse so that he could rest and the trio could keep going as fast as the horses would carry them across the plains.

It was a short, swift descent into hell for Seth, who was now riding at the end of the regiment, the position assigned to the Commander's most hated man. It had happened over a Droughtland girl. Seth hadn't known that the Commander was outside his girl's hut when he offered her a tenner just before the regiment was to leave. He knew it was against the rules, but so was all of this, and the girl had been so weak from hunger she'd fainted before he'd even unlaced his boots. He'd helped her to the bed, and then her little boy, barely old enough to hold his head up, wailed thinly from a box of straw in the corner. Seth had picked him up and set him on the young mother's chest, where he nuzzled for milk and found none.

Hers was the most depressing village so far. The few surviving children had the bloated stomachs and stick legs of those dying from starvation, and the young women were so exhausted from lack of food they could barely stand up in a line. Seth had felt sick at the thought of sleeping with any one of them, even the rather pretty blonde he'd been paired up with. When she led him back to the hut he'd been horrified to find she was a mother. She was fourteen, she said when she came to after fainting. The father was a Guardy, but she didn't know which one.

Commander Regis crashed through the door just as he was handing her the tenner. He yanked it away from the girl, who'd been staring at it in awe. It wasn't much, in fact it was nothing to Seth, but it was obvious it would keep her tiny village from death for a time. Without it they'd all soon be dead, given that the regiment had consumed what little the village had left.

"Are you insane, Maddox?" The Commander pushed the girl away, but she scrambled to take the tenner back. He punched her in the face and she crumpled to the floor with a terrified whimper.

"But sir, they're dying!"

"What do you care? Do you save every starving dog you see out here?"

"She's not a dog, sir."

"She's certainly no better than one!" Regis bellowed. He kicked the girl and she cried out, which sent her baby into a fit of breathless screams.

"Why are you beating her?" Seth knelt and felt where Regis had kicked her. She yelped as his fingers found her ribs. "She didn't do anything! Don't you have any mercy?"

"Mercy?" Commander Regis pulled Seth away from the girl and kicked her again, this time in the head, and hard. The girl lay sprawled out, eyes wide, silent. "Mercy?"

"Commander! Please, sir, stop!"

"Mercy is putting them out of their misery, isn't it?" Regis crossed the room and smacked the baby, who just cried harder, so he picked him up and threw him to the floor where he landed with an inhuman thud. Regis stormed out, dragging Seth behind him. "This is precisely why your kind aren't suited for this. When this tour is done, you'll never tour again."

Riding in the wake of his regiment, Seth could not stop thinking about the girl and her baby. Were they lying dead on the dirt floor of the shabby hut? Had they died because of him? Seth held the tenner he'd tried to give the girl above his head. It caught the wind of the storm the Commander had scheduled to stay ahead of the regiment so that the plains would be less dusty. When he was sure he wasn't being watched, he let the tenner sail off in the wind over his shoulder. Perhaps a Droughtlander as badly off as the girl would find it, or some orphan, or dying beggar. Seth didn't care who picked it up so long as he was rid of the cursed thing. He hadn't expected the Droughtland to be like this. He hadn't expected that he'd *care* about them at all. What was happening to him? What was wrong with him? Was he even cut out for this at all? He'd sent Edmund several letters asking if he could arrange for him to be "needed" at home for important state business. That way, it woudn't be a shameful discharge. Seth figured he'd go home, lie low for a while, and then set out to look for Eli on his own. But Edmund had ignored his pleas. Was he punishing him? If not, why wouldn't he bring him home?

15

⌘

Eli often found himself staring at the horizon, silently trying to coax any clouds in their direction. Second to missing Lisette, he missed weather. All weather—snow, hail, rain, storms, even the terrifying sight of an oncoming twister. It was as if the Droughtland had no weather at all, except for the snow in the mountains, and the wind, and the fog layering the increasingly chilly mornings. The occasional random smattering of rain from a front passing on its way to its designated Key never amounted to anything. And it seemed as if every single cloud was already spoken for, although Eli knew that wasn't possible.

Eli was off in his own little world, watching the horizon for weather, when Nappo roused his attention five days after leaving Trace to deal with Bullet.

"Disaster ahead, Eli."

Eli focused on the figure on horseback blocking the road in the near distance.

Trace.

"I'm not looking for trouble," Trace hollered. He opened his arms in a gesture of peace. "I just want to talk."

Nappo pulled Dawn tight up beside Saber. "Want to make a run for it?"

Eli shook his head. He could see for miles around, and saw nothing, but that didn't mean there wasn't an entire Guard regiment hiding out nearby, waiting.

"Stay on the horses," Eli said. "If he tries anything, we'll take off and hope we can get a good head start before his tired old mare can catch up."

Come to think of it, why would a Keylander spy be riding a drippy-eyed old mare with a bowed back and patches of hair missing? And how, with such a lame horse, could he have possibly caught up with them?

"Keep your eyes peeled," Eli added as Trace approached them. "He's up to something, you can be sure."

Trace pulled up his trouser leg, revealing a big, blood-soaked bandage. "You owe me for this. How about letting me slice the wretched beast from tongue to tail?"

Eli drew his knife, as did Nappo, and Teal too, for what his was worth. "What do you want from me?"

"I wonder what it is *you* think I want from you."

"A bribe? So you won't report me to the Guard?"

Trace let out a loud, obnoxious laugh. The boys checked in all directions in case it was a summoning signal to the others. "You think I'm a Keyland spy?"

"I do." Eli swallowed. "So how much for your silence? Obviously you're a rogue, so don't tell me you won't accept a bribe."

"I won't."

"Then we'll be on our way." Eli nodded for Nappo and Teal to follow. "If you want to take a message to my father, tell him he'll rot alive for what he did. Tell him I will make him pay. And tell my brother he's a fool not to see the truth. Tell them the whole of Keyland can rot alive for all I care."

"My, my." Trace raised his eyebrows and applauded Eli's little outburst as they passed him. "Very dramatic. How about I give you a nice little head start, a couple of hours? Is that sufficient to run away from the big bad Keyland spy?"

Eli slowed. "What the hell do you want from me?"

"You two," Trace pointed at Nappo and Teal. "Go on ahead."

"Eli?" Nappo still held his knife at the ready.

"It's okay," Eli said. "But don't go far. And keep your eye on me."

When Nappo and Teal were a little way off, Trace pulled his horse up close to Eli's. "Your mother asked me to keep an eye out for you."

"You're a liar!" Eli's heart sped up. "My mother is dead."

"I know. She was killed in the bombing at the gardens."

"She was." Eli stopped. "How do you know that?"

"A bombing orchestrated by your father, made to look like the rebels did it."

"Yes." Eli dropped his eyes to the saddle horn as a sudden shudder of grief came over him. "Yes. But how do you know about it?"

Trace lowered his voice even more. "Do the brothers know about you?"

Eli nodded. Trace straightened and stopped speaking in a whisper. "I was there visiting the cell when the news came that we had to clear out."

"You were *there*? In Eastern Key?" Still, Eli was skeptical. "How can I be sure you're not one of my father's men?"

"That day you came you were wearing green pants and a blue short-sleeved shirt. Your mother had you read the books all day."

"You were really there?" Was there any way that this was still a trap? How could he know all this, even if it was Edmund who sent him? "You saw me?"

"We all did."

"But how did you survive?"

"I was just passing through. I left the day the news came that the cell had to be dismantled. Before I left your mother asked me if I'd keep an eye out for you in case anything should happen to her. I told her I would."

"How did you find me?"

"You found me."

"In the mountains?"

"I saw you in Foothills Market first, when they let you out of the box. Once I found out you were headed for the mountains, I went ahead."

"Why didn't you say anything in the mountains?"

"I wanted to be sure you were out here with the right intentions, and I wanted to see how you were doing on your own."

"How am I doing?"

"You're doing well." Trace patted Eli's back. "A little soft for a Droughtlander, still got some of the Keyland self-righteousness you all are famous for. I like that you were going to look out for Althea."

"What really happened to her? You didn't sell her, did you?"

"She's in a good place." Trace looked across the plain, toward the horizon. "Someday you may see her again."

"You won't tell me now?"

Trace shook his head. "Go tell the brothers what I've told you. I'll ride ahead." He patted his horse. "This old beast doesn't move very fast any more."

"How did you catch up with us?"

"Eli, there are tunnels out here you'd never find, even if you spent your whole life looking," he said as he coaxed his old mare west.

ONCE THEY WERE CONVINCED that Trace was a real rebel, the brothers treated him as if he were a Droughtland legend come to life. Nappo wouldn't stop with the questions, and Teal followed the man around like he was tethered to him. Trace was patient with Teal, but less so with Nappo. After a couple of nights of travelling together—this time west with a purpose because Trace knew exactly where he was going—he grabbed Nappo's stash of poppy dust and dumped it in the fire.

Eli waited for Nappo to erupt, but Nappo just stared at Trace, a look of shock on his face.

"You know why I did that?" Trace plucked the little bone dust spoon out of Nappo's hand and threw it into the fire too.

Nappo looked beseechingly at Eli.

"He doesn't have the answers. Think for yourself." Trace put a hand on Nappo's shoulder. "What good are you to the revolution if you spend all your time sniffing dust, huh?"

"Everybody sniffs dust," Teal said, daring to come to his brother's defence, even if it meant challenging his new idol.

"Do you?"

"No, but I'm just a kid."

"So is Nappo."

"I am not!"

"Kid or not, not everyone dusts, and Triskelians don't. Ever."

"I been sniffing dust since I was eight," Nappo muttered, eyes on the ground. "Done me no harm."

"And done you no good either, has it?"

"Sure it has, makes me brave, and better at Seduce."

"You can be brave without it." Trace's tone was firm. "I won't be taking you to Triskelia so long as you still have cravings."

"I don't got no cravings," Nappo said. "I can stop dusting any time I want."

Trace stood and stretched in the shadows of the fire. "When's the last time you went two days without it?"

"Lots of times."

"Yeah?" Trace looked at Nappo, but Nappo kept his eyes on the ground. "Then you know what it's like to stop?"

"Sure I do."

"My brother can do anything he wants," Teal added.

"Good." Trace nodded slowly. "Then you won't need me looking after you. Good night, boys."

Once Trace was out of earshot, Eli whispered, "Are you okay?"

"That was a tenner worth of dust." Nappo's voice was shaky. "I really stuck my neck out to steal the bracelet I sold for that."

"*I* stole it," Teal said.

"I told you what to do, though."

"You *steal* for your poppy dust?" Eli lowered his voice even more. He couldn't say he was surprised, really, but he'd thought Nappo bought it with Seduce winnings made off of coins Teal begged for in the markets. "You ever steal from me for it? Should I be counting my money every night?"

"I don't steal from you, not since that one time."

"You're really going to quit?"

"Don't have a choice, do I?" Nappo shrugged. "It's all gone, and Trace says it's four days till the next market. Unless there's a camp in between."

"Well, you're better off without it," Eli said.

"What do you know about it?" Nappo looked up then, his gaze hard, his jaw clenched. "You've never even tried it."

"True." Eli looked away.

"So just leave me alone."

That night, Eli dreamt of a field of red poppies, and Nappo and Teal standing in the middle of it, gazing at an enclave wall in the distance.

ELI WOKE to Nappo screaming as though he was being ripped apart by a troop of night bandits. He pulled on his clothes and stumbled out into the dawn mist, knife tight in his fist, ready for a fight. He found Trace backing out of the brothers' tent. Eli rushed up to him, ready to drive the knife into the man's side.

"What did you do to him?" He lunged at Trace as he straightened. Trace held him off and twisted the knife out of his hand as Bullet barked and snapped at him.

"I won't be so forgiving if that dog comes at me a second time." Trace growled and bared his teeth right back at the dog. Bullet pulled his ears back and settled on his haunches, seconds away from springing on him. "Call him off."

"Bullet, leave it!"

Bullet sat. Trace let Eli go.

"Seems our friend lied about quitting before." Trace handed Eli back his knife. "Have a look."

Eli peeked in the tent and saw Nappo thrashing in his sweat-soaked sleeping sack.

"That's what happens when you quit."

"Is he going to be all right?"

"He'll live." Trace stoked the coals in the fire pit. "I've been minding him since the little one came to me, scared out of his mind. Nappo was screaming and clawing at him. You should see the boy's face. He's asleep in my tent."

Eli looked in on Teal. He was curled up in a tight ball in a corner of the tent, clutching his bit of rag, thumb in his mouth. His cheeks were criss-crossed with scratches, and his bottom lip was swollen and purple.

THEY CAMPED there for four more days, waiting for Nappo to recover from the vomiting and seizures. With each day Nappo grew more humble, until Eli began to wonder if the Nappo he knew no longer existed. Trace assured him otherwise, but whenever Eli looked at Nappo, drawn and pale, he wondered who the real Nappo was without the dust.

As they packed up camp and set out on the fourth day, Eli drew Saber alongside Nappo and Dawn. Nappo was carving a notch in a length of wood.

"What are you doing?"

"Marking each day."

"Until you get more dust?"

"No." Nappo half laughed. "Trace says it helps to keep track of how many days I've gone without it. He says when I fill this stick with notches, he'll throw me a party."

"You don't want it any more?"

"Sure I want it." Nappo slipped the stick into a saddlebag and put away his knife. "But I don't want to ever have to quit it again." He straightened in his saddle and looked Eli in the eye for the first time since the night he quit. "Besides, I want to be a Triskelian. I've changed, Eli."

There was an awkward silence, during which Eli decided it was time to change the subject.

"Race you?" He pointed to a boulder way off in the distance.

"On three." Nappo leaned forward.

"One, two . . . three!" The boys kicked their horses' flanks and galloped past Trace, and Teal, who was riding with him.

"Hey!" Teal hollered. "I want to race too!"

But the boys couldn't hear him and they didn't care, they were racing across the meadow, heads down, eyes on the mark, Bullet running alongside them, barking wildly.

16

lies buzzed at the crusty edges of Seth's eyes as he slipped in and out of consciousness, his fever a hot, raging river determined to pull him under. Between the horrific hallucinations he prayed he'd live long enough to forget, during the brief moments of lucidity, Seth couldn't help but relive the events that had brought him to this place and this crippling, cruel sick. At first the memory was kind, recalling the soft, cool wind that had carried the stench and heat of the village away, the fat raindrops plopping on the tin roofs, the comforting smell of wet earth. The rain was supposed to stay just ahead of them, but sometimes it lagged a little and they were caught in it. Seth didn't mind. Rain made him think of the Key, of home, of his room with all his things, of the servants waiting to do his bidding, of the lush, sprawling lawns, of wealth. Seth longed to stay with this part of the memory, but it inevitably surged forward, and he found himself face to face with the girl.

Commander Regis hadn't even bothered to hide his smirk as he paired the very last girl in the lineup with Seth after the feast in that tidy little village. She was bone thin, with sunken cheekbones and bald spots and a spine that curved so badly she had to walk with a cane.

"I'll pass, Commander," Seth said when the girl was pulled forward. "I'm very tired, sir."

"Hah!" Nord slung his arm around his rather beautiful Droughtlander. "He says he's tired, Commander."

"I don't need an interpreter, Nord." Commander Regis shoved Seth toward the girl. "You will do as the rest, or suffer the consequences."

Later, Seth would wish he'd suffered the consequences instead.

A GUARD WAS STATIONED outside the hut, which made Seth wonder if the Commander thought he might try to run away like the last poor kid to be Commander Regis's most hated. Seth had no such plans. He knew he wouldn't last a day on his own. He had tried to buy his way back into favour, a bribe to which Commander Regis had said, "Don't insult me."

But Seth was convinced the Commander could be bought. Surely it was just a matter of waiting it out. Let Commander Regis parade his power, and then Seth would offer again, with a much larger amount.

The girl sat on the bed, looking at him with such pathetic terror that he wanted to smack her, just so she'd look at him differently.

"I won't hurt you," he growled. "And I won't touch you either, so don't worry." Her expression relaxed into gratitude.

"Are you retarded?"

She shook her head.

"Can't you speak?"

She nodded.

"That was a question, so speak."

She lifted a hand to cover her mouth. Her fingers were dotted with warts. "I'd rather not," she mumbled.

"Why not?"

She removed her hand and opened her mouth. The girl had no teeth left, her gums were infected and rotting, and her tongue was swollen and white with thrush. The stench was worse than the fumes off the rotting corpse they'd come across the day before.

"Ugh, shut your mouth!" Seth plugged his nose and covered his own mouth.

The girl began to weep.

"It's not you," Seth said. "It's not. It's the smell."

"But that *is* me!"

Seth stifled a gag. "I mean, it's not your fault."

"Fault? How dare you talk about fault? This is *your* fault!" The girl's accusations pickled the air. "Your people are killing us!"

Seth scrambled for the door. He flung it open and gasped in the fresh air. Commander Regis stood on the step, hands clasped behind his back, grinning.

"Tsk, tsk. I do believe she spoke without being asked a question."

"No!" Seth tried to block the door. "I can handle it, sir."

Commander Regis shoved him out of the way and waved for two Guardies to go in ahead of him.

"Behead her, would you? Perhaps that will put an end to the unbearable stench and the slanderous allegations she'd be executed for anyway."

"Commander, please! It's not her fault!"

"Oh? You're on her side?" Commander Regis clamped a heavy hand on Seth's shoulder and steered him outside. "Do you believe it's our fault too? Is it our fault that these creatures live and die like vermin? Is it our fault that they're weak and sickly?"

"Sir, please don't kill her!" Seth shouted over the screams of the girl coming from inside the tiny hut. The girl's mother rushed down the path. Commander Regis nodded at another pair of Guardies, who held her back at a distance.

"What did I say?" the Commander bellowed at the first two Guardies, who'd come to the door for a gulp of air. "Behead her!"

"No! Alakina!" The mother collapsed to her knees, wailing. "*Alakina!*"

Seth knew better than to say anything more. His own life was at stake now, and by begging for the girl's life he was doing nothing to help himself. It may be too late already. His fate may be sealed.

From inside the hut there came a torturous thunk. The girl's screams stopped. The Guardies dragged out Alakina's headless body by her feet, a tidy wide ribbon of blood trailing back into the hut.

"Leave the head." Commander Regis grimaced at the body. "Give the rest of it to the dogs."

Seth leaned against the nearest wall and puked.

"So much more cost-effective than a trial," Commander Regis commented to his assistant as they wandered away. "And so much more efficient."

Seth wanted to kill him. He wished he had his gun, but they were all being guarded, along with the horses. They weren't allowed to have any weapons with them when they were paired off with the Droughtland girls, after an incident two years before when a girl took a gun from a sleeping Guard and killed him and ten others before shooting herself. If Seth had his gun, he knew he wouldn't be able to stop himself from putting it to the back of the Commander's head and blowing his twisted brains out the front. Especially because his own troubles were about to escalate. He could very well not have anything to lose. But there was always a chance, and so he held his tongue.

Instead, he spat out the bitter dregs of vomit, wiped his mouth, and ran to catch up with the Commander. Perhaps it wasn't too late to save himself, at least.

"I can't do this, sir. Please," Seth pleaded. "Please, sir, let me go."

"Where exactly?" Commander Regis had to practically holler to be heard over Alakina's mother's keening. "Would you get rid of her?" he yelled over Seth to a Guard at the hut.

"You're going to behead her too?"

"Maybe." The Commander clasped his hands behind his back and shrugged. "Maybe not. Now tell me, Maddox, where is it that you would like to go?"

"Home."

"Back to Daddy?"

"Yes sir."

"Then say it. Say that you want to go back to Daddy and tell him what a monumental failure you are."

The Commander's assistant chuckled, clearly enjoying all of this.

"Well," Commander Regis prompted. "Say it."

"I want to go back . . . " Seth cringed. " . . . to Daddy and tell him what a monumental failure I am. Sir."

"And then what? You'll tell him about all this?" The Commander shook his head. "He would be deeply, deeply ashamed of you. You know that, don't you?"

"Then let me go back to base. I'll work there. No one has to know what happened."

"Just can't hack it out here among the real men, can you?"

"I guess not, sir."

"Well, you guess right," Commander Regis said. "So, how about one last kick at the can, and then we'll send you on your way. How does that sound?"

"Thank you, sir." Seth shook Commander Regis's hand, all the while wishing he had the strength to crush every bone in it. "I'll speak highly of you to my father. I'll see to it that he arranges for new horses for your men, and new uniforms too."

Being with another Droughtland girl was the last thing Seth wanted, but he didn't argue as Commander Regis paired him up with a slender but not emaciated girl with bright blue eyes and full red lips. She was prettier than any of the others had been. At first Seth wasn't going to have sex with her, but then he found himself confusingly desperate to. Why did he feel this way? After what he'd just been through?

He shoved her onto the bed and felt overwhelming guilt as if he'd bathed in it. He was rough with her, and by the time he sent her away afterward the guilt was threatening to drown him.

The girl scurried out into the bright sunlight and looked back over her shoulder.

"Goodbye," she whispered.

"Just go." Seth hoped no one had seen or heard her speak without being given permission. It was just one word, but Seth was sure that would be all Regis needed to strike.

OF COURSE, she knew what he didn't. She was sick, although she hadn't broken out in the sores yet. It was the skineater sick. When the Commander summoned her she'd shyly reminded him of the results of the medic's test. He'd nodded, and told her that if she warned the blond soldier in any way he'd behead her whole family and then line her sickbed with their heads. Then he'd taken her to the dead girl's hut and made her see her friend's stinking head for herself. She let the soldier have his way. What did it matter if he'd hurt her? They'd both soon be dead anyway.

17

❦

At long last the ocean lay before them, the salt mist biting at their noses in the dark. Moonlit, the waters were endless, and angrily churning. Neither Eli nor the brothers had ever seen so much water before. Even though Eli's Key was just a two-day ride from the ocean, the eastern beaches were one long toxic mess of makeshift huts and all the accompanying human waste. Besides, it was a hotbed for arms traders. There'd been no seaside recreation along the eastern shores in over a century; the boardwalks had rotted and the roller coasters were a crumbling wreck. There had clearly never been a boardwalk here. This coast was wild and untamed and, coming upon it at night, it seemed almost threatening.

They stood atop a cliff watching the surf pound the rocks below with such force that the earth shuddered under their feet. It was the most awesome thing Eli had ever seen, and at the same time one of the most terrifying. It was like standing at the end of the planet and looking off into the rest of the galaxy. Teal wouldn't let Trace put him down. He was so scared of the ocean that he mashed his face against Trace's chest and refused even to look at it.

"Is it magic?" Teal asked later when Trace settled him into the tent. "Will it put a spell on us?"

"No." Trace tucked another blanket around him. Although it was warmer than the nights in the mountains, the damp in the air went right to their bones and made it feel much colder than it was. It was raining as well, the steady patter of it falling on the waxed walls of the tents.

"Will it swallow me up?" Teal clutched his rag tight in his fist, his eyes sleepy.

"No. It is majestic."

"You said it wasn't magic!"

"Not *magic*. Majestic," Eli called from Trace's tent, where he and Nappo were setting up for a game of Seduce.

"WHOSE RAIN is this?" Eli asked when Trace joined them.

"Might not be anybody's." Trace was playing two hands. "Lots of renegade weather this side of the mountains. They can't control all of it all the time. That's why there's so much green. Then again, it could be one of ours. We've got cloudminders too."

"Generating or stealing?"

"Both." Trace arranged his two hands of cards and frowned. "Now, are we going to play or chat?"

Eli had long since resigned himself to learning Seduce. He was getting better at it too, even though Trace said he took too long at each turn. Nappo, much to his own surprise, found that he was a much better Seduce player without the poppy dust. Trace was coaching both of the boys for a Seduce tournament that would be taking place in Triban. Triban was only a day's ride away now. Once they got there, they'd have a day's rest, and then the tournament would begin and last a week.

"But can't we skip it and go straight to Triskelia?" Eli asked when Trace had announced the plans. Eli still found the game confusing and dull, and he wanted to go to the real rebel front, not Triban. Triban was a false rebel front, a place used to sort out the true rebels from the extremist nutcases and Keyland spies who tried to break in by posing as Droughtlanders wanting to join the rebellion.

"After sixteen years, I think you can stand another short wait."

"But I didn't know there was anything to be waiting for all that time."

"No matter. We can't miss the tournament. This one in particular will keep us in money for months. We all have to eat, and there are a lot of mouths to feed."

WHEN ELI STEPPED OUT of his tent in the morning he took one look at the ocean and just about fell over. In the moonlight it was one thing, but the daylight revealed it to be far more awesome. There was literally no end to it. It was a massive, live beast that looked as though it could scale the cliffs and effortlessly pull them into its clutches, drowning them all.

Teal refused to come out of the tent until the surf's thunderous pounding stopped. Trace tried explaining that the surf never stopped, but Teal wouldn't hear of it, until finally Trace plucked him up and carried him kicking and screaming down the sandy trail to the shore. He set Teal down for a moment, just to pull off his boots and socks, and the boy scrambled back up the path. Eli and Nappo watched from the relative safety of the cliff as Trace grabbed Teal again and carried him back down and waded into the frigid water with him writhing in protest. Bullet sat at Eli's feet, looking up at him, whining.

"See?" Trace hollered up at Eli and Nappo, who both stared at the waves, waiting for them to pull Teal and Trace under. Trace whistled for Bullet. Bullet leapt to attention. The dog was obviously desperate to join Trace, but Eli couldn't imagine how a dog could survive that.

"Bullet, stay." The dog quivered, whining.

"You're going to kill him!" Nappo hollered. "Bring him back!"

Trace waded back onto the shore and put Teal down. Eli and Nappo watched in amazement as the little boy stripped off his own boots and socks and waded right back in. He and Trace splashed around, getting soaked with the salt water as well as the heavy rain that began to fall.

"I'm not going near it." Nappo went back to the fire and poured himself a mug of tea. "Those two are completely nuts."

Eli watched from the cliff edge for another moment, and then carefully made his way down to the beach. Bullet bounded ahead of him and straight into the waves.

"Bullet!"

A wave crested over the dog and sucked him farther out. Bullet paddled back to shore and shook his fur. He barked and barked, until Trace found a stick and threw it into the water for him.

Eli couldn't watch. Every time Bullet hurtled himself gleefully into the water, Eli was convinced it was the last time he'd see his dog. He walked along the beach, daring himself to get closer and closer to the water's edge until he could just kneel down and let the last lip of a wave wash over his hand.

Trace and Teal caught up with him, and Bullet too, although he was slowed up by the great big piece of driftwood he was dragging. At least he'd stopped his incessant barking. Teal's teeth chattered.

"You two better go back up to the fire and get on some dry clothes," Eli said. "Both of you are going to catch your death."

"Yes, Mother!" Teal said with a grin that drooped immediately. "Sorry, Eli."

"It's all right," Eli said as he hustled Teal up the hillside ahead of him. "We're both orphans, Teal. I'm not that fragile."

TRIBAN WAS A COLOSSAL MADHOUSE of Droughtland debauchery and decay unlike Eli had witnessed in all his time since leaving the Key. It was ten times bigger than the largest Key, but it looked as though it had grown in angry fits and starts rather than in the carefully planned manner of the Keys. Dust-delirious carousers and drunks high on ill intentions competed with fat scurrying rats for the largest population. Poppy dust was hawked out of ground-floor windows, street corners, back pockets, and at stands that outnumbered any other kind of ware for sale. Droughtlanders smoked it in pipes and papers and bongs; they snorted it; they rubbed it on their gums; they even cut themselves and sprinkled the wounds with it so it'd go straight into their bloodstream. It was a pageant of hell.

Trace warned the boys not to speak to anyone. He set Teal in front of him in the saddle and ordered Eli and Nappo to stay close as they rode along the tiny, stinking streets. Half-dressed women and bare-chested boys with rouged lips draped themselves in doorways and beckoned them as they passed, dancing provocatively to the buskers that hogged each corner, their music clashing.

Looking down one dark alley, Eli spotted a gang of men attacking another, smaller man. He had to leap off Saber and hold on to Bullet's collar so the dog wouldn't try to sort the men out with his teeth. In seconds the attackers were fleeing and the smaller man was on the ground, clutching his guts as blood seeped through his fingers and spilled onto the dirt.

"Get back on your horse and tie a rope to the dog," Trace hissed at him. "We have to keep moving!"

"But the man's hurt!"

"For good reason, probably," Trace growled as Eli fastened a rope to Bullet's collar. "Let's go!"

The city—the rats, the fights, the sextraders, the beggars, the orphans, the sick and the dying and the dead and the rotting—was a teeth-grinding nightmare. It all seemed louder, raunchier, meaner, sicker, and more depraved than anything Eli had ever seen or heard of, including an entire schooling component devoted to the seven deadly sins as represented in art and history. Trace tied Teal's beloved rag over his eyes so that he might at least be spared the sights.

At long last, Trace led them through an archway and into a small, tidy courtyard.

"This is a safe place." Trace climbed off his horse, untied Teal's blindfold, and lifted him down. A woman with a baby on her hip stepped out of a doorway and cried out with joy.

"You're back!" She embraced Trace. "Are you well? Have you been safe?"

"I'm fine." He kissed her and the baby. "My wife, Anya," Trace explained to the boys.

"You missed her first steps, Trace. Watch." She set the baby down and steadied her on her feet. "Go to Papa."

The baby toddled over, clutched Trace's leg, and stared up at the strangers. "And Charis, my daughter." He gave the toddler his hand and she swung up, nimble as a monkey.

"You are Lisette's boy, of course!" Anya hugged Eli hard. It was a long, tight hug. Eli stiffened. His mother had been the last to hug him like that, and the last to speak to him with the familiar French accent.

"Hi," Eli said, which seemed absurdly insufficient somehow.

Anya gazed in wonder at Trace. "How did you find him?"

"It wasn't so hard."

"*Mon dieu*! Look at you." Anya held Eli's shoulders, her smile slipping, weighed down by grief perhaps, and something else Eli couldn't quite peg. "You look just like—"

"Just like his mother, doesn't he?" Trace kissed Anya hard on the lips. "We're starving! Where's the feast?"

"*Je n'ai pas de* feast." Anya gave Trace a long look. "But there's leftover roast, and vegetables and cheese. I did not know when you would arrive, or who would be with you. I didn't think you'd find him so fast."

Trace and Anya stared at each other, their expressions tender yet slightly wary. Was that the look of lovers long parted, mourning the shared time and distance and experiences lost? Or was it something more, something one or both of them did not want to or could not say in front of him? What was this *You look just like Lisette*? He didn't, not really. Had they seen Seth? Had he been here? Had they done something with him? To him? Eli felt the familiar scurry of fear under his skin. He would trust no one. Not yet.

"There are loaves ready for the oven." She lifted Charis from Trace's arms. "I will go put them in while you boys settle the horses."

Just then, another small figure emerged from the building. It was Althea, the girl from the mountain camp! She waved shyly at Eli, and then followed Anya and Charis back inside.

TRACE AND HIS FAMILY didn't live in Triban. The old rooming house they stayed at belonged to the rebels, and was used to house them, although for all appearances it did look to be in business. An old man, half blind from cataracts, spent his days behind a little window by the front door, acting as proprietor. He peered hard at Eli as he and the others came inside.

"I suppose you look like her, don't you?" He blinked.

"You knew my mother?"

"Never met her, but—"

"Morley, meet Eli. Eli, Morley." Trace pushed Eli down the hall while he hung back to whisper something to the man.

AFTER ANYA SHOWED THEM to their rooms and they'd all had a chance to wash up and have a rest, except for Teal, who hadn't left Anya's side since meeting her, Nappo and Eli met at the top of the stairs to go down for supper.

"What do you think so far?" Eli asked in a whisper.

"Food smells great."

"I mean of this place, of Triban. Of *them*." Eli nodded down the stairs, at the bustle, the noise, the clatter. "Do you think it's on the up and up?"

"Don't know yet."

"But you don't think it's a trap or anything, do you?" Eli grabbed Nappo's arm as he started down the stairs ahead of him. "The food will wait, Nappo. Answer me, do you think they are who they say they are?"

"Sure, why wouldn't they be?"

"I don't know." Eli let go. "Something is odd. The way they're staring at me, like those guys when we came through the hall. They all just stared."

"I don't know. We're new faces. That's reason enough to stare."

"They don't look at you the same way." Eli shook his head. "Maybe this is a set-up. Maybe we should leave."

"Even if it is a set-up, I'm going to eat." Nappo jumped down two steps. "C'mon, I'm starving!"

"I'll be down in a minute." Eli sat on the top stair, still feeling uneasy. Bullet lay down beside him and rested his chin on Eli's thigh.

From the stairs, Eli watched Nappo enter the kitchen. A few people looked up, but not with any particular intensity or interest. A plump woman wearing an apron handed him a stack of plates to put around the table.

The group gathered in the kitchen was all ages, from a baby tucked into a pack on his father's back to old Morley from the front desk. They all looked healthy, and they all knew each other well enough to joke and harass each other in good-natured fun. A group of boys around Eli's age huddled around one end of the long table, going over sample Seduce hands in preparation for the tournament. Once Nappo was finished setting out the plates, he joined them.

Teal, who'd been tailing Anya around the hot kitchen, looked like a different kid. She'd given him a bath and combed out his braid. He kept a firm grip on Anya's skirt with one hand and a firm grip on his rag with the other. He looked younger even than his five years. Teal looked up the stairs and spied Eli.

"Come eat, Eli! There's biscuits an' stew an' roast an' pie!"

The room fell silent, all eyes on the stairs. This is what Eli meant. When it came to him, the atmosphere shifted. He didn't like it, but what could he do? He reluctantly descended into the kitchen. No one breathed a word while they all stared at him.

"What're they all looking at?" Teal pulled at Anya's skirt. "How come they're looking at him funny? He ain't got any sick on him or anything."

"Of course not." Anya put a tureen of stew on the table. "Everyone, this is Eli. He looks so much like his mother, don't you think?"

She had broken the spell. Everyone nodded and launched into stories about Lisette, how brave she was, the sacrifices she'd made to further the revolution, Eli's likeness to her. He guessed he did look like her somewhat. Definitely more like her than Edmund, thankfully. Eli soaked it all up, hoping to remember every word of it, feeling for the first time like things might turn out okay after all. Like he might have a home again someday.

Eli fed most of his meal to Bullet under the table. He just didn't have much of an appetite. He thought about Seth again. Even though they were twins, Seth had Edmund's blond hair. Would they say he looked like Lisette too? These were Lisette's people, so they would see her in them both of course. If that truly was the case. Eli hoped it was, even though a small part of him still felt a wariness he could not explain.

All through dinner, a young man among the boys at the end of the table kept looking at him out the corner of his eye. As the plates were cleared for dessert, Eli met his stare and held it.

"What are you looking at?"

"Nothing." He was tall and lean, his long blond hair in a ponytail, his arms tattooed from shoulders to wrists with thick black swirls and jagged lines. "It's just a little strange . . . that's all." He glanced at Trace, who was busy necking with Anya in front of the stove, Charis tugging at her skirt. "It's bizarre."

"He looks regular, don't he?" Nappo gathered the cards and shuffled them expertly. "A little pale, but regular."

"Yeah, regular," a guy with red hair said. "Sure."

"I'm Jack," the young man with the tattoos said. "And the carrot top is Gavin."

"Apparently you know who I am," Eli said.

Trace looked up just then. "Oy!" He came and leaned over them. "You better not be conspiring to cheat tomorrow. I'm on Eli's team, you know."

"You were going to be on ours!" Gavin cried.

"Got to keep an eye on this one." Trace winked at the others. "He's new at all this."

THE TOURNAMENT WAS HELD in a long hall built especially for such Seduce events. There were no windows to distract the players. The only light was the long metal rack of lanterns suspended above the tables. All along the walls were bunks for the players to take shifts sleeping, because once the tournament began, no one was allowed to leave. Spectators were not permitted, which angered Teal so much that he had to be carried, amidst a full-blown tantrum, away from the entrance by Anya and Althea, who would be back only to drop off food once a day for the players from the rooming house.

Eli sighed once the door shut behind him. He didn't want to play. He'd much rather spend the week with the others at the rooming house, but Trace wouldn't let him out of his sight, except for the night before, when he was locked in his room.

"To keep you safe," Trace had said. "We're all locked in, except Morley, who does the locking and keeps the keys."

The hall stank something awful, a mix of the limey stench from the waste pits at the back and sweat and poppy smoke. The ceiling crawled with a hovering cloud of it. Trace clamped a hand on Nappo's shoulder.

"Think you can handle this?"

"Sure." Nappo's eyes danced from pipe to pipe.

Trace frowned. "You're playing at my table."

"But I told Gavin and Jack I'd take your spot."

"There's plenty who can fill in." Trace steered Nappo and Eli to a corner where there was a little less dust smoking going on. "This is us. Get comfortable."

Eli looked around. The other players all knew Trace, and greeted him with bellowing hellos and hugs. They weren't rebels, though. Eli knew now that if they were they'd be goggling at him, at his likeness to Lisette. Did that mean he hadn't come across any rebels until now? That because no one had recognized him, none of the Droughtlanders he'd met was a rebel? Or were there rebels who wouldn't point themselves out to him, or who didn't know Lisette? That would make sense, given that she'd been in the Eastern Key for so many years. But then rebels came and went from the cell, and met her that way too. Eli tried to sort it all out, but it was a befuddled mess and would distract him from the game, so he set aside his questions and doubts for the moment. He tried to set aside his fear too, but that seemed a constant undershirt, sweaty and dirty, impossible to peel off.

The tournament began with the Seduce song sung by the gameminder, a portly man with a voice that carried far from his platform at the front of the hall. Everyone joined in, singing with more enthusiasm than a coliseum of Keylanders singing the anthem, and by the end everyone was stamping and cheering through the final verse.

Eli mouthed the words. Trace winked at him as he belted out the tune, singing loud enough for the both of them. Nappo was a terrible singer, off key and confident. Between the two of them, Eli figured no one would notice that he didn't know the words.

OH, BUT IT WAS SUCH A BORING GAME. And Eli's table seemed to play very slowly, which was probably why Trace had chosen it, so that Eli could keep up. The pace was nearly putting him to sleep though. He watched with envy as Jack left his table across the hall for his first sleep shift. It was another three hours of playing before a sleep replacement came to relieve their table. Trace let Eli go first.

When he stood, his legs ached. He and Bullet, who'd been lying at his feet the whole time, took a few moments to stretch. It was frowned upon to leave the table to pee, as the lineups for the waste pits were long and it slowed the game, so Eli hadn't stood for hours, and neither had Bullet. He let Bullet out a guarded side door to pee, while Eli hobbled to the back of the hall and got in a line. He'd been shifting his weight from one leg to the other for ages when a gang of boys budged in front of him.

"Hey!" Eli yelped as the biggest of the group, a dark-haired boy with a face full of pimples, shoved him aside. Eli sucked in his breath, desperate not to piss himself. "You can't do that!"

"Piss off, eejit." The boy smelled of body stink and poppy smoke. "Get it?" He started laughing. "Piss off? Hah!"

"Amon, leave him!" A smaller boy pushed through the herd. "Can't you see it? The resemblance?"

Amon fastened his eyes on Eli. Eli watched as the boy's jeering expression morphed into one of confusion. "Can't be."

The boy pulled Amon away. "Leave him, come on."

Amon shrugged off the boy's grip and frowned at Eli. "What's your name?"

"Eli."

"Eli what?"

Why were they asking? Did they know Seth? Were they spies? Or could these losers possibly be Triskelian kids seeing the family resemblance?

"Look, I really have to pee."

"I'm not finished with you!" Amon said as Eli backed away. The little one pulled on Amon, begging him to leave Eli alone. As for Eli, he rushed to a dark corner of the hall behind a bank of sleeping platforms and peed against the stone wall, one eye over his shoulder to make sure Amon and his gang hadn't followed him.

WHEN HE RETURNED to the table after a restless three hours of trying to sleep—made worse by Bullet constantly getting up, turning around in circles, and lying down again on Eli's feet and legs, and stomach at one point—Eli asked Trace if he knew who Amon was.

"Bad seed." Trace didn't look up from his cards. "Stay away from him."

After the tournament, when they were in private and it was safe to ask if Amon was a Triskelian, Eli would. There was something about him that made Eli particularly uneasy.

18

❦

The wounds of the skineater sick surfaced two days after Commander Regis and the rest of the West Droughtland Regiment pulled out of the tiny village, leaving Seth on his knees, begging in the dirt.

"Take me with you!" He was too weak to stand. He grabbed onto the Commander's boot. Commander Regis kicked him off with no less force than he'd use for a dog.

"He touched me!" Regis signalled for his assistant to wipe off his boot.

"I'll die here!" Seth wept. "Don't leave me!" He crawled in Nord's direction. "You can't let him leave me here!"

Nord stared down at him for a long moment, long enough for Seth to let a slip of hope peek through his terror. Seth stretched up a stiff, aching arm. "I can pay you. You won't be sorry."

Nord glanced past Seth to Commander Regis, who was now demanding a new pair of boots. Nord shook his head.

"Sorry, Maddox." He snapped his reins and took off.

Seth slumped forward, forehead in the dirt, as the regiment paraded out, the dust kicked up from the horses making him cough. He figured he would die there like that; the thin dust his only grave. He closed his eyes and thought of nothing at all.

BUT HE DIDN'T DIE THERE. He was left there for many hours, thirsty and sore, while the villagers sat in a circle and argued his fate, but he didn't die. As for the villagers, they were in no hurry to help the Keylander. Many of them wanted to leave him there and let nature take its course, but there were some who didn't. Some wanted to execute him, others were more merciful, though none so merciful as the lifeminder's apprentice.

"I'm sworn to do whatever I can to help anyone who needs it," she argued. Her name was Rosa, and she was just a year older than Seth. "Now you're telling me to do nothing?" She put her hand on her teacher's knee. "Just because he's a Keylander?"

The old lifeminder didn't reply. She was sworn by the same oath as Rosa, but this one time, with this blessed opportunity, a dying Keylander left at their feet like an offering, she wanted to worsen his death, rub salt and caustic powder into his wounds when they surfaced, which would be very soon. If she had her way she'd make his death come very slowly and with the most pain she could muster out of her concoctions. She searched inside herself for some sign of compassion. There was none, and she wasn't surprised.

"I'm supposed to ignore him?" Rosa asked again.

The lifeminder, who'd been beaten, or raped, or robbed, or left to starve or die from thirst, or a combination of the above by too many Guards to count, could only shrug.

"Some life is worth more than others."

"I guess we haven't gotten to that lesson yet." Rosa fought to keep her voice steady. She looked down the road at the heap in the dirt. "I thought I was duty bound to treat any creature who needs it, but I guess not, huh?"

The other villagers were silent.

The lifeminder sighed. "You are learning, even as we sit here and discuss it."

"Learning what?" Rosa stood. "That you're a hypocrite?" Again, silence.

"I won't have him in my house just to serve your childish ignorance!" Rosa's father yelled as Rosa stalked off toward their hut.

"Or in the yard, either," her mother whispered to him.

"Or in the yard!"

Rosa disappeared into the hut. She reappeared with a cart, her gloves and mask tucked into her basket of lifeminding supplies.

"Rosa, he's an animal!" her mother pleaded with her. "Don't help him."

"I set the dog's leg when it broke, didn't I?"

"Rosa." Her mother gripped her arm. "He'll die anyway. His fever hasn't been treated. That will make the wounds worse, you said so yourself, didn't you? Didn't you say that? Isn't that what the lifeminder taught you?"

"Each morning," Rosa said as she pulled away from her mother, "I'll need food and water for three. You can leave it at Mina's gate if you don't want to come to the door."

"You'd have him in Mina's house?" Rosa's mother shook her head, disgusted. "After he had his way with her?"

"She's so delirious, Mom, she'll never know."

"I didn't raise you this way."

Rosa hugged her. "Yes, you did."

Rosa slipped her mask on and walked past her father and the lifeminder and the others without looking at them. Her older brother hung his head. Her little sister ran after her, crying, until her father pulled her back. Rosa struggled, alone, to get the Keylander onto the cart. Once she had him balanced enough that she could pull the cart without him falling off, she took the long way around the village. She left the cart and the Keylander in the backyard and went in to check on Mina first.

She would die very soon. Her wounds smelled about a week away from death. There wasn't much Rosa could do for her. She was surprised that the Keylander wasn't worse off by now than he was. But then, maybe they knew something about it that Rosa didn't, although if they'd managed to develop a vaccine that could keep up with the constantly diverging strains, she would've certainly heard about it in the lifeminder gossip that spread through the markets like its own kind of virus.

Mina didn't stir while Rosa cleaned her and changed her dressings and poultices. That done, Rosa pulled the cart to the door and dragged the Keylander onto the only other bed. As she stripped him out of his sweat-soaked clothes, the villagers pelted the hut with stones.

"Let him die!" Mina's brother hollered from a safe distance.

"Get him away from my Mina!" Mina's mother's voice was choked with tears.

Rosa watched from the window. They wouldn't come any closer, and Rosa doubted that even the lifeminder would pay her a visit, malicious or kind. She went back to the Keylander. His eyes were open now. He blinked slowly at her.

"What's your name?" she asked.

Seth licked his lips.

"You're thirsty?" Rose tipped a cup to his lips. "Tiny sips, or you'll be sick."

Seth took a few swallows, and then licked his lips again. "Seth."

"I'm Rosa." Rosa straightened and pulled her shoulders back, hoping she looked formidable and stern. She didn't want to seem kind or merciful, so she added, "I'll be minding you until you die, which will be soon, I hope."

19

⚜

Thanks to Trace and Nappo, Eli's table came in sixth overall at the end of the tournament. Jack and Gavin's came in first. The cash pot was so huge that it took all the players from the rooming house to take it back there, except for what they paid to several burly acquaintances to help guard them and the wealth as they crossed the city.

Back at the rooming house, while the money was being counted at the kitchen table, Trace doled out the beer and toasted Jack and Gavin.

"To the best Seducers of the revolution!"

After a couple of pints of beer, Eli forgot all about his intention to ask Trace about Amon. Instead, he slouched in a chair and watched bleary-eyed as everyone danced and sang long into the night. He was tired, but he didn't want anyone to think he was a baby, so he forced himself to stay awake until all the children had fallen asleep one by one on cloaks and blankets and couches. He was still the first of the older ones to go up to bed. He was nearly asleep, but not quite, when he heard the key turn in his door, even though the celebration was carrying on full-tilt downstairs.

THE NEXT AFTERNOON Eli, the brothers, Althea, and Trace and his family left for Triskelia. Others would set off in a few days, and still others several days after the second group.

"So it's not so obvious," Trace explained once they were well clear of Triban. "We all take different routes, and none of us knows what the others' are." That morning, everyone who wanted or needed to go to Triskelia drew routes and leaving times out of Morley's hat. Trace hadn't smiled when he read the one they'd be taking, but now he grinned. "We got the most direct route of them all."

This was great news to Eli. Travelling in the cold rain and icy wind off the ocean made his bones ache and left him constantly struggling to get warm. It was hard to believe he'd ever missed rain at all. It was hard to believe that there were a million miles of this continent that were desperate for rain. And now, here, after personally knowing the troubles of extreme drought, he was tired of what little rain the rebel cloudminders could conjure. It didn't seem to matter how many layers he put on, or how often he changed his wet socks for dry ones, he was cold right through. The first night, he was too cold to sleep even a wink.

They'd camped at a poppy farm Trace knew the owners of, and even though Trace had Nappo set up his tent right beside his, Eli still heard him sneak out in the middle of the night.

In the morning, Nappo had dark rings under his eyes.

Trace sat in the mouth of his and Anya's tent and laced up his boots. He eyed the boys, who were drowsily nursing their tea by the fire.

"Didn't find any, did you?" He patted Nappo's head and then poured himself some tea.

"I didn't go looking."

"You did so. I heard you. But they got it good and locked up, not only 'cause I warned them about you, but to keep it safe from anyone else who's stupid enough to try."

"I had to pee, that's all."

"One hell of a long piss, then," Trace said. "What do you think, Eli? You think he was looking for dust?"

"I'm staying out of it," Eli muttered.

"Smart." Nappo left the fire. "Both of you can just leave me alone. I don't need this shit."

"Don't talk like that in front of the children," Trace said.

Nappo ignored him, wordlessly pulling down his tent and saddling up Dawn. He was ready to go by the time Anya was just giving breakfast to Althea and Teal. "I'm leaving. Which way are we headed?"

Trace shook his head. "We travel together."

"But I want to leave now."

"You will wait until we are all ready, and then we will leave. Together."

Nappo climbed off his horse. "You won't tell me?"

Trace thanked Anya for the plate of food she handed him and ignored Nappo.

"You're an ass, you know that?" Nappo stalked off toward a grove of trees at the back of the farm.

"I told you, don't talk like that in front of the children!"

"Maybe you're a little hard on him, love." Althea helped Charis steer her fork into her mouth.

"He's too easy to upset," Trace said through a mouthful of food.

"Then why not leave him alone?" Eli asked.

"If he wants to be a Triskelian, he'll have to develop a much thicker skin." Trace poured himself and Eli more tea. "We won't have him as he is now."

"But where else would he go?"

"That'll be his problem, if he doesn't change for the better."

"He'll change."

Nappo was halfway to the trees, walking fast and muttering to himself.

"I hope you're right." Trace nodded at Teal, who was vying for a position on Anya's lap beside Charis. "Because we'd keep the little one. He's a natural."

"How do you know?"

"He's like Althea. Scrappy and smart and almost fearless."

"That's why you took Althea? So she can become a rebel?"

Trace nodded.

"And myself?" Eli asked shyly. "Do you think I'll make a good rebel?"

Trace nodded again. "It's in your blood."

"It's in my brother's blood too."

"Don't forget." Trace eyed him. "You and your brother have your father in you too."

"Does that make me less of a rebel?"

"No, but it may be why your brother will never be a rebel at all."

"Back in Triban," Eli started hesitantly, "I thought you might've led me into a trap. I thought it might've been a set-up."

Trace smiled. "It's all a bit mysterious, isn't it?"

"Seth *is* after me." Eli pulled his cloak hood over his head as the rain started again. "There might be others after me too, I don't know. But if Seth ever finds me, he'll kill me."

"He won't find you."

"But what if he does?"

"I'd kill him first, before he could touch you or your—" Trace stopped. "Don't worry, Eli. He can't hurt you now."

Eli said nothing. He hadn't ever thought about actually killing Seth. That was a cold thought, even more chilling than the rain.

ELI TOOK UP the rear of the group when they set off again. He pulled out his knife and jabbed at the air. If Seth found him, Eli wouldn't be able to fight him off unarmed. He hadn't ever won a fistfight with his brother before Seth had Guard training, so there'd be no way he could fight him off now that he was a Guardy. But using his knife? Eli couldn't imagine stabbing his own brother. He closed his eyes and tried to imagine what it would take to ram the blade into his brother's stomach, like the man he'd seen bleeding to death in the alley back in Triban. The idea made his own stomach flip.

He opened his eyes. He just wouldn't be able to do it. Trace could, though. He could fight Seth. Perhaps, if it ever came to that, Trace could wound him enough to capture him, but not kill him. Eli had to admit that he'd rather Seth wasn't killed, even if it meant Seth would be a threat or a prisoner for the rest of his life. Eli was disappointed in himself. What about wishing him dead? What about wishing him that suffocating box at the Foothills Market? What about wishing his brother's bones into cutlery for the Droughtlander who caught him and orchestrated his death? It was different when it came right down to it. It was hard to want to kill the twin who you played with, fought with, and knew since conception, no matter how fraught the relationship, or how evil the twin.

BY THE SECOND DAY of travel Eli had given up trying to guess how far they were from Triskelia, and Trace wouldn't say. Eli tried to distract himself by taking in the sights, but they were keeping to a route with lots of sicks and dust smokers, and with sextraders lining the roads alongside beggars and travellers looking to hire a ride. On the morning of the sixth day Trace woke him early, the moon low on the horizon, the valley they were camped in white with plump fog.

"You might want to wash up," Trace whispered. "We'll be at Triskelia by nightfall."

"We're that close?" Eli was suddenly very awake.

Trace put his finger to his lips and nodded. "Don't tell the brothers."

"Does Anya know?"

"Of course. She's been on this route many times. Even Charis probably knows we're nearly there, but I don't want the others to know. That way, they'd have a harder time describing the route if they were ever captured."

"But they would never tell!"

"You never know," Trace said. "Torture can be a very effective tool."

Torture. The word alone seemed a punishment. Eli left it at that.

"I'm going to go check the traps." Trace patted his shoulder. "Don't go back to sleep."

ELI TOOK A BAR OF SOAP and a towel and clean clothes down to the river's edge. It was too cold to strip, so cold that Bullet wouldn't so much as dip a paw in or take a drink. Eli washed quickly, eager to get back to the fire. There was frost on the ground, and his breath hung in the cold air. He relished the idea of having a warm place to sleep that night. He decided it was too cold to wash his hair, so he wetted an end of the towel with water and soap and rubbed his head with it. That would have to do.

Anya beamed at him when he returned to camp. "You look very handsome."

"Thanks." Eli sat beside her. He hadn't ever been alone with her before. He didn't know what to talk to her about. She was breastfeeding Charis, which made him not want to look at her, but he felt her gaze on him. He glanced at her out the corner of his eye. She stared sadly at him.

"Is something wrong?"

"No. Nothing is wrong." She brushed his bangs away from his eyes. "You do look like your mother. I miss her."

"You knew her well?"

"Very well."

"As children?"

"Yes." Anya wiped a tear from her cheek as Nappo and Teal began rustling about in their tent. "Someday, I will tell you."

There was so much he wanted to know *now* though. "Did she ever love my father?"

"*Je ne sais pas*, Eli." Anya looked away. "I don't know." She rearranged the blanket around Charis and sighed. Finally, she shrugged. "Not at first, that much I know."

Teal emerged from the tent, rubbing his eyes and shivering.

"Go get on your cloak, Teal." Anya waved him back into the tent. "Eli, No matter what happens, no matter what you discover at Triskelia, you must understand that your mother loved you very, very much. She was forced to make sacrifices that no one should have to make."

Teal emerged again and ran full steam for Anya, his cloak half on. Anya scooped him into her lap with her free arm and snuggled him under the blanket with Charis.

As the others got up, and Trace came back with a rabbit to roast for breakfast, Eli thought about Anya's cryptic words. What exactly would he discover in Triskelia?

20

❧

In his more lucid moments, Seth begged Rosa to kill him.

"I can't live with these scars!" He groped for her, but she'd learned to stay well back from him when he was like this. "How can I go home?"

"You don't have to worry about that," Rosa said from across the hut, where she was mixing a paste for his wounds. "You'll be dead."

But would he? He should have died days ago, when his wounds were at their widest, but he was hanging on, and his wounds were starting to close up. It wasn't possible for him to survive, though. His fever had been untreated at first. No one survived if the first fevers weren't treated and the tinctures administered immediately. Mina had been treated, but she hadn't lived. Why should he?

"Bring me my gun!" Seth writhed on the bed, wishing he could get it himself. He would put it in his mouth and blow his head off. That way, there'd be no way this witch could keep him from death.

"They took it when they left you here." Rosa carried the paste to his bedside. "Now, stop moving so I can change your dressings." Before, when he was feverish more often than not, she would wait until he was out cold before changing the dressings, but these days he was lucid more often. This was a problem.

"No!" Seth knocked the bowl to the ground. "Let me die! Leave me alone!" He didn't look at her, couldn't look at her, this Droughtland wench who'd seen him like this, covered in seeping wounds, soiling his pants, crying for his maman, which Rosa knew was French for mother.

"Fine. I'll wait until you're sleeping." Rosa scooped the paste back into the bowl.

"Then I'll stay awake."

"If you like." Rosa shrugged. "I don't care." She left him, writhing and complaining, and went to the window where she spent many slow hours. She could see a slice of the courtyard from there. They were setting up the tables for a common meal. Someone must've caught some game, something large enough to feed everyone. A deer, perhaps, or a boar. Meat. She'd miss out, stuck there in Mina's hut with a dying Keylander.

Finally, near dark, Seth's eyes fluttered and he felt himself falling asleep.

"Get away from me," he mumbled as Rosa leaned over him.

"You've soiled yourself again." Rosa wished this business didn't always make her blush. "I need to wash your clothes." She pulled back the sheet, grimacing at the smell.

Seth struggled to wakefulness. "I'll do it myself." He shoved her away.

Rosa stumbled, surprised at his increasing strength. He was much stronger these days. Yet he should be closer to death. Was it that she was that good a lifeminder? Her older brother had always told her she should just settle for becoming a herbminder, but this, this just proved that she was a born lifeminder, didn't it? Or were Keylanders more immune?

Under the blankets, Seth wrestled out of his underlinen. "You think I didn't hear you laughing at it the first time?"

"I wasn't laughing." Rosa bit her lip. "That was a gasp."

"And then you laughed." Seth nearly wept from shame as he balled up his soiled clothes and handed them to her.

"You'll wash yourself?"

"Give me water and a cloth. I'll do it." Seth looked away. "Why did you gasp?"

"I've never seen one like that."

"It's bigger than usual?"

"Hah!" Rosa held the stinking bundle at arm's length. "You *would* think that." She went out the back to put the things in the wash bucket to soak in the sun.

"Then what is it?"

Rosa waited, her back to the door, giving him time to clean himself up. If he continued to get better the diarrhea would end soon, as it did with the few others she'd known who'd survived the skineater sick.

"It's misshapen."

Seth looked down at his penis. No one had said anything during basic training, and there'd been lots of opportunities to be ridiculed in the showers and barracks. None of the Droughtland girls he'd been with had said anything either. But then he hadn't asked what they thought of it, had he? Misshapen? Not possible. She was teasing, or was ignorant, or both.

"You've been cut," Rosa added from the doorway. "I've heard about it from the other girls." She was always hidden when the regiments came. Her village couldn't spare her should she catch a sick from a Guardy. "But you're normal, I suppose. For a Keylander."

"Droughtlander men are different?"

"Droughtlander men are better."

Seth fell silent. Why argue? When he was well enough he'd be rid of this girl, although what he would do with himself, he didn't know. Even though his wounds were healing they'd still leave wicked scars. He'd really rather be dead. He glanced across the hut at his pack. Had the Commander really taken his gun, or had she taken it and sold it, or hidden it somewhere?

He set the bowl of dirty water on the little table and very quietly slid his legs over the edge of the bed. He inched forward until his feet touched the cool dirt floor. He hadn't done anything more than sit up for weeks, so when he tried to stand he wasn't surprised to find himself slipping. He tried to steady himself on the table, but he just pulled it down with him, tipping the dirty water over him.

"Did you faint?" Rosa hurried inside. "Are you okay?"

"I tried to get up." Seth covered himself with his hands. "I tripped."

"You didn't trip." Rosa pushed the bowl away and offered him her hand.

"You're not wearing the gloves," Seth said as she helped him sit on a stool.

"You're not contagious any more." She poured hot water from the stove into a clean bowl and began washing the muck off his back.

"Then why doesn't anyone come?"

Rosa hesitated. "Because they still think you're dying."

"And if they knew I was better?"

"You're not better yet."

"But if they knew I was getting better?" Seth took her wrist, and Rosa let him.

"Mina's brothers would kill you." His eyes were green with flecks of hazel, still somewhat dilated from the sick. "And mine. And others too, my father among them, I fear."

"You *fear*?"

Rosa pulled away and handed him the cloth. "You can reach to clean the rest."

She washed her hands and began chopping vegetables for their supper. When her mother had come earlier with food, Rosa had been so proud about her lifeminder skills that she'd told her the Keylander wasn't contagious any more. She just had to tell someone, and she'd made her mother swear she wouldn't tell the others.

"Then you've done your job here." Her mother handed her the basket of food but would not meet her eyes. "Now let the others do what they need to do."

Mina's sick-ravaged body was out back, in a shallow grave Rosa had dug herself. They would give her a proper burial once the danger of contagion from the Keylander was gone. But Rosa knew that's not what her mother meant. Rosa looked past her mother at her father, who stood in the middle of the courtyard watching them with her and Mina's brothers. There was an energy about them, angry and fierce, like a heat rising from their skin. They badly wanted to get their hands on Seth. But what were her ethics if she nursed someone back to health only to send them on their way to a violent death?

Rosa stoked the fire under the oven and then stuck the vegetables in to cook. She glanced at Seth, who was wiping himself dry and pulling on clean clothes. Across the little hut, Seth could feel her eyes on him. He didn't have the energy to cover himself. Let her look, she'd already seen him at his worst. What more was there?

Rosa did look. Seth had been very muscular, never mind heavy, the day the Guard had left him behind. He'd since wasted away from the sick, and the wounds had ravaged his skin. He looked more like a Droughtlander now, or almost. His hair was still too short, and if he ever stripped, or was accidentally seen peeing, he'd never pass as a real Droughtlander. Even if Rosa could secret him away from the village, where would he go? He'd never be accepted in any Key, not now, not with the scars. Keylanders were so ignorant about the sicks.

But what would he do in the Droughtland? Would he off himself at the first opportunity? Should she just turn him over to the others and let them have him, rather than risk taking the side of a Keylander who claimed he just wanted to die anyway? Rosa's older brother had always said she was stubborn and bullheaded and always had to have things her way. But now, for once, she didn't know what she wanted. This was worse—not knowing where to go from here, how to make this turn into a happy ending, or at least one without any more harm coming to anyone, Seth included. And herself too. There were many in the village who would never forgive her for helping the Keylander.

[THREE]

TRISKELIA

21

༜

As night began to fall and Trace made no mention of setting up camp, Nappo and Teal guessed they were nearing Triskelia.

"We're almost there, aren't we?" Nappo scanned the dark horizon. "We're close, right, Trace?"

"Keep your voice down, boy," Trace growled.

"Aw, there's not even a rat out here, no one will hear."

"You have no idea what's out here." Trace pulled his horse alongside Nappo's and gripped his arm. "So keep your voice down, or I'll tie you to a tree and leave you and then you'll find out exactly how many rats there are out here."

Nappo shut up.

Eli wished they could go faster, but the cart carrying the children and their things moved slowly along the muddy trail, and Trace insisted that they all stay together.

WHAT HAD ELI EXPECTED to find after all these months of wondering, dreaming, hoping? He'd imagined a fortress with high stone walls rimmed with jagged glass, or a labyrinth of tunnels, or a roving camp of caravans. His hopes careened ahead, building mythical architecture worthy of admiration and awe out of the rocks and trees in front of him. When Trace called for him, and they rode ahead of the others for once, those same hopes went hurtling off the cliff they stopped at after a short ride through brush.

"There it is."

Far below, inland a ways from a wide river shimmering silver in the moonlight, across which a thick bank of fog was rolling in, lay a sprawling, disorganized mass of wretched shacks and huts dappled with thousands of lanterns and candles illuminating windows. The lanes, if you could name them as such, wound in nonsense routes like the path of a drunkard toward a crumbling group of dark stone buildings at the epicentre of the mess.

"That's Triskelia?" Eli wanted to weep. He wanted to get off his horse and fall to his knees and weep, and then when he was finished weeping, he wanted to head east and away from there as fast as Saber could carry him. He would live in the mountains, or in the foothills, but not in that cesspool. "That's it?"

But Trace was shaking his head. "The Colony of the Sicks," he said, watching as Eli struggled to keep the shock off his face.

"But Triskelia—"

"—needs protecting, doesn't it?"

"I don't understand."

It had stopped raining. Trace pushed his hood back. "Think of it this way. If you were your brother, would you want to make your way through that, if that's what you had to do to find out if there were any rebels in there?"

"Never mind Seth! I'm *me*, and *I* don't want to go through that to find out if there are any rebels in there."

Trace laughed. "It may look higgledy-piggledy, but there is a method to it all." He pointed out a lane that twisted between the shacks. "See that one there? The one that starts by the burnt shack? That's the safe-passage route, right now anyway."

"How can it be safe if it's surrounded by sicks?"

"Every single one of those people down there are Triskelian allies. Triskelians bring them here, sick, to help keep the Keylanders back. Many of them die here, but not at all in vain." He pointed out a tall structure at one edge, great pillars of smoke pumping out of its three chimneys and mingling with the fog.

"Crematorium?" Eli thought he could smell it, now that Trace had pointed it out.

"Just a big stove, really. If you want ashes, you take a scoop from the pile. That's those who die. The ones that don't, the ones who survive and aren't contagious, they move to the shacks that line a lane. When the whole lane is lined with safe shacks, it becomes the safe passage and the old route is retired. When it's time to change the passage, they move on."

"But how can you be sure they won't tell anyone where it is?"

"Some call it loyalty. Some call it fear." Trace flicked his reins and the horses started down the trail into the settlement, just as the others caught up behind them. "We have many skilled herbminders and lifeminders to tend to them, and clean water, and more supplies than they'd see in any village or market. Most who do survive wouldn't have if they hadn't come here."

"Where will we stay?"

"The buildings in the centre, that's Triskelia proper. What the Keylanders think is the hospital."

The buildings were tall, taller than the tallest buildings in the Eastern Key. And mostly dark, with just the odd light dotting the shadows. It almost looked abandoned, except there was smoke coming out of some of the chimneys, so at least there was the promise of a warm fire, if nothing else.

IT SEEMED to take hours to reach the centre, hours of the ceaseless noisy chaos of a sick colony, manufactured or not—the thin wails of babies, the moans and screams of the ill, the sloshing of soiled water tossed out of doorways, the random clatter of life lived by the most desperate and poor. Nappo had caught up to Eli, but he hadn't said a word.

"They say this is the safe way," Eli offered.

Nappo just nodded.

"Did Anya tell you?"

Nappo nodded again, his gaze fixed somewhere ahead, or somewhere imaginary, safe.

Eli fell silent, fear and anticipation dumbfounding him. What would it be like? What would happen now? Did this dark place harbour answers? At long last, Trace stopped the group in a damp stone entryway, the end lit by two lanterns. The horses' hooves echoed on the cobblestones, and each wet drip from the arch landed with a resounding plop.

"You were scared, even after what I told you." Trace shook his head. "You have to start to trust, Eli."

"I believed you."

"But you were scared."

"I wasn't scared!" Nappo offered.

"Don't lie," Eli said. "You were so! You couldn't even speak."

"You calling me a liar?"

"Then admit it, you were scared!"

"Don't call my brother a liar!" Teal yelled. "He's never scared! And neither me!"

"As if." Eli snorted. "I'd like to see you go two minutes without your blankie. You're just a baby."

"Don't call him a baby!" Althea put a protective arm around Teal.

"Ooo, Tealie's got a girlfriend." Nappo made kissing sounds.

"That's enough, everyone!" Anya shifted the weight of Charis, fast asleep, off her back. "We're all tired and hungry and cold."

Trace got off the horse and took Charis from Anya. He gave the older children a reproachful look that made Eli wish he'd kept his mouth shut.

Anya climbed off the cart and straightened her clothes. "Come on. All of you."

One by one the children climbed down from the cart or slid off the horses. Anya stood them in a line, youngest to eldest, while Trace led the horses and cart away. Anya smoothed out Althea's messy braids and buttoned up Teal's shirt correctly. She licked her palm and wiped a streak of dirt from Nappo's cheek.

"Get off me!" Nappo pushed her away. "Mother your own kid."

"We've been soft on you, Nappo." Anya pulled her arms into the warmth of her cloak and looked down her nose at him. "There is an expectation of respect here. I worry that you will fail."

"I don't fail."

"Dear Nappo," Anya said as the children's attention was drawn to two enormous wooden doors slowly creaking open nearby. "You've never been as challenged as you will be here."

IT WAS SO WARM inside that Eli's skin shivered with delight. The long hall was well-lit, with heavy tapestries covering the windows. Hundreds of people crowded along the sides of the room, all of them staring at the travellers.

Anya, Charis, and Althea were immediately swept into the bosom of a group of women and children who'd been waiting for them just inside the door. Charis was passed among the women and older kids, who covered her in kisses and held her high like a trophy while Anya and Althea were petted and hugged and welcomed and handed mugs of tea. Trace held back, although several men called to him and began approaching.

Trace stepped forward and the boys filed in behind him. When the men saw the boys, they all stopped and looked at one another.

One of them, a man with a ragged braided beard and stars tattooed on his temples, pointed and cried, "It's him!"

The crowd surged forward as though it was one curious being. The women stopped fussing over the baby and rushed forward in the throng.

"It is!" one of the women cried. "He's come!"

And then it was pandemonium. Everyone hurried toward the boys, pushing at each other, straining to get a look while Bullet barked madly, not sure who to fend off first.

"What do they want with us?" Eli screamed at the brothers as he backed toward the door.

Nappo and Teal stayed put, getting jostled into the mass as the crowd moved forward.

"It's not us!" Nappo cried, out of sight now. "It's you they're after!"

Behind Eli, Anya climbed up on a table and waved her hands. "Everyone, stop! Please, you're making him nervous!"

As soon as she spoke the crowd stopped and pulled back to either side of a long purple carpet that ran the length of the hall. Nappo and Teal pushed through from behind a group of boys and returned to Eli's side.

"What is it about me?" Eli pointed at the brothers. "You don't stare at them like that." No one looked away, but no one offered an explanation either. "What are you all staring at me for?" When still no one uttered a word, Eli shouted, "Tell me! What is it?"

AS HIS SHOUTS ECHOED off the stone walls, a small voice arose from the belly of the crowd.

"Welcome, child."

The crowd parted to let an old woman through.

Eli stared at her. Her cloak was crimson and purple, her white hair in a complex plait pinned atop her head.

Something about her was familiar. Did she remind him of someone? Had she been in the gardens that day? Had she known Lisette?

The woman reached a hand out to Eli and smiled warmly at him.

Eli felt a strange heat spread over him.

"I know you," he whispered. "I know you, don't I?"

She squeezed his hand. Her grip was firm, and warm. "Do you?"

"You seem familiar to me."

Someone in the crowd laughed. The old woman glanced sharply over her shoulder and there was silence again.

"Come." She took his arm and steered him down a long hallway that led off the great room. Behind them the crowd erupted, everyone chattering at once so that Eli couldn't make out anything that was said, although it was surely entirely about him. The old woman led Eli up several flights of stairs and into a small room with a fireplace in the corner. She pointed to a stool in front of the fire. "Sit, child."

Then Eli remembered where he'd seen her before. "You were my mother's cook!" Then he completed the thought. "But she didn't have a cook."

"I suppose I was her cook, in a way." She laughed. "But I was more than that. I am much more than that. Eli, I'm your grandmother."

Eli remembered screaming at Lisette to get away from the filthy Droughtlander she'd embraced that night. He remembered brushing off his arm where Lisette had touched him afterward. Her own mother. His *grandmother*. His grandmother, who he'd always thought had died years ago in a tragic fire.

"That night." Eli squeezed his eyes shut and swallowed hard. He did not want to cry. "I didn't know." He looked up at the old woman. "I'm sorry." Of course she was his grandmother—the high forehead, the narrow nose, the same full lips as his mother.

"I am Celeste," she said.

"I am Eli."

She winked. "I know who you are."

"What were you doing there that night?"

"You will find out in time." She put her hands on her knees. "Now, it is time to rest."

"There's so much to ask you." Eli felt faint with the desire to know. "I want to know everything. The boy who fell, who was he?"

Celeste crossed the room to the bed and turned down the blankets. She picked up a pillow and held it to her chest. "His name was Quinn." She hugged the pillow a moment more, and then fluffed it and set it down. "Enough for now."

"What do I call you? Grandmother?" The word felt strange on his lips.

"That is up to you. The others call me Nana."

"The others?"

"Your cousins, and your cousins' children."

"I have cousins?"

"Many."

"Here?"

"Some are here. You will meet them tomorrow." Celeste went to answer a knock at the door. She let in a stooped elderly man and took a tray from him. He puffed on a pipe, looked at Eli and did not smile.

Celeste spoke a few quiet words to him, and he left, closing the door firmly behind him.

"Who's that?"

"Tomorrow, Eli." Celeste set the tray on a table beside the bed and filled a mug from the steaming carafe. "Have some tea, then sleep."

"I can't sleep! Tell me everything!"

"Tomorrow can only come when today has been put to rest." She put the mug in his hands and leaned down to pat Bullet. "Now go to bed. Both of you."

When she left she locked the door behind her. Eli took a sip of the hot drink and moved closer to the fire, sure that he would be up all night, millions of questions poking and prodding him awake.

22

Rosa's mother did not keep the secret of Seth's miraculous recovery. She did for a while, all the time pressing Rosa to leave the hut and let Mina's brothers and the other angry villagers have their way with the Keylander, but the more her mother pushed, the stronger Rosa grew in her conviction that it was wrong to let Seth be killed.

"It's not because I like you," Rosa said to him as they planned a way of getting him out of the village. "I'd do the same if you were a dog." Her mother had come by earlier to tell Rosa that she'd tell the others that night, after her father returned with the other traders who'd been to market.

"When night comes, you must leave the hut." Her mother gripped Rosa's wrists. "If you do not, they'll suspect you've been harbouring him on purpose and they'll come after you."

When she said that, Rosa realized something horrible. Her mother hadn't laid eyes on Seth since Rosa had brought him to the hut. She hadn't seen how well he'd recovered, how even his sick wounds had healed better than most. They had scarred, yes, but several weeks ago. Now, except for the shorter hair, he could pass for any Droughtlander who'd survived the skineater sick. If she were to have given him over to Mina's brothers, she should have done so weeks sooner.

"They'll see me as a traitor." Rosa wrapped two mugs in a dishcloth and put them in a pack. It had been Mina's pack, as had all the things Rosa was putting in it.

"You were just doing your job." Seth had already finished packing. He sat on the edge of the bed, ready to go. "Tell them I was holding you captive. Tell them I was going to kill you."

"All the times I spoke with my mother." Rosa shook her head. "All the times she came to the window."

"She never saw me. Tell her I was on the floor, holding a knife to your stomach, ready to cut out your guts if you said the wrong thing."

"They would never believe that." She paused, a sack of nuts in one hand. "You should've been too sick for that. And I could've slipped you a sleeping powder any time. They all know you were at my mercy."

"For the record, I did not want your mercy."

Rosa ignored the dig. "There's no other choice. I have to leave." She fixed her gaze on him. "I don't want to go with you, you know."

"I know."

"Everything was fine before you came. You've ruined my life."

"And you ruined mine by letting me live."

Rosa scowled. "You can't sit there and honestly tell me you'd rather be dead."

"Than scarred like this and unable to ever go home?" Seth held out his ravaged arms. "Yes. I would rather be dead."

"Then why am I helping you escape? I could just go myself, and leave you to be dealt with by Mina's brothers, my father, all the villagers who'd like a slice of Keylander to nail on their door."

"You saved me from the sick." Seth shrugged. "That wasn't my choice. But to not be ripped apart by a pack of Droughtlanders, that is my choice now."

"We're not animals, Seth."

"You are, in a way."

"Would an animal have the knowledge to save you from the sick?" Rosa's cheeks flushed with anger. "Would an animal help you escape from death not only once, but for a second time?"

"You're not like the others."

"I am so."

"You're not."

"I am!" Rosa set her pack at the door. "The only difference is that I took an oath to help people. I can't break it. If I wasn't the lifeminder's apprentice, I'd be out there waiting to get a slice of you myself."

"I don't think that's true."

"Well, you can think whatever you bloody well want." Rosa pulled aside the curtain a tiny bit and peered out. "The minute I can get away from you, I promise you I will. And then you'll be on your own in the Droughtland. You won't last two hours. You'll get your wish. You'll die. It's only a matter of time. Satisfied?"

THEY LEFT OUT THE BACK while the villagers who'd stayed behind welcomed the ones who'd been to market. There were carts to unload, partners to embrace, children to sweep up and be covered in kisses by parents who'd been away. Rosa's mother was out there, welcoming back her father. As she fastened the packs onto a neighbour's horse she'd coaxed into the yard with a carrot, she could hear her little sister squeal with delight. Her father was probably swinging her onto his shoulders, like he used to do with Rosa when she was little.

When the horse was packed, she helped Seth out the back door.

"I could still leave you." They walked slowly, Seth steadying himself on her arm, his muscles atrophied and still fatigued from the sick, although he'd been exercising in the little hut for over a week in anticipation of this day. "I could leave, and let them have you." But she did not take her arm away.

She helped him up onto the horse.

"No saddle?"

"Where would I get a saddle?"

"Where'd you get the horse?"

"I stole it." Great shame filled her voice. "It's the only thing I have ever stolen, besides what we're taking from Mina. I will not steal more than I need."

Rosa helped Seth get settled, and then climbed up behind him and reached around to loop the reins around her palms. She hesitated, listening to the revelry coming from the courtyard. A group of men were singing a song she'd never heard before. That had always been her favourite thing the traders brought back from market: new songs, new stories, tales and music she immediately committed to memory.

"We go now, or we don't go at all," Seth said gently. "The decision is yours."

Rosa nodded. She snapped the reins and the horse took off at a gallop, through the little gate and across the plains toward the dark blue tail of dusk.

23

W hen Eli awoke the next morning he was foggy and confused and sore. He had not moved one inch during the night. He didn't know where he was and, for a brief second, who he was. He told this to Celeste, who'd come in to wake him, and she explained that she'd put a sleeping powder in his tea.

"You needed the rest." She drew the tapestry from the window, letting in a sharp light, diffused somewhat by the thick fog that blanketed the compound and the sick colony beyond. "There is much to see and learn. I'm not sure what should come first." She clasped her hands in front of her. "Breakfast, perhaps?"

"Yes, please." Eli rubbed the sleep from his eyes. "I'm starving."

"I think you should take your breakfast in here." Celeste looked around the room. "I think it's best to wait to meet the others."

"I'd like to have breakfast with the others, though. Why not?"

Celeste shook her head. "There are things you need to know before joining them. Shall I send the brothers up to eat with you? So you're not lonely?"

Eli nodded, wishing he could think of something to say to make Celeste change her mind. He wanted to push past her out the room and run up and down the corridors, drinking in the sights, meeting everyone, discovering this new world. But Anya came to mind, and her warning to be respectful, and so Eli forced himself to stay on the bed lest he get off and not be able to hold himself back from the curiosity that threatened to catapult him out of the room, despite his better judgment. Celeste left, coming back about half an hour later followed by Nappo and Teal, each armed with a tray piled high with food.

The brothers looked at Eli strangely as they put down the trays.

"What?"

Teal and Nappo looked at each other. "We can't say," Nappo finally blurted. "The old lady made us promise."

"About what?" Eli helped himself to a roll, still warm from the oven. He slathered it with jam and butter. "Are you my servants or something now? Is that why you won't talk to me?"

"Servants? Nuh-uh!" The brothers laughed. Eli felt a stab of envy. Already they knew more than he did. It wasn't fair.

"We shouldn't have secrets. If it hadn't been for me you wouldn't even be here, you know."

"We can't tell you," Nappo said. "Sorry."

"I wouldn't tell her if you did."

"Can't, Eli. Just this once." Nappo offered him an orange. "Okay?"

Eli took the orange and shrugged. What was more intriguing? Finding an orange in the Droughtland, or the secrets the brothers were keeping? Eli gave over to his hunger, setting aside his curiosity for the moment.

The food was a delicious distraction—grapefruits baked with honey and cloves, fat sausages, poached eggs with the brightest orange yolks, thick bread, a tub of butter and a pot of chocolate hazelnut spread, and strong coffee brewed with mint. Eli was so busy eating it didn't bother him that the brothers hadn't spoken since they'd filled their plates. Once they were all stuffed, though, Eli wanted to hear everything.

"Where did you sleep?"

Teal looked up at Nappo. Nappo nodded. "I think you can tell him that much."

"In a great big room with lots of kids, and bunk beds that went up to the ceiling that you climbed up a ladder to, and a woman that read us a story and an old man who passed round cookies and warm milk!"

"Both of you?"

Nappo shook his head. "I was with the older kids."

"The children all sleep together? Like an orphanage?"

Nappo nodded. "But they're not all orphans. Lots of them have parents here, but the children all stay together."

"Where do the parents sleep?"

The boys shrugged. In the silence that followed, Teal looked nervously at Nappo again. Nappo pretended to ignore him, but Eli saw it.

He crossed his arms and levelled the brothers a look he hoped would instill a little fear. "Tell me what it is you've been told not to tell me."

The brothers shook their heads.

"If you don't tell me, I'll tell them that you're nothing but scheming thieves."

Nappo grinned. "They like that sort of thing here."

Just when Eli was going to lose it and lunge for Nappo and beat the truth out of him, the door opened and the same little old man from the night before popped his head in.

"You two, come with me."

The brothers got up. "Later, Eli," Nappo said. "Hold on to your hat, friend."

"Bye, Eli!" Teal waved happily from the door. "I never told," he reported to the old man, who grunted at him and ushered him into the hall.

SOON THE OLD MAN was back. He took the seat across from Eli and put his elbows on the table. "You've guessed who I am?"

Eli shook his head.

"Come on." He packed his pipe with stiff, knobbly fingers. "I'm told you're the smarter one of you and your brother."

The door opened again, and Celeste came in. Perhaps it was the way she looked at the old man, or maybe it was the way he didn't even look up, let alone at her, when she came in that hinted at who he was.

"You're my grandfather, aren't you?"

"You can call me Pierre."

Celeste put a hand on the old man's shoulder. "Now that's not fair."

"There will be no discussion about it." Pierre lit his pipe. "He will call me Pierre."

There was no doubt; the man hated him already. Eli found no reason to feign fondness if Pierre wasn't going to.

"Yes, sir." Eli didn't even bother to try to keep the sarcasm out of his voice.

"Eli!" Celeste yelped.

The old man bristled. "What did you just call me?"

"I'm sorry." Eli swallowed. "It just slipped out."

"I doubt that." Pierre pushed back from the table. "Perhaps you are not the smarter of you and your brother. Or perhaps you are, and he is even worse, and we will have waited all these years for nothing."

Eli felt a sudden strange urge to defend Seth. He held his breath for a moment and the urge thankfully dissolved. He looked up as Pierre whispered something to Celeste.

She shook her head. "But Pierre, it's only fair that—"

Pierre held up his hand. "What, of any of this, is *fair*?"

Bullet growled, his hackles rising as Pierre raised his voice. Eli reached down and held his collar tight.

"None of this is fair." Pierre let loose a short, bitter laugh. "None of it! So don't you dare talk to me about fair."

Celeste took a deep breath and smiled thinly at Eli.

"I want you to meet someone very special." She waved at the door, where a small crowd had gathered in the hall. To Pierre, she said, "Would you ask the others to leave us alone?"

"They have the right to be where they want, don't they?"

"I'm sure they all have work to do."

"It's not my concern when they complete their day's work, so long as it's within the day." Pierre shrugged. "Isn't that what you always say, darling?"

Celeste frowned. "Indeed, Pierre. Forget I asked anything of you at all." She placed a hand on Eli's shoulder. "Eli, this will not be easy for you, but

I can think of no other way to do it." She nodded to the young man who was keeping the crowd from spilling into the room. "Let her in."

In that snap of an instant, Eli leapt to the unlikely conclusion that it was Lisette about to walk through the door. She was alive after all! Her death had been a plot, and she was alive, and now here she was, coming into the room on her own two feet, very much alive and not a scar on her!

It may well have been Lisette, for the girl coming in did look just like her. But she was much younger. Who was this? What was happening? Had he ever truly woken up from that night he'd curled up watching the garden rubble burn, or was this all a long, cruel nightmare in place of life?

Celeste took the girl's hand and coaxed her forward, all the while keeping an eye on Eli, who looked like he might tip right over. "This is your sister."

Eli shook his head. "I don't understand."

The girl bit her lip. She could not look at him, nor could he at her. Instead she knelt down and patted Bullet, who'd approached her as though he'd known her forever, and Eli stared at the window, wishing he was out in the thick white wet of the fog rather than in this stuffy room with an audience drinking in his shock, his confusion, even his dog's wandering loyalty.

Celeste's voice was soft. "It's true."

"By my father?" Eli squeezed his eyes shut, desperate for it all to fall into place in his mind.

"Yes."

The girl had still not spoken. Eli glanced at her, then past her to the crowd swarming at the door. A boy at the front stumbled and fell right into the room.

"Get out!" Eli rushed the door and kicked the boy until Pierre hauled him off. "All of you! Go away!" Eli pulled away from Pierre and ran at the door again, kicking at people until the crowd backed away enough that he could slam the door and bolt it from the inside. That done, he surveyed the three still in the room, the bitter old man who hated his guts, his grandmother with such a sympathetic look on her face that Eli wanted to slap her, and the girl, who Eli knew in his heart was much more than just a sister.

"How old are you?"

The girl looked up. "Sixteen."

Eli nodded slowly. "There were three of us."

She nodded.

"Why are you here?" Eli asked. "What happened?"

The three looked to one another. No one hurried to explain.

"Bullet, come." Eli snapped his fingers, bringing the dog to heel and away from the girl. "How is it that you're here, and I was not? How is it that you knew of me? You did know of me, didn't you?"

She nodded again.

"How is it that you knew of me, and I knew nothing of you? How is it that there were three of us, and Father only knows of two? He does think there's just me and Seth, doesn't he?"

Celeste and the girl nodded.

"It was a difficult pregnancy—" Celeste began.

"Of course it was!" Eli laughed. It was all so absurd. "There were three babies! I'm surprised she lived through it at all!"

"While she was pregnant," Celeste continued evenly, "we stacked the Key hospital with rebels, myself among them. We pretended that she needed to be confined to bed, in hospital for the last two months of the pregnancy. And then it became real; she did need absolute bed rest. We knew there were two babies, but we didn't know of the third."

"Who was first?" Eli asked.

"Seth."

"And then?"

"You."

"She was last?"

Celeste nodded. "If it had been you last, you would've grown up here. It was just the way things turned out. We had planned to fake your mother's death then. We were going to tell your father that she and the baby died."

"He didn't know that there were two?"

"We did not tell him." Celeste took a seat at the table where Eli had sat only half an hour before, eating breakfast, clueless. He wouldn't have even known what triplets were except that when one of his cats had had only three kittens in a litter Lisette had said they were triplets. She'd held them all in the palm of her hand, their eyes still shut, and named them Seth, Eli, and Sabine.

"Your name is Sabine, isn't it?"

Pierre and Celeste and the girl looked at each other in surprise. Eli told them about the kittens. "I'd thought it was what she would've named a girl, if she'd had one."

AND THEN, somehow, it became easier. Pierre left, for one thing, and with him left some of the tension. Celeste and Sabine and Eli sat on the bed as Celeste told the rest of the story.

The birth came early and went very wrong. After the boys, the birth-minders left to tend to them, and Lisette began to hemorrhage. Sabine, who no one had expected, was breach, threatening to come out feet first. While the griefminder, also a rebel sympathizer, was telling Edmund out in the hall that his wife and the baby had died in birth, Lisette began to scream.

"She's alive!" Edmund pushed past the griefminder into the room he thought she was in, but it was the room the boys were in, and Edmund was stopped in his tracks in bewildered shock.

"It's a miracle!" a birthminder cried, stepping away from the babies. "They're breathing!"

"There's two?" Edmund stared at the boys. "There's two! Twins!" Edmund shouted with delight. The babies began to cry, covering the squalls of the third baby, Sabine, who was whisked away before Edmund could discover her. At least she would go with the Triskelians. In the confusion, it's what Celeste thought Lisette wanted, but when Lisette discovered that the plan had been ruined, and that Edmund knew she was alive, and knew of the boys, she'd clawed furiously at Celeste.

"And the third? The girl?"

"She's gone."

"She died?" Lisette began to weep.

CELESTE SAID NOTHING for a while. She stared at her lap, slowly shaking her head.

"I considered telling her that yes, her little girl was dead, but I could not bear passing that false grief to my own daughter." Celeste put a hand on Sabine's knee. "I told her she'd gone with the birthminder, back to Triskelia. I told her the truth." Celeste looked at Eli. "I thought it was what she wanted. By the time I knew she would rather die than be separated from even one of you or have you separated from each other, it was too late to bring Sabine back. Edmund knew of only two babies. There is no story that could've brought her back without exposing everyone. Your mother never forgave me for sending Sabine away."

There was a stiff silence while Celeste cried quietly.

"Fate." Sabine put an arm around her grandmother and gave Eli a cool look. "That's why it was me without a mother and not you."

24

❦

Later that day, after Eli had had several hours by himself, during which he'd stared at the wall, trying to make sense of things, Sabine returned to Eli's room.

"Are you going to stay in this room forever?" She peered in. "You're not a prisoner here, you know."

"I thought I wasn't allowed to leave."

"Who told you that?" Sabine stepped in. Eli couldn't help but stare at her, of course. It was extremely odd, looking at a female version of himself, with slender girl's hips, and breasts, and hair to her bum, dark like his rather than blond like Seth's. Frankly, it unnerved him more than he could deal with. No wonder everyone had been looking at him strangely in Triban. It wasn't his likeness to Lisette they were marvelling at, but his likeness to Sabine.

"Did Papa tell you that?" she asked.

"He told me to call him Pierre."

Sabine shrugged. "He might warm up to you."

"And he might not, right?"

"And he might not." Sabine perched on the edge of the bed. She'd shed the long woollen cape from earlier, and the thick scarf she'd worn against the damp morning cold, and was wearing a short sleeveless tunic with a tight leotard underneath, accentuating the definition of the muscles in her arms and legs. Eli looked down at his own muscles, what little there was to look at anyway. His were nowhere near that defined, or strong.

"He blames you and Seth." Sabine crossed her arms, conscious of Eli's stare.

"For what?"

"For Lisette's not being able to return. For her death, probably."

"You were the third. Why not blame you?"

"He'd rather it was just me."

"You're his favourite," Eli muttered. "Lucky you."

"Only because I was here to be favoured."

Just as Lisette favoured Eli, and Edmund favoured Seth. There was no fairness in any of it. Eli hadn't thought about his father for a long time. What was he doing right now? It was dinnertime back east. Was he eating supper, normal as you please? Or maybe having a dinner meeting with Chancellor East? Was he even still Chief Regent, after everything?

If Eli had never left home, and none of this had happened, he'd be sitting down to dinner too, none the wiser. And Lisette too. She'd take her seat opposite Edmund and smooth her napkin over her lap. And after dinner, she'd play the piano for them in the parlour. And there'd be a fire in the hearth, and Seth and Edmund would have a game or two of chess while Eli sprawled on the couch with a stack of books and Bullet slept on the floor beside him. So this is what homesick felt like.

"Look, I don't really want to talk about this any more." Eli pulled on his sweater. He was cold, even if Sabine was dressed for a warm spring day, although it was nearly winter. "Are you going to show me around this place, or should I explore on my own?"

"I don't want to talk about it either. Besides," Sabine reached her arms above her head and stretched, "I have to lead a drop class in a little bit. You can come if you want."

"A drop class?"

"For the little ones," Sabine said. "You'll have to take it too, though, because you're new."

"What is it?"

Sabine raised her eyebrows. "You don't know?"

Eli shook his head. "No one's told me anything."

"Come on." Sabine took his hand and led him out of the room. "You've got a lot to learn. You might as well start with a drop class."

SABINE LED ELI through a maze of stairwells and long corridors, out across a little courtyard shrouded in fog and through to another building, even taller than the first. It was just one great room inside, so huge that the children at the other end looked like mice scurrying around beneath the rope net that ran the length and width of the room about ten feet off the floor, which was covered in thick mats. It was a gymnasium, or that was the closest thing Eli could relate it to, but with one glance up past the net Eli knew immediately what it was. A room strung with the wires and cables and swings of the trapeze.

"Welcome to the Night Circus," Sabine said.

"*The* Night Circus?" Eli gasped as he watched a small boy no older than Teal fall from such a height that he had time to sing a verse of a song before landing on the net on his back, arms and legs spread. "Is he okay?"

"Are you okay, Toby?" Sabine waved up at the boy.

"Yeah!"

Two women helped him to the edge of the net, where he swung over and dropped down, nimble as a squirrel. He ran over and clamped onto Sabine's leg.

"He looks the same as you. On'y he's a boy."

"That's right," Sabine said. "Eli, this is Gavin's brother, Toby."

"Hi Toby."

Toby scampered off.

"He's a little shy."

Eli watched the boy scramble up the scaffolding and rope ladders, telling everyone along the way that his cousin Eli was there to watch him.

"With new people, that is."

"Cousin?"

Sabine nodded. "You'll get used to that. There's a million of us. Papa and Nana had ten children."

Above them, Toby was stepping onto the highest platform. The dizzying height was enough to distract Eli from the subject of cousins. "He's not going to jump from there, is he?" From that far away Toby was as small as a pigeon. The actual pigeons that flapped about in the rafters above looked like tiny fleas in comparison. The birds flew Eli back to the night Quinn died. They'd been trained to bomb the acrobats, Eli was sure now, considering that the circus was used to performing with pigeons around. They'd been Maury's birds for sure, and Seth's name was written all over the stunt.

"He's one of the best," Sabine was saying. "He's showing off for your sake."

"Sabine." Eli had to look away, the image of Quinn falling making him suddenly queasy. If he watched Toby fall from that height he might actually be sick, and that would be humiliating. "Is this the very same circus that travels the Keys?"

"Watch him." Sabine waved at Toby.

"Is he looking at me?" Toby hollered, his voice a tiny echo.

"Yeah, he's watching." Sabine ribbed Eli. "Watch him!"

Toby brought his hands together over his head and dove off as if he were diving into water. He spun three somersaults and did two jackknives on the way down, and then flipped onto his back for as smooth as possible a landing from that height. Everyone watching cheered. Toby swung off the net, ran up to Sabine, and clamped onto her leg again.

"I was good, right?"

"You were a piece of absolute perfect, love." She kissed his head and pried him off. "I have to go teach the little ones, Toby. I'll see you at supper, okay?"

"Is he going to be at supper too?" Toby glanced shyly at Eli.

"That was awesome, Toby!" Eli knelt down as Toby backed away, wedging himself between Sabine's legs. "My name's Eli. You can call me that if you want."

Toby tugged at Sabine's tunic. "Is he gonna be at supper?"

Sabine shrugged. "I guess so. Why don't you ask him?"

Toby shook his head and ran back to the rope ladder.

"He'll warm up to you." Sabine led Eli to the other end of the hall.

"If Toby's not in the little ones' class, who is?" Eli asked.

Sabine stopped in front of a group of babies and toddlers, confined to a corner of the room by a little fence. "Say hi to your classmates, Eli."

EVEN THE BABIES WERE BRAVER than Eli. The dropminders, and Sabine was one of them, coached the babies, some as young as six months, in the art of dropping. Of course, at that age it was mostly dropping back into one of the minders' arms at the gentle push of another minder, but even the toddlers were comfortable dropping from three- and four-foot-high platforms into their minders' arms, especially Charis, who gleefully and repeatedly flung herself off the four-foot platform with extra zeal. Sabine set Eli up at a fifteen-foot platform, which meant he would be dropping five feet onto the net.

"It looks farther than five feet." Eli clung to the rope ladder as Sabine climbed up ahead of him.

"That's because you're looking down fifteen feet. You do it like this." She backed up to the edge of the platform so that only the balls of her feet and her toes were still on the board. "Lean forward just enough so you don't topple off before you mean to. Then arch and drop." She did just that. "Spread your arms and legs out when you land," she said as she fell onto the net. "It distributes the impact more evenly." She climbed up the ladder behind Eli. "Just keep it simple for now. You'll learn the fancy stuff later."

Eli wasn't worried about keeping it simple. He was worried about losing his breakfast or pissing his pants in fear. He climbed onto the platform and slid his feet in front of him until he reached the edge.

"Now turn around."

He slowly turned, wishing there was something to hold on to. The platform wobbled slightly.

"This thing's bouncing all over the place!"

"Never mind, just back up a little. I'll tell you when to stop."

Eli glanced down. All the babies were watching. Charis waved at him. He closed his eyes and stretched out his arms shoulder high to keep his balance.

"Don't tell me you're afraid of heights, because I won't believe it. Our family has been doing this for seven generations."

Eli opened his eyes. "Our family?"

Sabine rolled her eyes. "Didn't Lisette tell you anything?"

"Not about this." Eli stepped away from the edge. "Tell me now."

"Drop first."

"No, tell me first and then I'll drop."

"Tell you what?"

"About this." Eli looked down again and had to close his eyes. "Did my mother do this?"

"Yes, *your* mother did this, until she became a spy."

"Sorry. Our mother."

"Yes, *our* mother. Get used to it, Eli."

"And Celeste and Pierre?"

"And everybody, okay?" Sabine rolled her eyes again. "This is what we do. All of us. We're the Night Circus. That's one way we make money and get in and out of the Keys to pick up intelligence. Now drop."

"But why a circus? Why not an army? There are so many more Droughtlanders than Keylanders. We could just storm them."

"*We*, all of a sudden. Listen to you. Our number doesn't seem so impressive when you think of how many are dusters or are too sick or poor or without hope. Never mind that the Keylanders have almost all the guns. Right now it's about collecting intelligence, and so why fight for it when you can play?" Sabine waved him back to the edge. "Everything we learn for the circus makes us better fighters for when it will come to that. Okay?"

"But *when*?"

"I don't know, Eli, okay? I don't have all the answers. I don't even know all the questions. Everyone is waiting. Are you going to drop or not?"

Eli backed up, eyes closed. Later. He would learn more later. Like exactly *when* this revolution would begin. What were they all waiting for?

"Good. A little more . . . more . . . now lean forward!"

Eli leaned forward as he felt his heels leave the board. How can they play when there's so much evil to deal with out there? How can they be so complacent? Where is the battle? For the weather, the wealth, the world?

"That's it, good!"

Eli opened his eyes. He grinned. "This is cool."

"Just balance there for a moment and feel what it takes not to fall."

Eli bounced slightly. The board wobbled. "This isn't so hard."

Just then Toby ran up below him, beneath the net. "Hey, Eli!"

Eli looked down and lost his balance. He tipped off the platform and fell, whacking his ankle on the board as he did. He landed in an ungraceful heap on the net, his legs sticking through, his balls mashed against the rough rope. He tried to pull his legs up, but the pain was too much. He groaned and tipped forward, getting even more tangled. Below him the babies laughed and laughed. Toby stared up at him.

"I came to watch you drop," he said. "That wasn't a very good one. Want me to show you how?"

25

A week into their travels, and Rosa had come up with all sorts of reasons not to abandon Seth quite yet. He might get sick again—after all, he was still quite weak—plus he didn't know how to behave in the markets, he had the wrong accent, and no clue about travel routes, food, signs of sicks, when and when not to wear his mask, how to avoid or negotiate with night bandits, how to treat sunburns, where to find free safe places to sleep, where to get cleaner water. He didn't even know how to barter.

"If it wasn't for me you'd be dead!" Rosa yanked the horse's reins into a knot on the post.

"Look, I'm sorry I called your mother a bitch, okay?" On their way into this market they'd been recalling their time in Rosa's village, and from that, Rosa had begun reminiscing about her childhood, how she and her mother used to bake bread at the start of each day, before it got too hot.

"Those times were my favourite," Rosa had said. "I had her all to myself."

"She can't be that great," Seth had said. "She's the nasty bitch who forced us out here."

Rosa had pushed him off the horse and taken off at a canter. She only did that because they were within sight of the market. If they'd been in the middle of nowhere, she would've just pushed him off and scolded him. She'd never tell him that, though.

Seth caught up with her at the horse hitch rail at the edge of the market.

"It's your turn to stay with Honey." Rosa glared at him.

"Couldn't we just steal a lock?"

"No, we cannot just steal a lock." Rosa dug in her pack for a jug wrapped in a sweater at the bottom. Mina herself had painted it, in beautiful reds and blues coming together along the fish-shaped handle. "If you want a lock, you can figure out some way of earning enough money to buy one. You're going to have to anyway, because after this, we have nothing left to trade but the horse."

"We can't trade the horse."

"Exactly." Rosa slung her threadbare bag over her shoulder. "So while I'm getting us food and water, maybe you could come up with a bright idea or two."

SETH WENT TO SLEEP instead, awkwardly atop the horse, so there was absolutely no way anyone could steal her. He'd learned many things in the Droughtland so far, and one of them was how resourceful Droughtland thieves were. They'd steal your pinky finger without your even knowing, if they could think of a use for it. Secretly, Seth respected the thieves. Even when they'd lifted two loaves of bread and a pint of beer out of the basket he had over his arm without his noticing, Seth couldn't help but be awed with admiration, while Rosa nagged at him for not being more mindful.

HE WOKE UP to Rosa yanking on his ankle. She handed him a horse lock and a teacake and a mug of tea.

"You said we couldn't afford a lock."

She put her hands on her hips and grinned. "I got us jobs."

"Here?"

"Lock up the horse, and I'll show you."

Rosa led him to the pub. A large group of people milled anxiously outside the tent, some of them with napkins tucked into their shirts and plates of half-eaten food, others with bottles and mugs of all sorts of booze. Rosa pulled him past them all and inside.

"You're mad!" a tall man with a scrawny beard cried. "You'll die in there!"

"Ignore them," Rosa said as Seth tried to pull away.

"What are they talking about?"

"Trust me, I know what I'm doing."

The place was empty, and the reason for the crowd outside was clear. In the middle of the tent, between two tables, a girl lay on the floor face down, a tray beside her, plates of food and mugs of drink a broken mess above her head.

"She dropped dead while I was trading the jug at the bar." Rosa stepped closer. "I'm surprised you didn't hear the screams while that stupid lot climbed over each other to get out. They think it's catching."

"It isn't?" Seth judged the distance between himself and the door.

"Come look." Rosa knelt beside the girl and moved her blond curls aside. "See these bumps along her neck?" She lifted the dead girl's tunic and showed him more bumps lining her spine. "Born like that. Her mother would've had the sick and passed it to her when she was pregnant with her. It's not a catching sick unless you sleep with someone who's got it, but those folks out there didn't want to take the risk to figure out what sort of sick it was that took her."

"You're taking her job?"

"No, *you're* going to be the tableminder." Rosa rolled the girl over. Her eyes were open, her lips blue. Seth looked away. "I've got the job of cleaning this place, and then the lodge tent she stayed at, and the dust lounge she spent her evenings at. We'll be here a few days at least, or until you get fired. You probably don't have any experience as a table-minder, do you?"

Seth shook his head.

"Well, you better be good at pretending, because I told the guy that you grew up in a pub." Rosa grinned at him. "You wanted a job, didn't you?"

Seth opened his mouth to say that he'd had thieving in mind as a job of sorts, but he quickly decided against sharing that with her. He'd rather Rosa not think him any worse than she already did.

"Grab her ankles." Rose slipped her arms under the dead girl's. "We'll wrap her up in that." She nodded at an oiled tablecloth.

After they'd lugged the dead girl out the back, Rosa informed the crowd that the cleaning process would take quite a while. Then she bolted the door to the tent and she and Seth helped themselves to the abandoned food on the grill.

"They'd expect us to throw it out anyway," Rosa reasoned. "So it's not stealing."

They tidied a little, enough so it would look as though they'd gone over the place thoroughly. Rosa had Seth wipe down all the bottles and kegs and mugs and plates with a damp cloth soaked in a thyme and basil tincture, which Rosa explained was antibacterial.

"I don't want to cheat them that badly," she said. "This way the pubminder is sort of getting his money's worth. Smells like it anyway."

Seth was quiet as he worked, looking for things to pocket that the pubminder wouldn't notice. When he squatted down to lift another tray of mugs onto the bar, he spotted a bag embroidered with pink and purple rabbits. Probably the dead girl's. Seth popped his head up to check that Rosa was still wiping tables across the tent. She waved.

"We can move on after a while," she said, going back to her work. "We won't stay here forever, if that's what you're brooding about."

"I'm not brooding." Seth raised his voice as he squatted out of sight. "Just working away, lost in thought."

"I get like that too," Rosa said as Seth rummaged through the pack. "My mind just takes off, following whatever rabbit trail it fancies." A hand mirror! He hadn't seen any mirrors in the Droughtland. What was it worth? What could he get for it?

Then he remembered his scars. He'd seen his reflection in windows, and pools of water, but not yet in the clear honesty of a mirror. He looked and then quickly looked away. There was no surprise, and no going home. It was that bad. He was disfigured beyond explanation. A monster. How could Rosa even look at him without retching?

He let the mirror drop to the floor and lifted his boot to smash it. But as much as he hated it for recording his demise, it was worth something. He picked it up, brushed it off, and pocketed it, along with the numbness he felt. He kept rifling through the bag as Rosa prattled on.

Five ones. She must've just been paid. The ultimate find, though, was a knife with two blades, one pencil-thin and pointy, the other wide and stubby and sharp on both sides. Rosa, and most everybody, had one just like it. The handle was well worn, made of bone that warmed fast in Seth's grip. He slipped the knife and the money into his pocket and left the girl's hairbrush and sweater in the bag. He stood up then, with the bag.

"Look, it must be hers." He wanted to tell her about the mirror. It might reflect his ugliness, but it would be kind to Rosa, who was very good looking, for a Droughtlander. Rosa was always gazing at herself in basins of water or warped candle-lit windows. She would love to have the mirror, but Seth resisted. It was stolen, and it was valuable.

"Put it back, Seth."

"It's a nice bag." Seth shook it. "Well made. Nice rabbits on it. Girly. Sure you don't want it?"

"Definitely not." Rosa shook her head. "Taking dead people's things brings bad luck."

"You took Mina's things."

"I had no choice." Rosa wrung her rag out. "Besides, I did get bad luck. I'm stuck with you aren't I?"

"So funny I'm dying over here."

"Don't make dying jokes."

"Don't this, don't that." Seth tucked the bag back under the bar. "You sure you're a lifeminder and not a childminder?"

"And if I was a childminder," Rosa smirked, "what would that make you?"

IT WAS AFTER DARK when they announced to the crowd that they were finished. As people meandered back inside, the pubminder pulled them aside.

"I can't tell you how thankful I am. You saved my pub." He pressed a fistful of money into Rosa's hand. "We took a bit of a collection. There's double what I promised you there. You're a brave couple of kids. In a clean market, it's hard to find anyone willing to do that sort of dirty work."

"Thank you—" Seth started. Rosa kicked him, although not so hard that the pubminder would notice.

"Thank you, mister." She smiled at him. "We'll burn the body, and then I'll send Seth back to tablemind for you while I get started on the lodge tent."

As they dragged the girl's body, bound tightly in two tablecloths, out into the black empty night beyond the market, Rosa whispered to Seth, "You were going to call him that word, weren't you?"

"What?"

"That word the Keyland soldiers call the commanders."

"Sir? I was not," he said, although he most certainly was. "I'm not that stupid."

"You better not be," Rosa said as she let down her end of the body and reached for the kerosene. "Right. Here's good. Got a match?"

26

✧

li's ankle was only slightly bruised, but his ego fared far worse. After that first drop he'd hardly been able to stand when he was helped down from the net. His balls had never hurt so badly in all his life, not even when Seth had kicked him there on purpose.

While his ego and balls and ankle recovered, he watched the drop classes, determined never to screw it up again. He wished he was happy for Teal and Nappo, who took to dropping as if they'd done it forever, but inside he felt he should be better at it than they. He was determined that soon he'd be climbing the rope ladder again and dropping like a pro—after all, the circus was in his blood for generations, not theirs.

ELI NO LONGER had a private room. He bunked with the other kids his age, the boys and girls together, which Eli thought was a stupid idea. He could hear some of them climb into each other's beds after the dorm-minder said his good night. Maybe the revolution needed lots of babies; after all, why else would they go about looking for orphans to bring back and train for the Night Circus? Besides, it wasn't like they had to do much to raise them. Most of the time the children were kept together, brought up collectively, loved and taught by everyone. Ultimate responsibility for the children's daily lives—food, clothes, education—fell to the childminders. But children did spend time each day with their parents, from late afternoon through supper. Parents had few, but important, duties toward their children—love them, enjoy them, cherish them.

It all seemed so *pleasant*. Where was the urgency? Where was the drive to overthrow the Keys? Celeste said that the night Quinn died was going to be the start. The plan was for Lisette and the boys to leave with the circus, but then Quinn died and the plan fell apart. Eli didn't want to tell her that there was no way Seth would've ever left with Lisette. And how was she going to do it, anyway? Fake a kidnapping? Tie the boys up and take them against their will? Even Eli wouldn't have gone willingly. Not then. Not without knowing. This revolution had too many *not yets*. Not yet, we need all our spies home first. Not yet, we're working on an important cloudminder mission. Not yet, the Guard has more guns now. Not yet, we need more people.

What Eli knew about battles of any kind is that there would be terrible losses. People die in war. It's a fact. Unfortunately, it seemed to be a fact that Triskelia wasn't willing to deal with. They wanted a quiet revolution, strategy versus violence. It would never work. Eli would convince them otherwise. He knew better. He'd been a part of the world they wanted to overthrow. It would take violence. And there would be death. Lots of death. Triskelians, mostly. He was sure.

He debated violence versus vision with anyone who'd engage with him, but it was like talking to a wall. The time would come to start the revolution, deaths and all, and he would see to it that it was soon. In the meantime he was damned if he wasn't going to become a star circus artist. Especially if he wanted to sneak back into any of the Keys. He had to be able to perform in order to go on tour.

Eli left the dorm one night, tiptoeing past Nappo, who'd started to snore since arriving in Triskelia, probably from the weight he'd put on from all the good food. Eli was glad his bunk was at the other end of the room. He made his way to the drop gym. In the dark, with no lanterns lit, the trapeze looked like the skeleton of a massive beast. Eli started climbing. He passed the five-foot drop and kept climbing, up to the ten-foot.

It was in his blood. He had to be good at this. His heart pounded as he backed toward the edge of the board. He'd been watching, studying. It was all about precision. Precise movements. Precise intentions. Precise skill. His heels left the board. Eli leaned forward and kept himself from falling. He felt the same rush he had that first time, only this time it was less fear, more determination and excitement.

"One, two, three." Eli arched back and dropped. He kept his eyes open as he fell. It was like flying. It was flying! He landed, arms and legs spread, on the net with a satisfying bounce.

"Yes!" His triumphant cry echoed up to the rafters. A flock of pigeons rustled above, startled from sleep. Below the net he heard a dull clapping. Eli stepped to the edge of the net the same way Toby did, placing the middle of his foot squarely on each rope section. He swung off with a slightly sloppy overhead flip, just like Toby. Someday he would thank the kid.

"Who's there?" Eli squinted into the dark.

Whoever it was was carrying a small lantern and was coming closer. It was Pierre, Eli could now see, his sharp features made even sharper in the glow.

"It's pretty stupid and inconsiderate of you to try a stunt like that, being as untrained and unskilled and untalented as you are."

"You can't have been watching then, because I did it perfectly." Eli hadn't seen Pierre since the day he'd met Sabine. Sabine told him to ignore the old man's bitterness until he came around, which she promised to work on. But here he was, impossible to ignore. "Are you going to tell on me?"

All infractions were reported to Zenith. She wasn't so much the leader of Triskelia, there was no specific leader, but she was the oldest woman by many years and was respected by all.

Pierre laughed. "So Zenith could have you sweeping the halls for an evening? I wouldn't waste my breath."

"Did you follow me here?"

"What if I did?" Pierre lit his pipe and started walking away. "I'm on watch. Part of my duty, if you must know."

Eli had to admit that even Edmund had never been so petty and sarcastic in his admonishments.

"Any time you feel like being nice to me, go right ahead," Eli said as Pierre disappeared into the dark, only the small glow of the lantern betraying his presence. "All right, old man?"

"Any time you feel like going back where you came from, go right ahead." Pierre's voice was stone. "All right, little boy?"

"Looks like I came from *here*."

"You'd like to think that, wouldn't you?" The glow disappeared around a corner and Pierre's voice grew distant. "You're half enemy, Eli. That makes you unique here in a way I don't envy."

Eli growled in frustration. He wanted to go after Pierre, grab the old man by the shoulders and shake the bitterness out of him.

"You're my grandfather!" Eli yelled into the darkness. "Doesn't that mean anything to you?"

There was no answer beyond the echo of his own voice and the quieting flutter as the pigeons settled back down to roost.

OTHER THAN PIERRE'S apparent hatred of him, which Sabine tried to convince Eli would eventually soften, Eli slid into life at Triskelia with great ease and little effort. He got used to seeing twins—there were many in their bloodline—but he and Seth and Sabine were the only triplets in recent memory. The only triplets who had survived, that is. One of Eli's aunts had given birth to triplets three months before they were due. They had died, and so had she. No one told Eli this kind of information except for Sabine, who answered his many questions in exchange for Eli telling her all he could about life in the Eastern Key, about Lisette, and Edmund, and Seth, who she was most interested in. She often sat on Eli's bunk and examined Seth's stony gaze in the photograph he'd taken from Edmund's study.

"I'll never meet him, will I?" Sabine said one day as the two of them took a break from Eli's training. She was teaching him the high swing, which involved swooping across great distances, fifty feet in the air, passing double-ended batons of fire back and forth. The others juggled the batons too, but that was a long way off for Eli. For the moment they had blown out the flames and were still, the swings swaying side by side. Sabine sat cross-legged on the narrow bar, her arms draped loosely around the ropes. Eli tried to look just as comfortable on his swing, but he wasn't. He was holding on to his ropes with white knuckles, and it felt like the bar was cutting off the circulation to his legs.

"You don't want to meet Seth, trust me."

"I do want to meet him." Sabine rolled a sooty baton along her thigh. She looked over at Eli. "It seems only right that we should be reunited, don't you think? Maybe he'd see things differently after meeting me?"

"Seth will never see things differently. He's pure Guard. It'd be as impossible as trying to make a Droughtland rebel into a Keyland—"

Sabine's look stopped him mid-sentence. "Like Maman."

"That's not the same."

"It is, in a way."

"She was still a rebel. You're only proving the point that even if Seth did appear to have changed his ways, he'd still be loyal to his original cause, the Keyland Guard. Just like Maman was loyal to Triskelia all along."

"I don't think you're being fair."

"You don't know him." Eli pumped his legs a little to get the blood flowing. "And besides, the only way the three of us will be reunited is if he hunts me down. Which he probably will, knowing him. I, for one, hope he's dead."

"Don't say that! No matter what, he's our brother."

"You wouldn't defend him if you knew him."

"I didn't know you before, yet every time Papa would say bad things about you, I stuck up for you and Seth. Both of you."

"Well, you can stop sticking up for Seth," Eli said as he swung past Sabine. "He's not worth it."

"Funny," Sabine said as he passed her again. "That's what Papa says about both of you. Still."

WHILE EVERYONE WAS WAITING for dessert that night after supper, Zenith stood with help from her attendants—twins, incidentally; a brother and sister about ten years older than Eli and Sabine. The twins, Ruben and Riva, whistled for everyone's attention. It took several minutes before the great hall quieted enough that the soft-spoken elder could speak.

"There has been great joy at the recent return of one of our young." Her rheumy gaze fell on Eli. "He is a very good boy."

Eli blushed as his friends around him elbowed him playfully. Sabine patted him on the head as if he were a dog.

"What a good boy," she said.

Under the table, Bullet barked happily at the words he thought were meant for him. Eli hushed him.

"It is only fitting that we celebrate his safe return," Zenith continued. "Not only because we are glad he is with us after so long, but also because of who he is, grandson of Pierre and Celeste, son of Lisette Fabienne, a great rebel, whose tragic death we have mourned together."

The air in the room fell from playful to sombre in the few seconds it took for the words to sink in. Somewhere in the back of the hall a very new baby started to cry. The father stood to take the baby outside, but Zenith waved for him to stop.

"The child can stay, Kahlib." Zenith nodded her head as the young father sat, rocking the baby in his arms. "We are a community, always. We never shut out our own. If we were hiding that child from the Keylanders, and she began to cry, then the rest of us would sing to conceal her." Zenith looked again at Eli. "Your mother was dear to everyone here, but I know she was most dear to you, child."

Eli felt a lump forming in his throat. His eyes began to tear. He did not want to cry, not in front of everyone.

"It's okay, Eli." Sabine put her arm across his shoulders.

"To us," Zenith continued, "she was sister, daughter, ally, friend, and mother in spirit to Sabine. But to Eli, she was always and only *mother*. That was her most important relationship, being mother to you and your brother."

Eli, and everyone else for that matter, shifted their eyes to Pierre, who was pushing his chair away from the table. He left the dining hall with heavy steps and not a word. Zenith didn't see him go, or if she did, she chose not to pay him any attention.

"Tonight, I am announcing a feast and celebration in the name of Lisette, a chance for Eli to recognize and honour his mother's life, and her death."

The room filled with excited chatter.

"A feast!" Toby cried. "We haven't had one in so long!"

Jack, who'd arrived from Triban just two days before, put a firm hand on Toby's shoulder. "Quiet, little monster." He eyed Eli, who was staring at his dessert while everyone around him lost themselves in talk about what they'd wear and all that needed to be done in preparation for the celebration. "Are you all right, Eli?"

"I don't think so." Eli stood. Bullet stretched under the table and stood too. "I think I'll go to bed early."

"But what about your dessert?" Teal said.

"You can have it."

Eli slipped between the long tables to the dark edge of the room. He leaned against the cold stone wall and watched everyone. For the first time since arriving at Triskelia, Eli felt as though he shouldn't be there. He wasn't sure why; maybe because he hadn't been there when they honoured his mother the first time, or maybe it was deep embarrassment at being singled out by Zenith, or maybe it was triggered by Pierre's leaving the room in such a public way that cemented his disapproval and absolute refusal to accept Eli.

Eli wanted to leave, not just the hall, but Triskelia itself. He didn't belong here. It was already complete without him. And as far as any revolution was concerned, the people of Triskelia would never be "ready." They were always waiting for something. Their people to come home, the crops to be brought in, the sick to be tended. And, ultimately, a peaceful plan. They had committees and caucuses, planning and strategizing, when all Eli wanted to do was amass an army and storm the

Keys and get the revolution started. But Triskelia wasn't willing to send its people to slaughter, and so the planning continued. And here Eli was, wanting to flood the Droughtland with the blood of those responsible for his mother's death. He and his violent thoughts had no home here. Maybe it was the Edmund in him that filled him with murderous desire; maybe—because of his father's blood—he would never truly belong here.

He watched from the shadows of the corridor. A merry pageant. A fairy tale come to life. The Droughtlanders were waiting for Triskelia, and here was Triskelia, drunk on their blessings.

There was Sabine and her gorgeous best friend Zari, heads together, gossiping. Jack and Gavin bounced a giggling Toby between them, and quiet, dark-eyed Lia, Zari's sister, staring down at a novel in her lap while Nappo leaned across the table trying to get her attention with some trick he could do with a spoon. And little Teal, finishing Eli's pudding and starting in on his brother's, which did not go unnoticed by Althea, who was off at a run to tattle to Anya. Was there any room for Eli at all? Life was already full to brimming from what he could see.

He crept along the wall in the dark, praying no one would stop him. He hoped he could sleep off this terrible feeling of restless unease. He hoped he would wake in the morning with the same excitement he'd woken to since the morning after his first bungled try at the drop—the unbridled joy at being at Triskelia, the same eagerness to perfect the circus arts that had been in his blood for a hundred years.

He was just about to turn into the corridor that led to the dorms when he felt a hand light on his shoulder.

"You're upset." It was Zenith, alone, leaning heavily on her walking stick. "Was it something I said?"

"No, ma'am." Eli winced as he heard himself say yet another forbidden word. He sighed heavily. "I'm sorry. I didn't mean to call you that."

She took his hand. Hers was dry and leathery, her grasp so light that if Eli hadn't done his part in holding it, her hand would've dropped.

"It's all right, child. I know you mean well. I know it is a term of respect in the Keys. Take my arm." She crooked her arm. "I've told Ruben and Riva that you will see me to my room."

"You knew I was leaving?"

She winked at him. "I thought you might."

"How did you know?"

"Never mind." She started shuffling forward, so Eli had no choice but to follow, supporting her. They stopped to light one of the lanterns left on the shelves at the mouth of the corridor, and then they carried on their way. Zenith walked very slowly. They'd gone only half the length of the first hall and already Eli was annoyed. He just wanted to be left alone with his thoughts. Zenith was Triskelia, lovely and slow moving. A wonderful, charming sloth. When they finally arrived at her door, she patted his hand again.

"You are impatient with me."

"No, not at all."

"Someday, you too will be this old, child."

"I wasn't impatient."

"Then intolerant, perhaps?"

Eli decided it was best not to reply.

"Tolerance and patience is something you will grow into," she said as Eli opened her door. "It comes easily to the children raised here, as they spend a great deal of time with the elders. I hear that in the Keys, the elders are put away in a lodge, all together and yet alone from their kin?"

Eli nodded as he helped her into her room. It was deliciously warm, by far the warmest spot he'd encountered in all of Triskelia, although he'd been told the infirmary was kept warm too. Nappo had told him that much when he'd been stitched up after catching a pole tip on a fall and slicing his arm open. This reminded Eli that, besides his humiliating ball smash and bruised ankle, he'd yet to acquire an injury in learning the circus arts. And while he was secretly proud that he'd avoided injury so far, at the same time he hated that it set him apart from the others, who each wore the story of their first circus injury like a badge of honour, a symbol of acceptance.

"Did you ever meet Edmund's parents?" Zenith asked, bringing Eli back to the present.

"No."

"Not ever?"

Eli shook his head.

"But they're alive?"

"Yes. They live with the elderminders."

"Where?"

"I don't know where exactly." Eli swallowed. Only now did that seem strange and wrong. "They moved there before my brother and . . . before we were born."

It had never seemed odd to Eli that no one ever visited elder Keylanders. It was a commonly held belief that at that age, after a long, full life, they just wanted to be left alone. Eli imagined that if Chancellor Southeast didn't keel over pretty soon, her Chief Regent would probably lock her up with the elderminders, against her wishes or not.

"How sad." Zenith slowly lowered herself into a chair by the fire. "But at least you have your grandparents here."

"But Pierre—"

"Pierre never learned the patience and tolerance I spoke of earlier, even though he was raised in the old Triskelia. I hope you will be patient and tolerant of him despite his behaviour. He is controlled by grief and love, the two pulling fiercely at each other."

"Love?"

"For Lisette and Sabine."

"And Nana?"

Zenith shrugged. "I am tired, child. And so are you. We must all sleep well. Preparations for the celebration will begin in the morning. There's lots to be done."

Zenith's eyelids grew heavy and her head started lolling to one side. Eli let himself out, and as he climbed the stairs to the dorm, the sounds from the dining hall echoed from far below. By the time he climbed into bed he could hear only silence. He would stay for the celebration out of respect for Celeste and Zenith. Then he would decide whether to leave Triskelia and go live in the markets. As he fell asleep, he thought of the mountain camp where he'd met Trace, and of Foothills Market where he'd nearly lost his life. He knew enough now; he could manage all right in the Droughtland. Perhaps he would start the revolution for real. He was sure he could mobilize the Droughtlanders. It could be done. It *had* to be done. Perhaps that's what he needed to do to avenge his mother's death—to *be* the revolution.

In the morning he woke up somewhat refreshed, yet the sense of not belonging lingered. And what a stupid idea he'd fallen asleep with. Being the revolution? Daylight showed the impossibility of that idea. Perhaps Zenith would let him join one of the cloudseeder camps where they worked to perfect the science and to battle the Keys for the skies, or maybe she'd let him be an orphan seeker, like Trace. That way he'd still be part of Triskelia, but he could live away from all the painful reminders of his past and how he didn't quite belong. Maybe he could even team up with Trace; that way he might stand a fighting chance if Seth were ever to find him, and he surely would, knowing him.

27

𑁋

The pubminder was very nice about firing Seth, although he wouldn't look him in the eye as he did it.

"You might be a bit rusty, right?" The pubminder kept his eyes on the broom as Seth swept up another mess of broken crockery, the remains of a tray of mugs he'd tipped onto the floor. "I mean, I'm sure you were a good tableminder for your pa. He probably had better trays, and a real floor, made of wood, not this uneven dirt full of stones to trip on."

"I am sorry," Seth said. He was, too, but not for the pubminder. For himself, because every time he'd tripped, slipped, screwed up on an order, or dumped a mug of beer or a plate of stewed dumplings onto one of the patrons' laps, his humiliation peaked. As the laughter boiled Seth would blanch with fury. And if a patron was infuriated there was no recourse for Seth. Whether he was left with a black eye or great throbbing bruises, there was nothing he could do. Payback just wasn't possible, not even when one particularly large and particularly drunk patron twisted his arm behind his back with such force that it popped right out of its socket. Beyond being let off for the rest of the day so that Rosa could wrench it back in place, Seth was expected back at work in the morning to serve the very same man breakfast. He'd had to carry the tray with his left arm, which he was useless with, which meant he had to move as slowly as a half-wit to ensure he didn't end up with another limb jerked out of place.

This was not who Seth was in the world. He was a Keylander! These filthy Droughtlanders should be on their knees begging him for mercy. He'd like to be beholding them all from the other side of his gun, his fingers tingling like they did when he was just about to pull the trigger. When Seth closed his eyes at night, he pictured the man who twisted his arm sobbing, pleading for Seth to spare him. And then Seth blew his head off. In the half-dream there was no carnage, just the glory of domination oozing onto the floor like blood.

In his short time with the Guard he'd never actually killed anyone, but he knew that if he had to, or if he got the chance to, he'd do it without so much as a twinge of guilt or hesitation. These Droughtland beasts all deserved to die. Or nearly all of them. Not Rosa, of course. But the rest of her family, absolutely. And maybe not the pubminder, who was just a hard-working man, and not his daughter and grandkids, who were harmless and kind to Seth.

Sometimes, when Seth allowed himself to think of all that he'd lost, he wondered what would happen if he just went home and tried to explain it all. But whenever he toyed with that possibility it included taking Rosa with him, no matter how hard Seth tried to shake her out of the picture. How could that ever work in real life? She was a Droughtlander. Seth repeated that to himself often. She's just a Droughtlander. Just a Droughtlander. But if that was the case, why did he catch himself imagining a Keyland marriage, both of them in the luscious red robes, all of the Eastern Key rejoicing? It would never happen, and furthermore, Seth failed to see why it should. It was not possible to fall in love with a Droughtlander, even one as civilized and beautiful as Rosa. It was just a crush, probably because she saved his life. He'd heard of people being kidnapped and falling in love with their captors. This was probably no different. Misplaced affection just because she knew a few potions.

"I've been fired," he said to her that evening as she came in the door.

"I heard," she said. "His daughter told me."

"So there's nothing for me to stay here for."

"You want to leave?"

"What a stupid question! Of course I want to leave! I'm out here to find my brother." Seth downed the rest of his tea and banged the mug on the table. "And I won't find him here, will I?"

"Don't yell at me."

"What, you think I want to be a crap tableminder for the rest of my life? If I'm going to even have 'a rest of my life' then the first thing I need to do is find my brother and kill him."

"What a terrible thing to say!"

Seth shrugged. "Suck it up, that's the truth."

"Fine. Then go."

"You wouldn't come with me?"

"No." Rosa shook her head. "Not if the only thing you want in life, a life that I saved, by the way, is to kill your brother. I've had to give up my brother because of you. A brother I love. I thought you were starting to change."

"Just because I let some Droughtland pig nearly break my arm and I didn't slice his balls off while he slept?"

"Don't be gross."

"Don't think I didn't want to kill that pig, Rosa. The only thing that stopped me was that if I had the rest of them would've turned on me."

"This is true." Rosa stared hard at him. "So perhaps you are changing. You made a smart choice in place of a stupid one."

"And the smart choice regarding Eli is to find him and kill him before he can ruin my father any more than he already has. Perhaps if I manage to prevent that disaster, Father would understand and let me back."

"With the scars?"

"He just has to understand that the scars aren't what you get the sick from."

"You think you're the first to try to convince a Keylander of that?"

For a moment, Seth was silent. Then he got up and began collecting his things from around the tiny room he and Rosa shared in the lodge tent. Rosa sat on the edge of her cot, watching him.

"You're staying?" he said when he'd packed everything.

"I'm not sure," Rosa said. "I'm almost done here, but why should I come with you?"

"I don't know. Because." Seth cinched his pack shut. "We travel well together?"

"We fight all the time."

"But when we're not fighting, we travel well together. Don't we?"

"I suppose."

Seth squirmed under Rosa's intense stare. She was waiting for him to say something in particular, and he didn't know what it was, although he thought he had an uncomfortable inkling.

"Why should I go with you? This is a clean market, for the most part, and I've made friends here. Perhaps the pubminder will let me take your job."

"He filled it before I'd even left. Some traveller from the south."

"Tell me, Seth." Rosa leaned back on the mattress, her hands behind her, pushing her chest out. She crossed her slender bare legs. "Why do you want me to go with you?"

Seth squeezed his eyes shut, trying to shake the desire to run his hand along her thigh. Would it be any different from the other Droughtland wenches he'd had? Yes. Yes, he argued with himself. Because you don't think of her as just so much Droughtland meat. He swallowed, crossed his arms tight across his chest, and looked at the door. "Just because."

"As a guide? Shouldn't you be paying me for that?"

"No, not as a guide."

"As what, then?"

"As my friend?"

Rosa laughed. "Your *friend*." She sat still for another moment, not sure of what to say, then she began packing.

"So you are coming with me?" Seth tried to keep the elation out of his voice. He hadn't realized until this very moment the dread he felt at the prospect of losing Rosa.

"As your *friend*," Rosa said. "If that's what you want to call it."

She sounded mad, but Seth couldn't understand why. She'd be just as sickened at the thought of their being more than friends. Seth might have to admit his confusing feelings for Rosa to himself, but he was honourable enough not to share them with her, or, even worse, force them on her. She would be horrified, disgusted. She would leave him for sure if she knew what he was really thinking.

"As my friend and teacher." Seth forced some confidence into his voice. Perhaps she wanted some acknowledgment for the savvy that had kept them both alive this far. "You're far more than a guide. You're a mentor, Rosa. There's so much I have to learn from you."

"Whatever." She slipped her pack onto her shoulders and opened the door. "I'll meet you at the horse hitch."

THEY HAD LITTLE TO SAY to each other over the next few nights of travel, and when they stopped to rest as the heat of each day grew, they often took bunks as far away from each other as they could. As Seth tossed and turned in the underground bunkers, often a lot less cooler than the traders promised, he wondered if Rosa would just decide to leave him soon anyway. Why should she stay? He couldn't pay her, he couldn't be honest with her, and he was a constant threat to her safety. When he woke, in the blessed cool of night, he was always surprised and deeply happy that she had stayed to travel with him another night.

28

꩜

An air of festivity had taken over Triskelia and preparations for the celebration and feast were in full swing. Regular practices had slackened so that everyone could participate by making decorations and working on the acts they'd perform for the celebration. Eli didn't get out of regular practice though. Sabine and Jack made him work doubly hard so that he'd be ready to perform for the first time on the night of the celebration. Anya was sewing his costume to match those of Sabine and Jack and the others who formed their troupe. He wouldn't need a mask yet. They used them only when they performed in dirty markets and in the Keys.

"The masks," Anya explained at yet another fitting for his costume, "are as much to keep the Keylanders nervous of us as they are to make sure we stay anonymous so that we can switch people out of the cells as we go."

"Maybe I could use Quinn's mask to save you having to make another one?"

Anya shook her head. "That was his and only his. They're like a signature. Have you seen the display by the library?"

"Yes." They lined each shelf of a tall cabinet, masks so lively and colourful he half expected them to break into song.

"Those are the masks of the ones who've died performing. Like Quinn."

"There's so many!"

Anya didn't look at him. "Keylanders make sure of that. Taking our nets. Sabotage. Blood thirst."

Eli's cheeks heated with shame. "It's true. I'm sorry."

"Small words for such monumental loss," Anya murmured.

"I am sorry."

"We all are."

"That night, when Quinn died," Eli said, "there was a girl. She was going to scream at the Chancellor. I thought he was going to have her killed, but I don't think he noticed."

"That was Sabine," Anya said through teeth clenched holding sewing pins. "Hasn't she told you?"

"She was there?" Eli reeled from the idea that his triplet had been right before his very own eyes and he hadn't known. He'd heard of other twins who could feel their sibling's emotions, or knew where they were, or could read each other's thoughts. Not only was he a twin who didn't have that gift, not that he'd want to know where Seth was or how he was doing—although it would be handy to know if he was on his trail—he was a *triplet* without the gift. How underwhelming. Sabine had actually been there, and he had barely noticed her and felt nothing between them.

"They were partners in the fly act." Anya took the pins from her lips. "But they were more than that too. They were inseparable. Best friends."

"Was he her boyfriend?"

"No, he was Jack's."

Eli shifted uncomfortably on the stool. Jack was bent? Then did that mean Gavin was his—

"*Mon dieu.*" Anya sat back on her ankles. "That's a terrible thing to be in the Keys, isn't it?"

Eli nodded. Benders, as they were called in the Keys, were executed if they were discovered. There were so few babies born to Keylanders that to not partner with the opposite sex was seen as a crime against the state. Eli had heard of some who'd gone in front of the Star Chamber and been given another chance to procreate, but most were executed and their usually shocked and horrified wives and husbands assigned to new ones. Eli's very last female tutor had been exposed as a bender. She'd been executed, along with her lover, who was a widow, her orphaned child taken in by a couple who couldn't have children of their own. Eli had been only six, but he remembered feeling disgusted when their new tutor explained what had happened in more detail than necessary.

"You'll have to get used to it, Eli. It's normal here." Anya looked up at him. "You won't treat him differently now, will you?"

Eli shook his head, because he knew he had to.

"How do I know you won't?"

"I'll try, Anya. That's all I can promise. Where I come from it's illegal."

"Let me remind you that you come from here, in a way. And besides, you would've found out sooner or later. There's lots like that here."

"There are?" Eli felt sick. Who else? Had they been eyeing him in the dressing room? In the showers? The dorm? What about his troupe? What about when Jack had to hold his hands, or lift him, or put his hand around his waist as they practised the fly act? Although it was in the air, it was like they were dancing together the way they swooped and dived as Gavin and Sabine worked the pullies. Eli loved the fly act the best. Now he would have to quit it.

"You can't be here and hate them." Anya stood. "And there's no sense being mad at him."

Eli nodded.

"You're the one who has to change."

"Why shouldn't *they*? They're the benders, not me."

"That's not a word we use here." Anya shook her head. "You won't last long with that attitude."

Eli said nothing. He added this new information to his growing list of reasons to leave Triskelia, along with the fact that Pierre had rifled through his things and helped himself to Lisette's opal ring. Eli had confronted Pierre about it, but he'd said he'd given it to her in the first place and was just taking it back. When Eli went to Zenith for help, she'd told Eli that Pierre must truly feel that he needed the ring if he'd degraded himself so much as to steal it. She'd actually told him to use the experience as an opportunity to forgive. As if. *Forgive*. Triskelians did far too much of that, in Eli's estimation.

"Mind the pins." Anya gestured for him to get out of the costume. Eli pulled the tight body suit off, careful not to disturb where Anya had pinned on the flames that started at the ankle and wrist. Now he hated the outfit he'd been so eager to acquire before. He hated that it was so tight, his crotch an obvious bulge. Probably some bender freak had invented it.

"If I discover that you're treating Jack or any of the others poorly," Anya was saying, "or even differently, I'll tell Zenith. She'd expel you for that."

And would that be so bad? Eli held his tongue, knowing full well that Anya sensed his unspoken reply.

"I think you should go now." Anya slipped the costume onto a hanger.

That was fine with Eli. He pulled his pants on and left with his shirt under his arm. Once out in the hall, far enough away from the costume room that she couldn't hear, Eli spewed every nasty bender curse he could think of, plus a few he made up on the spot. He didn't say them loudly though, for fear someone coming down the hall might hear.

LATER, Eli told Jack he was feeling nauseous and couldn't do the fly act with him.

"Actually, you know what?" He struggled to keep his voice even as the troupe assembled around the pit of cushions above which they practised their act. "It kind of makes me nauseous every time. Maybe I'm not cut out for it?"

The troupe stared at him.

"It makes you sick?" Sabine took her eyes off him and looked at the others. "Have you ever heard of that before?"

"Not from one of our own," Gavin said.

"Not from anyone with circus blood," Jack added.

"I don't mean *every time*." Eli hadn't meant to alienate himself completely. "It's just lately. I just feel a little woozy these days."

Jack put his arm over Eli's shoulder. Eli stiffened. Jack looked over at Gavin. Gavin lifted his eyebrows and slowly folded his arms across his chest.

"Okay, then." Jack made a great production of removing his arm. "Maybe Zari could take his place for now and Sabine could teach him the pullies?"

"My shoulder still hurts when I fly," Zari said. "The masseuse says it'll be a few more weeks. Sorry."

"And why should he learn the pullies before learning to fly?" Sabine frowned at Jack. "Everyone learns to fly first."

"I wouldn't trust him if I was flying and he was pulling." Gavin nodded. "He doesn't know the first thing about it."

Lia, who rarely said anything, spoke up then. "Maybe he should just sit out for the celebration."

"No, I—" This wasn't going the way Eli had planned. "I just don't want—"

"Don't want what, cousin?" Gavin leaned forward. "What don't you want, huh?"

"Me," Jack said. "He wants a different partner, don't you, Eli?"

Eli hesitated a moment too long before saying, "No. That's not it."

"Hang on." Sabine held up her hands as everyone tried to speak at once. "Everybody just stop for a minute." She grabbed Eli's wrist. "Why do you want a different partner? Jack is the best. That's why we paired the two of you up, so you could learn from him."

"Guess why," Gavin said harshly.

"I asked Eli," Sabine said.

"I'm not good enough, and—"

"As if!" Zari cried. It was common knowledge that Eli was taking to flying as if Lisette had been teaching him in secret all his life. In fact, Pierre had gone so far as to accuse Eli of lying when he said that she hadn't. He was spreading all sorts of rumours to that effect.

"I can tell everyone here why you're acting like a freak." Gavin pushed in front of Sabine. "You want me to tell them, or will you?" When Eli didn't respond, Gavin shoved him. Eli stumbled back toward the cushion pit. "I think you should tell them. Tell them, *Master* Eli." As he spat the word "master" he shoved Eli again, harder, sending him backward into the pit.

Gavin and the others lined the edge and stared down at him.

"Tell them!" Gavin yelled.

Eli lay on his back on the pillows, trying to think of a way to get out of this situation without offending Jack or infuriating his bodyguard or boyfriend or whatever Gavin was.

"Because I'm leaving!" Eli rolled over as he said it so that the others couldn't see his misery. "Face it, I don't belong here. There's no point in teaching me any of this."

"You can't leave!" Sabine jumped into the pit with him. She picked up a cushion and hit him. "You just got here!"

The others jumped in too, and the whole troupe attacked Eli with the cushions. Soon everyone was laughing, and the conversation slipped out of mind, or so it seemed.

"But I still don't have a partner," Jack reminded them all as they climbed out to get on with the practice. "Eli?"

"Sorry, Jack." As much as Eli wished he didn't mind, he did. He just couldn't. Not with all the touching required. "Maybe when my nausea goes away?"

Gavin glared at him. Eli looked away.

Jack put an arm around Sabine's shoulders. "Sabine?"

"I don't fly any more," she said. "Not without Quinn. You know that, Jack."

"And I'll say it again," Jack said. "Maybe it's time that you did." He grabbed hold of the long thick loops that hooked snugly under the flyers' armpits. They dangled at the ends of elasticized ropes, and when the pullies lifted them up and let them drop it made it look as though the performers really were flying. He held them out to her.

"No way." Sabine slapped the loops away. "Not without Quinn." She turned and walked away. Jack ran after her for a few paces but then stopped.

"Then you'll never fly again, Sabine!"

Sabine turned. "Then so be it, Jack."

THE SCENE BETWEEN Jack and Sabine sobered everyone up and made them forget about Eli altogether, or so it seemed. Eli sat on a bench along the wall and watched Jack and Gavin practise together while Zari and Lia worked the pullies. Jack and Gavin swooped up and then spiralled down in intricate patterns, coming together and pushing away with such grace that they looked like plumes of smoke twisting in a soft breeze. Eli wondered again if they were lovers. He guessed they were, given the fact that they spent all their time together and the way Gavin had stuck up for him so fiercely. Eli knew that Gavin knew the real reason Eli didn't want to fly with Jack. He could only hope he'd keep it to himself.

Eli watched the practice for a while, but his troupe was ignoring him and his tentative shouts of encouragement, so he crossed the long room to watch Nappo practise the human pyramid with his troupe.

"You gonna join our group?" Teal asked while he waited to clamber to the top as the smallest member.

"Maybe," Eli said. Teal and Nappo had been assigned to the clowning troupe, which didn't have to perform nearly impossible physical feats. It was more about comedy and slapstick. The whole point of the pyramid, for example, was the hilarity at its collapse. The only thing the members had to do was learn to roll and fall safely, and to comically exaggerate their movements. The only one who had to be precise was the captain, whose charge was to catch Teal when he fell.

"I'm not going to be in this group forever, you know," Teal said. "I'm going to be a flyer, like you."

"I'm not anything you want to be like, Teal." Eli shoved his hands into his pockets and turned away. "Be like yourself. You're already better than me."

29

❧

Seth and Rosa received a very strange reception when they arrived at Foothills Market. A hush smothered the market bustle around them as they headed first for the breadminder for something to eat. They could see Thomas gawping at them from the other end of the market, as were many of the other stallminders. Most, however, only stared for a second before regaining their composure and carrying on as normal. As they neared the breadminder, Thomas, still staring, leaned over and whispered something to his wife. She dragged Tasha out for a quick look, and then tossed Seth and Rosa a brief scowl and whipped the shutters shut across the counter.

"We're closed!" she hollered from inside.

"The less business for you, mister!" Seth banged on the shutters. "We won't be back, you can thank your wonderful customer service for that."

Inside, Thomas and his wife and the daughter who'd been pining for Nappo ever since they'd left argued in harsh whispers that Seth and Rosa could not decipher.

"Leave it, Seth." Rosa pulled him away. "We'll find something else to eat."

IT DID NOT TAKE many more odd looks and wide eyes for Seth to know that Eli had passed through here.

"Do you know what a twin is?" he whispered to Rosa as they sat at a table beside the sweetminder stall drinking warm honeyed milk, since the day was cool enough for it.

"Of course I know what twins are." Rosa shook her head. "After all this time, do you really think I'm that stupid?"

"Well, I haven't seen any twins out here—can you blame me?"

"I attended a miscarriage once where there were two babies. Most don't make it to birth or much past it."

"Eli is my twin."

"Really." Rose furrowed her brow. "And exactly why haven't you mentioned that before?"

"He might be my twin, but if I could have it any other way, I would. I didn't want you to think we had any psychic connection, or soul connection, or whatever Droughtland mumbo jumbo you could think up to try to convince me that he's worth sparing. I hate him. Plain and simple." Seth shrugged. "And besides, I didn't think you'd know what I was talking about."

"And that's why people are staring, because he's been here."

Seth lowered his voice even more and leaned close. "Not only has he been here, I think he's made friends. I think that's why they're trying not to stare, so I won't guess that he's been this way, or so that they can carry out some instructions he left with them or something. We're in danger here, Rosa."

He looked up at the breadminder's stall. The shutters were open again, and a crowd had gathered and were murmuring among themselves, every once in a while glancing over at Rosa and Seth. The daughter seemed the most riled up of them all. Seth had to wonder about that.

"This is going to be a problem."

A panic slowly crept into Rosa's eyes as she glanced over at the crowd. "What are they going to do?"

"I don't know. If they didn't befriend him, if they discovered he was a Keylander and killed him, they'll kill me too. If it comes to that, I'll say I forced you to guide me out here. Maybe they'll spare you. If he made allies, and told them to keep an eye out for me and to stop me from pursuing him, then I'm in trouble and he's likely fine." Seth put his hand over Rosa's as she nervously toyed with the paper under their sweets. "No matter how you look at it, you have to calm down." He checked the growing crowd. They weren't murmuring any more, they were arguing, loudly. And the girl was flapping her arms and crying now.

"He's Guard, Daddy!" Tasha cried. "Nappo said!"

"Get them!" Thomas hollered.

At that, Seth and Rosa leapt to their feet. Seth tipped the table over, giving them a gain of just seconds.

"The horses!" Seth grabbed Rosa's hand.

They ran through an alley between two stalls and along the backside of the market as the crowd fumbled after them in a disorganized mass. They had to let go of each other to clear a heap of dirty laundry, and after that Seth lost sight of Rosa as she turned back into the market ahead of him.

When he made the turn the sight of Thomas gripping Rosa in a neck hold stopped him short. Her feet dangled as she choked and gagged and tried to pull free. Seth glanced over his shoulder. The crowd was nearly upon them, the breadminder's wife in the lead.

Seth didn't even think about it. He reached under his shirt for the dead girl's knife and flicked it open, a blade at the ready at either end.

"All the trouble you and your brother have caused this market." Thomas squeezed harder. "And still more. I'll break this traitor's neck if you don't put that knife down."

Seth took aim and threw the knife, praying the hulking man was slower than he was. Rosa screamed as the knife spun neatly through the short distance at her and dug into the only piece of Thomas that wasn't somewhat shielded by Rosa, his thick forearm at her throat.

Thomas howled and dropped Rosa. She crumpled to the ground and clutched at her throat, gasping. Seth pulled her up and shoved her toward the horse she'd bought with the money from her job at the market.

"Go! *Go!* I'll catch up."

Thomas was on his feet now, fuelled by pain and anger.

"You're already a dead man!" Thomas yanked the knife out, threw it to the ground, and lunged for Seth.

Seth ducked, scooped up his knife, and plunged it into the man's side.

Thomas reeled back, clutching his side. He collided with his wife, who did her best to break his fall to the ground. Blood gushed onto the dirt.

"Daddy!" Tasha dropped to her knees beside her father.

The crowd surged toward Thomas, forgetting Seth for the precious seconds he needed to slice Honey's reins from the hitch and race after Rosa, who was a shrinking cloud of dust in the distance.

30

❦

A group was sent from Triskelia to Triban to bring back supplies for the feast and to give the Triskelians in Triban enough advance warning to organize their way back in time for the festivities. This was one reason why the celebration wouldn't happen for weeks, so that other Triskelians could safely travel from wherever they were without arousing suspicion, which would surely be the case if everyone came at once. Not everyone could come anyway; some had to stay behind to keep track of the Guard's movements, and of course, some were on missions far, far away, and still others were cut off in near absolute isolation at the cloudseeding labs in the wilderness, atop mountains where they were engaged in a laborious, tedious war of weather.

Gavin went with the group to Triban, which Eli was glad for, because ever since Eli had dumped Jack as a fly partner Gavin had not stopped glaring at him. Eli was training with Zari now that her shoulder had healed. With Gavin gone, Eli was back to worrying about less important things, like when he'd get his first injury. He was the butt of many jokes, most told in good humour but many with an edge of disapproval and envy, fuelled by Pierre, who rather enjoyed pitting people against Eli whenever he got the chance.

One of Pierre's cronies, the chief tumbler, called up to Eli one day as he and Zari rehearsed the sequence they would perform on feast day.

"Hey up there! Look at you, mister I-don't-got-no-battle-scars!"

Eli flew through the air and hooked arms with Zari, the two of them spinning in tandem.

"Ignore them," Zari whispered as she pushed away and Sabine tugged at the pulley, swooping her high up above him. Zari never spoke when they flew, so Eli was caught off guard. He lost track of his sequence and did a back flip in place of the forward somersault that would've positioned him to catch Zari on her dive down. He scrambled toward her, kicking the air uselessly.

"Uh-oh!" another tumbler hollered. "He's gonna drop her! He's gonna, yes he is!"

And he did. Zari raised her eyebrows at him as she sailed past his open arms and landed in the pillow pit below.

"Letting go!" Jack called up to him. "Drop ready?"

"Drop ready," Eli replied miserably and positioned himself to drop.

Jack loosened the pulley and Eli dropped to the cushions.

"Right, you lot!" Jack strode toward the tumblers now that his hands were free. "Piss off and leave us alone."

The tumblers ran off, laughing.

"I see you again," Jack called after them, "I'll tattoo 'loser' onto your foreheads, got it?"

Zari frowned at Eli in the pit. "Why don't you just do it and get it over with?"

"An injury?"

"What else would I be referring to?"

"But I thought that was cheating."

"What's worse?" Sabine reached a hand to Eli and helped him up. "That they might think you cheated getting your first injury, or that they'll always think you're showing off?"

"I don't know," Eli said. "Which *is* worse?"

"I wouldn't cheat," Jack said. "Some people go years without a first injury. I was nearly two years into a touring circuit before I got mine."

"Was it bad?" Eli asked.

"It was great." Jack pointed to a jagged tattoo that ran the length of his left forearm. "They gave me this. See where the line's broken in two places?" Jack grinned. "That's where the bone broke. In two places."

Eli cringed. "I meant, was it bad going all that time with no injury?"

"Pure hell. After the first year no one would even talk to me, except my troupe."

"And if you had to do it all over again, you still wouldn't cheat?"

"Nah," Jack said. "Those that cheat, they're treated differently anyway, for giving in under pressure. If there's anybody that Zenith thinks less of, it's those who cheat at their first injury."

"I suppose it is cowardly," Sabine said. "After all, who are you *not* to be as gifted as you are? So what if you threaten people who are less gifted."

"Who are you *not* to shine?" Zari linked arms with Sabine. "That's what Zenith always says."

"Besides," Sabine said, "those who are caught cheating end up with all the crappy jobs."

"I'll definitely wait, then." Eli looked over at the tumblers who were practising three-high roll-offs on a long mat across the hall. Even if he wasn't going to stay in Triskelia forever, he didn't want to be demoted. Not to a tumbler, and not to worse.

When he'd first arrived in Triskelia it appeared as if everyone was equal and no one was held in any higher regard than anyone else—except that elders were revered and respected as wiser and were looked to for advice. That idealistic image faded quickly. Everyone supposedly took turns performing the menial jobs such as shovelling horseshit, emptying the waste pits, and cleaning the buildings from floor to ceiling, but Eli had noticed that the circus performers were rarely assigned such duties.

JUST BEFORE PRACTICE one morning, Anya came to find Eli to give him his costume. It was grand, with blood-red flames shooting up the legs and arms and stars embroidered with silver thread at the elbows and around the neckline. Eli thanked her and dashed into the dressing room to try it on.

As he pushed open the door, Zari covered herself with a towel and screamed at him.

"Eli!"

Sabine peeked out from behind a makeup mirror. "You could've knocked!"

"Sorry! Sorry." Eli turned his back to let Zari get properly dressed. How badly he wanted to watch, though. He'd be humiliated to admit how much time he lay awake at night imagining what she looked like beneath her clothes. "Are you done? Can I show you my costume now?"

"Patience, patience," Zari muttered. "You can look now."

All she'd put on was her underlinens. Eli stared at the loose satin ribbon criss-crossing her breasts. Beneath it was a triangle of smooth brown flesh. A perfect, most kissable place. He stared.

Sabine smacked him lightly on the cheek. "You better get comfortable with us like this, Eli. Those costumes might be flashy, but they're really uncomfortable."

"Come on, then." Zari pulled a shawl over her shoulders. "Put it on. Let's see."

"Okay, wait." He slipped behind a changing screen and stripped off his clothes. He had to take his underlinens off too, since it would look like he was wearing a diaper if he didn't. For the few seconds he was buck-naked before he tugged on the costume, he stared down at his dick and wondered if Triskelian girls—say, Zari, for example—would ever consider someone who'd been cut. He yanked the slick material up his body and slid his arms in. He smoothed the material over his abs, which had become neatly defined since he began training, and turned to admire himself in the mirror.

Something was wrong. None of the other boys or men looked like that, their bits squelching around like two mandarin oranges and a sausage in a wax paper bag. Worse though was that the slick fabric was making his sausage stand at attention.

"Come on!" Zari rapped on the screen. "Let's see."

"No!" Eli bent over to cover himself. "I'm not ready."

"Come on." That was Lia. "We've only got the pit for two hours."

"Who all is out there?"

"Everyone," Jack said. "Sabine brought us all in for the unveiling."

That did the trick; nothing like the thought of a bender to send his willy into chilly exile. Eli sighed with relief and straightened. He pulled his shoulders back and strode out. He struck his tag; the wink and finger-snap that would be his trademark way of addressing the crowds on tour. He looked over his shoulder at himself in the mirror and couldn't help but dog-whistle at his own image. Man, did he ever look sharp.

"Eli, no!" Zari cried. Behind her the others groaned and shook their heads.

"You never whistle in the dressing room!" Sabine put her hands to her mouth. "It's very bad luck."

"I didn't know." Why wasn't anyone looking at his fabulous costume? "Isn't it great?"

"Yeah, it is." But Sabine's eyes were locked on Jack.

Zari at least was looking, or staring, more like. Why was she staring? Eli became acutely aware of the fabric of the costume again. No, he ordered himself, absolutely, positively not right now, no! Sabine jabbed Zari with her elbow. "He looks really good, doesn't he, Zari?"

"He looks great." Zari tugged at Lia, who was nodding her agreement, and the three girls backed toward the door. "The costume looks great, really."

"We're going to warm up," Sabine said quickly. She widened her eyes pointedly at Jack, who was having a hard time suppressing a smirk. "Jack has something to tell you, don't you, Jack?"

Jack coughed back a laugh and nodded.

"Wait!" Eli took a step for the door. He didn't want to be left alone in the dressing room with a bender. "I'm coming with you."

"Uh, no." Sabine pushed him gently back. "Trust me, Eli. You're not ready." And with that she shut the door, leaving Eli and Jack alone.

Eli looked at Jack. Jack looked at Eli.

"Eli, Eli, Eli." Jack grinned.

"Uh, I forgot something," Eli said as he ducked behind the screen.

"You sure did." Jack followed him and poked his head around the corner.

Eli turned his back to him. "What do you want, Jack?"

"We've got to work this out, Eli."

"Work what out?" Eli tried his hardest to look clueless.

"There's two things going on here." Jack came behind the screen and sat on a little stool in the corner. Eli prayed no one would come into the dressing room to find them like this. It seemed intimate. Wrong. "Do you want me to start with the one about me? Or the one about you?"

"I don't know what you're talking about." Eli sat on the narrow bench beside the mirror, as far away from Jack as possible. He draped his clothes over his lap so that Jack wouldn't have anything interesting to look at.

"I'll just go ahead then and start with the one about you." Jack reached into his pocket and pulled out a shallow dish of turned wood lined with felt. He tossed it at Eli. "The girls were staring at you because you didn't have your balls in one of these. All the guys wear them, hadn't you noticed?"

"Why would I even be looking?" Eli was instantly horrified. Of course they'd wear something like that. Of course, of course. Of course! It was no different from the football players in the Keys. Was it humanly possible to be more of a fool? Eli doubted it very much. He'd reached the pinnacle of idiocy. "Anya didn't give me one."

"That's because you don't get them from her." Jack reached over to give Eli a reassuring pat on the knee, but Eli cranked himself away.

"Don't."

Jack pulled his hand back. "You get them from the woodminder."

"Well, thanks." Eli wanted to evaporate right then and there and be done with it. There was no point going on in life after a humiliation of this magnitude. "Now, would you excuse me so that I can die of a fatal case of embarrassment?"

"You know that Droughtlanders don't get cut, right?"

"Yeah. Trust me, I know." Eli stared at the floor. Oh, please, to just bloody well evaporate and be bloody well done with it.

"So you'd probably want to know that we could tell you were cut, just then. Through the cloth. It was kind of obvious."

Eli put a hand to his forehead and rubbed hard before forcing himself to look at Jack. Jack pulled in a grin, but not before Eli caught it.

"You're enjoying this, aren't you?"

"Not at all, I would die if I were you right now, especially considering your crush on Zari."

"Then why are you grinning?"

Jack shrugged. "To tell you the truth, which will also bring me to my other reason for talking to you, I'm delighted to see you get a little bruised after how you've been treating me lately."

"What do you mean?"

Jack rolled his eyes. "You going to play stupid? Or do you think you might actually be able to take a little responsibility for your ignorance?"

Now Eli's cheeks were flushing again, only not in embarrassment, but in rage.

"I don't know what you're talking about, Jack."

"Tell me, while looking me in the eye, that you haven't treated me differently since you found out that Quinn was my boyfriend. Tell me you're okay that I'm bent."

Eli looked up, surprised at hearing Jack say the word.

"I happen to like the word," Jack said, sitting back against the wall. "Well?"

"Where I come from—"

"You come from here, Eli."

"But where I was raised—"

"You're not there any more. You're here now, and if you're going to be a member of the Night Circus, or a rebel, or even a Droughtlander, you're going to have to change your attitude. Benders are a legion out here, and if I wanted I could have you lynched for your backward Keyland ideas."

"I'm sorry, Jack. I am trying."

"And that's why I haven't let Gavin beat the Keylander out of you. So far, anyway." Jack folded his arms. "You know he desperately wants to?"

Eli nodded. "I guessed that much."

"I'm going to take this opportunity to tell you one more thing." Jack stood. "I'm only going to tell you this once. I find you entirely unattractive. You're scrawny and gangly and have a pimply back, and all that's besides the fact that you hate queers. If you're at all worried that I'm going to put the moves on you, you can rest assured that I'd rather die by skineater sick first. Okay then, see you at the pit."

And then he was gone, leaving Eli with the jockstrap, wondering how it tied on. He was also left to wonder this: if a bender found him so repulsive, did that mean girls would think he was gross too? Did Zari think he was unattractive?

NO ONE WAS SURPRISED when during practice—not even half an hour after he'd whistled in the dressing room—Eli stumbled after Zari did a pitch-back off his shoulders. He fell off the platform and hit his wrist on the bar of the swing he was meant to catch. There was a satisfying crack, and then a hot rush of pain. Eli landed in the pit and lifted up his broken wrist for all to see.

"I did it! My first injury! And it wasn't on purpose!"

The troupe glowered at him.

"But it wasn't! You all saw!"

"Great timing, you idiot." Zari yanked herself out of the fly straps. "Now who'll I fly with at the feast?"

"You never whistle in the dressing room," Sabine said. "Everyone knows that!"

"Everyone," Lia murmured as she climbed down to take a look at the break.

"Exquisite timing, Eli." Jack put his hand to his forehead and shook his head. "This is just great."

"Well, what's done is done." Sabine jumped into the pit with the first aid kit. "Let's get you out of here."

"I've messed everything up, haven't I?" Eli's wrist started to throb heinously. "I've ruined the fly act for the feast."

"Yeah, you did." Sabine splinted his arm and secured it in a triangle bandage across his chest. "But life goes on." She looked up at Jack as she said it. "We'll figure something out."

"But I won't get to perform at the celebration, will I?" Now his wrist felt like someone was slicing it with a dull knife in slow, steady drags.

Sabine shook her head. "Doesn't look like it."

"Could we postpone it?" After all, it was in honour of *his* mother.

"With all the planning and everyone coming?" Zari offered Eli a hand out of the pit. "As if! I think the pain is making him wonky. Let's get him to the lifeminder."

31

⟨⟩

Seth took to Seduce with the same natural talent and speed that Eli had taken to the circus arts. Days after he and Rosa had fled from Foothills Market they'd come upon the same mountain camp that Eli and the brothers had, although none of the same people were left to recognize Seth. They rested there, keeping an eye on their backs. It would seem, so far, that no one from the market had followed them.

Rosa taught Seth the game, and then after a few rounds she'd grown bored and gone to bed. When she awoke at dawn, cold and stiff, a foot of snow having fallen in the night, she wasn't surprised to see that Seth was still playing at the main fire. He won and lost a lot of money that night, but in his mind it was an investment. This was something he could get rich by, he was sure.

The other players told him about the recent tournament in Triban, although none of them had been there. Several of them were on their way there now, though, to participate in smaller tournaments, less organized but with much bigger stakes. There were cash prizes, yes, but you could come away with land, or horses, or slaves. Seth's Droughtland opportunities were suddenly endless and exciting.

"We'll go there next," he said as he helped Rosa pull down the tent.

"I don't know, Seth. It sounds rough and dirty."

"This whole place is rough and dirty!"

"Still," Rosa said. "I'm uneasy about it for some reason."

"You're uneasy because of what happened in the market," Seth whispered. "That's perfectly understandable. We *killed* a man."

"We don't know that he's dead, but you did nearly kill *me*! That's what makes me uneasy. Where did you get that knife, and when did you learn to use it like that?"

"I bought it. As for using it like that," Seth shrugged, "I've had practice."

He meant his time as a Guard initiate, and basic training of course, but he wasn't about to mention either.

THERE WAS PLENTY of work for Rosa in Triban. After they'd settled at a lodger's and had treated themselves to new masks—top of the line according to the maskminder—Rosa chose an intersection of five lanes in the market district where she set up a little table and waited for the sick and wounded to come.

And come they did. The characters who formed the line waiting for her services repulsed Seth. He kept well away from the pussy human wrecks, and was more than happy to run around fetching the herbs and cloths and clean water Rosa sent him off for as the cash came pouring in. At the end of the first day Rosa collapsed onto her bed and exclaimed, "This is a very lucrative place to be, isn't it?"

"And to think you didn't want to come." Seth was washing up with a pail of warm water, getting ready to go to the Seduce den at the end of the street, which he figured was as good a place as any to embark on his new career as a Seducer.

"Maybe it wasn't such a bad idea."

"Are you saying I was right and you were wrong?" Seth pulled off his shirt, checking covertly to be sure that Rosa was watching. She had been, lately, at any opportunity. Seth was beginning to hope that she might be attracted to him in the same way he was to her. She just wasn't like other Droughtlanders. And after all this time out here, even he was realizing they were more than animals.

"Maybe."

"Man, I wish I had a witness right about now." Seth pulled on a clean shirt. "Will you come with me tonight?"

"No." Rosa collapsed on the bed. "I'm exhausted. You go. Make us rich."

She said *us*, make *us* rich. "I'll do that." Just a few minutes later, when he was ready to leave, Rosa was already fast asleep, hands together under her cheek. Seth took the blanket from his bed and covered her with it. She didn't even stir. He watched her breathe steadily for another minute and then leaned down and kissed her forehead. She opened her eyes.

Seth reeled back. "Sorry!"

"It's okay, Seth." Rosa reached for his hand. He let her take it, and then he let her draw him closer. She pulled him nearer until his face was just above hers, and then she lifted her head and kissed him on the lips.

As far as Seth was concerned, that was the first real kiss he'd ever experienced. Never mind the village girls, this was brand new. This was a brand-new star in the galaxy. Rosa smiled and pushed him away.

"I'm really too tired to be doing this, or maybe that's why I did it." She stifled a yawn. "I have to sleep now and you have to go, or I'll stay up being nervous." She closed her eyes again. "Okay?"

"I'm going." Seth swallowed. "Soon." He wanted to kiss her again, but she rolled over, her face almost touching the wall. Seth sat on the edge of her bed until her breathing levelled into sleep, then he backed out and quietly closed the door. He stood in the hall for a while, too bewildered to move, until he finally made his way down the winding stairs to the street, the memory of the kiss locking a ridiculous smile on his face. He had to work hard to get rid of it, lest strangers think he was a foolish goof not worthy of picking for a game of Seduce. But in the end, reciting the fact that he was a Keylander and she was a Droughtlander did it. Barely though, because it was getting to the point where he just didn't care. His ideas about Droughtlanders were getting confused, as was his grasp on Keyland ideas and politics. If it wasn't for the fact that his main goal was to destroy Eli, he wasn't sure what he'd have left to believe in.

THE FIRST TABLE HE JOINED was too ruthless even for Seth. The glowering men there wagered wives and daughters and deeds to vast tracts of land in regions Seth had never heard of. He excused himself, pretending he had to pee. He left that den, hurried down the street, and disappeared into the next one.

The next table he joined was much more suited to him. He played several rounds, losing all of them spectacularly. Soon, he had no money left to wager. He gave up and pushed his chair away from the table, preparing to leave, but the winner of the last round stopped him.

"Haven't you got anything of value to wager?"

Besides his knife, there was only the dead girl's mirror. He pulled it out and set it on the table. The other players stopped their cussing and smoking and set their mugs of booze down to pass the little mirror between them. Seth watched how each man looked at it. Each one of them wanted it very badly. The winner caressed it in his big hands, rubbing the smooth carved back of it with his thumb.

"This is a fine thing to wager." He set it on the table in front of him. "How much is it worth?"

The men stared hungrily at the mirror.

"You tell me," Seth said.

"Hah!" The winner stroked his filthy beard. "I don't think so. Misters?"

The other men reluctantly pulled their eyes off the mirror.

"What say we have a little tourney for this pretty prize here? Winner takes the mirror and whatever pot there is, and if this mister wins, he takes the pot and—"

"And what?" Seth folded his arms. "What have you got that equals my treasure?"

"A plot of land. A small one, up north on the water." The winner set a tattered piece of paper on the table. "There's the deed. My name is Bristol."

"Maddox." Seth had worked hard to break the habit of shaking hands, but still, he felt his hand instinctively rising. He picked up the mirror instead. "You're on."

Bristol announced the tourney to the rest of the den.

"It's a rare piece of finery," Bristol boasted. "Guaranteed to woo your lady, or, if you prefer, it would fetch a pretty pile of cash on the market." He took the mirror and tilted it so that it caught the light and reflected on the dark faces of the other Seducers.

"My mom had one of them," an old fellow at the next table said, leaning over and reaching for the mirror. "Let's have a look?"

"I don't think so. No." Seth took the mirror back and slipped it in his pocket. "I'll hold on to it until there's a winner."

Bristol rubbed his hands together and winked at the old man. "No worries, mister, this lad is all over the map when he plays. Might very well be you with it in your pocket at the end of the game."

Seth bristled. "How do you know I haven't been holding back?"

"For your sake," Bristol said, "let's hope you have."

Seth appraised his hand—not bad to start out with. He and Rosa could make a farm on that land up north. They could build a house. He hoped the land was perched high, with lots of sunlight and rich soil.

HALFWAY THROUGH THE GAME, two burly men crashed through the crowded den and pulled one of the players at Seth's table out to the street by his ears.

"Debtminders," Bristol muttered, eyes on his cards. "Can't even let the poor man finish the round."

"He might'a won this time," another player said, and then he half stood and addressed the players queued along the walls. "Need a player. Only one!" he added as half a dozen surged forward.

Seth sized up the young man with the fiery red hair now sitting across from him. The new player was staring at him just as hard.

"What are you looking at?" It came out more bitter than Seth had intended, but he was doing very badly. At least before he'd still had the mirror to give Rosa, and now both the mirror and the farm were unlikely.

"Nothing, mate." The new player grinned. "I'm Gavin. Pleased to join your table, albeit crippled with a lousy hand." He waved the cards abandoned by the last player.

"Maddox," Seth offered. "Also crippled by a lousy hand, albeit my fault."

"You're crippled by far more than the cards you're dealt, my young friend," Bristol said, topping up Seth's mug from the pitcher.

"I'm no friend of yours," Seth growled. "Just play the game."

HE LOST rather spectacularly again. Gavin took the pot, and the mirror, and then offered to buy Seth a consolation supper at a pubhouse a short walk from the den. Seth agreed to join him, only because he didn't want to lose track of the mirror. He hoped to win it back shortly, as soon as he had something to get into a game with. He wondered if Rosa would lend him some money, just a little bit to get started again.

"Who you got there?" a boy asked at the corner, stepping out from the alley where he'd been playing craps with a gang of ratty-looking boys gathered around a burning barrel.

"None of your business, Amon." Gavin quickened his pace. "Come on, Seth. Let's go."

"Hey! He looks just like—" Amon called after them. "Wait up, Gavin!"

"I look familiar?" Seth stopped. "Why do you say that?"

Amon shrugged. "A little money might help me remember."

"Leave him." Gavin tugged at Seth's sleeve. "He's a liar, and a cheat. And a junkie."

"Oh yeah?" Amon hollered as Gavin ushered Seth down the steps of a pub at the end of the block. "You better watch out, Gavin, I got way more friends in this city than you!"

GAVIN SEEMED VERY INTERESTED in Seth, even though Seth fed him lie after lie about being a Droughtlander from Rosa's village. Gavin wanted to know how he'd come to be in Triban, and where he was going next, and did he have any brothers or sisters back in the village?

"One. A brother." Seth set his knife and fork down and levelled his gaze at Gavin. "He's the reason I left the village. I need to find him, to tell him that our father is very ill and wishes to see his son once more before the sick takes him. We look exactly the same, only his hair is dark. His name is Eli. Eli Maddox. Maybe you've heard of him?"

"Hmm. Can't say I have." Gavin pushed his plate away. "But I wish you the best of luck in finding him. I hope your father recovers."

"Thank you."

"I'll keep an eye out for your doppelgänger." He dropped a handful of cash on the table. "Well, I've got an invite-only tourney across town to get to. Maybe I'll see you around." And with that he left, taking with him Seth's small hope of winning the mirror back for Rosa.

Once outside, Gavin waited in the narrow gap between two buildings to see which way Seth would go. Seth came out shortly and headed back the way they'd come. He walked slowly, looking down each alley. Gavin followed at a distance, stopping when Seth did. From a dark doorway, he watched Seth approach Amon when he finally found him. He watched them talk for a while, and then he hurried away in the opposite direction, to the horseminders.

Tasha, her heart full of relief that her father had fully recovered from Seth's attack, packed a horse and rode into the mountains, slipping away from Foothills Market without saying goodbye to her parents, or her sister, or anyone. She didn't want anyone to stop her. She had to be strong. She had to find Nappo. She was pregnant. By him.

He would marry her. She'd bring him back to Foothills Market and he could work for Thomas and they would have a wedding, bigger and more beautiful than her sister's. She headed up the mountain pass, alone, the snow falling thick and quiet.

She'd been to the mountain camp. Sometimes kids from the market went up there, just to get away, play some Seduce, smoke some dust. Mostly in the summer though.

She arrived at the camp, found some people she knew from the market, set up her tent, and chose a game to join. As the moon rose the air grew even colder, and every exhale was marked with white.

It was after midnight when the ambush happened. An army of Guard horsemen, guns drawn, stampeded from all directions into the camp.

Everyone scattered, until the first shots were fired and the first Droughtlanders fell, their blood screaming in the snow, their bodies lifeless.

"Nobody move!" Commander Regis sat tall in his saddle, gun raised. His men corralled the motley crew of campers into a trembling mass and surrounded them. Tasha was more furious than afraid. She would not die here. Not without Nappo. Not before she could meet their baby. Not before their wedding. And who was this man anyway?

Commander Regis looked the group over, and then shook his head.

"He's not here." He whispered something to his assistant. And then louder, to his munitions man, "How are we for bullets?"

The man shook his head. "Dwindling, sir."

"Knives then." Commander Regis turned his horse around. "Conserve the bullets."

And so the slaughter began. There was nowhere to go, and no way to fight back. Tasha swallowed her screams and dropped to her knees, clutching her belly protectively. As her fellow Seduce players fell around her, she fell too, as if she'd been gored. In small movements, she worked herself nearer to a fat man, his guts spilling out of his belly in a steamy mass. She bloodied her hands and clutched her throat, wiping the blood on her neck and down her cloak. She pulled the man's cape over her face and lay very still while the screams fell like shooting stars around her and the snow bled red with death.

WHEN THE SCREAMS STOPPED, and Tasha was left tangled in a heap of cold, stiffening corpses, she forced herself to remain still. The Guardies hadn't left. They were wandering the camp, taking what little there was to take—food, trinkets, whatever money they could find.

The one in charge, the one who'd given the orders, strode through the camp, obviously angry.

"How hard is it to find Keylander twins out here? We know he's been this way." He was very close now. Tasha held her breath. "I want to know more about the Droughtland bitch he's travelling with. And I want the truth from the Chief Regent. If he wants his boys brought in, I want to know the real reason why!"

Nappo's friend! And the one who'd stabbed her father! This was about them! She had to warn Nappo. He was in danger travelling with Eli.

She waited, the cold creaking right into her bones, the bodies hardening with rigor, until the rumble of the regiment faded into silence and the only sound that was left was her pounding heart. Had this hurt the baby? The panic? The fear? She stood, shivering and stiff, her hands clutching her belly. She did look at the bodies, of course she did, there was no way she couldn't have, but she didn't really see them. She saw darkness, and the moonlit shadow of forest, and a million stars above all telling her to go home.

Tasha stumbled out of the camp on foot—they'd taken the horses—back toward Foothills Market. Back toward home, where she would tell everyone what she'd seen. And then she'd set off again to find Nappo, and nothing would stop her this time.

32

The only one who felt sorry for Eli's broken wrist was Bullet. The dog kept nudging his cast and looking up at Eli with the most pathetic stare. As for everyone else, they carried on without so much as a nod in his direction at getting his first injury, although the harassment had thankfully ended. Eli had been assigned to help the childminders until his wrist healed.

"But I could stick with my troupe and learn from watching," he'd said to Zenith when she told him he was expected in the nursery the morning after he broke his wrist.

"Normally, I would concur," Zenith said, "but with preparations in full swing, we need you in the nursery to free up one of the other minders to help in the kitchen."

"I hate kids?"

"You do not," Zenith said. "You're just feeling sorry for yourself."

At least he got Charis to keep an eye on. She pulled him around the nursery, showing off his cast to the other children. He let her draw all over it with crayons and climb all over him like he was a trapeze. It wasn't that bad, actually. If he was going to be honest, he'd have to admit it was a thankful break from the ruthless training regime of the troupe.

Three days later the situation got even better. Nappo showed up.

"Reassigned until after the feast." He lifted Charis onto his shoulders. "They don't need the new tumblers. I don't mind. Really."

Both of them could spot each other's bruised egos from across the room.

"Think of it as a holiday," Eli suggested.

"Yeah. I guess."

They made the best of it anyway. The nursery was a cheery, vibrant place where the kids were encouraged to play all day with paints and blocks and dress-up clothes. There was a tot-sized gym at one end of the attic nursery where the little ones could practise tumbling and dropping and hanging from the bars. The best part of the day was after the midday meal when the children settled for naps on thick mats under small quilts. An elder told them all a story, and then another sang them lullabies until they were all asleep and blissfully quiet.

Eli and Nappo would do their share of tidying up, and then slip out and sit on the landing and marvel with each other about Triskelia and all that had happened since they met. And when they ran out of things to say about that, they talked about Zari and Lia, and how one day the four of them would form their own act together, and their children would be born in Triskelia, and would take to the circus arts like they were born with an extra part in their brain that held all they'd ever need to know about it.

They didn't talk about the revolution though. Now that they were here, welcomed and happy and fed, and with crushes to distract them and the circus arts to learn, Eli started to understand how complacency happened, and why no one wanted to upturn the utopia for what would be a long, brutal haul to freedom for every Droughtlander. Eli told himself it would happen, that he would *make* it happen. Just not yet. After the celebration, perhaps. Maybe then the time would be right.

And the boys never spoke of Seth, either, and the fact that he was likely still out there, hunting for Eli. It was a magic time, and the first since leaving the Eastern Key that Eli had managed to forget about his brother.

THAT IS, until Gavin arrived home in the middle of the night, having ridden straight from Triban after meeting Seth. He was the one who woke Eli and pulled him from his bunk.

"Get up!" Gavin chucked Eli's boots at him. "You're coming with me!"

"But Jack and I—" Eli fought to pull himself out of the deep sleep he'd been in, a dream where he was performing the fly routine without the straps and pullies and Zari had been flying right beside him. "Jack and I sorted it out. Didn't he tell you?"

"This isn't about Jack." Gavin tossed Eli a sweater. "It's about your brother. He's in Triban, and I think he's heading this way."

GAVIN LED ELI to Zenith's quarters, where Trace and Jack and Sabine and Celeste and about twenty others were already gathered. Pierre was there too, leaning casually against the wall, keeping his distance. Eli glanced at him.

"All your fault," Pierre muttered. "Happy?"

"Eli." Celeste reached out to him. "Come sit by the fire with us."

"What happened?" Eli gratefully accepted the mug of tea someone handed him. "What's going on?"

Gavin explained his encounter with Seth, and his subsequent meeting with Amon.

"That kid from the tournament," Trace reminded him when it became apparent that Eli had no idea who Gavin was talking about. "You remember, the one who gave you a hard time."

"Ah, him." Eli vaguely remembered.

"He's our cousin," Sabine said. "Only he's been banished from here."

"One of the few we've lost to the dust," Zenith said.

"He's a dust runner now." Trace leaned forward. "And a traitor. We think he'll tell your brother where you are. For the right price."

"But Seth *can't* know where Triskelia is!" Panic drew its icy fingers up Eli's spine. He shivered. "He'll tell Edmund. And then the Guard will come and destroy everything!"

Everyone was silent, eyes on Eli.

"He's had the skineater sick," Gavin said. "I don't think he's in the Guard any more."

"Or he's lying, and he's a plant," Trace said. "It could be makeup."

"He can't come here." Eli shook his head. "He has to be stopped."

"What a brilliant idea." Pierre clapped. "Oh, thank you Eli. We never would've thought of that on our own."

"Pierre," Celeste murmured. "Don't."

"I'll stop him myself." Eli's stomach flipped at just the idea. "Whatever it takes. I'll do it. I got us into this mess. Pierre is right. It is all my fault."

"Not really," Sabine said, but that was the only out offered.

"We'll go with you," Jack said.

"We'll send out five groups." Trace unrolled a map onto the table. Eli squeezed his eyes shut as everyone gathered around it. He opened them quickly, hoping he'd be back in bed, waking up for real. No such luck. It was true. It was his fault. If Eli hadn't left the Key, Seth wouldn't have followed him.

"We'll sweep the most likely routes." Gavin traced one with a finger. "The routes even Amon would remember."

"This area is impassable unless you have a proper guide." Trace crossed off a section of the map. "Amon won't send him that way, unless he wants Seth dead. In which case we don't have to worry about killing him."

Killing him? The idea was cold water in the face. Eli shivered. Even though he hated Seth, probably more than anyone in Triskelia could—even Pierre—Eli still shrank from the idea of killing him. He shook his head, disagreeing with his own thoughts. Now was not the time to be weak! He had no choice. If it came to that, he prayed he could do it. Kill his brother. It was a thunderous thought. Eli shook his head again, reminding himself that if Seth found him first, it would be Eli who would be dead.

"Are you okay?" Zari laid a hand on his shoulder.

"What about the celebration?" Eli swallowed hard, remembering Seth's gun jammed against his throat, and then his arm against his throat, pinning him to the wall. He coughed. "It's so soon."

"Eli?" Zari said in wonder. "Is that really what's on your mind?"

"Hopefully we'll sniff him out fast," Trace said. "Kill him quick and be home in time for it."

Zenith watched the remaining colour drain from Eli's cheeks. "And if there is no need to kill him, or if it takes longer than we hope, the festivities will wait," she said. "Don't worry, Eli."

"We leave now." Trace rolled up the map. "Gather your packs and assemble in the courtyard. We can't wait to stagger our departures."

"Then Triskelia is already doomed," Pierre said.

"I did check it out, Pierre." Trace glared at him. "The trailminders are confident that there've been no Guardy spies for several weeks. And the colony leaders agree."

"And if they're wrong?" Pierre glared back at Trace. "If this is all part of a trap?"

"Then perhaps you should inventory our defences while we're gone." Trace looked away, slapping the rolled-up map in the palm of his hand as if it were a weapon. "Let's go!"

Eli hung back until the room cleared, except for Zenith and Trace.

"Don't kill him, Trace." Eli hated himself for saying it. All these long months, nearly a year he'd wished Seth gone, and now he was sick at the thought of it actually happening. It was one thing to wish his brother a sick, or a crippling Guardy accident, or faceless, angry Droughtlanders beating him into a vegetative state, but murder?

"If you don't want to go, no one will force you to," Zenith said. "Or think less of you. And killing him is only an option if there is no other."

"No! No, I want to go. But can't we just capture him and keep him here as a prisoner?"

"Triskelia comes first," Trace said. "We'll do what needs to be done."

Zenith patted Eli's good arm. "Hopefully, violence will not be necessary."

THE FIVE GROUPS rode out that night, the sound of pounding hooves growing distant the farther each group travelled along their separate routes. Two of the groups were led by men Eli didn't know. Trace led another group, Gavin the fourth, and Sabine led the fifth with Eli, Zari, and Nappo. Their group took the same route Eli had first come with Trace, and as they climbed up the steep bank out of the valley—Bullet leading the way, happy to be travelling again—Eli looked back at the chaotic dapple of lights that he now called home and wondered if he'd ever see it again. He expected he'd be killed if his group found Seth first. Silently, Eli prayed Trace would have to kill him after all. Perhaps that would be for the best, however conflicted Eli felt about it.

33

S eth brought Amon back to the lodge and woke Rosa.

"We're leaving," he said. "I know where my brother is!"

Rosa rubbed her eyes and blinked as Seth lit the lantern. She noticed Amon at the door and sat up suddenly.

"Who's he?"

"This is the kid who told me."

She studied Amon's filthy clothes, his raw, blistered, dust-sniffer nose, and his fingers, pitch black from kneading poppy grease into blocks to sell to those too poor to smoke anything else. "And you believe him?"

"He knows. Don't you, Amon?"

"I saw him with my very own eyes."

Seth began throwing their things into the packs.

"Wait, hold on." She grabbed her pack from him. "I'm not going with you on a mission to kill your brother."

"As it turns out, I might not have to kill him after all."

"You expect me to believe that after everything?"

Seth pulled Amon all the way into the room. "This kid claims to know more about my family than you will ever believe. Before I do or do not kill Eli, I have to find him, and when I find him, first I need to find out how much of what Amon says is true."

Rosa scowled at Amon. "And what did this . . . this *kid* tell you?"

"That he can take us to Triskelia. And that my mother is from there."

"Your mother. From Triskelia." Rosa shook her head and planted her hands on her hips. "And you believe him? Just because he says so?"

"He recognized me because of Eli! He says Eli is there. He says I have grandparents, cousins, aunts and uncles."

"Seth, please, think about what you're saying." She put a hand on his arm. "How can you believe that? You're a—" She glanced at Amon and stopped herself.

"You can say it," Seth said. "Amon knows I'm from the Keys."

"I don't know, Seth." Rosa narrowed her eyes at Amon. "He hardly looks trustworthy."

"Hey, just you wait a—"

"Shut up." Seth put a threatening finger to Amon's chest. "Just shut up." He turned to Rosa. "I don't trust him, but we have to go and find out. I have to know! If what he says is true, then Eli just might live, for a while anyway. And if what Amon says is all a lie, I'll kill Eli, and then I'll take great pleasure in slitting Amon's throat."

Amon swallowed, but didn't say a word.

"Don't talk like that," Rosa said. "It's terrible."

"Look, Rosa. This kid has told me things that Eli tried to tell me back home. And if what Eli was saying was true, then I am very wrong about what kind of man my father is. I have to find out for myself."

"So this isn't a death mission so much as a mission to seek the truth?" Rosa pulled the blankets off and stood, hands on her hips. "Can you promise me that you won't kill your brother?"

"I promise I won't kill him right away."

"But you still might?"

"Rosa, this might be a set-up. Amon might be part of a trap Eli has set for me. I might have to kill him out of self-defence."

"But you don't *intend* to kill him any more?"

"I *intend* to speak to him, and to the others Amon told me about."

"I can't believe you're taking the word of a filthy dust hook. Look at him!"

"Hey," Amon said. "You're speaking to a first cousin of Mister Seth Maddox, so watch it."

"Cousin?" Rosa's jaw dropped. "You don't really believe him, do you?"

"I have had the most incredible evening, Rosa." Seth pulled her to the door, draped her cape over her shoulders, and handed her her mask. "I'll tell you everything on the way, or Amon can. He's coming with us."

34

On the second day out of Triskelia, about midday, it began to snow. As the snow continued to fall, Eli's group fell silent. The only sound was the horses' hooves crunching on the frosty ground. If Eli hadn't been so keenly aware of why they were out in the bush in the first place, he might have enjoyed himself on what any onlooker would've thought was a wintry ride in the woods with a group of friends.

"It's so cold." Zari rubbed her mittened hands together after it'd been snowing for a couple of hours. "Let's stop and make tea."

Everyone agreed that a hot drink was a brilliant idea. They warmed their hands over the fire and waited for the melting snow in the kettle to boil. After tea and a few cookies each, they set off again, Sabine riding beside Eli, Zari and Nappo following behind. Nappo had sulked all their first day out because Sabine hadn't picked Lia to come with them too, but he'd chilled out a bit since, and was a little more bearable to be around. Although they were all getting a little tired of hearing about how great Lia was.

"He's pretty lovesick, eh?" Sabine said.

Eli shrugged.

"You sure haven't said much since we left," Sabine said. "Are you afraid?"

Eli nodded. "If you knew him, you'd be afraid too. And if you knew Edmund, and how much like him Seth is, you'd be terrified."

"Are you terrified then?"

Eli nodded again. "There's one thing that might stop him, you know."

"Me, right?"

"I can't help but think that if he lays eyes on you he'll have no choice but to realize how much he doesn't know or understand yet."

"Let's hope I'm the first one he sees then."

"Let's hope he freezes to death in the snow first," Eli said.

"You don't really want that, do you?"

"I don't know what I want," Eli said. "This Amon, is he likely to tell him anything more than where I am?"

"Amon is pretty unpredictable. I have no idea what he may or may not have told Seth, or how much of it is true."

Eli and Sabine rode along silently for a while, listening to Zari and Nappo argue about who was the best at each circus art. Then, as night fell, they stopped and set up their tents at the edge of a small frozen lake. After they'd eaten the four of them went out onto the lake and played on the ice, skating in their boots, crashing into one another and laughing in the moonlight, watching Bullet scramble gracelessly across the ice, his four legs slipping and sliding like a foal trying to stand. Eli enjoyed himself in the moments between when he remembered why they were out there, and for those brief reprieves from terror, he was thankful.

THE NEXT MORNING Eli woke very early. It was still dark out, and dreadfully cold, but he needed to pee, so he pulled on all the layers he had and went out into the crisp dark dawn. Bullet followed him at his heel, and after Eli peed he realized he wouldn't fall back to sleep and would rather take a head-clearing walk by himself before the others woke. He headed out onto the lake at first, but Bullet had such a hard time on the ice that he eventually just flopped over and refused to go any farther until Eli turned them around. They walked south of the lake instead, down the path the group would set out on later.

After a while Eli stopped, the light of day creeping through the forest, dappling the morning in shards of light and glinting off the icicles weighing down the boughs. This was as quiet as the world would ever get, and Eli soaked it up, shivering at a distant crack that broke the reverie, the gunshot-loud crack of a branch snapping off under the weight of melting snow. He turned and headed back to camp, Bullet bounding ahead of him in eager anticipation of breakfast.

About halfway back to camp Bullet stopped and turned back on the path ahead of Eli. Ears straight, tail hovering at an uneasy half-mast, he started barking.

"What is it?" Eli scanned the dense forest on either side, straining to hear what Bullet was hearing.

Bullet let out a low growl, his hackles rising. He ducked his head, ready to charge, but still Eli couldn't see or hear what he was focused on. And then Bullet took off, down the path away from camp, at a dead run.

"Bullet!" Eli ran after him, but the dog had disappeared over a ridge and was out of sight now. "Bullet! Get back here, boy!" Eli crested the ridge just as a terrible yelp pierced the air. He scrambled to keep his footing, but didn't, and landed on his knees, staring in horror at the sight far below him. There was Bullet, collapsed on his side at the foot of the hill, blood staining the snow around him like a cape, and Seth atop a mangy horse, towering over the dog.

Eli slid down the hill and sank into the bloody snow beside Bullet.

"What did you do?" Eli didn't look up for a reaction or wait for an answer. He pulled out the hot, slippery knife and put pressure on the wound with his hands. He could not, *would* not, look at his brother.

"I'll take that." Amon scooped the knife away before Eli could think straight. His brain had begged for him to stab his brother, but his heart argued for him to keep his hands where they were.

"Told you it was him." Amon handed the knife back to Seth, who'd pulled his hood up to conceal his scarred face. "Didn't I?"

Eli shrugged off his cloak, pressing a corner of it to Bullet's wound and draping the rest of it over the dog to keep him warm.

"The dog was going to attack me," Seth said, in the same patronizing tone he'd always used with Eli. "What else was I supposed to do?"

"It's true," Amon said. "The bitch was racing for him, teeth bared and everything."

"It's a male dog, genius." Rosa climbed off her horse. She knelt and lifted the cloak off Bullet. Eli pushed her away.

"Don't touch him!" He couldn't keep from weeping a moment longer, as much as he did not want to cry in front of Seth. "Get away from us!" Eli lowered his face, burying it in the warmth of Bullet's neck. He listened to the dog's shallow panting, his soft, resigned whine.

"Fool." Seth got off his horse. "You haven't changed a bit, Eli. What happened to your arm?" He tapped the cast. "Stop your blubbering for a minute."

"Leave us alone." Eli could not stop crying. "Just go away. Please, please, please go away."

"Still a begging little crybaby," Seth said. "Some things never change."

"Seth," Rosa said, but then stopped, as she wasn't sure what to say next.

Seth shoved Eli. "If you'd stop your crying and get off the dog, Rosa could have a look at him and see if she can do anything."

Eli looked at the girl. She tried to smile warmly at him, but was still unnerved at how very much he resembled Seth.

"Who are you?"

"She's a lifeminder." Seth shoved Eli again, and hard. "Now get off the dog, Eliza." Seth turned away and climbed back onto his horse.

When Eli heard the name he'd not been called in so long, he felt something in him snap with a sharp, invigorating pain. Keenly aware of his intentions, he brought out his own knife and in one fluid motion flicked the wider blade open, turned and plunged the knife through Seth's pants and as deep as it would go. Seth arched back and screamed. The knife stopped hard when it hit bone. Eli dragged it down.

"Stop! Stop it!" Rosa ran for Seth, but Eli yanked the knife out of his brother and pointed it at her.

"Don't move." He switched the knife into the hand with the cast and held it as best he could. With his good hand he grabbed Rosa and forced her onto her knees beside Bullet. He switched the knife back to his good hand and held it in front of her face.

"After, do you hear me? *After* you have tended to Bullet to *my* satisfaction, you can go to him." Eli's voice shook, but the hand with the knife was steady and sure.

Rosa couldn't take her eyes off Seth, who'd fallen forward on his horse and was clutching his thigh, blood spurting between his fingers.

"Do it! Or I'll knife him again, somewhere where it will stop his screams permanently."

"Ah!" Seth clenched his teeth, rocking back and forth. "Do what he says, Rosa!"

"Stop moving!" she called to him as she turned back to the dog. "Amon, get something to staunch the blood."

"What?"

"Put pressure on it!"

Eli stood behind Rosa, positioned so that he could keep an eye on Seth and Amon as well as her and Bullet. He kept the knife pointed at the girl, but his eyes on Seth. Seth had his eyes squeezed shut while Amon helped him slide off the horse and onto the snow. His hair was longer now, and hung across his face.

"You're loving this, aren't you?" Seth said through clenched teeth. "I swear, I will—"

"Yeah, yeah." Eli rolled his eyes. "You'll get me for this. That's what you were going to say, right?"

"You have no—"

"Blah, blah, blah," Eli said. "I have no idea how badly you will get me for this? That's it, isn't it? You are so tediously predictable, Seth."

Seth opened his eyes and glared darkly through his greasy hair at Eli, stirring Eli's familiar fears until he reminded himself that he had the knife, and that it was Seth lying in a growing pool of bloody snow, not him.

Then Seth pushed his hair out of his face and his hood fell back. Eli gasped, getting a good look at him for the first time.

"You *have* had the sick! For real!"

Seth didn't know what to say, the threats he'd had at the ready evaporating in the heat of pain and the equally hot glee of Eli's smug expression.

"Hah!" Eli wished the others were there to see this. "You got the skineater sick! You're not in the Guard any more at all, are you?" He laughed to himself again.

"You have to hold the dog still." Rosa struggled to keep Bullet from getting up.

"It's okay, boy," Eli said as he strong-armed the dog into submission. "You'll be okay." Eli had another look at Seth. He hardly looked like himself—the hair, the scars, the pale blue pallor of shock.

"And the mangy horse, that's no Guardy horse, and you're not wearing a uniform! This whole time I thought you had an army with you, and here you are, all pockmarked and covered in welts with only a scrappy dust hook to do your bidding! Hah!"

"Quit gloating for a moment and hold him tight." Rosa muzzled Bullet with a strip of cloth. "I'm starting the stitches."

"Hang in there, boy," Eli murmured in his ear. Bullet whined, his eyes wide with fright. Eli tightened his grip as Rosa pierced the skin and Bullet thrashed. "Do you do his bidding too? Are you his slave? Did he buy you with his daddy's money?"

Rosa narrowed her eyes at him. "I am no one's slave." She blushed as she said it though, which made one thing certain. Eli dropped his jaw for a second and then began laughing uncontrollably.

"You have a *Droughtland* girlfriend? You? Seth Edmund Maddox?"

"Shut up!" Seth yelled through clenched teeth.

"The same Seth Edmund Maddox who used Droughtlanders for BB gun target practice from the watchtower?"

"Shut up!"

Rosa hesitated in her stitching. Bullet thrashed again, weakly, his breathing fast and unsteady.

"It's okay, bud. It's okay." Eli held him firmly and soothed him with praise. "Now finish what you were doing," he ordered once the dog was somewhat calm again.

Over in the snow, Seth writhed in pain while Amon weighed down on the wound.

"How are you doing over there, Seth?" If it weren't for Bullet's injuries, Eli could almost imagine enjoying this. "You can have Rosa in a second. That's your little Droughtland girlfriend's name, isn't it? Rosa?"

"She's not my girlfriend!" Seth screamed as Amon pulled away one soaking shirt and replaced it with another. "She's nothing!"

Rosa glanced up, her cheeks red. "Don't take off the bandages when they're soaked, Amon." She spoke calmly. "Just add the other one on top."

"Sorry." Amon took off the new one, replaced the old one, and put the new one back on top while Seth screamed in agony.

Rosa looked down at the bloody snow as if she might pack it into a gruesome snowball and hurl it at Seth. She let the needle and thread drop, and set her hands in her lap.

"Keep going." Eli waved the knife in her face. "Finish properly and put a bandage on."

Rosa shook her head. "No."

"No?" Eli wondered what he could possibly say next. "But you have to."

"No, I don't, and you can't make me." Rosa stood and slapped the knife away. She strode back to her horse and climbed into the saddle. "As for you, *Master* Seth, you can bleed to death for all I care."

As she galloped away, Sabine and the others crested the ridge behind Eli.

"Stop her!" Eli screamed.

Nappo took the cue and set off after Rosa, whose retired workhorse and conflicted emotions did not stand a chance against Dawn's speed and Nappo's determination. Rosa stopped before Nappo had to make her stop, and the two of them came back peacefully just as Zari and Sabine got to Eli.

While Rosa reluctantly dismounted and knelt to finish stitching Bullet's wound, Sabine leapt off her horse.

"Oh, Eli, what's happened?" She knelt beside Eli and Bullet, for the moment forgetting about her sibling bleeding in the snow, the one she'd once been so eager to meet. "Will he be okay?"

Rosa looked up and gasped. "It's not possible. I'm not really seeing this! The three of you . . . it can't be! There were *three* of you?"

"Poor Bullet." Sabine stroked Bullet's head and ignored Rosa's shock.

"He doesn't know," Rosa murmured. "The boy didn't tell him about you." She glared at Amon, who couldn't go anywhere, stuck as he was stopping Seth's bleeding. Amon kept his eyes on the snow, hiding his shameless smirk. "And when were you going to tell him, huh? When? Not until you'd made a fool of him? Is that it?"

"What?" Seth struggled to sit up. "Who is she?"

"There were really three of you?" Rosa stared at Sabine, marvelling. "What's the word for that?"

"You!" Seth screamed at them from across the little clearing, now near hysterical with pain and anticipation. "Look at me! Make her stand up and look at me!"

Sabine pulled her hood up and caught Eli's eye.

Eli shrugged. "You must've expected as much."

"What a mess."

"Who is she?" Seth twisted in the snow, pulled at Amon's cloak. "Bring her to me!"

As Rosa tied a bandage over Bullet's wound, her hands shook from the shock of seeing the three of them all at once. "I can't believe it," she whispered. "If I didn't know better, I'd say it was some kind of sorcery."

"There's no magic," Eli said. "Now, if you've finished with my dog, you can help Seth."

The mention of Seth jolted Rosa out of her astonishment. "And if I don't want to?"

Zari came up behind her, her own knife at the ready. "You will do it anyway, and under my supervision."

"It's creepy." Rosa stood, very slowly, her eyes locked on Sabine. "Creepy is the only word I can think of."

"Let me see her face!" Seth screamed again, his voice cracking with all the jagged emotions that heated his blood as it pulsed hard out of his wound, careening him dangerously close to shock. "Look at me, I beg you!"

"Now who's begging?" Eli stepped out of the way for Sabine to go to him. "He's all yours."

"Shut up!" Seth screamed. "Make her look at me!"

"He's talking to you," Eli said. "Here's the moment you've been waiting for."

"Now that it's time," Sabine took Eli's hand in hers, "I don't know that I want to meet him after all."

Just then, Seth erupted in a toxic cloud of curses as Rosa pulled the bloody cloths away from his wound and poured an antiseptic tincture over it.

"Well, you sure have been made the fool, Seth." Rosa scrubbed hard at the congealed blood, and then she remembered. "Triplets. That's what you're called."

Seth writhed, in too much pain to speak at all.

"Now or never," Sabine muttered, dropping Eli's hand and going over to get a look at her long-lost brother as Rosa tried to hold him still.

"You have to be still while I stitch you up."

"Don't tell me what to do, you wretched bitch!" He swung a punch at Rosa and missed as he laid eyes on Sabine. A moment later he passed out, leaving a thankful silence ringing in the crisp air.

35

~⚬~

Sabine had Zari return to Triskelia at once to have messengers sent out informing the others that Seth had been captured. After she'd searched Amon for dust and emptied two vials of it from around his neck, she assigned Nappo the task of keeping Amon under thumb.

"But he's going to be coming down!" Nappo glanced uneasily at the scrawny kid he'd just tied to a tree. "He's going to be freaking."

"I've heard you know a thing or two about that," Sabine said.

Nappo bit his lip. "So that means I got to babysit him through it?"

Sabine smiled at him. "I'm sure you'll both be fine."

"Can't we just send him back to Triban?"

"Not this time." Sabine shook her head. "He's already had his last chance twice. If he hadn't been one of Zenith's favourites when he was little, he'd be in chains already."

THAT BIT OF ORGANIZING DONE, Sabine squatted beside Seth and took a long intense look at her unconscious brother.

"He's much more charming like this," she said to Rosa, who was sitting on a log some distance away, munching on a strip of dried meat.

Rosa stared at her warily. "He's not charming, ever."

"Then why do you stay with him?"

Rosa shrugged. "I don't know."

WHEN HE WOKE, Seth was furious to discover that he was draped over his horse like a sack of oats, his hands and feet bound tightly.

"Hey! What is this?" He craned his neck to get a look around. Amon was now on the horse behind his, sitting up, his hands tied to the saddle horn. "What the hell's going on?"

Nappo brought up the rear of the group. He gave Seth a little wave.

"Piss off!" Seth spat at the snow. "Where's Eli?"

Up ahead, Eli stopped at the sound of his brother's protests, and all the other horses followed suit. Eli trotted back. "What do you want?"

"Back there, there was a girl, like us. I didn't dream it, did I?"

Eli rode off without a reply and stopped beside Sabine, who still had her hood up. "He wants to see you."

Sabine sighed. "I suppose we should just get it over with, don't you think? If I were him, I'd be going mad. I did go mad, that first night you came and no one was allowed to see you, not even me."

"I'll get him off his horse." Eli gently shifted Bullet's weight so that he wouldn't fall off the horse when Eli dismounted.

ELI SHOVED SETH off the horse without untying the ropes, so Seth crashed onto the trail flat on his back.

"My leg!" he howled, writhing in the snow. "You bastard!"

"If that were the case, you'd be one too," Eli said. "Unfortunately, Edmund is indeed our father. To all three of us." He waved for Sabine to come forward.

Sabine pushed her hood back and dug her hands nervously into her pockets. The two of them looked at each other, and then, to Eli's amazement, Seth started to cry.

Rosa got off her horse and ran to him. "Is it your leg?" She knelt to unwrap the bandage, but Seth pushed her off and rolled away so that no one would see him cry. But that just made his knife wound worse, so he struggled onto his back again and gave up trying to hide his tears. He flung his head back and cried openly, the tears rolling down his cheeks. Eli tried to remember Seth's ever crying before, but he couldn't, not even around Lisette's death. But then again, he'd thought she'd abandoned them. He maybe still did—that wouldn't last much longer.

"I don't believe this!" Seth wailed.

"Hah!" Eli nudged Seth with his boot. "It's all making sense now, isn't it? And you didn't believe me! Look at you," he continued. "You stupid bull-headed—"

Sabine put a hand on Eli's shoulder. "Stop," she whispered. "Imagine what he must be going through."

"I know exactly what he's going through!" Eli's reply was gruff. "I've already been through it, thank you very much."

Sabine frowned at him. She knelt beside Seth and put her hands over his.

"My name is Sabine," she said. "There were three of us. I'm your sister."

"That can't be." But Seth knew it was true in that instant, even before that instant. He'd known there was something about her when he first laid eyes on her, even when he couldn't see her face. He hadn't known what it was then, but he knew it was enormous.

"Well, it's true. Deal with it." Sabine untied his legs so that he could ride properly, but not his hands. Eli wouldn't allow it, and she had to admit that Eli knew Seth a lot better than she did.

Eli rode ahead while Sabine explained how it came to be that they were meeting like this, the three of them. Seth listened intently, of course he did, this was a brand-new history that spat in the face of everything he knew to be real. And what did all of this say about Edmund? What kind of man was their father? He'd known him to be cold, even cruel at times, but a murderer? Could it be? He was struck silent with confusion and awe at the strange turns life was taking.

A couple of hours later, his leg aching and throbbing, his eyes began to droop. Sabine left him to rest, and rode ahead alongside Eli.

"He seems okay."

"I don't know." Sabine had meant his leg, but Eli didn't. "You can't tell with him."

It was obvious Seth had changed—the scars were proof enough—but how much and to what end?

Eli kept a careful eye on his brother as Eli and Sabine set up the tents that night. He glanced back at the fire, where Rosa was tending the kettle and Amon was writhing and jittering with the first itchy tendrils of withdrawal. Nappo sat on the log beside him, cleaning his fingernails with his knife.

"What about Rosa?" Eli said. "We should tie her up. What if she goes off for help in the middle of the night?"

"She won't do that."

"How do you know?"

Sabine gave Eli the best deadpan look she could manage. "She's a Droughtlander, you fool. Why would she do anything to help the Guard discover Triskelia? Hmm? Why would she?"

"She's with a Keylander, isn't she? Maybe she's really a Guardy. How do you know she's not?"

Sabine shook her head again. "Your head has gone mushy. Take a look at her. I bet I could count the square meals she's had in all her life on one hand. And that's how I know she's not a Keylander. Satisfied?"

Eli was not satisfied in the least, but Sabine was in charge, so he opted to shut his trap and pray that she was right.

BEFORE DAWN, Eli awoke to the sound of a cavalry of horses pounding toward them at full speed. He tore out of his tent and rustled Sabine awake while Seth feigned sleep beside her, his head covered with the sleeping bag, not sure if he should hope it was the Guard or not.

"Listen!" Eli cried.

"It's probably Trace," Sabine mumbled, yawning.

"And it might not be!"

"And if it isn't, what are you so worked up about?" Sabine pulled on her cloak and followed Eli out of the tent as the sound of the approaching horses grew louder. "There's nothing we can do about it, Eli."

Seth was alone in the tent now. He sat up, his leg a loud, fresh complaint. Was it the Guard? And what would happen if it was? What did Seth want to have happen? What would he say to them? How could he explain himself?

Eli and Sabine joined Nappo, who had stayed up by the fire all night with Amon. Amon had finally stopped puking and was now in the clutches of a bad case of shivers under a pile of blankets as close to the fire as he could get without seating himself directly in it.

"What do we do?" Nappo asked, eyes on the trail.

"Ah, there you go." Sabine nodded as a horn call echoed off the hills. "It's just Trace." She poked Eli. "Told you so. Now, I'm going back to bed for a while. You guys can put the kettle on," she said. "They've probably brought food with them. Save some for me, okay?"

In the privacy of the tent, Seth exhaled, relieved. For the moment, he wanted peace, and for the moment, he had it. Sort of. He flopped back and closed his eyes, pretending to be asleep as Sabine crawled back into her sleeping bag beside his. Whose side was he on, anyway? He had to admit, he wasn't sure. Not after everything. Not after meeting her.

36

⁂

U pon their return to Triskelia, Trace handed Seth over to Zenith, who handed him over to Tagoi, the trialminder, who secreted him away immediately. Pierre demanded to see him, and when he was denied, he got into a terrible scrap with two of Tagoi's men. Eli also heard from Lia, who'd been informed by her cousin who worked in the laundry below Celeste and Pierre's quarters that they'd had a vicious row and Pierre had stormed off in the middle of the night.

"Supposedly on a hunt," Lia said, "but he packed the horse as if he was never coming back."

As for Seth, no one was permitted to see him. No one knew where he was being kept, not even Celeste, and no one knew how long he would be kept there. But they did know what he was going through, as it was the same series of challenges and trials they put any traitor through to find out if they were capable of changing their ways or should be banished, as Amon had been, twice, or imprisoned, which was rare.

More forgiveness, or the chance for it anyway. This was the way of Triskelia. It didn't mean that Eli himself had to forgive Seth. As far as he was concerned, it was just another way that Triskelia was putting off setting the Droughtland free.

EVERYONE GATHERED in the dining hall when it was time for Amon to report the moral inventory he'd come up with after two weeks in isolation.

"I hate this," Amon said as he unfolded his list on stage in front of the crowd. "Makes my skin crawl, all of you staring at me like that." When no one said anything, he muttered, "Okay, fine, here we go."

The crowd listened respectfully, if not dubiously, as Amon went on to itemize every single bad or shady thing he'd done since the last time he'd gone through the trials.

After nearly an hour, he paused, tapping the paper. "Now, you see, I'm not sure about this one here." He squinted at it, reading from the page. "I wrote, 'I didn't tell Seth about Sabine.'" He looked over at Zenith. "But does that count? I was keeping it as a joke. To surprise him, you know? Was that bad?"

Zenith smiled at him. "This is your list, Amon. You decide what belongs on it."

"I guess I think it counts, because of how upset he got, huh?" He looked to Zenith for confirmation, but she just kept her smile steady and nodded for him to continue.

When he was finally done, everyone remained silent for the Gaze, five minutes during which Amon had to stand there receiving everyone's stare. He squirmed and shuffled his feet through it, and when it was over, let out a deep satisfied sigh as Tagoi hurried him off the stage and back to wherever it was the trialgoers were kept.

A FEW DAYS LATER they gathered again, this time for Seth's moral inventory. Eli's skin crawled with disgust that Seth would even have a chance to make amends.

"He looks awful," Sabine whispered to Eli as Seth was ushered onto the stage.

"Looks like he's going to be sick," Nappo said.

"That's good, though," Jack said. "It means he cares."

"So what?" Eli muttered. He wasn't sure if he wanted Seth to care or not. He wasn't sure one little bit if he was willing to share Triskelia with the brother he'd hated all his life, and who had hated him even more. Eli imagined Seth being better at all of it, better at the trapeze, the tumbling, the juggling, and better at the girls. Eli looked across the table at Zari, who was staring up at Seth. She felt him watching her, and turned to him.

"He's a bit pale, isn't he?" she said.

When she said that did she mean, Aw, poor Seth all cooped up by himself in some dark cell, or did she mean, Now Eli, you're far more handsome than he is? Now that Seth was here, Eli had been spun back to his old familiar world of self-doubt and insecurity.

ON THE STAGE, Seth cleared his throat and didn't bother with any kind of introduction.

"I never respected my mother," he began. The crowd, accustomed to the standard tediousness of these proceedings, at the petty wrongdoing most trialgoers started out with, grew still and attentive, as if they might erupt in boos and hisses and drive him from the stage. He was referring, after all, to their treasured Lisette. How could anyone not have respected her?

"I was cruel to her," Seth continued. "I hated her a lot of the time." Tension thinned the air. His voice choked, but he covered it with a cough and continued, eyes on the papers shaking in his hands. "I always hated my brother."

Eli felt a shiver rush through him. Never in his life had he witnessed Seth like this. Vulnerable. Small.

"And I was cruel to him too. Very cruel."

Zenith tapped her cane on the floor to get Seth's attention. "Look up when you speak, child."

Seth dragged his eyes off the page and forced himself to look at Eli before he continued.

"I would've killed my brother had I found him sooner."

AND SO IT WENT, a sixteen-year inventory of ill will.

Eli was almost bored, and certainly not surprised at any of it, until it got to the past year.

"I blackmailed my father."

"I bought my way onto the Droughtland regiment so that I could hunt down Eli myself."

"I raped six Droughtland women."

Eli sucked in his breath and looked around the room. How could it be that everyone could just listen, seemingly without passing judgment? By this point Eli was ready to leap onto the stage and rip his brother's throat out with his bare hands in front of everyone.

Rape? He couldn't just stand up there, say it, and be forgiven, could he? Eli looked around him, at everyone still listening attentively. Why wasn't anyone saying anything, doing anything?

"This is bullshit!" Eli pushed his chair back, the sound of it cutting through the ceremonial quiet. All eyes turned to him.

"Stay where you are, Eli," Zenith said. But Eli stood. He couldn't stay and listen to this! He wouldn't be a part of this process that seemed so unjust and unfair.

Zenith banged her cane on the stage floor. "Eli, sit!"

Eli sat, full of rage. Seth stared at him from the stage, but with what in his eyes? Not anger, not envy, certainly not love, or even kindness or guilt. It was a sad, blank stare that Eli did not recognize.

"I stole from many Droughtlanders," Seth continued. "I don't know how many."

"I resented the girl who saved my life. I thought she was beneath me, and—" Seth frowned at the page, fighting back whatever emotions he was boxing with. He forced the next bit out in a rush. "And when I started to love her, I didn't tell her and that was very, very wrong of me."

Beside Zari, Rosa began to cry.

At that point, Zenith tapped her cane on the floor again. "Stop there, Seth. We will continue this at another time."

DURING THE GAZE, Seth stood with his shoulders militarily straight, his hands clasped behind his back. He surveyed the room, a sea of faces, open and generous and kind and excruciatingly naive. His time in the cells below the main hall had taught him a little something about Triskelia.

They weren't to be feared. They were cowards, waiting for the so-called perfect time to start their so-called revolution. He doubted they had anything to do with the bombing. What that meant then, he didn't know.

What he did know was that he could teach them a thing or two about the art of war. This waiting, their fears, would shackle them forever. Waiting was always worse than the actuality. Something needed to happen. Something to wake these people up. And no leader? What kind of utopian bullshit was that? With crippled, gentle Zenith as the nearest thing to it? Seth shook his head, but then caught himself. She was no leader. She was just a withered old woman. Useless and tired. She should be packed off to the elderminders, so that the rest of them could get on with it.

These people needed a real leader. One who could command them into action. Someone like himself. He could do it, even as conflicted as he was about everything.

These people were the enemy, or so he'd been taught.

And his father was his hero. Right?

And the Guard was the bastion of justice.

But it just wasn't that clear any more.

One thing remained true, though. Seth was meant to lead.

Was this his destiny? To lead these people? To transform this pathetic heap of pacifists into warriors capable of overtaking the Keys?

Without a leader, without a clear vision, they would never get anything accomplished. They needed a leader, and he could be it. Here, his scars were a commodity, a badge of honour. They were worth a lot. He was no fool.

During the Gaze, Eli stared hard at Seth, wishing for his brother to be mysteriously struck dead on the spot. It would be merciful. It would save everybody the awfulness of his existence. Zari stared furiously at Seth too, one arm draped protectively across Rosa's shoulders, who wept quietly beside her and did not participate in the Gaze. Sabine, who couldn't bear to look at her brother either, not after all the awful things he'd admitted to, patted Rosa's back and stared at the floor.

A WEEK LATER it was time for Amon's amends, but all Eli saw of that was the bit that had to do with him. Eli was let into Zenith's room. Amon was set up by the fire, where he'd been receiving people for two days and making apologies. Beside him, Zenith was quilting a baby blanket for the baby that was due to be born any minute now. Without looking up, she nodded at Amon. Amon looked at a notebook in his lap, placing his finger on a line.

"Sorry I led Seth to you," Amon said. "I shouldn't have done that."

Eli shrugged. "But you did."

"So I'm sorry." Amon squirmed uncomfortably in his chair. "Friends?"

"Definitely not." Eli waited for Zenith to look up. "Is that it? Can I go?"

"You may go."

Amon checked his name off his list as Eli left the room.

In the hall, Eli took a deep breath. He did not trust Amon. Ever since that first time at the Seduce tournament. He was as shifty as they come, and the worst kind of shifty, the kind that can shimmy their way back into people's trust only to crack it from the inside yet again.

WHEN IT WAS TIME for Seth's amends, the only people around to apologize to, other than Triskelia as a whole, were Eli and Rosa. Eli waited outside Zenith's door for Celeste to come out. She and Zenith were receiving the amends on behalf of Triskelia.

She emerged in tears and embraced Eli fiercely. "Oh, I wish your mother could see the three of you together like this!"

"We're not together, Nana."

"You will be." She gripped Eli's shoulders firmly. "And soon."

Eli took another minute to organize his thoughts before going in. Did Celeste mean that she was going to recommend Seth be allowed to stay? Eli would have to give a recommendation in the end too, and Rosa. Surely two against one would have him exiled, even though Celeste was an elder.

SETH KEPT HIS EYES on the floor as Eli made his way to the chair by the fire. Zenith was still working on the baby quilt, although the little girl had been born four days earlier.

Eli sat, his eyes steadfast on Seth, who still hadn't looked up from the slate floor.

Zenith glanced up from her stitching. "Look up, child."

Seth shook his head. "I'm so tired." His voice was thin, and he spoke in a near whisper. "Can't I do this tomorrow?"

"No. Now look up, or I will come over there and make you look up." Zenith winked at Eli and picked up her needle. When Eli looked back at his brother, Seth was looking at him, his eyes red around the rim, as though he'd been crying, or hadn't slept, or had been ill. Eli wished all three on him. Eli took in the sick scars that cut a shocking pattern across Seth's face and grimaced.

"Don't look at me like that." Seth ducked his face.

Zenith tut-tutted from the other side of the fire. "Stick to what you rehearsed with me, child."

There was a long silence while Eli waited for Seth to begin and Seth waited for the words to come to him. He wasn't sorry. He wanted to be, or he thought he did, but he just wasn't. He could pretend for Zenith. He respected her that much. He could pretend for all of Triskelia—he wasn't a fool when it came to self-preservation, but he alone knew the truth. He wasn't sorry. And he would still cock a gun at Eli. In fact, he'd love to put a gun to Eli's temple right about now. Pow. Dead.

Without looking up, Zenith prompted, "I'm sorry, Eli, for . . . "

Seth folded his arms across his chest as if he needed to hold himself back. "I'm sorry, Eli, for giving you such a hard time."

Eli waited for more, but there was none. "That's it?" he finally said, flopping back in his chair. "That's all you have to make amends for?"

Zenith appraised Seth sternly. "And?"

"I'm sorry, Eli, for being such a terrible brother." He raised his intonation at the end, like it was a question. Eli leapt on that.

"Oh, I'm supposed to confirm that for you?" Eli jiggled his knee. "You're not quite sure that you were a lousy brother, a mean, cruel, sadistic prick. Is that specific enough?"

Seth took a deep breath and continued. "I'm sorry, Eli, for not believing you about Mother." There was a slice of truth, a small one, a glimmer. "Maman, I mean."

Eli slumped a little at the mention of Lisette. "I bet you are. Look at all the crap you could've avoided if you'd just come with me when I confided in you."

"You wouldn't have wanted me to come with you."

"I would've let you come anyway," Eli said, and meant it. "It might've been safer."

There was another long silence, and then Seth said, "You seem to have done pretty well on your own, Eli."

"Surprised?"

Seth nodded. "Honestly, I didn't think you'd survive long enough for me to find you."

Zenith looked up again. "I believe you have much more to say to your brother, Seth. The two of you can talk about other things afterward."

"Sorry, Zenith." Seth got back to his list of amends, and started from where he'd left off.

WHEN ELI FINALLY LEFT Zenith's room, Rosa was waiting in the corridor to take her turn.

"What will you recommend?" She took Eli's good arm in both her hands and gripped it hard.

Eli didn't know what to say. Going in there he knew he'd recommend Seth be exiled, but now he wasn't so sure. Seth was different, that much Eli was certain of, but different in what way? Was he remorseful only because he was caught? Or was this change real? Was he worthy of Triskelia? Or would he ruin it for Eli?

"Exile him, Eli," Rosa said before Eli had formed an answer. "He's done such terrible things. This place is far too good for him. Send him away," she begged. "I thought he would change, but he hasn't. And there's so much more than I knew! If I had known everything, I wouldn't have stayed with him."

Eli pulled away from her. "You make your own recommendation, Rosa, and I will make mine, and Nana will make hers. Then the elders will decide. You do what you need to do."

Zenith opened the door then and gently pulled a reluctant Rosa into the room.

"Please, Eli," Rosa said as the door closed behind her. "Please? Exile him?"

37

❧

"Face your people," Zenith said, tapping Amon's butt with her cane to get him to shuffle forward before she announced the verdict to the crowd, who were all waiting silently, the flickering lanterns casting long shadows over their heads. No one was particularly surprised with the result, although there had been a few small wagers that even Zenith's capacity for forgiveness must have an edge to it somewhere.

Amon wasn't exactly exiled for a third time, but he was assigned to be Trace's apprentice orphan seeker; he would be under constant supervision to ensure that he didn't start again with the dust and would always have a worthy task to keep his idle mind busy. Amon beamed at Trace, who levelled a cool gaze back at him, humbling him immediately.

" 'Bout time I got sorted out," he said, nodding as Zenith finished with the verdict.

"The day you truly get sorted out," Zenith said, "is the day we will throw a feast in your honour, child."

"Really?" Amon glanced around as the crowd laughed. "You really mean that?"

"I do," Zenith said. "But how will I know when the day has come?"

"Oh, I'll prove myself." Amon took the old woman's hand in his. "You just watch, Zen-Zen. I'm going to stay off the dust this time."

Eli didn't buy Amon's act for one minute, and looking around, it would seem he wasn't alone, but Zenith beamed at Amon. She let Amon kiss her on the cheek, and then steered him away and waved for Seth to come out of the dark shadow of the corridor, where he'd been waiting with Tagoi.

"Face your mother's people." Zenith gestured for Seth to turn away from her and toward the crowd.

Eli felt the pitch of anticipation flatten. She hadn't said *your people*, like she'd done with Amon. She'd said *your mother's people*. She was setting him apart, a sign that he did not belong. Was it a hint of what was to come? She was going to exile him?

Eli tugged on Sabine's arm and whispered, "But I recommended that he could stay!"

"You did?" Sabine stared at him, eyes wide with surprise.

Eli hadn't told anyone, other than Zenith, what he'd recommended. He was ashamed that he couldn't bring himself to exile Seth after all he'd done, that there was a large part of him that wanted his brother near, even though Seth had caused him such grief all his life. He had to admit that it was mostly curiosity that influenced his decision; he wanted to know who his brother would become. That, and his own experience with second chances. It was his attempt to live the Triskelia way of forgiveness. He didn't have to like it, but it felt like it was what he was supposed to do.

Before either of them could say anything more, Trace placed a heavy hand on their shoulders, hushing them both.

"Seth Edmund Maddox, son of Lisette," Zenith began, her voice taking on a chilly formality.

Eli suddenly felt a peculiar twinge. He glanced at Sabine. She nodded at him, eyebrows raised. Eli tapped his chest. It felt tight, as though someone was pinching his skin and pulling away. Sabine nodded vigorously, patting her own chest as her face blanched.

On the stage, Seth put an unsteady hand to his chest too. He tried to keep any expression from his face, although he was certain he was moments away from exile from this place he'd become so intrigued by, so inspired by. Where would he go? How would he survive? He didn't want to leave! He wanted to *know*, about Sabine, the truth about his parents, about everything. His chest boomed with pain.

In the crowd, Eli and Sabine leaned on each other, whispering.

"You feel it too?" Sabine doubled over, and then straightened immediately, not wanting anyone to notice. Eli could only nod. "What's happening?" Sabine said as she doubled over again, groaning.

The pain intensified, ultimately drowning out Zenith's voice altogether. Eli and Sabine couldn't stand it any longer. The two of them collapsed at the same moment Seth's knees buckled on stage and he fell forward into the crowd. The three of them blacked out, a violent ringing raging in their ears.

MUCH LATER, they awoke within moments of each other. The three of them looked around for each other in the dark.

"Where are we?" Seth's voice was hoarse.

"The infirmary," Sabine said. "Eli?"

"I'm okay," Eli said from the bed across the aisle. He sat up as his eyes adjusted to the dark. "What happened?"

"It must be some kind of sick." Seth's heart pounded and his muscles ached at the reminder of the last time.

"If it's a sick, why are the other beds empty?"

"No." Sabine shook her head. "It isn't a sick."

"Then what?" Seth sat up and was relieved to find that he wasn't nauseous or weak. He felt fine. Better than fine. He felt great. "And why all three of us at once?"

"It happens to Ruben and Riva," Sabine said. "A connection, between twins. Or triplets, too, I guess. When I was little the other kids used to sit me down and get me to close my eyes and try to find you."

"Find us?" Seth said. "But you knew where we were."

"Not like that. Like Ruben and Riva can. Sometimes they can 'see' each other when they're apart." The doubt was obvious in her voice. "They say they can feel what the other's feeling. But I never could. I'd pretend that I could, but it wasn't real. At least I don't think it ever was."

"Nah," Seth said, half-heartedly. "It's nothing like that. Is it?"

"How would you explain it, then?" Sabine felt in the dark for the lantern on the bedside table. She found matches in the drawer and lit it, a soft orange light illuminating the three of them. Across the aisle, Eli was silent. "What do you think, Eli?"

"I never thought we had any kind of connection, but now that I think about it, I remember one time," Eli began, not sure if he wanted to continue with the fragment of memory that was floating to the top. "When we were five. Seth was missing, and even though I hadn't seen him at all that day, I told Maman that he was in the reservoir. Do you remember, Seth?"

"I remember falling in. And I remember I couldn't reach the ladder to climb out. I remember getting too tired to swim any more. And I remember how cold it was. But I never knew it was you who led them to me."

"And this time, just before I blacked out," Eli said. "I was worried about you. I was worried that you'd be exiled."

"So was I!" Sabine said.

"Me too." Seth rubbed his face in his hands. "So am I exiled or not?"

"I don't know." Sabine peeked out the window to look at the moon. "It's the middle of the night. We should sleep. They'll tell us in the morning."

BUT THE THREE OF THEM couldn't sleep. They speculated on why only now they felt a connection. Why not before, when Sabine had tried thousands of miles away, lost to them, and why not ever between Eli and Seth, except for that one time?

"Because we hated each other," Eli said, as if that was explanation enough.

"And I would've ignored anything like that," Seth added. "But I'm glad you didn't, or I would've drowned."

"I just told them where you were. It's not like I knew it was weird that I knew where you were. I was just answering Maman's question. It didn't occur to me until now that there was anything special about it."

"But now we're together," Sabine suggested, "and you two are . . . well, you don't hate each other still, do you?"

Eli and Seth didn't look at each other.

"Never mind," Sabine said. "It's not going to happen overnight. I'm not naive."

"Don't hold your breath," Seth said. "There are years and years of history between us."

"You have no idea, Sabine." Again, Eli remembered his brother's arm at his throat. The click of the trigger. His pants hot with urine.

"Well, same to you." Sabine's tone was sharp. "If I could've traded with you, either of you, both of you, I would have, so don't tell me about *history*."

THEY WRAPPED THEMSELVES in blankets and sat cross-legged on Eli's bed and talked all through the night, only getting up to watch the sun rise over the hills, soaking the long stretches of cloud a deep rose and the emerging sky a robin's egg blue. Zenith found them sitting together on the window ledge and told them before they had to ask that Seth was welcome to stay in Triskelia, if that was his wish.

38

⟊

Of course he agreed to stay, but what was his wish, really? Did he want to stay? Was there something for him here? He wasn't sure, especially after Rosa left. She hadn't even waited to say goodbye. She hadn't given him a chance to speak to her in private. If she had, he would've begged like never before. He would've made it up to her. He would've proven that he had changed. He would've apologized, and then apologized again, and again. But she'd left without telling anyone during the night he and Eli and Sabine had spent in the infirmary. If they'd gone to the window just a little earlier, he might have seen her on her horse, making her way along the complex path through the sick colonies and up the mountainside the way they'd come together not so long ago. He might've been able to stop her, but the chance had passed and he hadn't even known it had existed. He spent more time than he would ever care to admit wondering what could have been between them and where she was now. Even the upcoming feast couldn't distract him from wondering where she was, and if she was well.

The feast had been put off long enough, what with Seth's arrival and the trials, and now it was going to happen in just a matter of days. Celeste put Seth to work straightaway, which he had to admit helped the heartache a little. She assigned him to the group building giant elaborate lanterns out of coloured rice paper and willow branches bent and cut and fashioned into stars and moons and dragonflies, all sorts of shapes. The one Seth was helping with was a giant jolly effigy of Zenith sitting in her chair. The designs were complex and the work meticulous, so Seth had much to learn in a very short time, and he was thankful for the distraction.

Eli's cast came off, but his arm was still too weak to perform, so he went back to childminding, and Sabine spent her days coaching the others as they rehearsed the fly act. At the end of each day, each of the three had only to close their eyes and take a deep breath and most times they would know exactly where in the labyrinth of corridors and rooms and stairwells the other two were. If it came, the knowledge landed with a thunk in the same spot in their chest that had burned with pain the night of Seth's verdict. There was no pain there now, only an awareness of not being alone in the world. They hadn't told anyone else about their ability to sense each other, not Zari, or Nappo, not anyone. In truth, it embarrassed them, and between them, they decided something like that could quickly become corny if the others knew. It would become nothing more than a party trick, and to them it was so much more, although none of the three could define what it was exactly.

ON THE DAY OF THE ACTUAL FEAST there was no more work to be done; the decorations had been hung, the food was ready to be tucked in the ovens and set out on the tables, and the troupes that were performing were as ready as they'd ever be. Everyone could take the entire day to get themselves ready for the event, which would carry on from sunset through to the morning.

Very few people were in the hall for breakfast. There was nothing hot to eat, either, just cold dishes laid out on a long table at the end of the room.

"Unless you want to make it yourself," Sabine explained, stacking a plate with bread slathered in jam. She grabbed a handful of nuts that had been roasted the night before. "Kettle's on the stove, if you're looking for tea or porridge." She put a spoonful of loose tea into her mug and headed for the kitchen, calling behind her, "I'm taking my breakfast upstairs."

"Wait." Eli caught up with her. "I have something for you." He pulled out Lisette's pearl choker. "It was hers."

Sabine set her plate and mug down and took the choker, letting the pearls slide over her fingers. "Eli, are you sure?"

"Well, I'm not going to wear it."

Sabine lifted it to her neck and turned. "Do it up?"

Eli did, and then she collected her breakfast.

"Thank you."

"And thank you," Eli said as she backed away, the familiar pearls at her throat making her look even more like Lisette.

SETH HADN'T KNOWN about the choker, and Eli didn't want to tell him. He wanted it kept small and special between him and Sabine, and so he was grateful to find Seth conveniently distracted by the sight of Nappo and Lia coming into the hall wearing each other's sweaters. Seth nudged Eli as he sat back down.

"Check it out."

Eli leapt right in. "Your bunk was empty last night, Nappo," he said as Lia went in search of a pot of tea after telling Nappo what she wanted from the food table.

"This is a big place." Nappo screwed his eyes shut, trying to remember what Lia had requested. "Lots of places around here to sleep rough."

"You were sleeping rough?" Seth said. "Sure." He and Eli laughed.

Teal hugged Nappo's waist. "You slept rough last night? Where? Can I come next time?"

"No, you can't." Nappo squatted and let Teal climb up for a shoulder ride to the food table. He glowered at Eli and Seth.

"Keep your nose out of my business." He tried to sound serious, but his frown quickly cracked into a stupid grin. Eli and Seth laughed at him as Lia came back to the table, a blush rushing up her cheeks.

"What? Did you tell them anything?"

"No! No, I didn't," he implored, and then tossed at the brothers, "Just shut up, okay? Please? Do me the favour?" And then he took off for the food table, Teal whooping from his shoulders.

MOST EVERYBODY SPENT THE DAY RESTING, or preparing themselves; bathing, doing each other's hair, deciding what to wear. Eli played ball in the courtyard with Teal and a handful of other children, until a bell Eli had never heard before sounded at sunset. It came from across the court-yard, where several other children were jostling for turns swinging from a thick pull hanging from a bell tower above. The children were dressed in golds and silvers and purples and reds, the girls' hair done up in elab-orate twists with jewels dangling from the knots, the boys with capes to their knees, and all of them in fancy shoes with shiny buckles. It was time to get ready. Eli shooed the ball players inside and up to their dorms.

The boys in Eli's dorm were all rushing to add the final touches to their costumes. Anya had made Seth and Eli matching costumes, which at first had annoyed the brothers. They were thankful to her face, especially considering how excited she was about her creation, but they hadn't been dressed alike since before they were old enough to push each other over.

"What do you think?" Seth leapt onto the bed and swaggered the length of it.

The pants were made of dark blue leather, so blue it looked black in the lantern light. Silver trim lined the outside seams. The top was a vest of black leather, with silver cord to lace it together at the top, although Seth had left his loose.

"It's all right," Eli muttered as he struggled to pull his own vest over his shoulders. It wasn't something he'd ever be caught dead in, given the choice.

"Well, I like it." Seth dropped to the edge of the bed and pulled on a pair of big black boots. "It makes us look like rogue pirates, or adventurers."

"Don't forget your wings, rogue boy." Eli tossed them at him. Anya had sewn together countless leather feathers she'd had one of her appren-tices cut out of thin black leather. She'd fastened the wings onto a frame that attached to two straps that secured to epaulettes on the shoulders of the vest. Seth handed the wings back to Eli so that he could fasten them on for him.

"And your beak," Eli said as Seth got up to leave without it.

The dance, to be held following the circus performance, was a masquerade ball. Seth tucked the mask, a black leather beak stitched onto a dark blue leather eye mask with more feathers at the corners, into his pocket. The pants were so tight though that the bulge looked weird.

"I'll carry it," Seth said, pulling it out. "Are you coming?" He glanced around as the others streamed out in full costume. "Man, some of these costumes are bent."

Eli let the comment go, more interested in getting comfortable in all his tight, creaky leather gear than educating Seth about Triskelian ideas on benders. Let him figure it out the hard way. He yanked the vest down over his abs as best he could with his one good hand.

"Well?"

Seth stared at him.

"Come on, Seth. Tell me if something looks dumb."

Seth silently followed Eli out of the dorm and down a flight of stairs, to the one mirror that the three floors of dorms had to share. When he'd jostled his way to a spot where he could get a good look, he grimaced. "It all looks dumb on me, doesn't it?"

The look on Seth's face could only be described as incredulous.

"Where did you get those muscles?"

"It's all the circus stuff, probably." Eli felt embarrassed for some reason, and he was angry with himself for it. He'd worked hard to look like this. He wasn't about to let Seth deflate him now. He steeled himself. "Go for it, Seth. Hit me with your scathing wit."

"No." Seth shook his head. "I'm not . . . you don't have to . . . it's just that I have to admit, if you had bet me, before everything, that you'd ever be stronger than me, I would've bet everything I had that that would never happen. Now look at me. I've been scrawny ever since the sick."

Rather than having to agree, Eli let himself be jostled away by the crowd of others wanting a look in the mirror. The brothers headed back for the stairs. Halfway up, the air between them awkward, Eli lunged playfully at Seth, fists up. "Afraid I might beat you up now?"

Seth slapped Eli's fist away, a little too hard to be friendly. "As if."

"Come on, admit it, it's freaking you out a little." Eli was trying to be playful, but he could tell by the icy glare Seth let slip that if it went any further, Seth would try to prove it wasn't just brawn that made a winning fighter. Eli dropped the subject and turned so that Seth could attach his wings from the back.

The room emptied, and still the brothers stood there, silent, Seth's shame and humiliation like a wall rebuilding itself between them.

"Seth?"

"What?" His tone was thin glass.

How badly Eli wanted to go in the direction Seth was pulling them, to that place they knew so well, of wicked barbs and gut-churning insults, of petty slights and gargantuan hate. They had come so very far, only to know all the shortcuts back. Eli was sure he could win now that he was stronger on the inside and out, but he sacrificed his pride in favour of keeping the shaky peace between them, if not for himself, then for Celeste and Sabine, and everyone else in Triskelia.

"Come on," Eli offered instead, "you know that the minute you start on the trapeze, you'll be twice as big as me, like always."

To his credit, Seth fastened Eli's wings in place of a barbed response. This truce, if it was one, if that's what a white flag looked like, was sinewy thin and as taut as heat. Talking to Seth was like learning a foreign language. Eli felt adrift, as if he were searching for words in a language he would never comprehend.

DOWNSTAIRS, the dining hall was filled with people feasting and preening in their fancy dress. The servers and childminders and songminders worked in rotations so that everyone could enjoy the feast. Eli didn't eat much, afraid that his pants might burst. Sabine, Zari, and Lia came down after Eli and Seth and Nappo had long finished eating. Sabine was wearing the choker. Eli watched Seth. He didn't seem to notice or recognize it.

"They're being dramatic," Nappo whispered as the girls paused on the stairs, ensuring that the boys had their eyes on them. "That's what Lia told me, that she wants to make an *entrance*."

"I see," Eli said, but he didn't really. Poor Lia didn't stand a chance beside Zari, who was far more beautiful than the others. She was wearing a silver gown with blue brocade accents and tight sleeves with no shoulders. The bodice hugged her narrow hips and then dropped to a full skirt that made her look absolutely regal as she walked with Lia and Sabine toward the boys.

After Eli had made awkward comments on all three girls' costumes and the sisters had left for the food table, Sabine poked Eli in the chest.

"I know what you're thinking."

"You do not."

"You wish I didn't," she said and flounced off after them.

AFTER EVERYONE HAD EATEN, the crowd slowly drifted into the gymnasium, which was decorated with the same elaborate swaths of shimmering fabric and cities of tiny candles as the Keyland performances had been. Eli felt what was now the increasingly familiar pang in his chest. He glanced over at Sabine, at the tears on her cheeks. The last time she'd seen the circus finery was the night Quinn had died. Seth looked over, his eyebrows raised in confusion. He tapped his chest and shrugged. Eli shrugged back. Some things Seth would have to discover on his own, like who Quinn was to Sabine and Jack and all of Triskelia.

Seth hadn't included any part of Quinn's death in his moral inventory, not his role in releasing the pigeons, which Eli was sure he'd orchestrated now, or how he'd thrilled in the blood and the grief of his very own kin. It was as though he'd forgotten about it.

Once again, Eli marvelled that Sabine had been so close that night, and yet Eli had had no clue, no mysterious pang, not even if he thought back and tried to make it up. He closed his eyes and tried again to remember something. He'd watched Sabine, out of all of the performers, but that could've been because she'd come so dangerously close to insulting Chancellor East and potentially losing her life for it.

That night was vivid in Eli's memory. Eyes still closed, he turned his head as if he were back sitting in the balcony seats, and there was his mother before the fall, leaning forward, eyes bright, cheeks glowing with what Eli now knew was so much more than the flush of entertainment. She smiled at him, put a hand on his knee. *Watch, watch, mon fils! Look what they can do*!

If he could go back to that moment, he would change so much. If he could go back to that moment before the fall . . . Quinn's bashed-in head flashed into view, Sabine's screams banged between his ears, both solid markers of a reality Eli could not change. He opened his eyes, the warmth and noise bringing him back to the moment, the celebration, the feast—back to his life that was so different now.

Riva and Ruben helped Zenith into the centre ring. A spotlight swung onto her from the rafters.

"Such beautiful food—thank you to everyone who had a turn in the kitchens." She raised her hands, and the crowd erupted in cheers for the cooks that went on and on until Eli's hands began to go numb with all the clapping.

Zenith lowered her hands and the cheering stopped. The old woman turned slowly, steadying herself with her cane as she admired the decorations. "And the work of magicians! Triskelia never looked so grand!" And again the crowd broke into cheers.

When there was silence again, Zenith continued. "Lisette Fabienne," she said, her voice strong. "Say it with me, the name of our treasure, our dear." She raised a hand, and the many hundreds of people said it with her, "Lisette Fabienne!"

Eli shivered as his mother's name echoed up the towering stone walls. Sabine reached for his hand, and Seth's with her other, staving off the pain that was thumping in their chests.

"There is no happiness at the loss of our Lisette, but there is happiness in the reunion of her children." Zenith gestured for the three of them to come forward. Trace gave Sabine a gentle push, and the crowd parted as she led her brothers into the ring. Again the crowd erupted in cheers as Zenith patted their hands and smiled at each of them in turn.

When the cheering died Zenith nodded to Anya, who sent Charis tottering into the ring balancing a flat pillow in her hands with exaggerated seriousness. The crowd bit back laughs when she nearly toppled over the ring rim. Zenith nodded to Ruben, and then to Riva, and the three of them each untied a silver medallion from the pillow.

As the medallions were fastened around their necks, the triplets lifted them to look at what they'd been given. It was the Triskelian symbol, the triangle with a wave curling away from each corner, but there was a unique spiral inside the triangle, pulling in from the corners. Stamped into the silver of each strand of the spiral was one of their names. *Seth*, *Elijah*, *Sabine*.

"Pierre made these for you after you were born," Zenith said. "I don't think he thought it would be so very long before you would be reunited. I am sad that he is not here to give them to you, and I hope he will come back and let himself get to know Eli and Seth for himself, independent of his grief for Lisette."

"Thank you, Zen-Zen," Sabine murmured for the three of them.

"To be honest," Zenith leaned forward on her cane, speaking so that only the triplets could hear, "I did not know of the medallions all this time. No one did. But when Pierre left, he left them for you. I think he would have liked to have presented them to you himself, but his grief cripples him. Perhaps with time," she said, then straightened and turned to face the east entrance.

"And now, our tribute and farewell to Lisette. As the sun rises in the east, it brings with it light." On cue, the lanterns and candles were snuffed, plunging the enormous room into darkness. A procession of lanternminders entered, each one carrying a lantern hung from sticks high above them so that the lanterns appeared to be floating in the dark. Some lanterns were so big it took two or three bearers to carry them. As they wound their way gracefully through the crowd, Eli stared, slowly realizing that he was seeing the story of Lisette's life. There she was, a ghostly, glowing sleeping infant at the front of the procession, followed by caricatures of Pierre and Celeste, and all the things and people dear to her, some represented on trapezes, others just as large smiling faces. There was a shaggy dog, several horses, many characters and things Eli didn't recognize. Then their father appeared, an eerily accurate portrait, with harsh eyebrows and an intelligent gaze.

"There's Edmund!" Seth whispered harshly. "How dare they?" And he lunged forward to pull down the glowing effigy.

Sabine and Eli held him back. "Leave it alone, Seth," Sabine said.

"You of all of us know better," Eli muttered. "He's a part of us."

"But he—" Seth started, and then stopped when he saw what was coming next.

Three identical babies, swaddled and asleep, and then a Keyland wall, so long that it was carried by eight people and so tall that it leaned and tipped as the lanternminders walked under its weight. Then they shifted position so that two of the babies were caught behind the wall and the third left outside, with the adult Lisette puppet lantern embracing the third until the Celeste puppet pulled the baby away, leaving Lisette to fall in place behind the wall, head bowed in grief. It was silent, but so telling.

Eli could not watch the rest of it. He stared hard at the floor, the lanterns reduced to bobbing lights reflecting off the slate at his feet. He willed himself not to cry. He willed away the lump in his throat and the pounding in his chest that was not his siblings' echo in himself but just the rude, jarring thump of tremendous sadness. He looked up again only when the procession finally exited out the west doors.

"And as the sun sets in the west, so she takes with her the light of our Lisette," Zenith said as the last of the lanterns disappeared, leaving the room in darkness once more. "We will now have a moment of silence so that we can each remember her privately."

Quiet and darkness closed in, the atmosphere stiff and solemn. As his eyes adjusted to the dark, Eli looked around at the thousands of people, their heads bowed, all with Lisette in mind. Eli wanted to run. He wanted to flee up to his bunk and be alone, but he couldn't make his way out without upsetting the ritual and drawing attention to himself, so he closed his eyes and gave up, waiting for an assault of painful images to slap him even further into grief. But all he saw was his mother at the piano, stumbling over a piece that she couldn't get right. He could hear it! He could hear *her!* She was laughing, plonking hard at the keys, making up some silly nothing of a song in place of the one she was botching.

And then Zenith closed the silence with three taps of her cane, and the lanterns and hundreds of candles were relit as she nodded up to the rafters. Not only one but three spotlights flashed on, moving in sweeping figure eights across the room.

"And now," Ruben said as Riva helped Zenith out of the ring, beckoning the triplets to follow, "prepare yourself to be dazzled, amazed, and amused as the fantastic Night Circus performs for you!"

The crowd roared with delight, bursting the grave, contemplative cloud that had settled with the lantern procession. Troupe members scuttled away to get ready, Jack pulling a stunned Sabine along with him, and the others moved back and up into the steep seating that climbed the walls. Eli and Seth let the crowd sweep them along to a bleacher halfway up the wall. It was a good spot, almost eye level with the trapeze.

ELI WAS FASCINATED by Seth's reaction to the performances. Seth had seen the circus time and time again, but this time he watched it with a purpose. He hardly said a word, and instead put his elbows on his knees and scrutinized the troupes' performances. He was studying every move, Eli knew. He was deconstructing the choreography so that he could perfect himself. And he likely would. He had a kinetic intelligence Eli did not. And the circus was in his blood too. How he wished Seth would be crap at all of it. He should be, Eli figured. It was only fair. There ought to be one thing he could do better than Seth.

"I can do all this, you know," he mumbled as they watched a highwire walker do a somersault with a seamless landing on the narrow wire twenty feet above ground. "I'd be up there, only my arm isn't strong enough yet. I broke it. Doing that."

Seth ignored him, which was probably good, because Eli hadn't learned the highwire yet, although he was sure he could master it if he tried.

Then it was time for the fly act. Jack and Zari and the others ran into the ring, waving at the cheering crowd.

"That's my troupe," Eli told Seth.

"Yeah, you told me." Seth's eyes were glued on the action below as Jack helped Sabine into the straps.

"Hey! Sabine's going to fly?" Eli pointed. The crowd rustled, realizing what was happening. Eli turned to Seth, who hadn't clued in. "You don't get it—she hasn't flown since Quinn died that night in the Key. She said she'd never fly without Quinn."

Seth's hands dropped in his lap. "The Droughtlander," he whispered, the colour draining from his face. "Sabine was there? That night?"

"Yeah, that night. That night when you made them turn him over so you could get a better look, remember?"

"But no one's said anything."

Eli shrugged. "I guess that's the beauty, or ignorance, of forgiveness."

"Maybe no one knows it was me?"

Eli shook his head. "They remember."

Below, Gavin and Lia yanked on the pullies, sweeping Sabine and Jack up into the air. Eli let the subject drop. But he would return to it. He wanted to hear it from Seth. He needed to know exactly what happened that night with Maury's birds, and how much Seth had to do with it. But for now he turned his attention to the performance.

Eli had never seen the fly act executed with such astounding grace. Watching Sabine and Jack together showed Eli how much more there was for him to learn. With them, it was as if there were no ropes, no pullies, no straps—nothing except two fluid spirits twisting together and pushing apart like tendrils of sweet smoke. The haunting melodic solo of a strange instrument accompanied them, a long clay pipe the performer stood behind, blowing into, the bottom resting on the floor.

When Sabine and Jack were lowered at last, there was a charged silent moment, and then the stands of people leapt to their feet and cheered louder than they had all evening.

"Sabine! Sabine!" they chanted, clapping and stomping on each syllable of her name.

In the ring, Sabine kept her eyes downcast as Zari helped her out of the rigging. Once they were loose, Jack took her hand and stepped forward.

"Sabine! Sabine!" The crowd was relentless in their praise.

Jack dropped her hand and pushed her forward. Sabine stood alone in the spotlight for a moment, her hands at her sides, as her name was chanted over and over, until she took another step forward. The spotlights followed her. She took a deep bow and then straightened up and threw her hands in the air. The crowd broke their chant and went into a frenzy of applause as she did a perfect back flip, the tag she'd always kept for the end of a performance she was particularly happy with.

39

꜠꜡

While Triskelia bathed in the glow of celebration, the night winding slowly toward dawn, and everyone making their way, drunk and blissful, to their own and each other's beds, Commander Regis amassed his men on the ridge above the Colony of Sicks. From the shadows of the forest he surveyed the constellation of lights spreading out below. There was a safe route, there had to be. But at this point it didn't matter. He turned and wandered through the sprawling fireless camp. Thousands of men—he had to admit, he wasn't sure exactly how many—hunkered restlessly, waiting for his command to storm the Colony of Sicks and, ultimately, Triskelia. To think such myth and power had been given to a snivelling bunch of peace-loving cowards holed up in a crumbling old hospital. And it was all the Droughtlanders had. Once he levelled it there would be no threat. It was like revealing a false god. It was like putting an old dog out of its misery. It could not be this easy, but it was turning out to be just that. Easy.

Except for the collateral damage. He'd lose most of these men, if not from the sicks, then in combat. But even that wasn't a big deal. Most of them were on disciplinary probation for some reason or another, and a chunk of them were Droughtlanders who'd been recruited from the villages and didn't know they were going to be demolishing Triskelia. But with guns at their backs they'd do what they were told, and that's all that mattered. So maybe *recruited* wasn't quite the word. *Forced* might be more appropriate. It was a move Commander Regis took sadistic pleasure from. Send them in with guns at their backs and guns in their faces and watch them fight for their lives. Animals.

The cannons were set up and ready. Almost forty of them were positioned around the colony. Commander Regis glanced at his watch. Twenty minutes. It would be like watching dominoes fall from barely the breath it would take to blow out a birthday candle.

ELI FOLLOWED SETH back up to the dorms. They were the first back to the room, and so Eli decided to confront him about that night at the circus, back in the Key.

"What exactly did you have to do with Quinn's death?"

Seth was tugging his way out of his costume. "What are you talking about?"

"The night of the circus. The boy who died. His name is Quinn. I know you had something to do with it."

"Well, you're wrong." Seth pulled on a sweater, and then a coat.

"Who did you whistle at then?" Eli pressed on. "You gave someone a thumbs-up. It was Maury, wasn't it? You two had a plan to set those pigeons loose, didn't you? They were trained to go after Quinn, weren't they?"

"I don't remember, okay?" Seth made his way to the door.

"Where are you going?"

"For a walk."

"In the middle of the night?"

"To clear my head." Seth felt his heartbeat quicken as the familiar friend called anger opened her bleary eyes. "Do you have a problem with that?"

"You're lying to everyone. You set those birds loose in the stadium, didn't you? You made him fall. It's your fault he died!"

"They were Maury's birds." Seth shrugged. "At the time, it seemed like a good idea."

"Then you admit it!" Eli rushed him, pinning him against the wall. "Why didn't that make it into your amends, huh?"

Seth grabbed his arm and tried to twist Eli off him, but Eli put all his weight into pinning Seth still. "You *will* admit it. You *will* beg for forgiveness. And I *will* make you."

"I don't think so." Seth sucked in his breath and shoved Eli off him with such force that Eli fell backward. Seth didn't waste a second; he threw himself onto Eli, pinning his arms with his knees and grabbing his throat in one hand. "You will never tell me what to do." Seth punched him hard, his knuckles complaining instantly. "And I have as much right to be here as you do, so don't think you're some kind of Triskelian princess. I have plans for this place. You might fit right in, sitting on your ass like everyone else while the Keys carry on, having everything, but I'm the one who'll make things happen here! Whether they want it or not, this place needs a leader, and whether they want it or not, the revolution has to start sometime!"

Eli worked his jaw. "Get off of me."

"You watch." Seth climbed off him. "I'll make the revolution happen. You'll never do anything. You and the rest of these cowards, thinking you're so much better than the Keylanders, yet you're no different! You have everything, and the Droughtlanders still have nothing. How is that different?"

"We feed them, and help them." Eli sat up and spat out blood. "And there are plans to—"

"Yeah, endless plans. Show me one person here willing to get their hands dirty."

"*Bloody*, you mean. There's a big difference." Eli yawned his jaw. "The revolution will happen, Seth. When I got here, I was like you. I thought the same way, but you'll come to realize it's better this way. Safer. Smarter."

"Sure, Eli. And who's the sheep now?"

"The revolution will happen." Eli let the remark go, for now. His jaw smarted, and he didn't want another blow. "In good time."

"There is no 'good time'! Don't you get that?"

"It will happen. I know it will."

"Yeah, you keep telling yourself that, princess." Seth slammed the door behind him as he left.

ELI SAT ON THE EDGE OF HIS BED and explored his jaw. His teeth felt loose, but none so much that they'd fall out. Did things ever really change? Did people ever really change? Was Seth any different at all, or had he just shifted his very same toxic self to new environs? More devastating a notion, had Eli himself really changed? After all he'd been through, had he changed at all?

This revolution. Had Eli just slid into the easiest way of thinking about it? The path of least resistance? Seth was right, just as Eli had been when he first arrived. There was no *good time*. And Eli had just gone along with the idea of *not yet*. And why? Because he was lazy, and scared, and did not want blood on his hands. Eli looked at his hands. They were bloody now, with his own blood.

Who was he? It was a huge question, or worse, maybe just a small question, with an even smaller answer. Where would the answer come from? Had he come all this way only to meet himself, unchanged?

At that moment Commander Regis's cannons exploded simultaneously and the world around him crumbled into chaos. Eli was knocked to the floor as the windows shattered and stone broke from the walls in a dusty rain.

He made his way to the window. The Colony of Sicks was on fire. *The garden. Where was his mother?* Eli shook his head, but the vision didn't disappear. Fire, smoke, and screams like sirens slicing the night. People fled on foot, dropping in the streets as mounted gunmen stormed the winding lanes, firing freely.

More screams from downstairs, people shouting. Eli fumbled over debris, crouching with each bomb blast. He made his way to the main hall where Trace stood on a table, his forehead bleeding. He yelled over the gunfire, which was getting louder, closer, with each pop.

"Hide the children wherever you can, but not all together!" He braced himself as another explosion shook the room. "Everyone who can, follow me to the munitions room!" He leapt down and led a group out into the night. Eli followed them to a bunker filled with guns.

"I thought we didn't have weapons," he said as he was handed a rifle.

"Not enough," the man said.

"I don't know how to use this."

The man grunted, took the rifle back, and handed Eli a machete. "Better?"

Eli and his machete were shoved back up into the night, where the gunfire and screams were escalating.

"What's happening?" Eli yelled. No one answered. He was shuffled along to a narrow back entrance and told to stay there and not let anyone in. Eli flattened himself against the damp stone wall, keeping to the shadows. Everywhere he looked there was fire. And piles of Droughtlanders dead in the streets, or dying, reaching up for help. But there was no one to help, only Guardy after Guardy, slaughtering everyone in their path.

Eli trembled uncontrollably. He tried to tighten his grip on the machete, but his hands shook. He held it tight with both hands as a couple of Guardies approached out of sight, their voices growing louder. They would have guns. He would have to surprise them if he was going to live. He crouched, steadying the machete at what he hoped would be waist high to them. As their footsteps closed in, he turned out of the shadows and wielded the long blade, eyes squeezed shut, no idea where he was landing it. He was cutting through something though, resistant yet supple. There was the pop of a gunshot. Then another.

Eli opened his eyes. He'd gutted the one man, who was crumpling to the ground, holding himself, and had sliced deep into the side of the other—the one who'd fired his gun at Eli. Eli put a hand to his shoulder; it came away wet with blood. Then a white-hot pain slammed up his neck from his shoulder and he passed out.

DAWN CAME ANYWAY, despite the death begging it not to. Eli awoke to raven song, cruel and mocking. A pigeon roosted on a laundry line across the lane, cooing at him. He would fly away if he had wings. Why did the birds stay? Eli's shoulder throbbed, but had stopped bleeding. He flexed his fingers. They still worked. He sat up. It was quiet. No gunfire. No explosions. Just the metallic hangover of gunpowder and smouldering fires. Yet still there were screams, although they were tired, and fewer, and utterly hopeless.

THE GUARD WAS GONE, and in their wake nothing but devastation. Eli turned in circles, bewildered, numb, until someone grabbed him and pulled him back toward the compound. It was Gavin. A bloody rag around his arm, gun slung across his back, limping. He pulled Eli along and didn't say a word, to him or to the three children trailing behind them, whimpering and filthy.

What was left of Triskelia was barely enough to know it had ever existed in the first place. One wall of the main building stood, windows blown out, but that was it. The rest had been bombed, reduced to a mountain range of rubble. Who was under there? Trapped? Dead? Where was everyone?

Eli yanked free and dropped to his knees at what was left of the dining hall, just a dump of busted timber and brick. He grabbed onto a beam and heaved, but there was no give.

"They might be in there!" he cried as Gavin pulled him away. "We have to find them! We have to get them out!"

Still Gavin said nothing. He shoved Eli ahead of him until they came to a small crowd of shaken, wide-eyed Triskelians. There was Sabine! And Celeste. The three clung to each other.

"Where's Seth?" Celeste asked.

Eli shook his head.

"You haven't seen him?" Sabine started to cry in earnest.

He shook his head again. *Seth*.

The Guard.

Who had revealed Triskelia to them?

Eli opened his mouth to speak, but the crowd was moving.

"We have to leave." Celeste took his hand. "In case they come back."

"But what if there are others? Still alive?"

"They will find us." Celeste took Eli's other hand. She held them both tight. "We must leave."

"But Triskelia—"

"It's ruined, Eli." Sabine took the hands of two children covered in so much soot that Eli couldn't tell who they were. Celeste let go of Eli's hands to take a wailing baby offered to her.

Anya was beside them then, carrying Charis in her arms, but there was something wrong. Charis's head flopped to the side and her skin was grey. She was dead.

Eli put his eyes on his feet and willed himself to just walk. One foot in front of the other. Ignore the pain in his shoulder, and the horrors dancing around him like cruel jesters. Just walk. And that's what he did, falling in behind a line of hastily packed caravans and horses and an exodus of stunned, surviving Triskelians, all dragging their spirits behind them like balls and chains.

40

W hen Edmund got word of the ambush, he was just finishing supper. His Chief Regent came in to report what had come over the wire.

"Chancellor! It's happened." Phillip flapped the paper in his hand. "Triskelia has fallen!"

Edmund pulled his napkin from his lap and folded it. He placed it on the table beside his plate and sighed.

"Good." He stood, brushing the crumbs off his lap. "This is very good."

Allegra, hands clasped across her pregnant belly, looked up at him. "Should I go?"

"No." Edmund kissed her forehead. "We'll go to my office. Stay, my dear. Have your tea."

Edmund left the room, with Phillip at his heel like a puppy.

"There was no sign of the boys," he whispered as they strode down the hall.

"Silence!" Edmund swung open the door to his office, shoving Phillip in ahead of him and slamming the door shut.

"Sorry, sir. I—"

"*Never* mention my sons outside of this room." He sat at his desk. "Is that understood?"

"Yes, sir. I'm sorry, sir."

"I don't want your skinny little apologies. I want your obedience."

"Yes, sir."

There was a light knock at the door.

"Enter!"

It was Allegra, her tummy entering the room ahead of her. "Cousin!" Phillip kissed her on the cheek and smiled. "Is the baby kicking?"

"Yes. A lot." Allegra took Phillip's hand and placed it on her belly. "Feel him?"

"Him?"

Allegra nodded. "I just know it's a boy."

"Darling," Edmund said through gritted teeth. "Is there something you need?"

"I want to sit in, if you don't mind."

Edmund laughed. "This is state business."

"My grandfather always let me sit in."

"Well, he chose me to replace him as Chancellor, and so I do things a little differently." He stood, took her arm gently, and escorted her into the hallway. "I love you too much to have you worry about state business."

"I love you too, Edmund."

He kissed her. "I'll meet you in the parlour. Soon, my dear."

"All right." Allegra stood on tiptoes to kiss him once more. "I'll keep the tea hot."

BACK IN HIS OFFICE, Phillip was still grinning. "So exciting, a baby!"

"Give me the wire."

Phillip handed it to him and waited, hands clasped behind his back as Edmund read it silently.

"No survivors? Not one?"

"Commander Regis did an excellent job. We should consider a promotion."

Edmund dropped the paper onto this desk. "I will be in charge of the *shoulds* around here."

"But Chancellor East always—"

"I am Chancellor East now," Edmund said. "And I would not have you as my Chief Regent if he hadn't stipulated that it be so. I would advise that less is more, if you feel the need to speak at all."

"Yes, sir."

"Sit."

Phillip sat. "You must be so excited about the baby. I know I—"

Edmund steepled his fingers and silenced Phillip with a look.

"Take notes." Edmund sat back in his chair as Phillip organized his pen and paper. "Wire Commander Regis a reply. Tell him he will be rewarded for such a successful mission, and request of him that he carry on looking for Eli and Seth. Include, clearly, that he is to maintain the secrecy of that aspect of his mission."

Phillip looked up, pen poised.

"That is all. Go."

As the fog rolled in along the river and the clouds hung heavy in the sky, the survivors of the Triskelian massacre trudged up the valley. Eli looked back once, and only once, for the rubble was a terrifying wasteland, and he thought he could see the spirits of the dead climbing out from the ruins and lurching up into the mist.

Acknowledgments

A bouquet of long-stemmed thanks to Christianne and her book clı
for their feedback and careful reading of the manuscript, with spec
thanks to the brilliant young minds of The Wormers, The Book Jack
and especially Cozey J. Gemms. Thanks also to the Canada Council
the Arts for their generous and continued support. Finally and n
importantly, a mountain range of appreciation belongs to Benja
Owens, this story's first and most enthusiastic fan.

RETRIBUTION

BOOK 2 IN THE TRISKELIA TRILOGY

The much-anticipated second book in the Triskelia trilogy, *Retribution* is a futuristic cautionary tale.

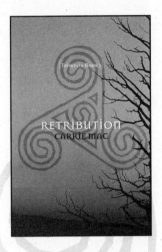

KEYLANDERS:
Brought up with privilege and protection

DROUGHTLANDERS:
Forced to survive in a parched wasteland

With thousands dead after the Triskelian massacre, Eli and Sabine flee with the survivors. Days later Eli's twin brother, Seth, is rescued from the rubble and discovers that people think the ambush was his fault. In exile, he creates an army in hopes of toppling the Keys once and for all, and to prove the massacre isn't his doing.

"Young adult devotees of fantasy will gallop through The Droughtlanders *and be chomping at the bit for the next instalment."*

–**Quill *& Quire*** **magazine**

Visit www.triskelia.com   penguin.ca